The AMAZING WORLD OF
GUMBALL™
CHEAT CODE

ROSS RICHIE...CEO & Founder
MATT GAGNON......................................Editor-in-Chief
FILIP SABLIK.................President of Publishing & Marketing
STEPHEN CHRISTY.......................President of Development
LANCE KREITER...................VP of Licensing & Merchandising
PHIL BARBARO..VP of Finance
BRYCE CARLSON...Managing Editor
MEL CAYLO...Marketing Manager
SCOTT NEWMAN.................Production Design Manager
IRENE BRADISH.............................Operations Manager
CHRISTINE DINH.................Brand Communications Manager
SIERRA HAHN...Senior Editor
DAFNA PLEBAN...Editor
SHANNON WATTERS...Editor
ERIC HARBURN...Editor
WHITNEY LEOPARD...............................Associate Editor
JASMINE AMIRI......................................Associate Editor
CHRIS ROSA..Associate Editor
ALEX GALER...Assistant Editor
CAMERON CHITTOCK.........................Assistant Editor
MARY GUMPORT.....................................Assistant Editor
MATTHEW LEVINE....................................Assistant Editor
KELSEY DIETERICH...............................Production Designer
JILLIAN CRAB...Production Designer
MICHELLE ANKLEY...................Production Design Assistant
GRACE PARK..........................Production Design Assistant
AARON FERRARA.........................Operations Coordinator
ELIZABETH LOUGHRIDGE ....Accounting Coordinator
JOSÉ MEZA...Sales Assistant
JAMES ARRIOLA....................................Mailroom Assistant
HOLLY AITCHISON...............................Operations Assistant
STEPHANIE HOCUTT ....Marketing Assistant
SAM KUSEK.....................Direct Market Representative

THE AMAZING WORLD OF GUMBALL: CHEAT CODE,
June 2016. Published by KaBOOM!, a division of Boom
Entertainment, Inc. THE AMAZING WORLD OF GUMBALL,
CARTOON NETWORK, the logos, and all related
characters and elements are trademarks of and © Turner
Broadcasting System Europe Limited, Cartoon Network.
(S16) All rights reserved. KaBOOM!™ and the KaBOOM! logo
are trademarks of Boom Entertainment, Inc., registered
in various countries and categories. All characters,
events, and institutions depicted herein are fictional.
Any similarity between any of the names, characters,
persons, events, and/or institutions in this publication
to actual names, characters, and persons, whether living
or dead, events, and/or institutions is unintended and
purely coincidental. KaBOOM! does not read or accept
unsolicited submissions of ideas, stories, or artwork.

For information regarding the CPSIA on this printed
material, call: (203) 595-3636 and provide reference
#RICH – 665293. A catalog record of this book is available
from OCLC and from the KaBOOM! website, www.kaboom-
studios.com, on the Librarians Page.

BOOM! Studios, 5670 Wilshire Boulevard, Suite 450, Los
Angeles, CA 90036-5679. Printed in USA. First Printing.

ISBN: 978-1-60886-842-1, eISBN: 978-1-61398-513-7

The AMAZING WORLD OF GUMBALL

CHEAT CODE

created by **BEN BOCQUELET**

script by **MEGAN BRENNAN**

art by **KATY FARINA**

colors by **WHITNEY COGAR**

"HIDDEN VALUE"
by **JEREMY LAWSON**

letters by **WARREN MONTGOMERY**

cover by **SEAN "CHEEKS" GALLOWAY**

designer **JILLIAN CRAB**

assistant editor **MARY GUMPORT**

editor **SIERRA HAHN**

with special thanks to **MARISA MARIONAKIS, RICK BLANCO, CURTIS LELASH, CONRAD MONTGOMERY, MEGHAN BRADLEY,** and the wonderful folks at **CARTOON NETWORK.**

additional thanks to **MATTHEW LEVINE** and **GRACE PARK.**

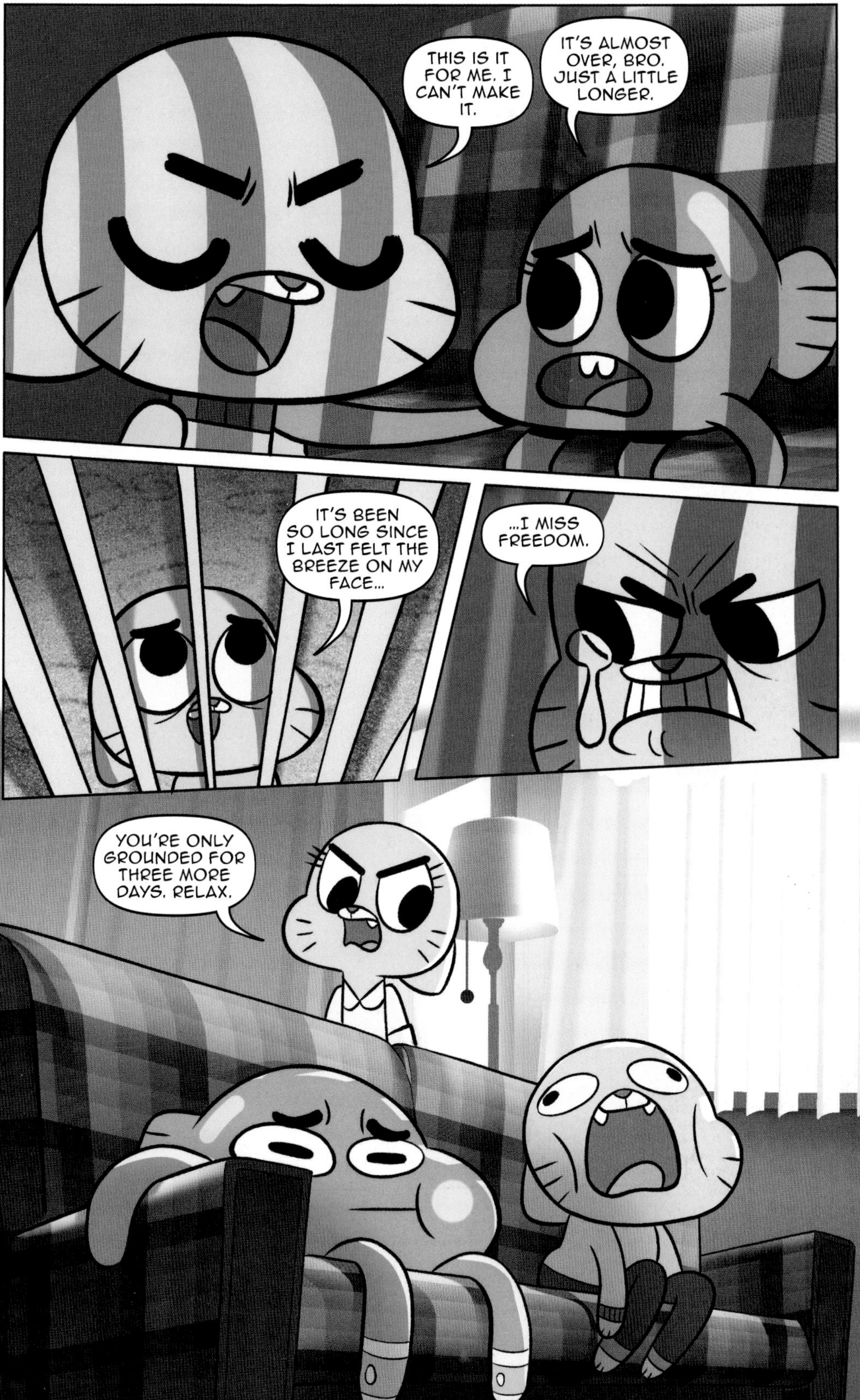
THIS IS IT FOR ME. I CAN'T MAKE IT.
IT'S ALMOST OVER, BRO. JUST A LITTLE LONGER.
IT'S BEEN SO LONG SINCE I LAST FELT THE BREEZE ON MY FACE...
...I MISS FREEDOM.
YOU'RE ONLY GROUNDED FOR THREE MORE DAYS. RELAX.

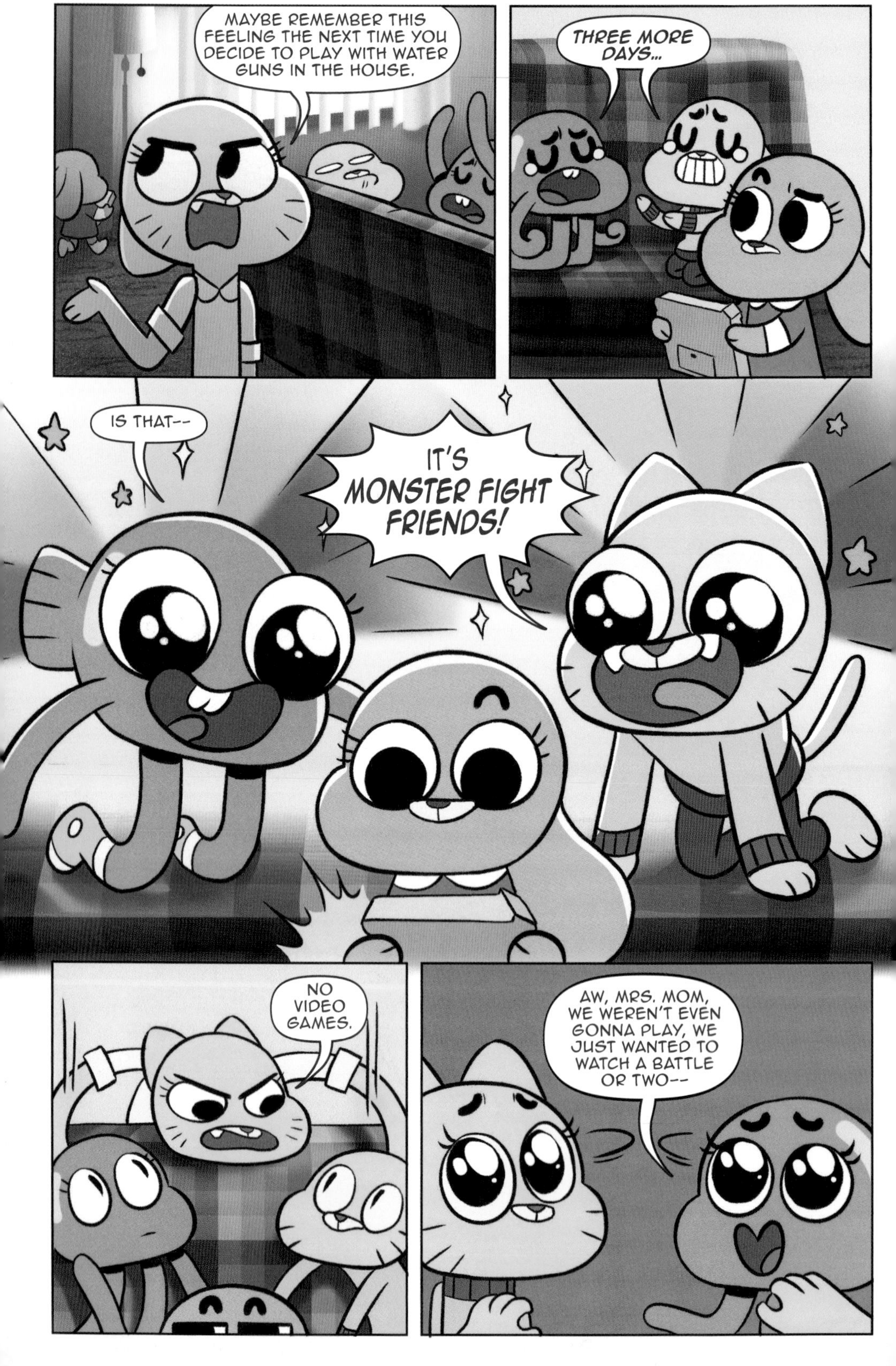
MAYBE REMEMBER THIS FEELING THE NEXT TIME YOU DECIDE TO PLAY WITH WATER GUNS IN THE HOUSE.
THREE MORE DAYS...
IS THAT--
IT'S MONSTER FIGHT FRIENDS!
NO VIDEO GAMES.
AW, MRS. MOM, WE WEREN'T EVEN GONNA PLAY, WE JUST WANTED TO WATCH A BATTLE OR TWO--

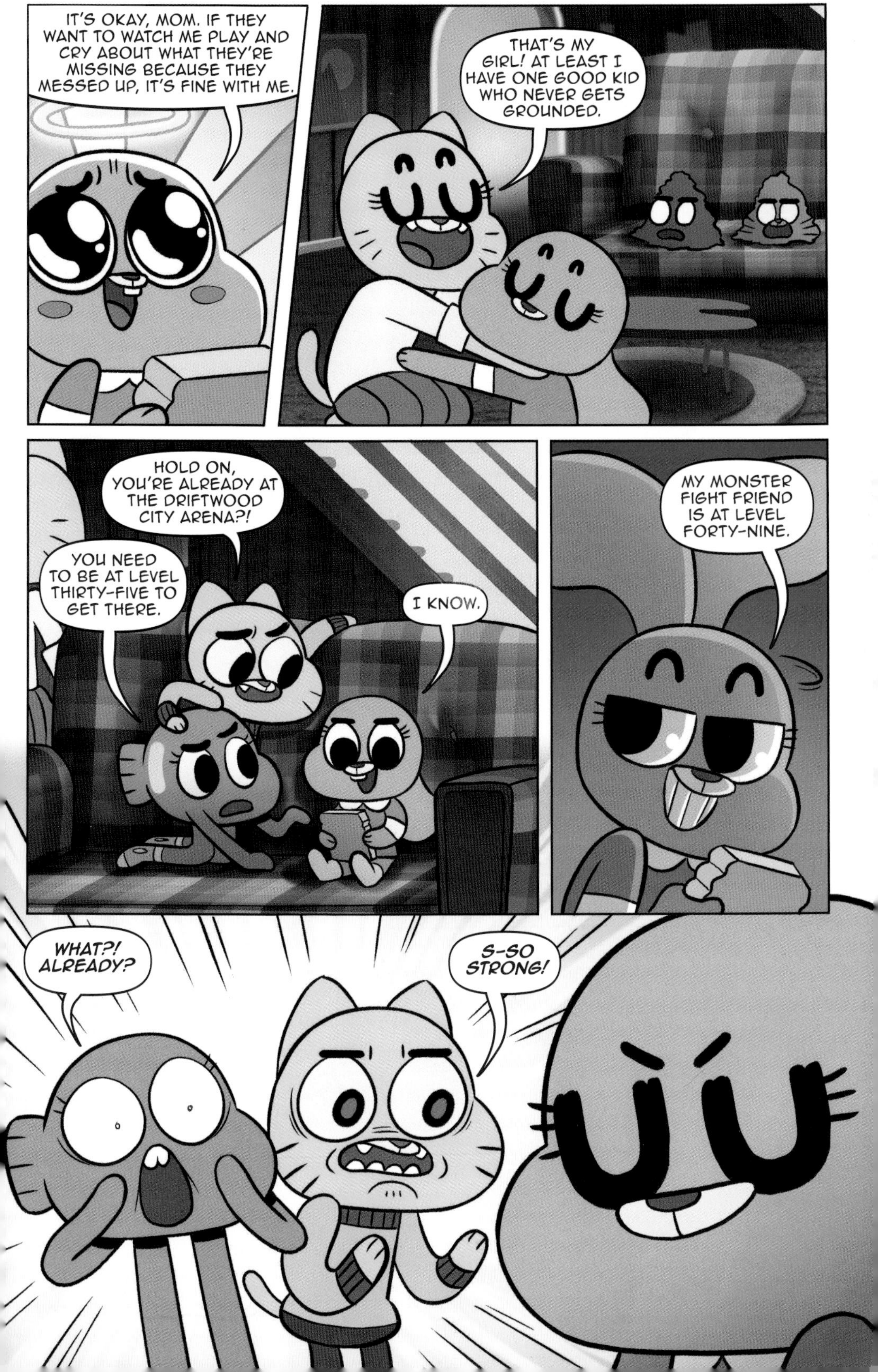
IT'S OKAY, MOM. IF THEY WANT TO WATCH ME PLAY AND CRY ABOUT WHAT THEY'RE MISSING BECAUSE THEY MESSED UP, IT'S FINE WITH ME.
THAT'S MY GIRL! AT LEAST I HAVE ONE GOOD KID WHO NEVER GETS GROUNDED.
HOLD ON, YOU'RE ALREADY AT THE DRIFTWOOD CITY ARENA?!
YOU NEED TO BE AT LEVEL THIRTY-FIVE TO GET THERE.
I KNOW.
MY MONSTER FIGHT FRIEND IS AT LEVEL FORTY-NINE.
WHAT?! ALREADY?
S-SO STRONG!

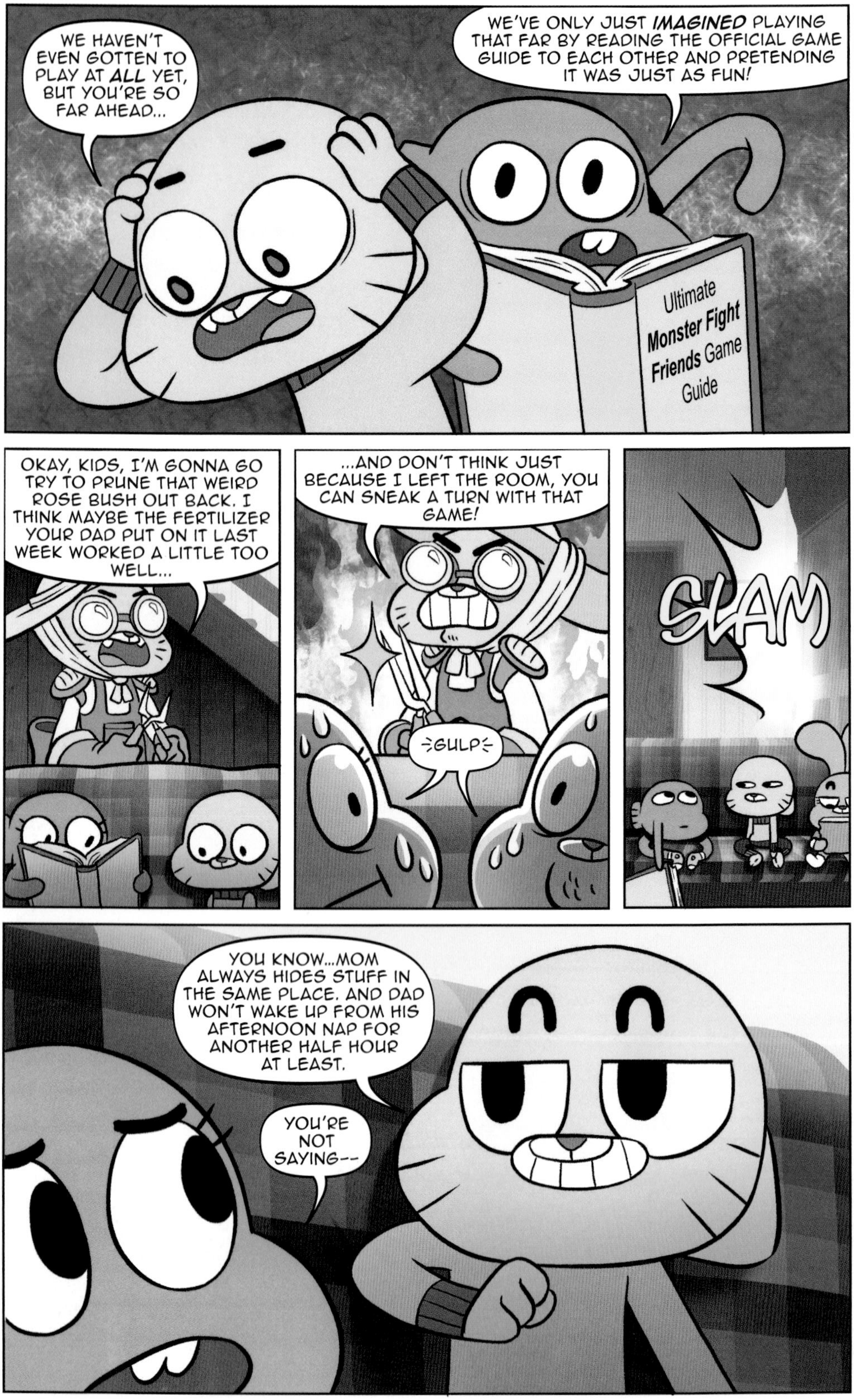
WE HAVEN'T EVEN GOTTEN TO PLAY AT ALL YET, BUT YOU'RE SO FAR AHEAD...
WE'VE ONLY JUST IMAGINED PLAYING THAT FAR BY READING THE OFFICIAL GAME GUIDE TO EACH OTHER AND PRETENDING IT WAS JUST AS FUN!
Ultimate Monster Fight Friends Game Guide
OKAY, KIDS, I'M GONNA GO TRY TO PRUNE THAT WEIRD ROSE BUSH OUT BACK. I THINK MAYBE THE FERTILIZER YOUR DAD PUT ON IT LAST WEEK WORKED A LITTLE TOO WELL...
...AND DON'T THINK JUST BECAUSE I LEFT THE ROOM, YOU CAN SNEAK A TURN WITH THAT GAME!
GULP
SLAM
YOU KNOW...MOM ALWAYS HIDES STUFF IN THE SAME PLACE. AND DAD WON'T WAKE UP FROM HIS AFTERNOON NAP FOR ANOTHER HALF HOUR AT LEAST.
YOU'RE NOT SAYING--

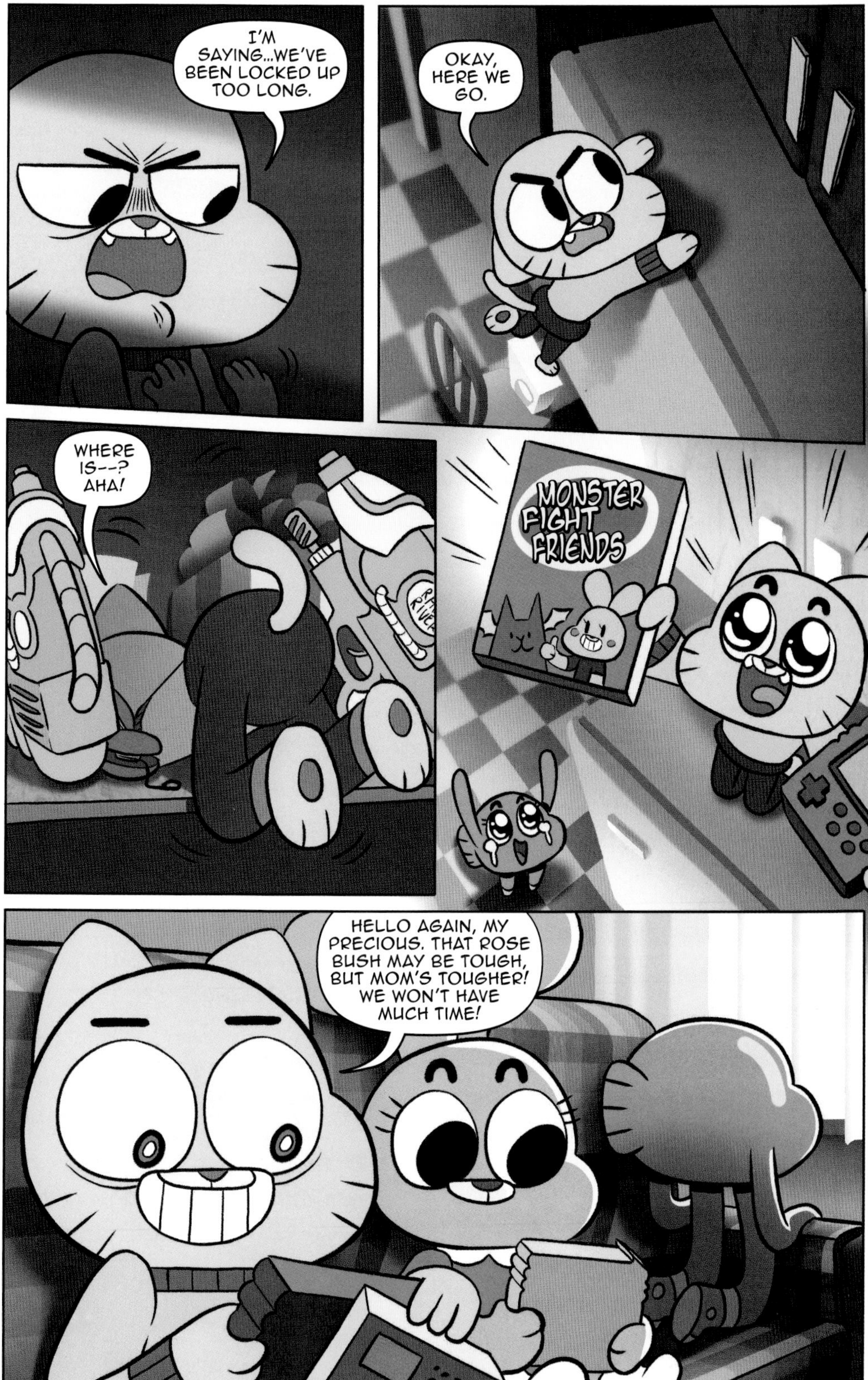
I'M SAYING...WE'VE BEEN LOCKED UP TOO LONG.
OKAY, HERE WE GO.
WHERE IS--? AHA!
MONSTER FIGHT FRIENDS
HELLO AGAIN, MY PRECIOUS. THAT ROSE BUSH MAY BE TOUGH, BUT MOM'S TOUGHER! WE WON'T HAVE MUCH TIME!

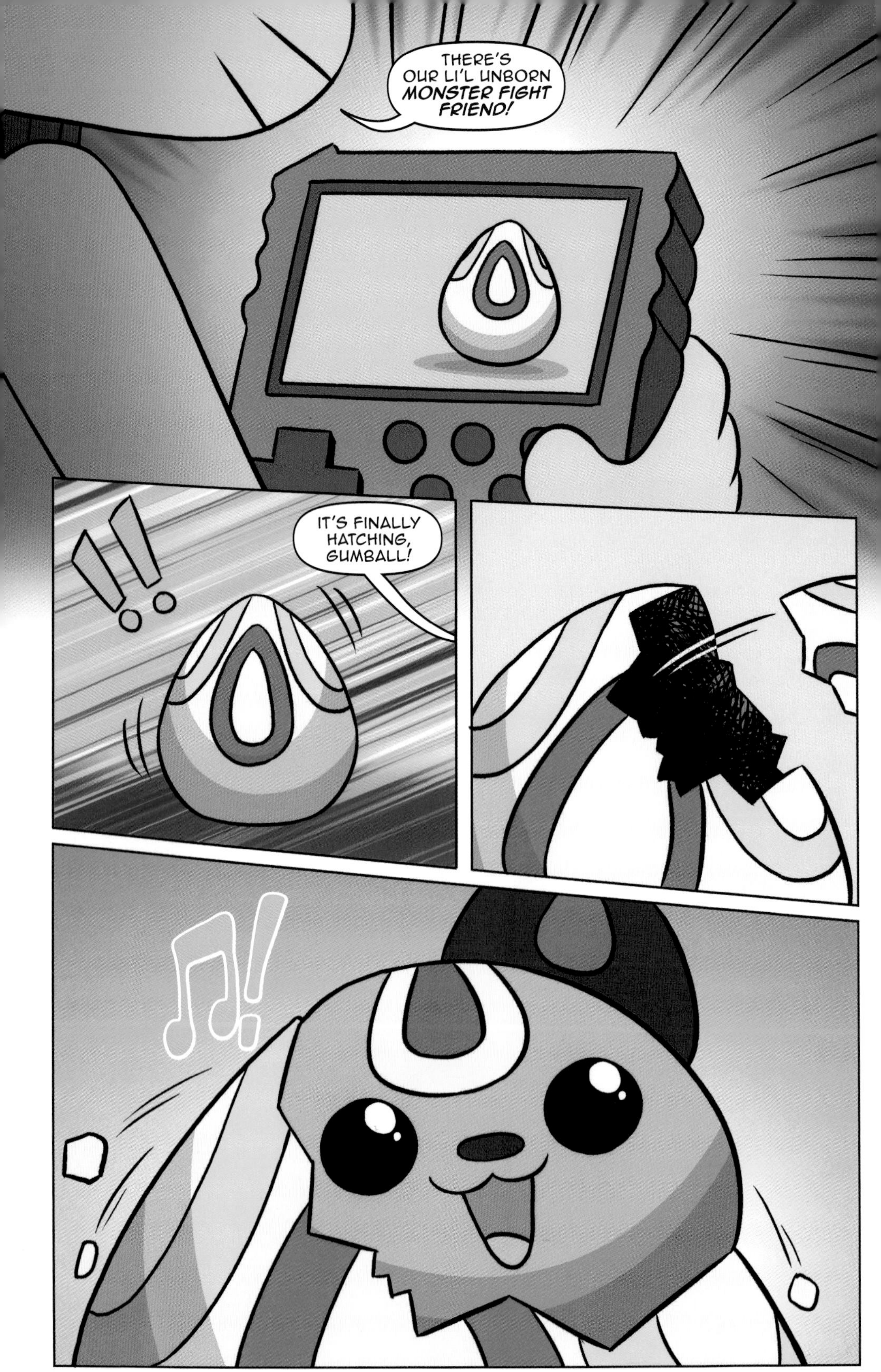
THERE'S OUR LI'L UNBORN *MONSTER FIGHT FRIEND!*
IT'S FINALLY HATCHING, GUMBALL!

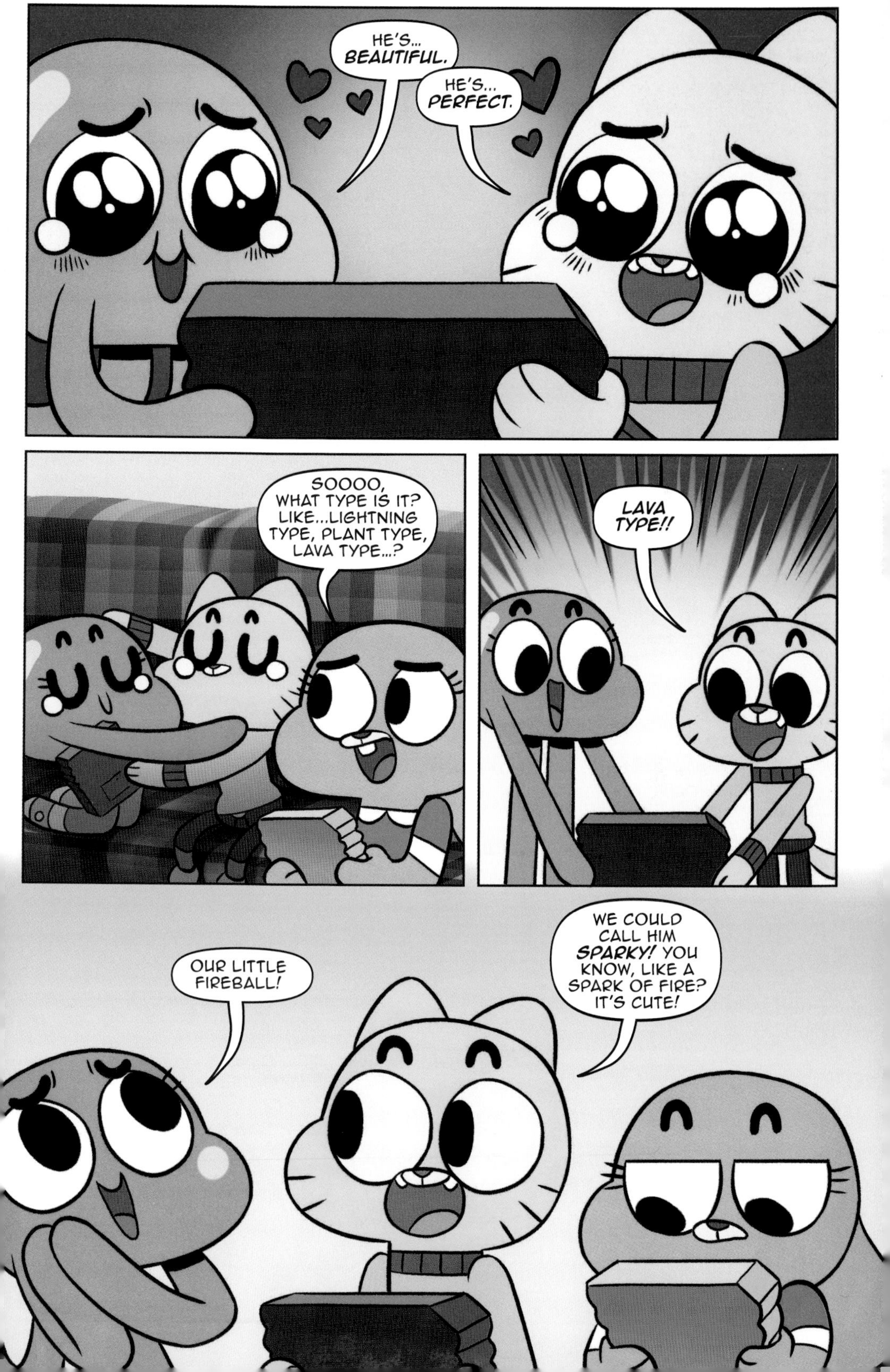
HE'S... BEAUTIFUL.
HE'S... PERFECT.
SOOOO, WHAT TYPE IS IT? LIKE...LIGHTNING TYPE, PLANT TYPE, LAVA TYPE...?
LAVA TYPE!!
OUR LITTLE FIREBALL!
WE COULD CALL HIM SPARKY! YOU KNOW, LIKE A SPARK OF FIRE? IT'S CUTE!

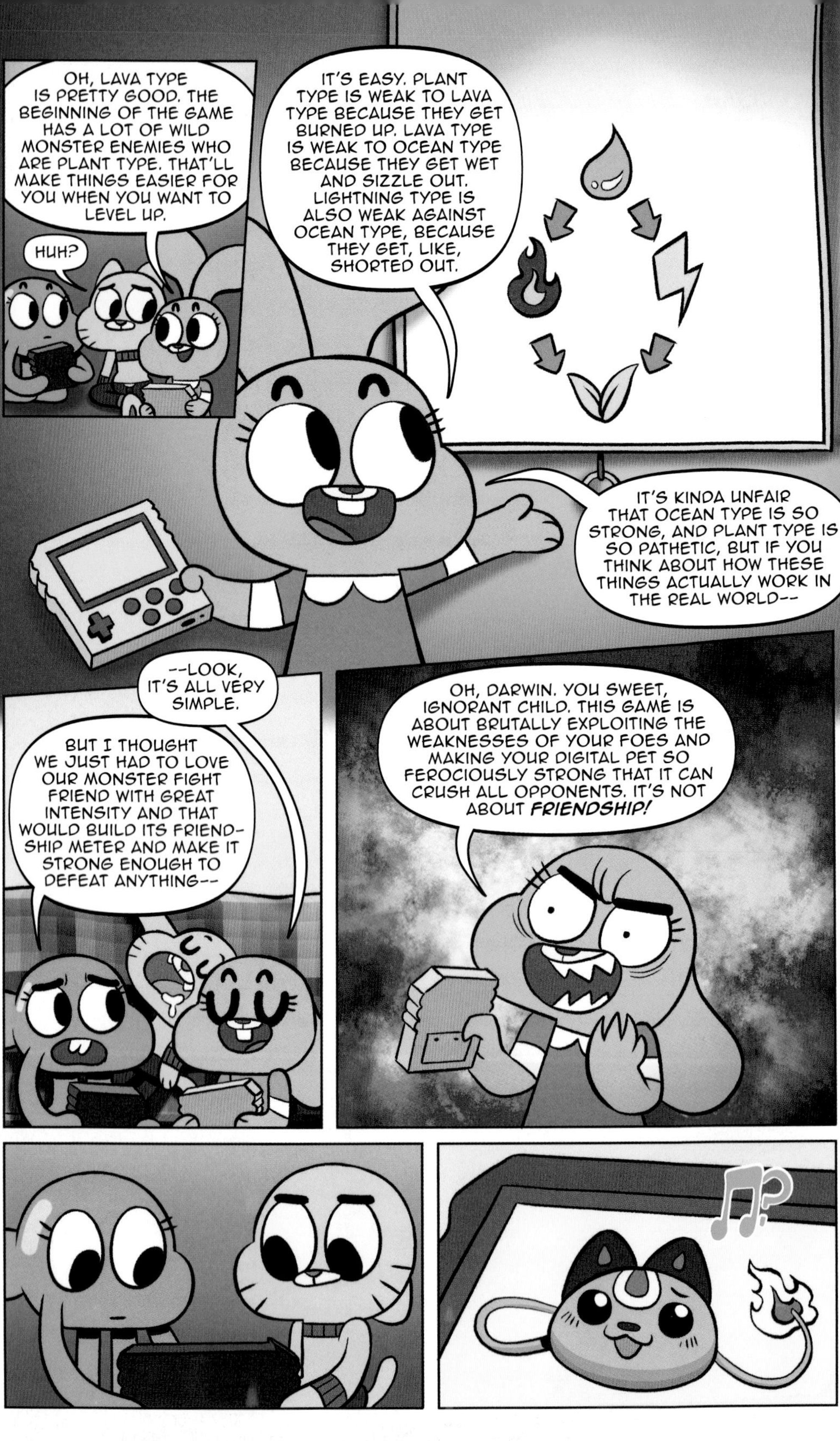
OH, LAVA TYPE IS PRETTY GOOD. THE BEGINNING OF THE GAME HAS A LOT OF WILD MONSTER ENEMIES WHO ARE PLANT TYPE. THAT'LL MAKE THINGS EASIER FOR YOU WHEN YOU WANT TO LEVEL UP.
HUH?
IT'S EASY. PLANT TYPE IS WEAK TO LAVA TYPE BECAUSE THEY GET BURNED UP. LAVA TYPE IS WEAK TO OCEAN TYPE BECAUSE THEY GET WET AND SIZZLE OUT. LIGHTNING TYPE IS ALSO WEAK AGAINST OCEAN TYPE, BECAUSE THEY GET, LIKE, SHORTED OUT.
IT'S KINDA UNFAIR THAT OCEAN TYPE IS SO STRONG, AND PLANT TYPE IS SO PATHETIC, BUT IF YOU THINK ABOUT HOW THESE THINGS ACTUALLY WORK IN THE REAL WORLD--
--LOOK, IT'S ALL VERY SIMPLE.
BUT I THOUGHT WE JUST HAD TO LOVE OUR MONSTER FIGHT FRIEND WITH GREAT INTENSITY AND THAT WOULD BUILD ITS FRIEND-SHIP METER AND MAKE IT STRONG ENOUGH TO DEFEAT ANYTHING--
OH, DARWIN. YOU SWEET, IGNORANT CHILD. THIS GAME IS ABOUT BRUTALLY EXPLOITING THE WEAKNESSES OF YOUR FOES AND MAKING YOUR DIGITAL PET SO FEROCIOUSLY STRONG THAT IT CAN CRUSH ALL OPPONENTS. IT'S NOT ABOUT ***FRIENDSHIP!***

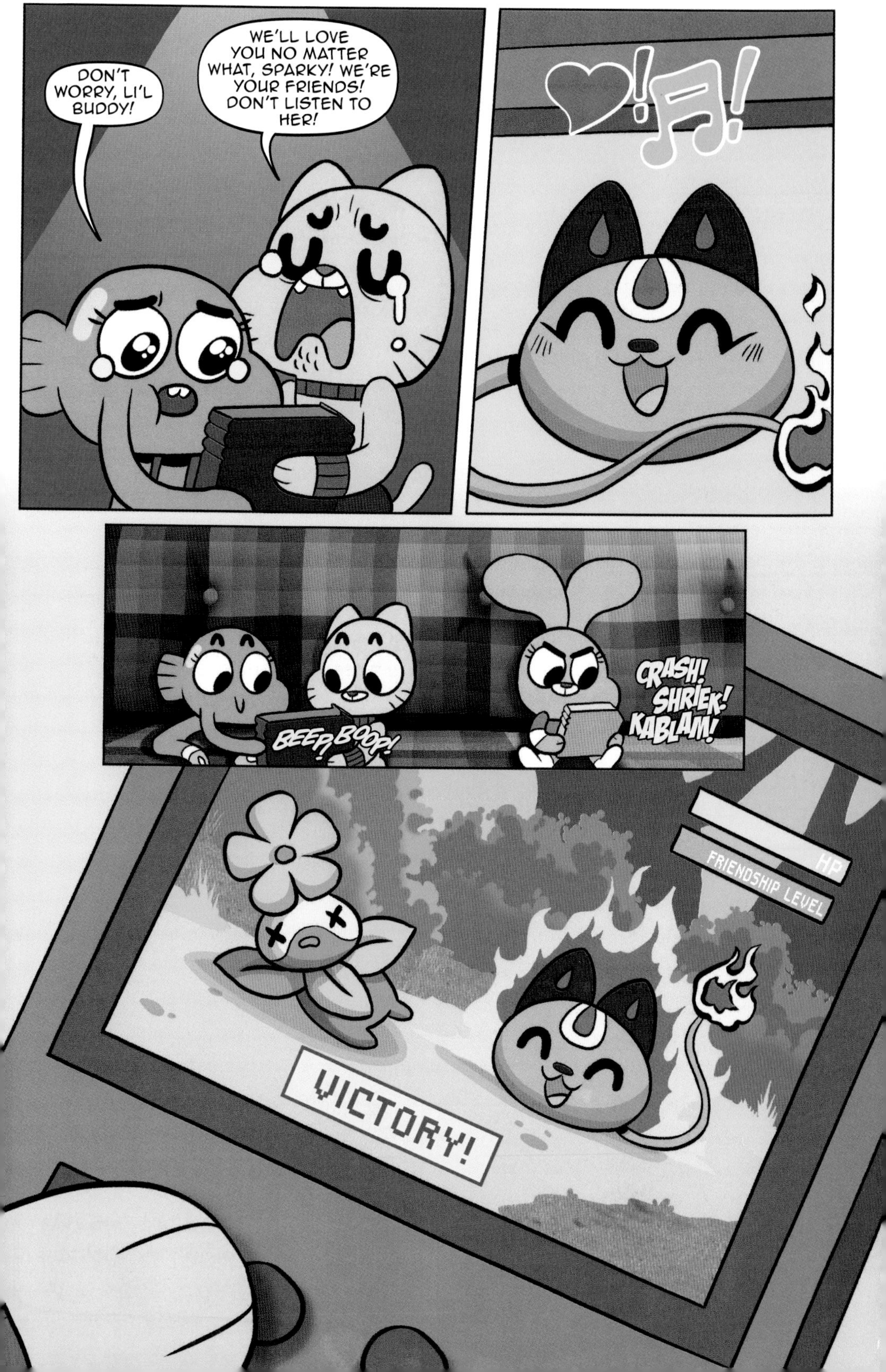
DON'T WORRY, LI'L BUDDY!
WE'LL LOVE YOU NO MATTER WHAT, SPARKY! WE'RE YOUR FRIENDS! DON'T LISTEN TO HER!
BEEP! BOOP!
CRASH! SHRIEK! KABLAM!
HP
FRIENDSHIP LEVEL
VICTORY!

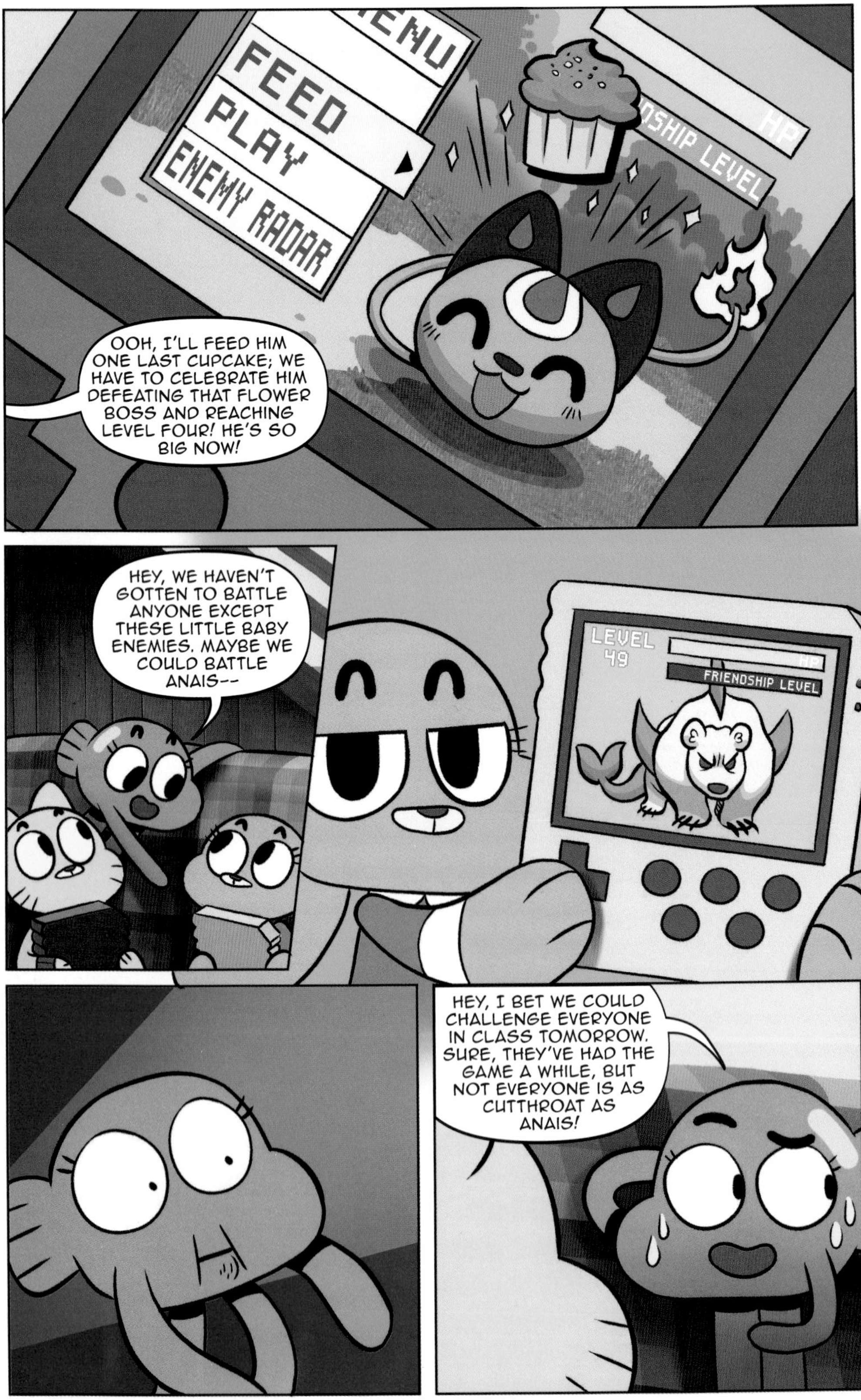
MENU
FEED
PLAY
ENEMY RADAR
HP
FRIENDSHIP LEVEL
OOH, I'LL FEED HIM ONE LAST CUPCAKE; WE HAVE TO CELEBRATE HIM DEFEATING THAT FLOWER BOSS AND REACHING LEVEL FOUR! HE'S SO BIG NOW!
HEY, WE HAVEN'T GOTTEN TO BATTLE ANYONE EXCEPT THESE LITTLE BABY ENEMIES. MAYBE WE COULD BATTLE ANAIS--
LEVEL 49
HP
FRIENDSHIP LEVEL
HEY, I BET WE COULD CHALLENGE EVERYONE IN CLASS TOMORROW. SURE, THEY'VE HAD THE GAME A WHILE, BUT NOT EVERYONE IS AS CUTTHROAT AS ANAIS!

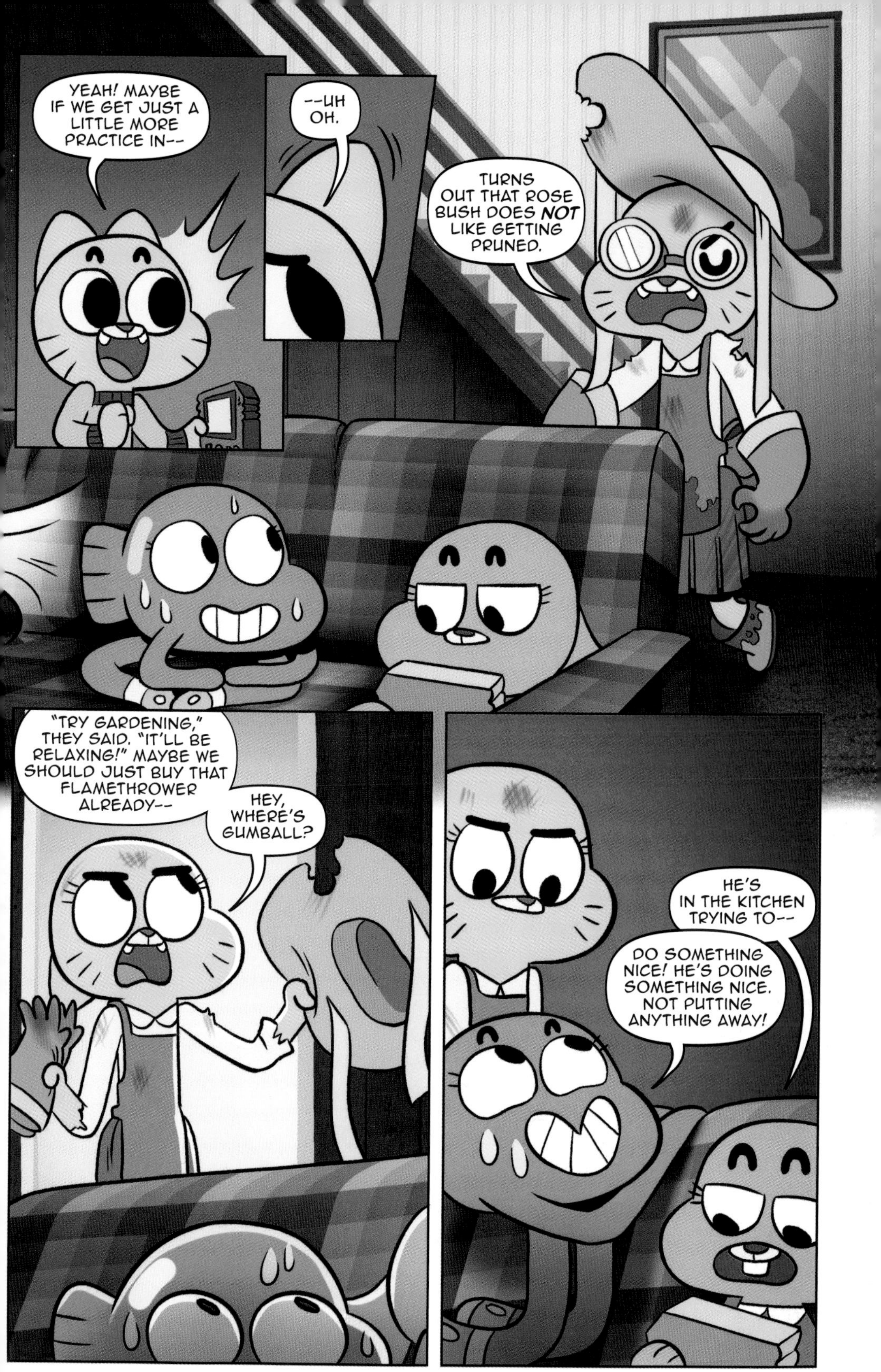
YEAH! MAYBE IF WE GET JUST A LITTLE MORE PRACTICE IN--
--UH OH.
TURNS OUT THAT ROSE BUSH DOES NOT LIKE GETTING PRUNED.
"TRY GARDENING," THEY SAID. "IT'LL BE RELAXING!" MAYBE WE SHOULD JUST BUY THAT FLAMETHROWER ALREADY--
HEY, WHERE'S GUMBALL?
HE'S IN THE KITCHEN TRYING TO--
DO SOMETHING NICE! HE'S DOING SOMETHING NICE. NOT PUTTING ANYTHING AWAY!

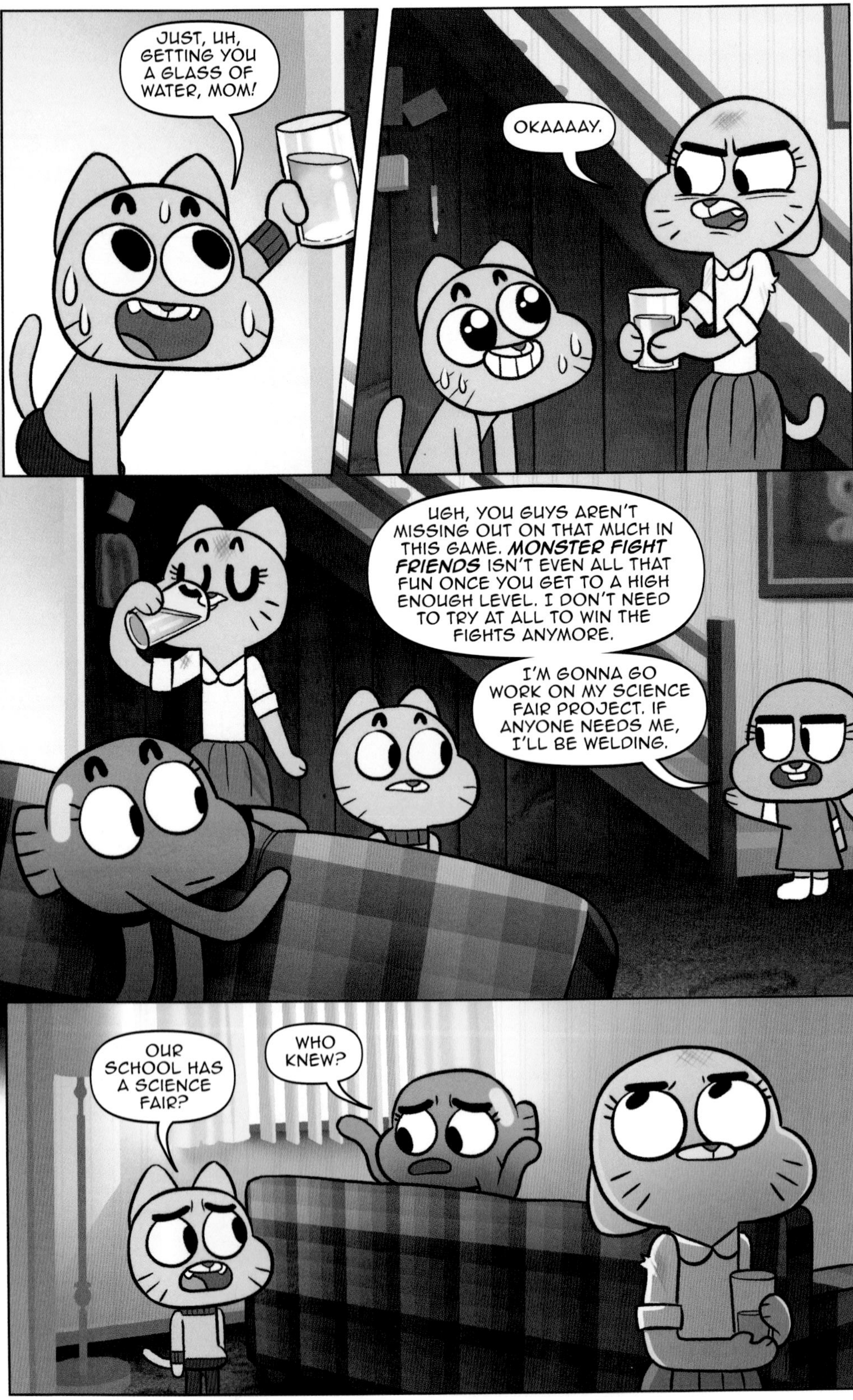

JUST, UH, GETTING YOU A GLASS OF WATER, MOM!
OKAAAAY.
UGH, YOU GUYS AREN'T MISSING OUT ON THAT MUCH IN THIS GAME. ***MONSTER FIGHT FRIENDS*** ISN'T EVEN ALL THAT FUN ONCE YOU GET TO A HIGH ENOUGH LEVEL. I DON'T NEED TO TRY AT ALL TO WIN THE FIGHTS ANYMORE.
I'M GONNA GO WORK ON MY SCIENCE FAIR PROJECT. IF ANYONE NEEDS ME, I'LL BE WELDING.
OUR SCHOOL HAS A SCIENCE FAIR?
WHO KNEW?

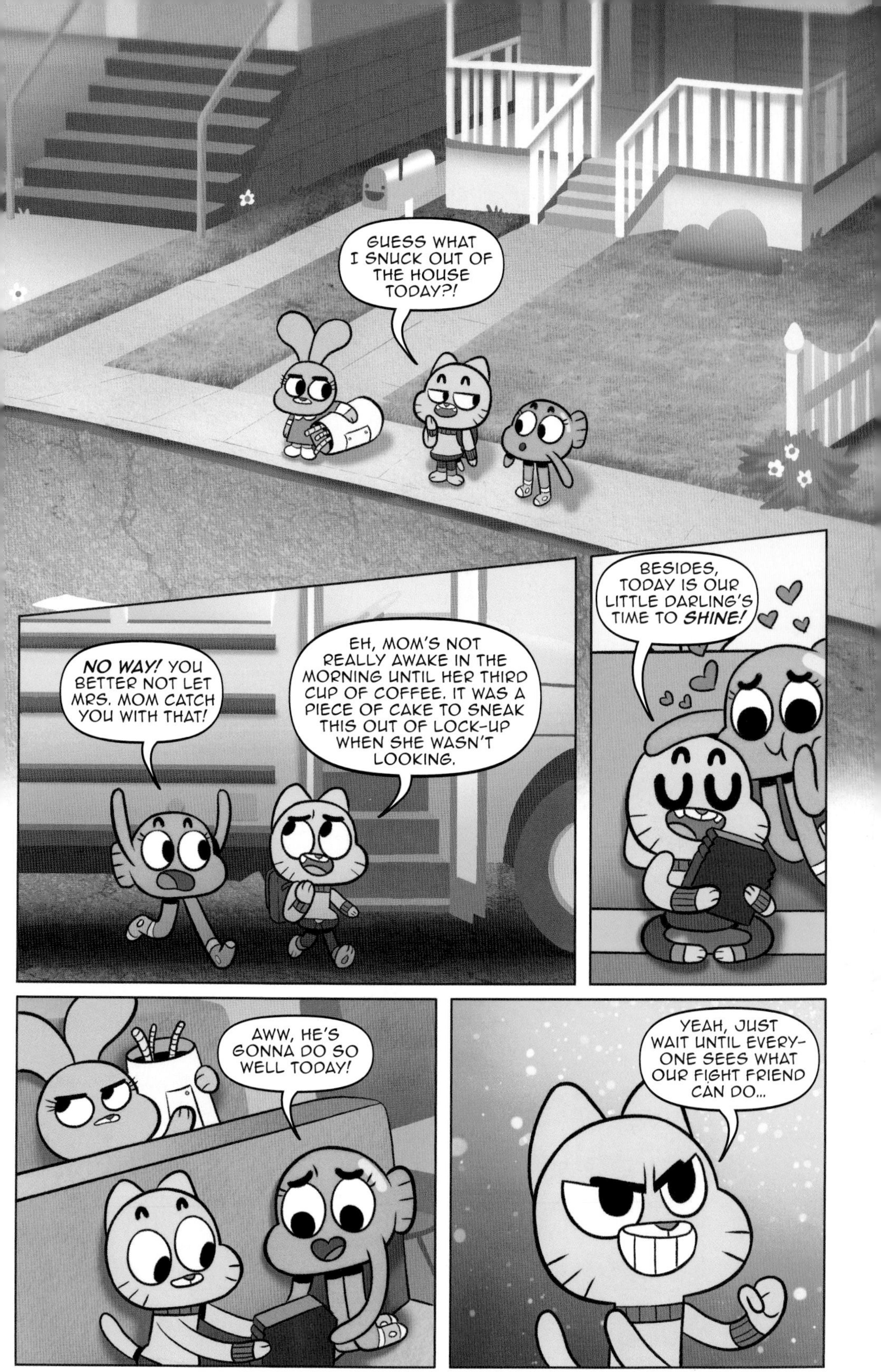
GUESS WHAT I SNUCK OUT OF THE HOUSE TODAY?!
NO WAY! YOU BETTER NOT LET MRS. MOM CATCH YOU WITH THAT!
EH, MOM'S NOT REALLY AWAKE IN THE MORNING UNTIL HER THIRD CUP OF COFFEE. IT WAS A PIECE OF CAKE TO SNEAK THIS OUT OF LOCK-UP WHEN SHE WASN'T LOOKING.
BESIDES, TODAY IS OUR LITTLE DARLING'S TIME TO SHINE!
AWW, HE'S GONNA DO SO WELL TODAY!
YEAH, JUST WAIT UNTIL EVERYONE SEES WHAT OUR FIGHT FRIEND CAN DO...

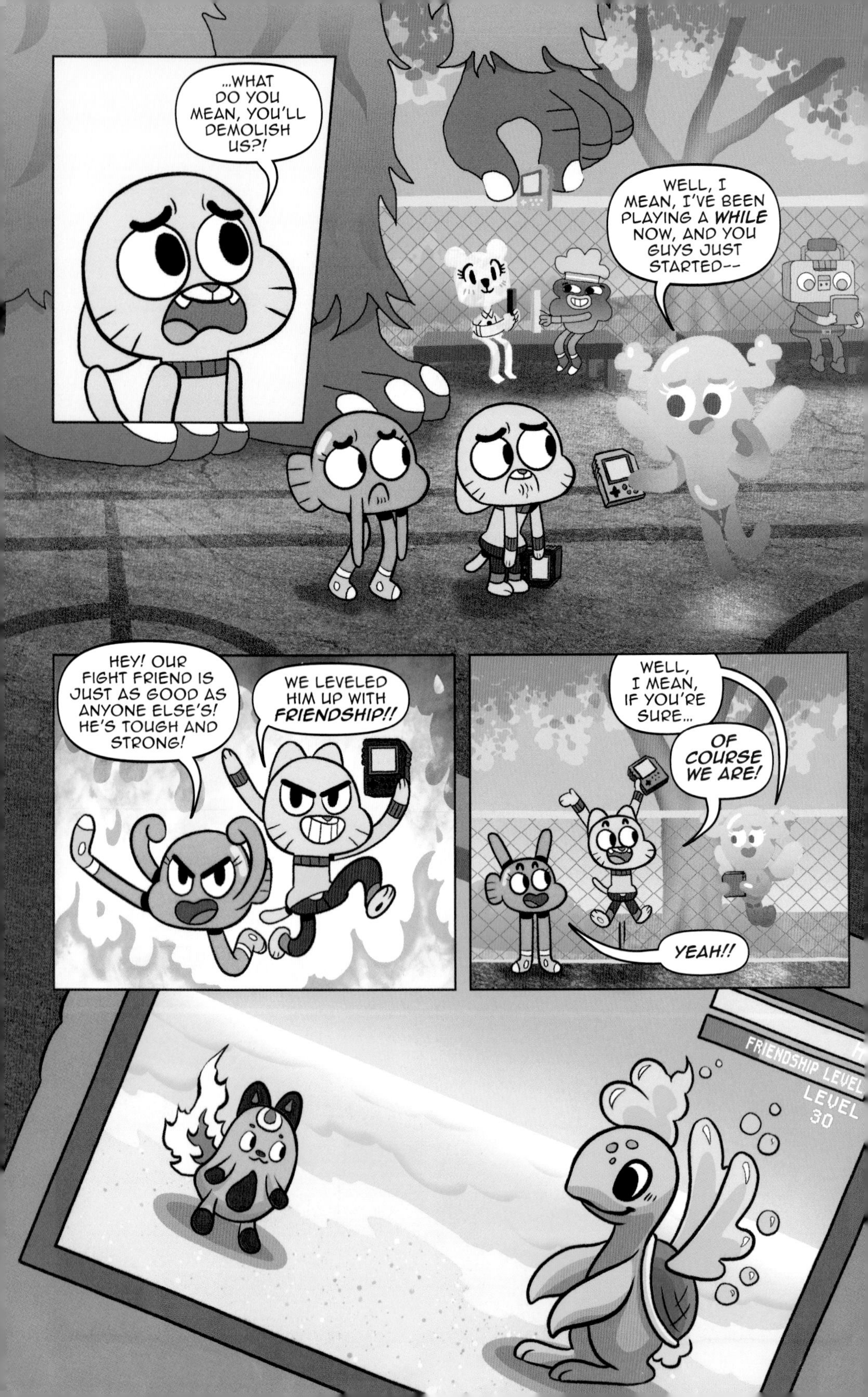
...WHAT DO YOU MEAN, YOU'LL DEMOLISH US?!
WELL, I MEAN, I'VE BEEN PLAYING A *WHILE* NOW, AND YOU GUYS JUST STARTED--
HEY! OUR FIGHT FRIEND IS JUST AS GOOD AS ANYONE ELSE'S! HE'S TOUGH AND STRONG!
WE LEVELED HIM UP WITH *FRIENDSHIP!!*
WELL, I MEAN, IF YOU'RE SURE...
OF COURSE WE ARE!
YEAH!!
FRIENDSHIP LEVEL
LEVEL 30

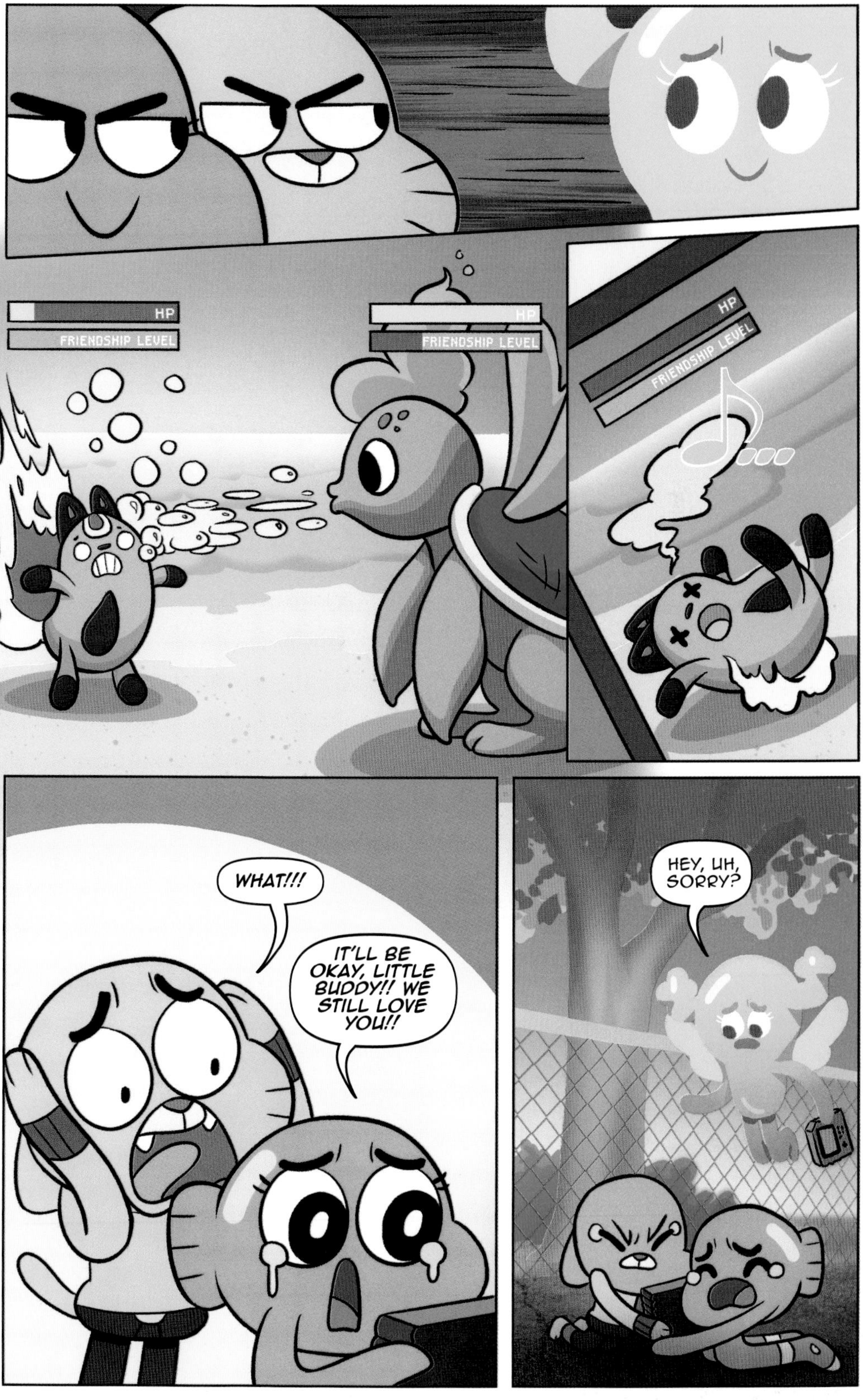
HP
FRIENDSHIP LEVEL
HP
FRIENDSHIP LEVEL
HP
FRIENDSHIP LEVEL
WHAT!!!
IT'LL BE OKAY, LITTLE BUDDY!! WE STILL LOVE YOU!!
HEY, UH, SORRY?

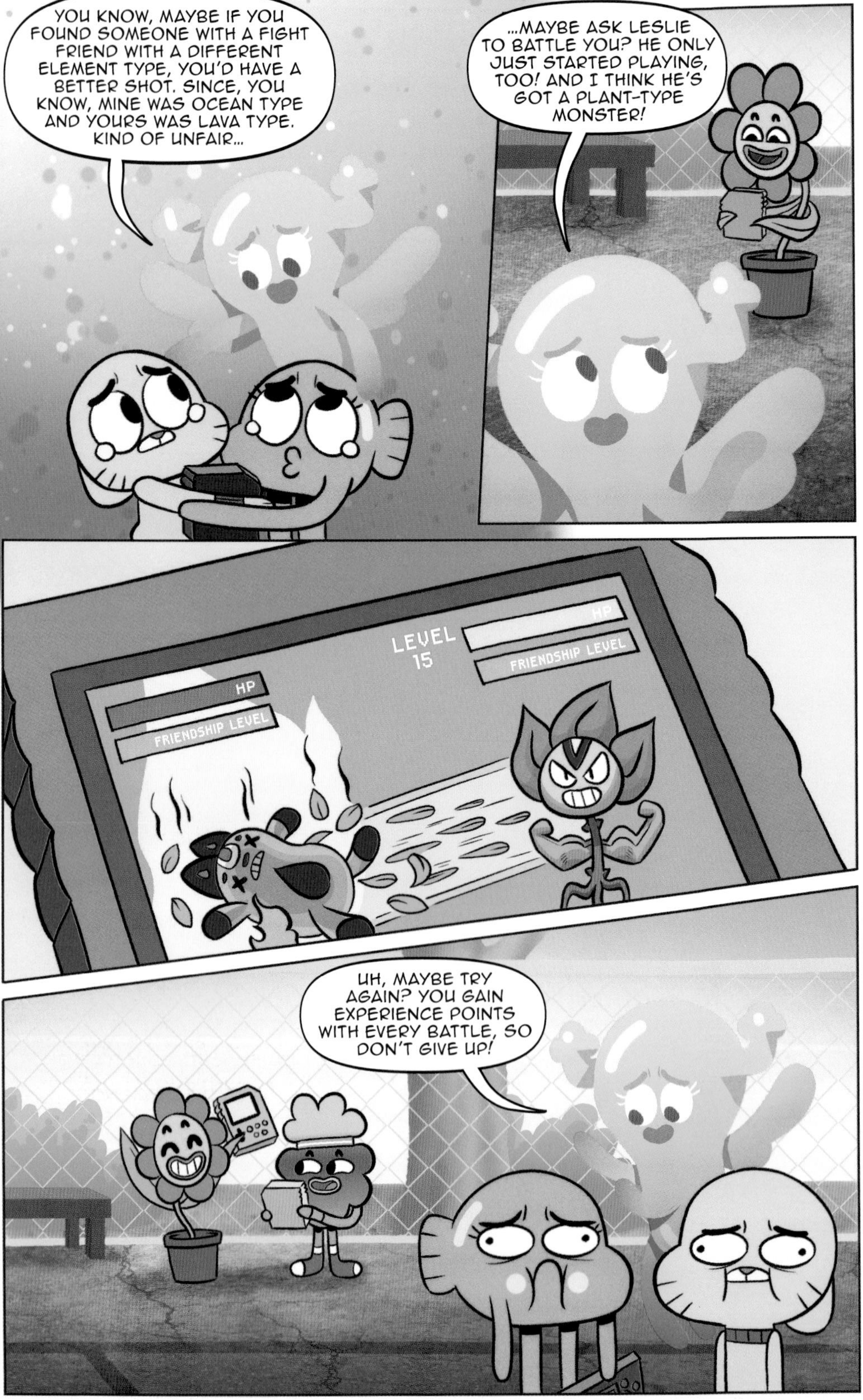
YOU KNOW, MAYBE IF YOU FOUND SOMEONE WITH A FIGHT FRIEND WITH A DIFFERENT ELEMENT TYPE, YOU'D HAVE A BETTER SHOT. SINCE, YOU KNOW, MINE WAS OCEAN TYPE AND YOURS WAS LAVA TYPE. KIND OF UNFAIR...
...MAYBE ASK LESLIE TO BATTLE YOU? HE ONLY JUST STARTED PLAYING, TOO! AND I THINK HE'S GOT A PLANT-TYPE MONSTER!
LEVEL 15
HP
FRIENDSHIP LEVEL
HP
FRIENDSHIP LEVEL
UH, MAYBE TRY AGAIN? YOU GAIN EXPERIENCE POINTS WITH EVERY BATTLE, SO DON'T GIVE UP!

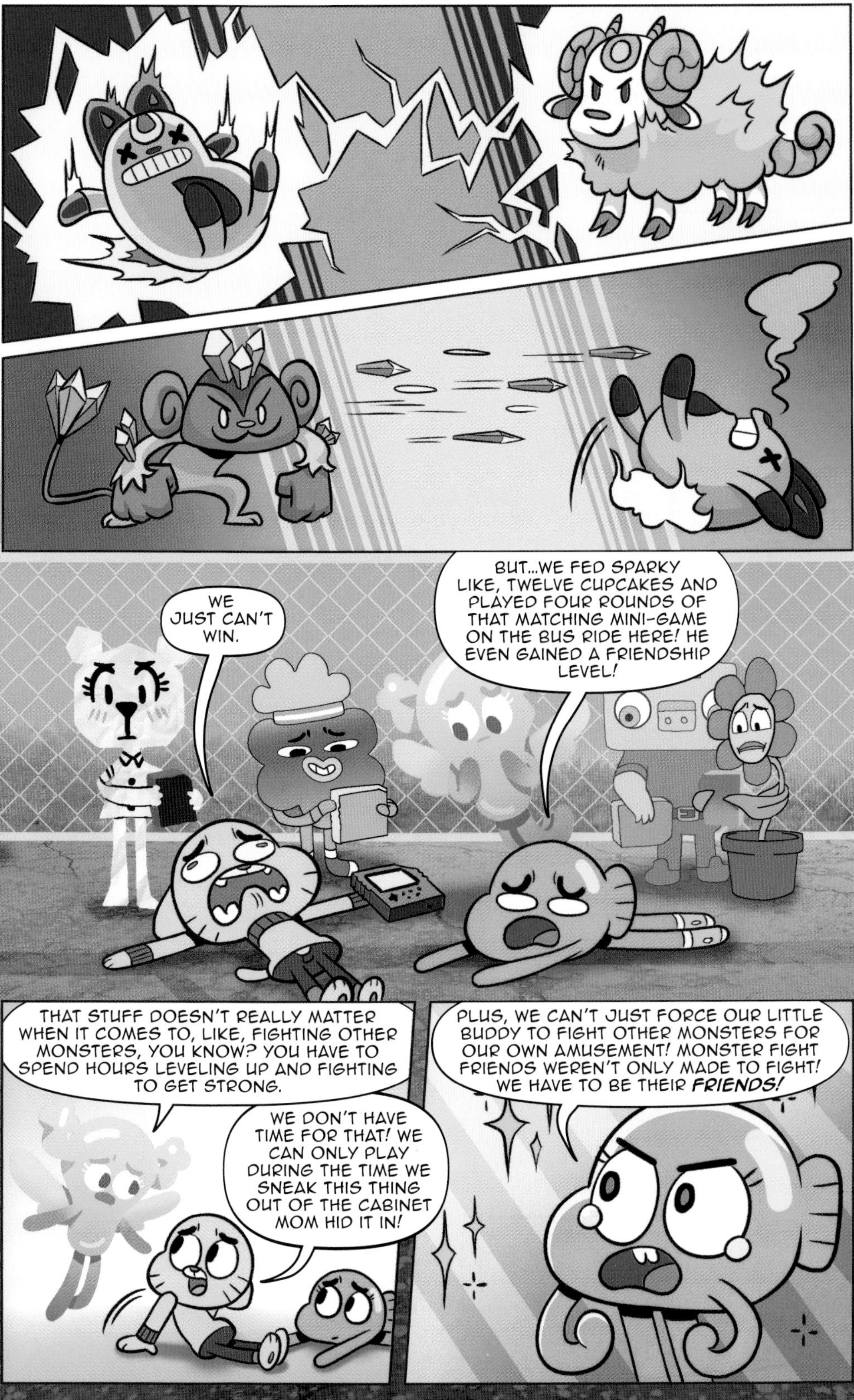

WE JUST CAN'T WIN.
BUT...WE FED SPARKY LIKE, TWELVE CUPCAKES AND PLAYED FOUR ROUNDS OF THAT MATCHING MINI-GAME ON THE BUS RIDE HERE! HE EVEN GAINED A FRIENDSHIP LEVEL!
THAT STUFF DOESN'T REALLY MATTER WHEN IT COMES TO, LIKE, FIGHTING OTHER MONSTERS, YOU KNOW? YOU HAVE TO SPEND HOURS LEVELING UP AND FIGHTING TO GET STRONG.
WE DON'T HAVE TIME FOR THAT! WE CAN ONLY PLAY DURING THE TIME WE SNEAK THIS THING OUT OF THE CABINET MOM HID IT IN!
PLUS, WE CAN'T JUST FORCE OUR LITTLE BUDDY TO FIGHT OTHER MONSTERS FOR OUR OWN AMUSEMENT! MONSTER FIGHT FRIENDS WEREN'T ONLY MADE TO FIGHT! WE HAVE TO BE THEIR ***FRIENDS!***

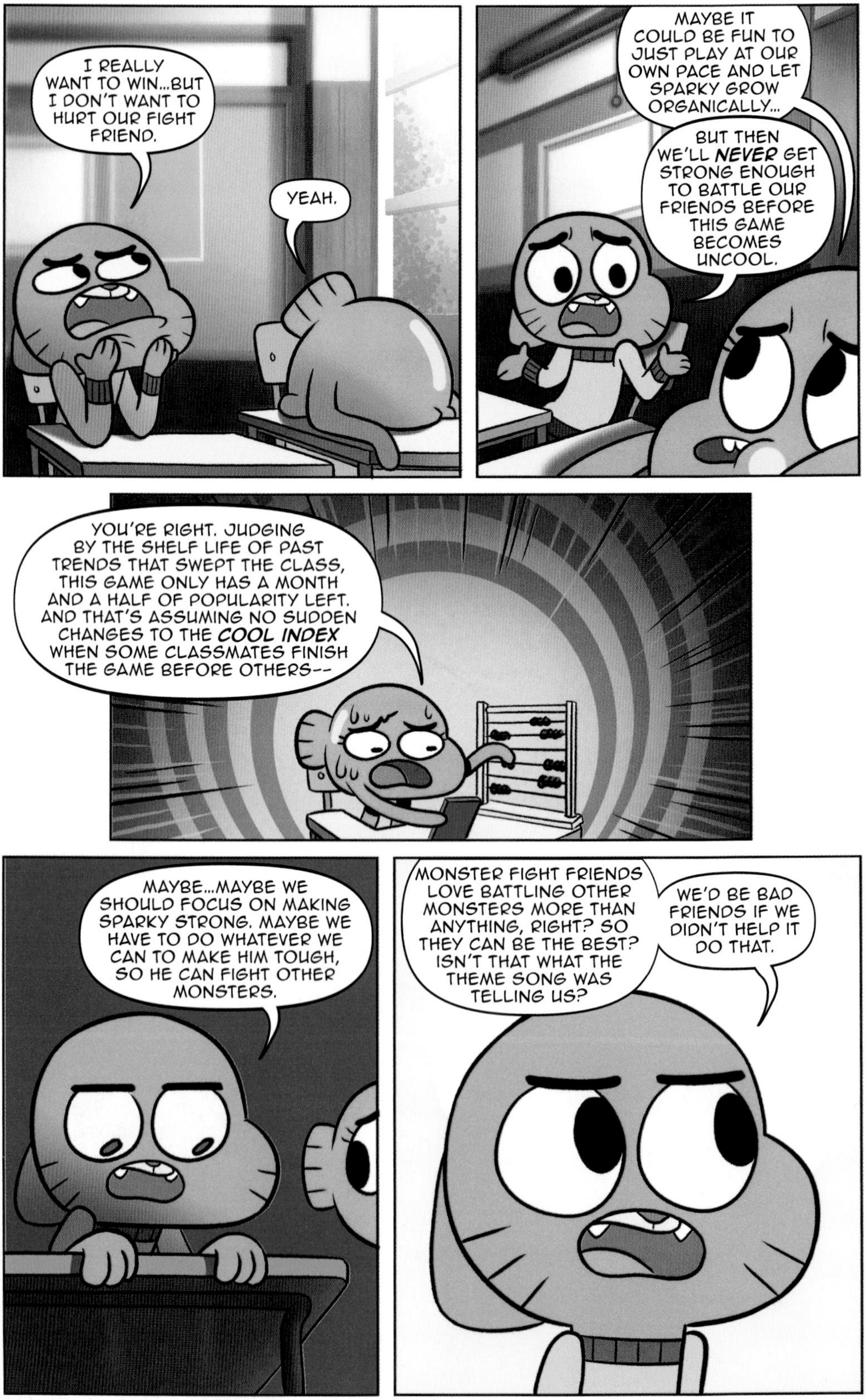
I REALLY WANT TO WIN...BUT I DON'T WANT TO HURT OUR FIGHT FRIEND.
YEAH.
MAYBE IT COULD BE FUN TO JUST PLAY AT OUR OWN PACE AND LET SPARKY GROW ORGANICALLY...
BUT THEN WE'LL NEVER GET STRONG ENOUGH TO BATTLE OUR FRIENDS BEFORE THIS GAME BECOMES UNCOOL.
YOU'RE RIGHT. JUDGING BY THE SHELF LIFE OF PAST TRENDS THAT SWEPT THE CLASS, THIS GAME ONLY HAS A MONTH AND A HALF OF POPULARITY LEFT. AND THAT'S ASSUMING NO SUDDEN CHANGES TO THE COOL INDEX WHEN SOME CLASSMATES FINISH THE GAME BEFORE OTHERS--
MAYBE...MAYBE WE SHOULD FOCUS ON MAKING SPARKY STRONG. MAYBE WE HAVE TO DO WHATEVER WE CAN TO MAKE HIM TOUGH, SO HE CAN FIGHT OTHER MONSTERS.
MONSTER FIGHT FRIENDS LOVE BATTLING OTHER MONSTERS MORE THAN ANYTHING, RIGHT? SO THEY CAN BE THE BEST? ISN'T THAT WHAT THE THEME SONG WAS TELLING US?
WE'D BE BAD FRIENDS IF WE DIDN'T HELP IT DO THAT.

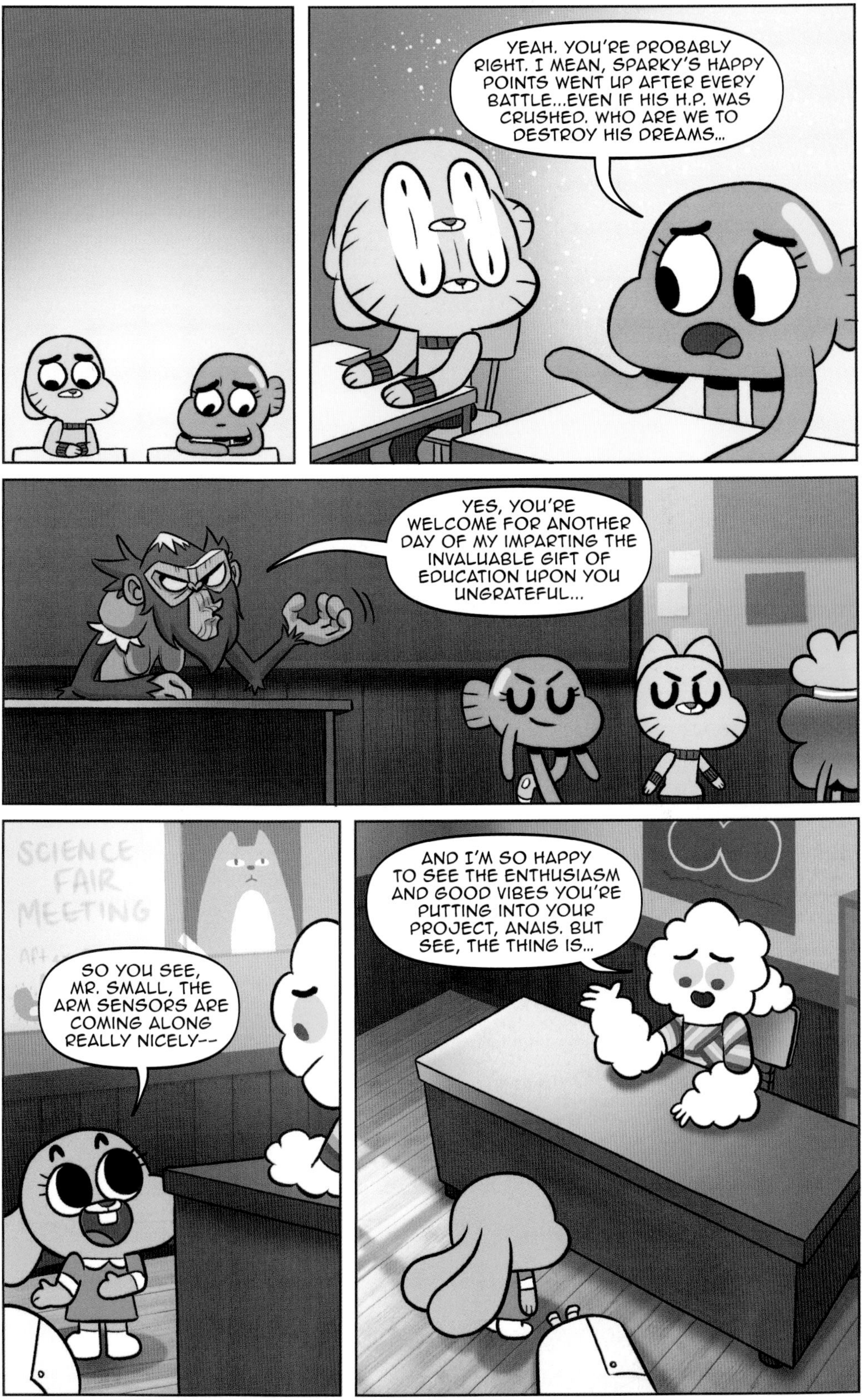

YEAH. YOU'RE PROBABLY RIGHT. I MEAN, SPARKY'S HAPPY POINTS WENT UP AFTER EVERY BATTLE...EVEN IF HIS H.P. WAS CRUSHED. WHO ARE WE TO DESTROY HIS DREAMS...
YES, YOU'RE WELCOME FOR ANOTHER DAY OF MY IMPARTING THE INVALUABLE GIFT OF EDUCATION UPON YOU UNGRATEFUL...
SCIENCE FAIR MEETING
SO YOU SEE, MR. SMALL, THE ARM SENSORS ARE COMING ALONG REALLY NICELY--
AND I'M SO HAPPY TO SEE THE ENTHUSIASM AND GOOD VIBES YOU'RE PUTTING INTO YOUR PROJECT, ANAIS. BUT SEE, THE THING IS...

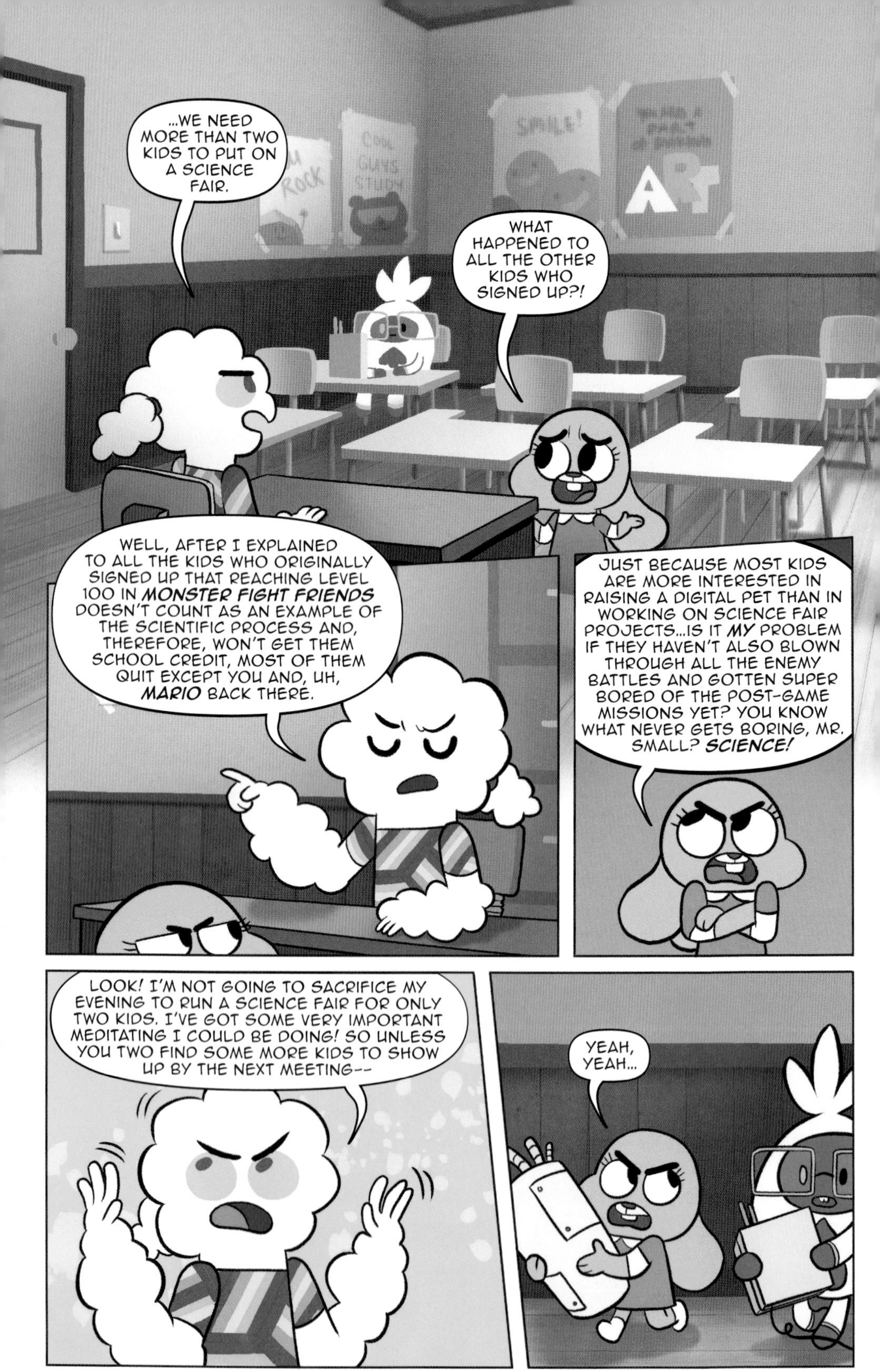
...WE NEED MORE THAN TWO KIDS TO PUT ON A SCIENCE FAIR.
WHAT HAPPENED TO ALL THE OTHER KIDS WHO SIGNED UP?!
WELL, AFTER I EXPLAINED TO ALL THE KIDS WHO ORIGINALLY SIGNED UP THAT REACHING LEVEL 100 IN MONSTER FIGHT FRIENDS DOESN'T COUNT AS AN EXAMPLE OF THE SCIENTIFIC PROCESS AND, THEREFORE, WON'T GET THEM SCHOOL CREDIT, MOST OF THEM QUIT EXCEPT YOU AND, UH, MARIO BACK THERE.
JUST BECAUSE MOST KIDS ARE MORE INTERESTED IN RAISING A DIGITAL PET THAN IN WORKING ON SCIENCE FAIR PROJECTS...IS IT MY PROBLEM IF THEY HAVEN'T ALSO BLOWN THROUGH ALL THE ENEMY BATTLES AND GOTTEN SUPER BORED OF THE POST-GAME MISSIONS YET? YOU KNOW WHAT NEVER GETS BORING, MR. SMALL? SCIENCE!
LOOK! I'M NOT GOING TO SACRIFICE MY EVENING TO RUN A SCIENCE FAIR FOR ONLY TWO KIDS. I'VE GOT SOME VERY IMPORTANT MEDITATING I COULD BE DOING! SO UNLESS YOU TWO FIND SOME MORE KIDS TO SHOW UP BY THE NEXT MEETING--
YEAH, YEAH...

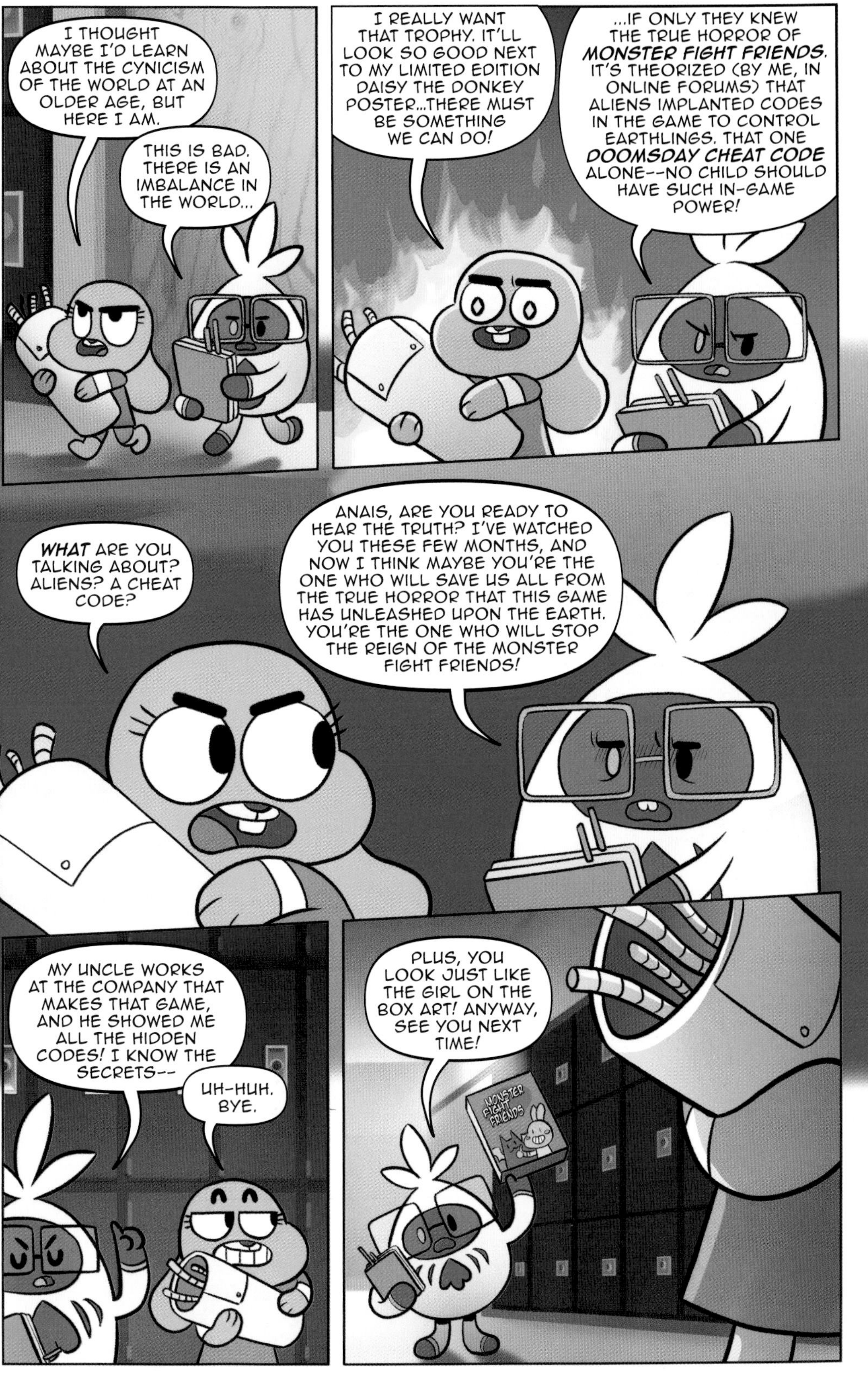
I THOUGHT MAYBE I'D LEARN ABOUT THE CYNICISM OF THE WORLD AT AN OLDER AGE, BUT HERE I AM.
THIS IS BAD. THERE IS AN IMBALANCE IN THE WORLD...
I REALLY WANT THAT TROPHY. IT'LL LOOK SO GOOD NEXT TO MY LIMITED EDITION DAISY THE DONKEY POSTER...THERE MUST BE SOMETHING WE CAN DO!
...IF ONLY THEY KNEW THE TRUE HORROR OF MONSTER FIGHT FRIENDS. IT'S THEORIZED (BY ME, IN ONLINE FORUMS) THAT ALIENS IMPLANTED CODES IN THE GAME TO CONTROL EARTHLINGS. THAT ONE DOOMSDAY CHEAT CODE ALONE--NO CHILD SHOULD HAVE SUCH IN-GAME POWER!
WHAT ARE YOU TALKING ABOUT? ALIENS? A CHEAT CODE?
ANAIS, ARE YOU READY TO HEAR THE TRUTH? I'VE WATCHED YOU THESE FEW MONTHS, AND NOW I THINK MAYBE YOU'RE THE ONE WHO WILL SAVE US ALL FROM THE TRUE HORROR THAT THIS GAME HAS UNLEASHED UPON THE EARTH. YOU'RE THE ONE WHO WILL STOP THE REIGN OF THE MONSTER FIGHT FRIENDS!
MY UNCLE WORKS AT THE COMPANY THAT MAKES THAT GAME, AND HE SHOWED ME ALL THE HIDDEN CODES! I KNOW THE SECRETS--
UH-HUH. BYE.
PLUS, YOU LOOK JUST LIKE THE GIRL ON THE BOX ART! ANYWAY, SEE YOU NEXT TIME!
MONSTER FIGHT FRIENDS

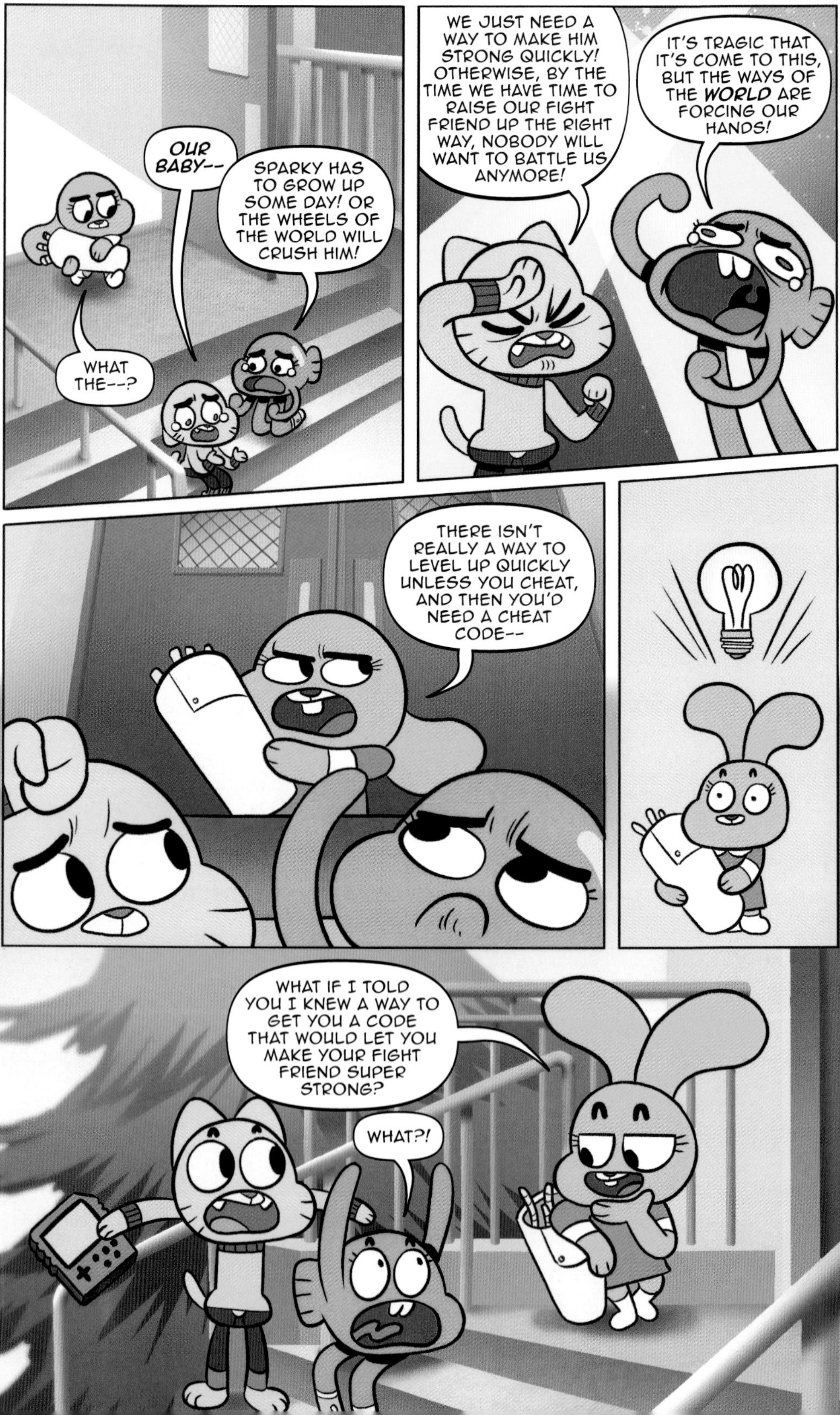
OUR BABY--
SPARKY HAS TO GROW UP SOME DAY! OR THE WHEELS OF THE WORLD WILL CRUSH HIM!
WHAT THE--?
WE JUST NEED A WAY TO MAKE HIM STRONG QUICKLY! OTHERWISE, BY THE TIME WE HAVE TIME TO RAISE OUR FIGHT FRIEND UP THE RIGHT WAY, NOBODY WILL WANT TO BATTLE US ANYMORE!
IT'S TRAGIC THAT IT'S COME TO THIS, BUT THE WAYS OF THE WORLD ARE FORCING OUR HANDS!
THERE ISN'T REALLY A WAY TO LEVEL UP QUICKLY UNLESS YOU CHEAT, AND THEN YOU'D NEED A CHEAT CODE--
WHAT IF I TOLD YOU I KNEW A WAY TO GET YOU A CODE THAT WOULD LET YOU MAKE YOUR FIGHT FRIEND SUPER STRONG?
WHAT?!

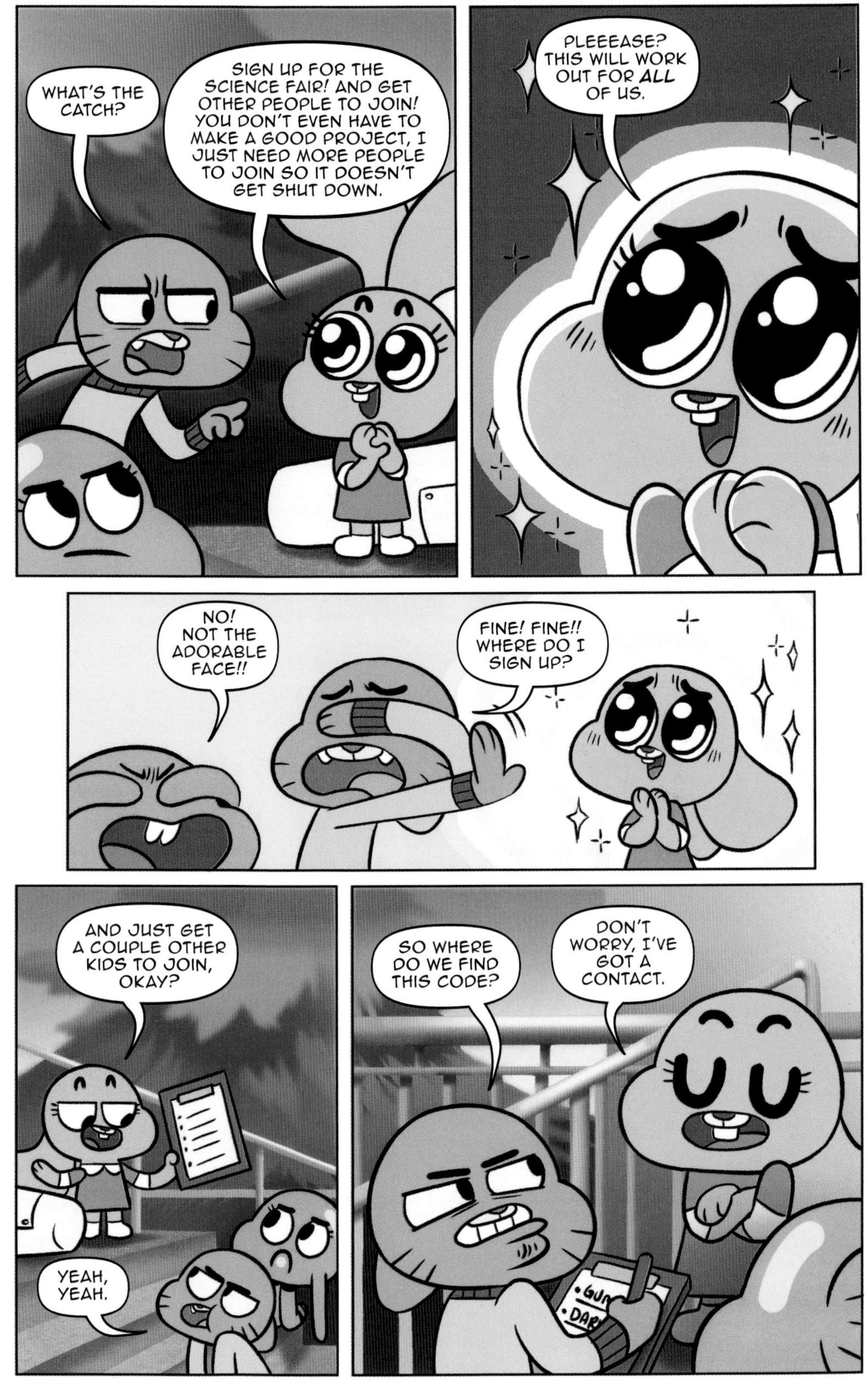
WHAT'S THE CATCH?
SIGN UP FOR THE SCIENCE FAIR! AND GET OTHER PEOPLE TO JOIN! YOU DON'T EVEN HAVE TO MAKE A GOOD PROJECT, I JUST NEED MORE PEOPLE TO JOIN SO IT DOESN'T GET SHUT DOWN.
PLEEEASE? THIS WILL WORK OUT FOR ALL OF US.
NO! NOT THE ADORABLE FACE!!
FINE! FINE!! WHERE DO I SIGN UP?
AND JUST GET A COUPLE OTHER KIDS TO JOIN, OKAY?
YEAH, YEAH.
SO WHERE DO WE FIND THIS CODE?
DON'T WORRY, I'VE GOT A CONTACT.

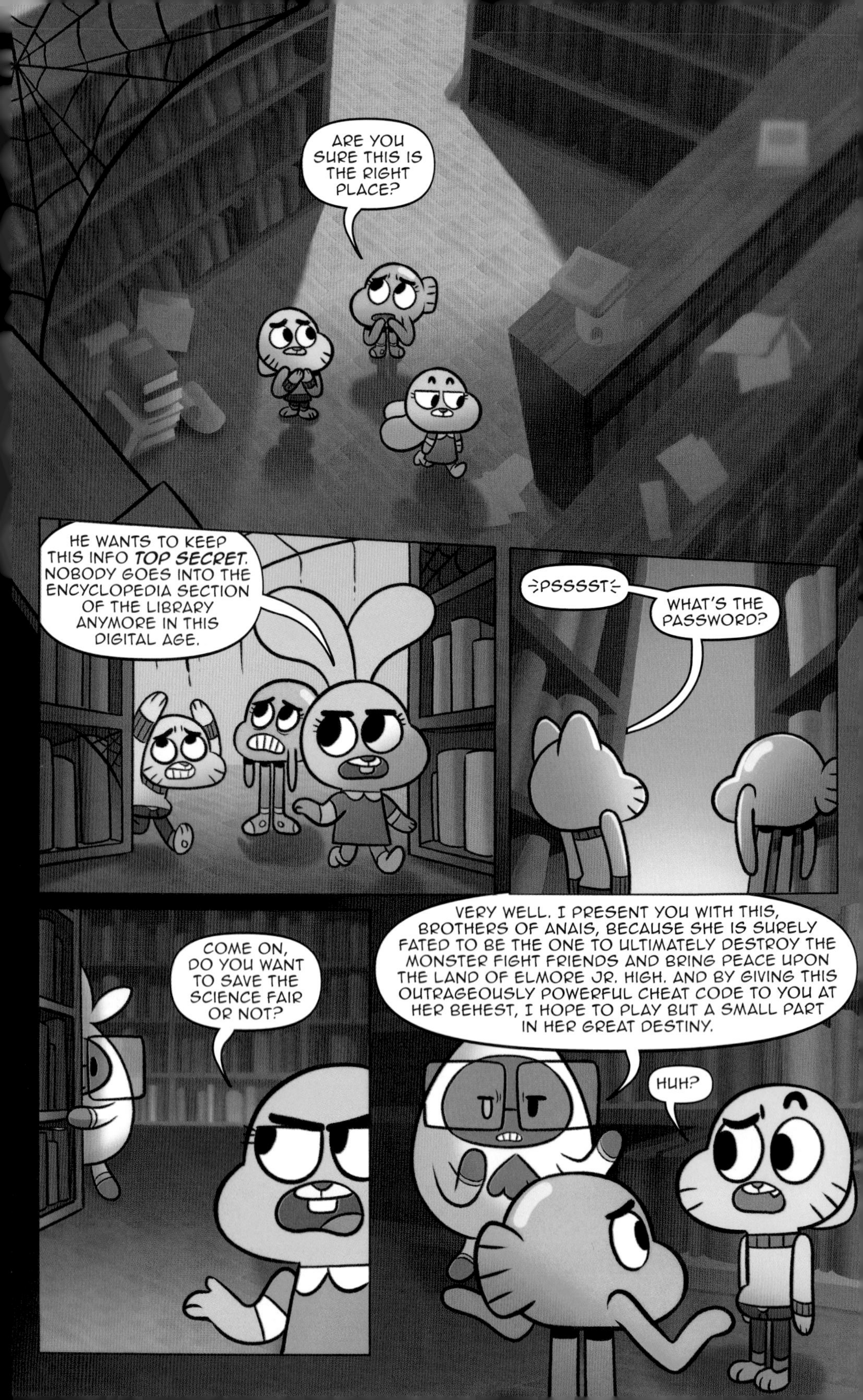
ARE YOU SURE THIS IS THE RIGHT PLACE?
HE WANTS TO KEEP THIS INFO TOP SECRET. NOBODY GOES INTO THE ENCYCLOPEDIA SECTION OF THE LIBRARY ANYMORE IN THIS DIGITAL AGE.
PSSSST
WHAT'S THE PASSWORD?
COME ON, DO YOU WANT TO SAVE THE SCIENCE FAIR OR NOT?
VERY WELL. I PRESENT YOU WITH THIS, BROTHERS OF ANAIS, BECAUSE SHE IS SURELY FATED TO BE THE ONE TO ULTIMATELY DESTROY THE MONSTER FIGHT FRIENDS AND BRING PEACE UPON THE LAND OF ELMORE JR. HIGH. AND BY GIVING THIS OUTRAGEOUSLY POWERFUL CHEAT CODE TO YOU AT HER BEHEST, I HOPE TO PLAY BUT A SMALL PART IN HER GREAT DESTINY.
HUH?

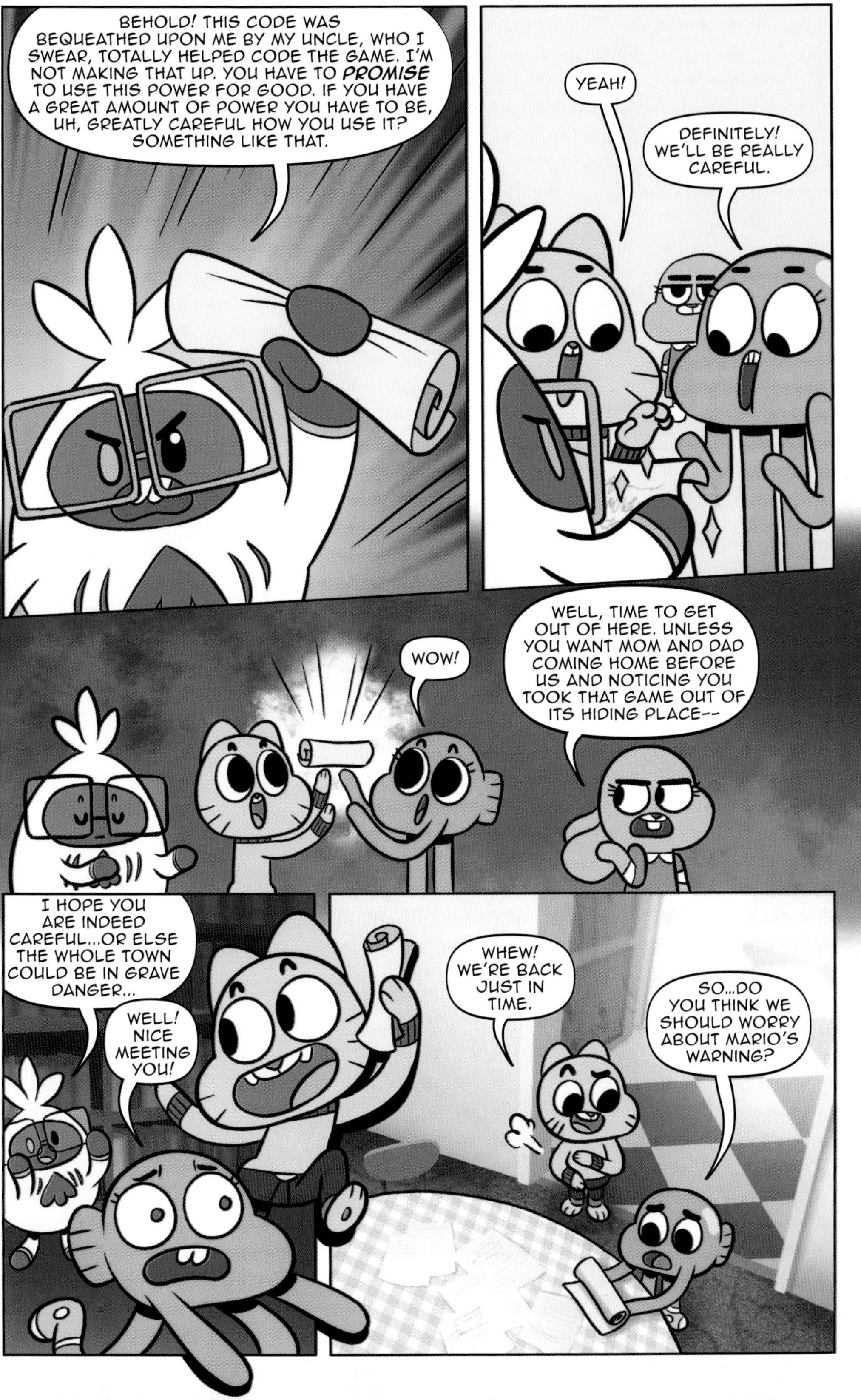
BEHOLD! THIS CODE WAS BEQUEATHED UPON ME BY MY UNCLE, WHO I SWEAR, TOTALLY HELPED CODE THE GAME. I'M NOT MAKING THAT UP. YOU HAVE TO PROMISE TO USE THIS POWER FOR GOOD. IF YOU HAVE A GREAT AMOUNT OF POWER YOU HAVE TO BE, UH, GREATLY CAREFUL HOW YOU USE IT? SOMETHING LIKE THAT.
YEAH!
DEFINITELY! WE'LL BE REALLY CAREFUL.
WOW!
WELL, TIME TO GET OUT OF HERE. UNLESS YOU WANT MOM AND DAD COMING HOME BEFORE US AND NOTICING YOU TOOK THAT GAME OUT OF ITS HIDING PLACE--
I HOPE YOU ARE INDEED CAREFUL...OR ELSE THE WHOLE TOWN COULD BE IN GRAVE DANGER...
WELL! NICE MEETING YOU!
WHEW! WE'RE BACK JUST IN TIME.
SO...DO YOU THINK WE SHOULD WORRY ABOUT MARIO'S WARNING?

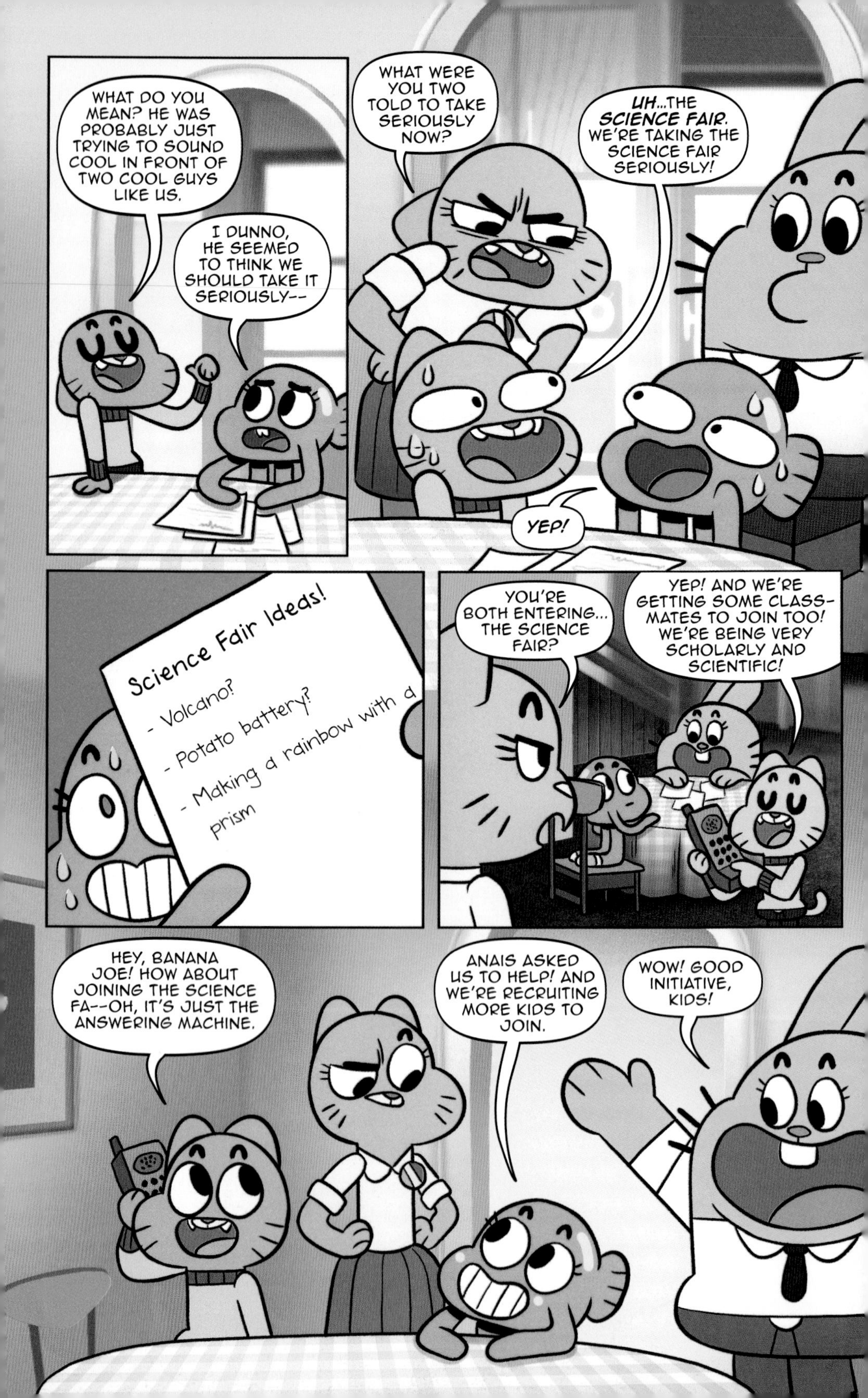
WHAT DO YOU MEAN? HE WAS PROBABLY JUST TRYING TO SOUND COOL IN FRONT OF TWO COOL GUYS LIKE US.
I DUNNO, HE SEEMED TO THINK WE SHOULD TAKE IT SERIOUSLY--
WHAT WERE YOU TWO TOLD TO TAKE SERIOUSLY NOW?
UH...THE SCIENCE FAIR. WE'RE TAKING THE SCIENCE FAIR SERIOUSLY!
YEP!
Science Fair Ideas!
- Volcano?
- Potato battery?
- Making a rainbow with a prism
YOU'RE BOTH ENTERING... THE SCIENCE FAIR?
YEP! AND WE'RE GETTING SOME CLASS-MATES TO JOIN TOO! WE'RE BEING VERY SCHOLARLY AND SCIENTIFIC!
HEY, BANANA JOE! HOW ABOUT JOINING THE SCIENCE FA--OH, IT'S JUST THE ANSWERING MACHINE.
ANAIS ASKED US TO HELP! AND WE'RE RECRUITING MORE KIDS TO JOIN.
WOW! GOOD INITIATIVE, KIDS!

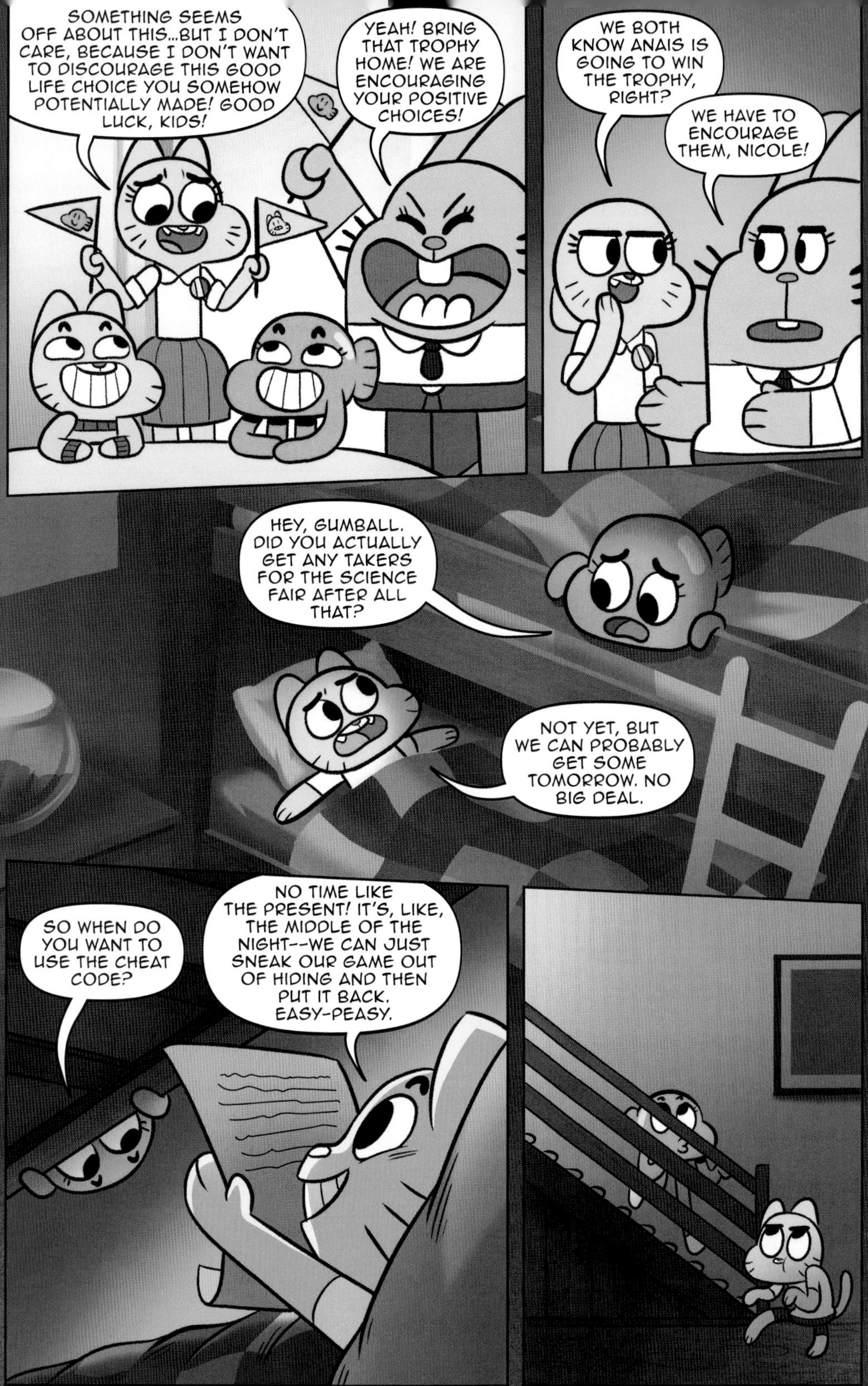
SOMETHING SEEMS OFF ABOUT THIS...BUT I DON'T CARE, BECAUSE I DON'T WANT TO DISCOURAGE THIS GOOD LIFE CHOICE YOU SOMEHOW POTENTIALLY MADE! GOOD LUCK, KIDS!
YEAH! BRING THAT TROPHY HOME! WE ARE ENCOURAGING YOUR POSITIVE CHOICES!
WE BOTH KNOW ANAIS IS GOING TO WIN THE TROPHY, RIGHT?
WE HAVE TO ENCOURAGE THEM, NICOLE!
HEY, GUMBALL. DID YOU ACTUALLY GET ANY TAKERS FOR THE SCIENCE FAIR AFTER ALL THAT?
NOT YET, BUT WE CAN PROBABLY GET SOME TOMORROW. NO BIG DEAL.
SO WHEN DO YOU WANT TO USE THE CHEAT CODE?
NO TIME LIKE THE PRESENT! IT'S, LIKE, THE MIDDLE OF THE NIGHT--WE CAN JUST SNEAK OUR GAME OUT OF HIDING AND THEN PUT IT BACK. EASY-PEASY.

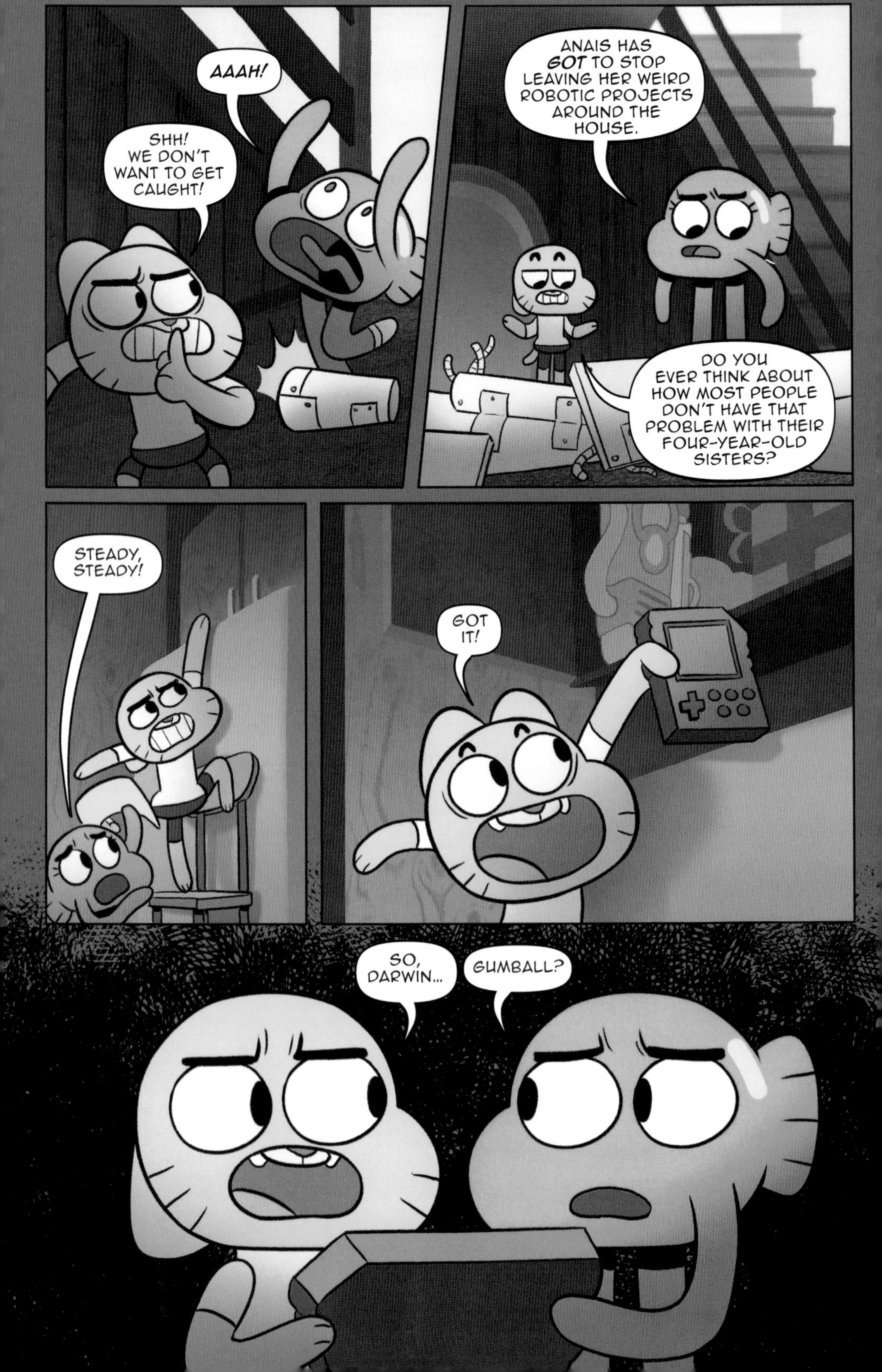
AAAH!
SHH! WE DON'T WANT TO GET CAUGHT!
ANAIS HAS *GOT* TO STOP LEAVING HER WEIRD ROBOTIC PROJECTS AROUND THE HOUSE.
DO YOU EVER THINK ABOUT HOW MOST PEOPLE DON'T HAVE THAT PROBLEM WITH THEIR FOUR-YEAR-OLD SISTERS?
STEADY, STEADY!
GOT IT!
SO, DARWIN...
GUMBALL?

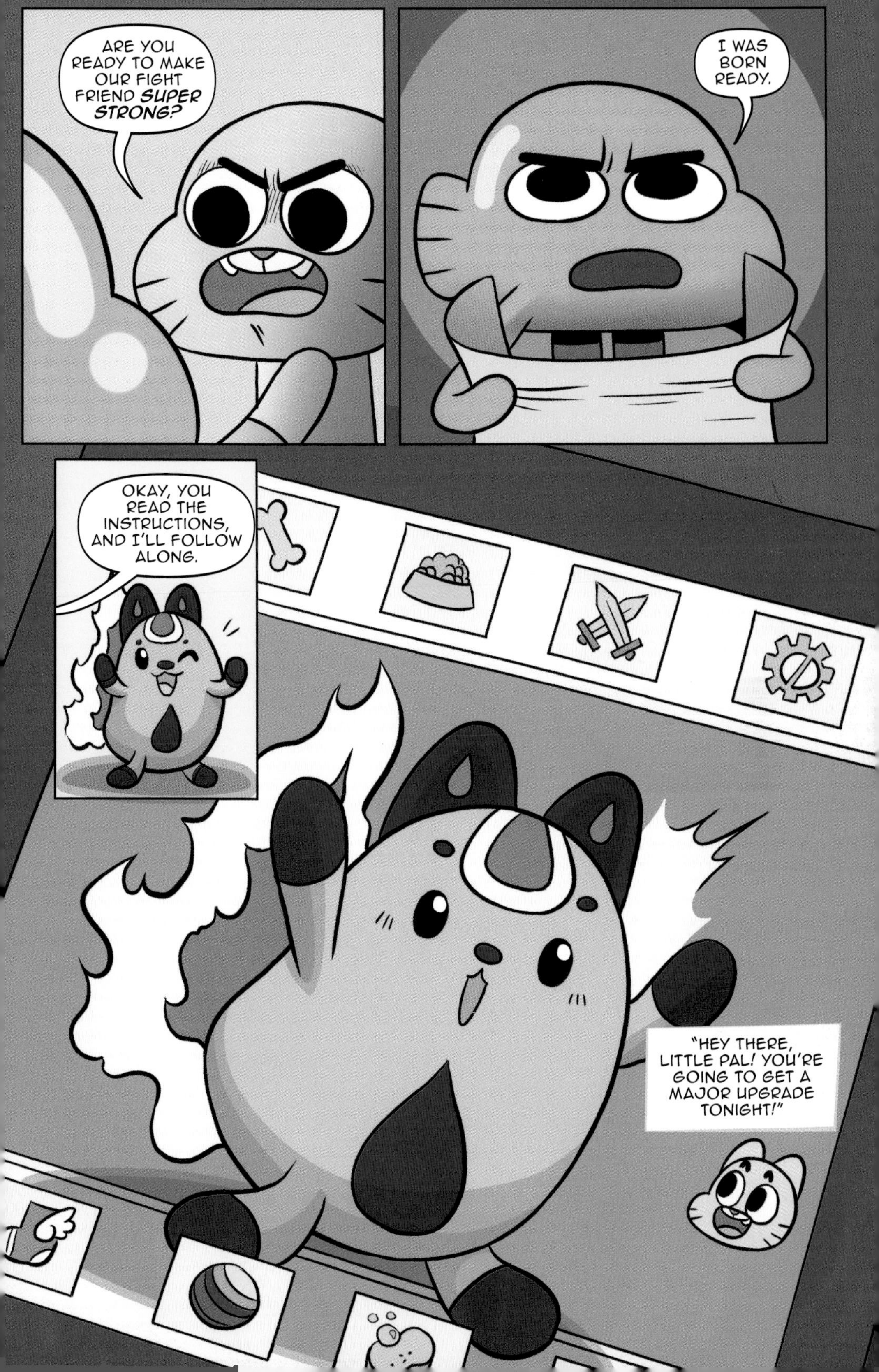
ARE YOU READY TO MAKE OUR FIGHT FRIEND **SUPER STRONG?**
I WAS BORN READY.
OKAY, YOU READ THE INSTRUCTIONS, AND I'LL FOLLOW ALONG.
"HEY THERE, LITTLE PAL! YOU'RE GOING TO GET A MAJOR UPGRADE TONIGHT!"

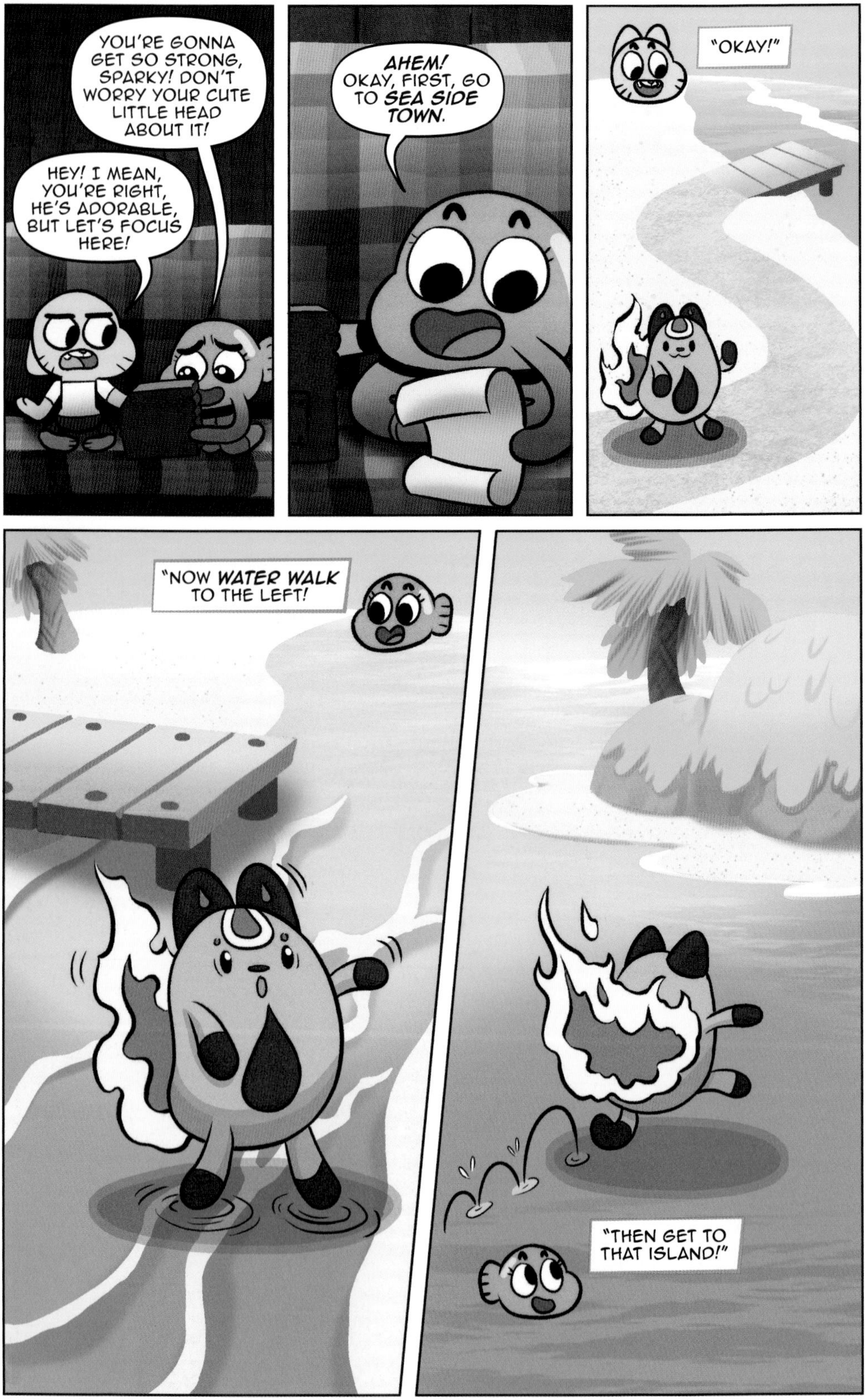
YOU'RE GONNA GET SO STRONG, SPARKY! DON'T WORRY YOUR CUTE LITTLE HEAD ABOUT IT!
HEY! I MEAN, YOU'RE RIGHT, HE'S ADORABLE, BUT LET'S FOCUS HERE!
AHEM! OKAY, FIRST, GO TO SEA SIDE TOWN.
"OKAY!"
"NOW WATER WALK TO THE LEFT!
"THEN GET TO THAT ISLAND!"

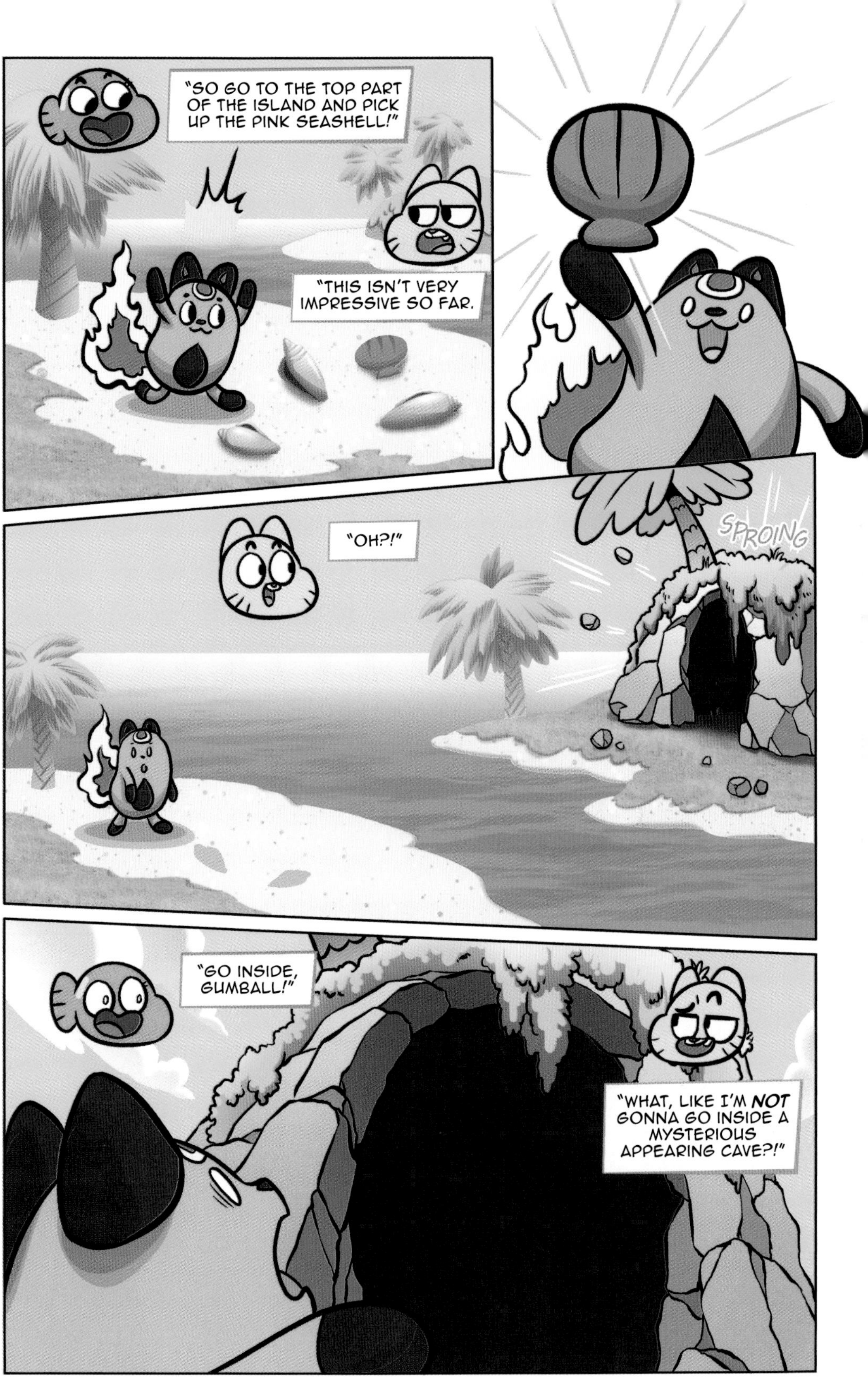
"SO GO TO THE TOP PART OF THE ISLAND AND PICK UP THE PINK SEASHELL!"
"THIS ISN'T VERY IMPRESSIVE SO FAR.
"OH?!"
SPROING
"GO INSIDE, GUMBALL!"
"WHAT, LIKE I'M NOT GONNA GO INSIDE A MYSTERIOUS APPEARING CAVE?!"

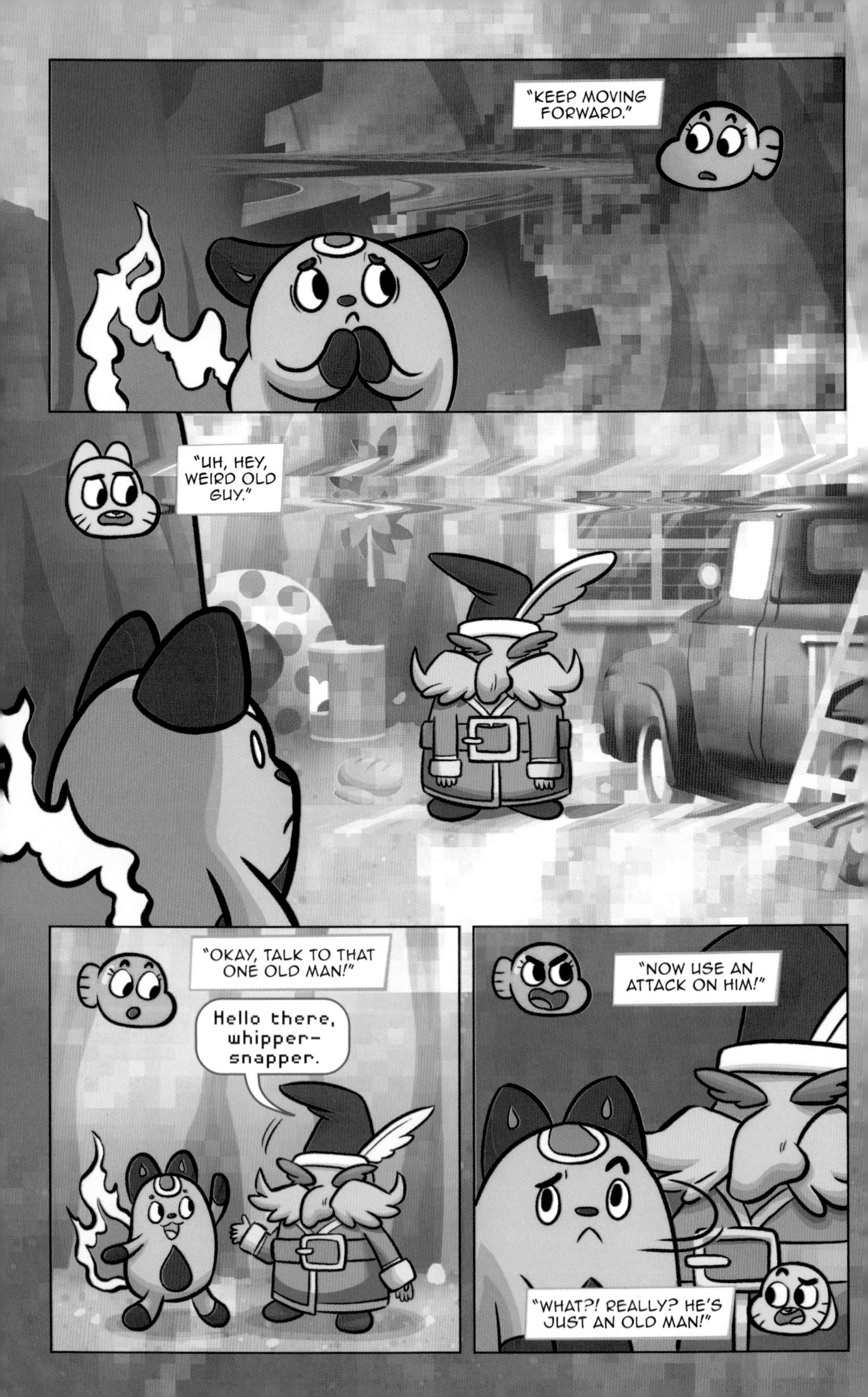
"KEEP MOVING FORWARD."
"UH, HEY, WEIRD OLD GUY."
"OKAY, TALK TO THAT ONE OLD MAN!"
Hello there, whipper-snapper.
"NOW USE AN ATTACK ON HIM!"
"WHAT?! REALLY? HE'S JUST AN OLD MAN!"

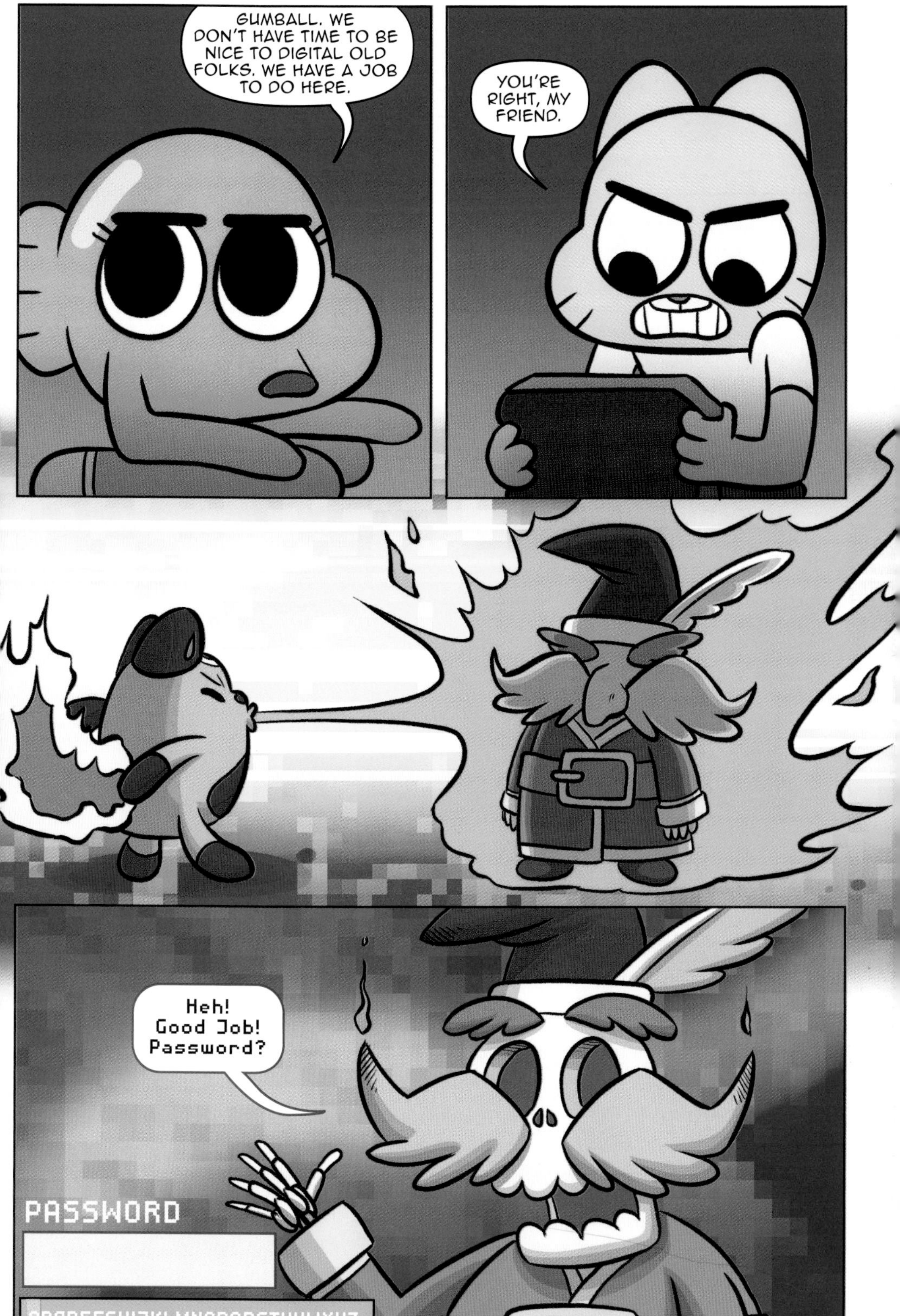
GUMBALL. WE DON'T HAVE TIME TO BE NICE TO DIGITAL OLD FOLKS. WE HAVE A JOB TO DO HERE.
YOU'RE RIGHT, MY FRIEND.
Heh! Good Job! Password?
PASSWORD
ABCDEFGHIJKLMNOPQRSTUVWXYZ

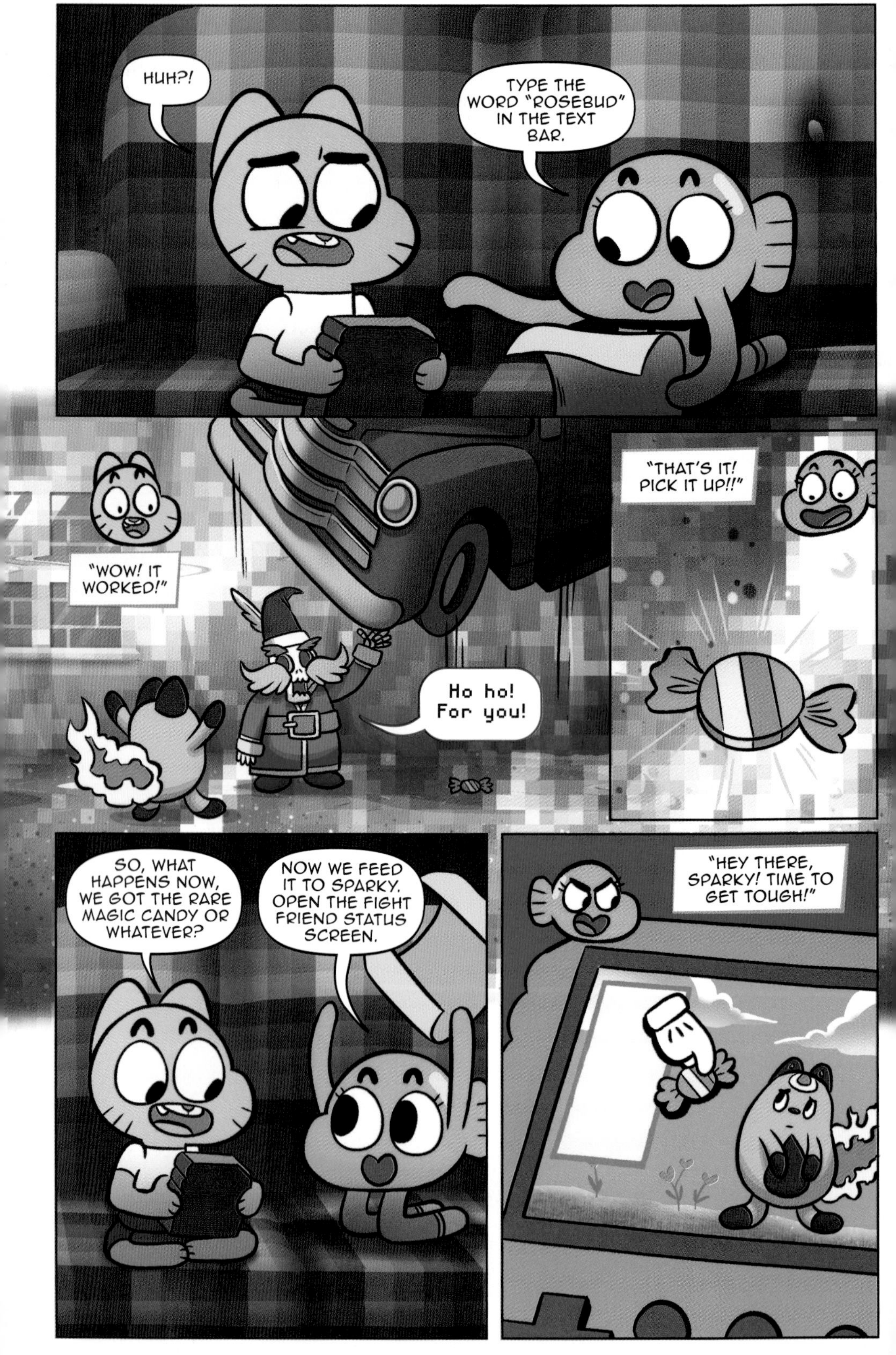
HUH?!
TYPE THE WORD "ROSEBUD" IN THE TEXT BAR.
"WOW! IT WORKED!"
Ho ho! For you!
"THAT'S IT! PICK IT UP!!"
SO, WHAT HAPPENS NOW, WE GOT THE RARE MAGIC CANDY OR WHATEVER?
NOW WE FEED IT TO SPARKY. OPEN THE FIGHT FRIEND STATUS SCREEN.
"HEY THERE, SPARKY! TIME TO GET TOUGH!"

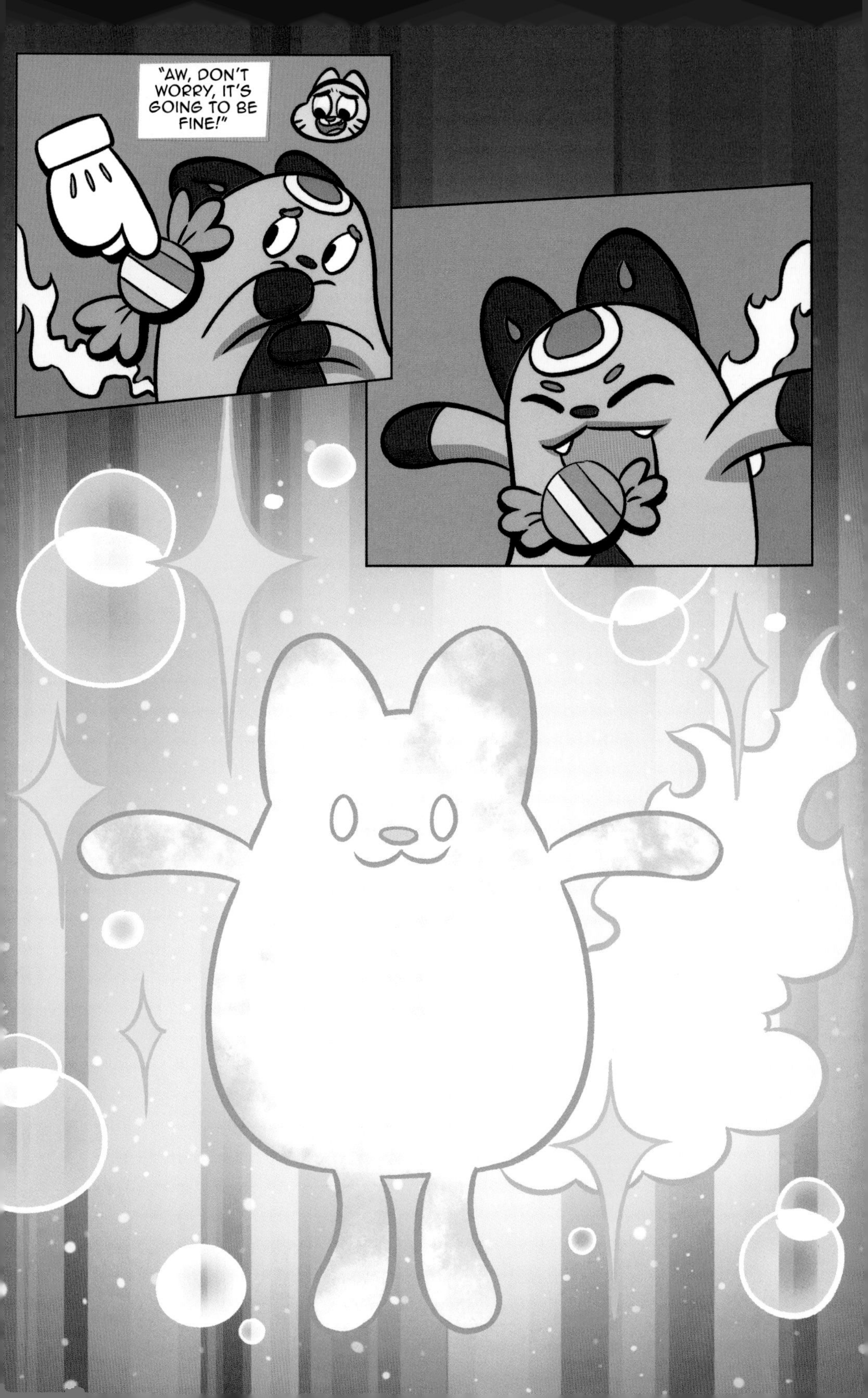
"AW, DON'T WORRY, IT'S GOING TO BE FINE!"

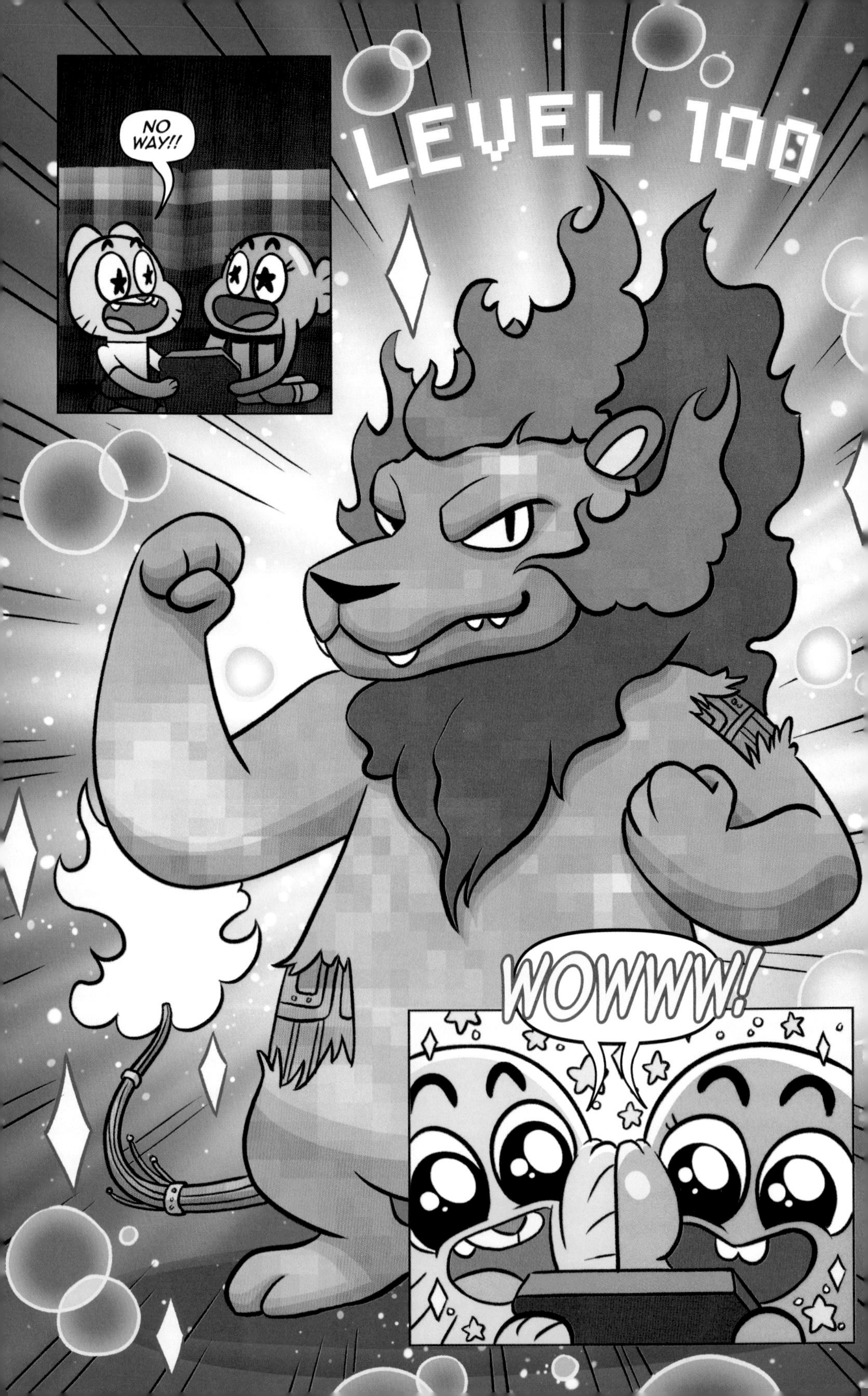
NO WAY!!
LEVEL 100
WOWWW!

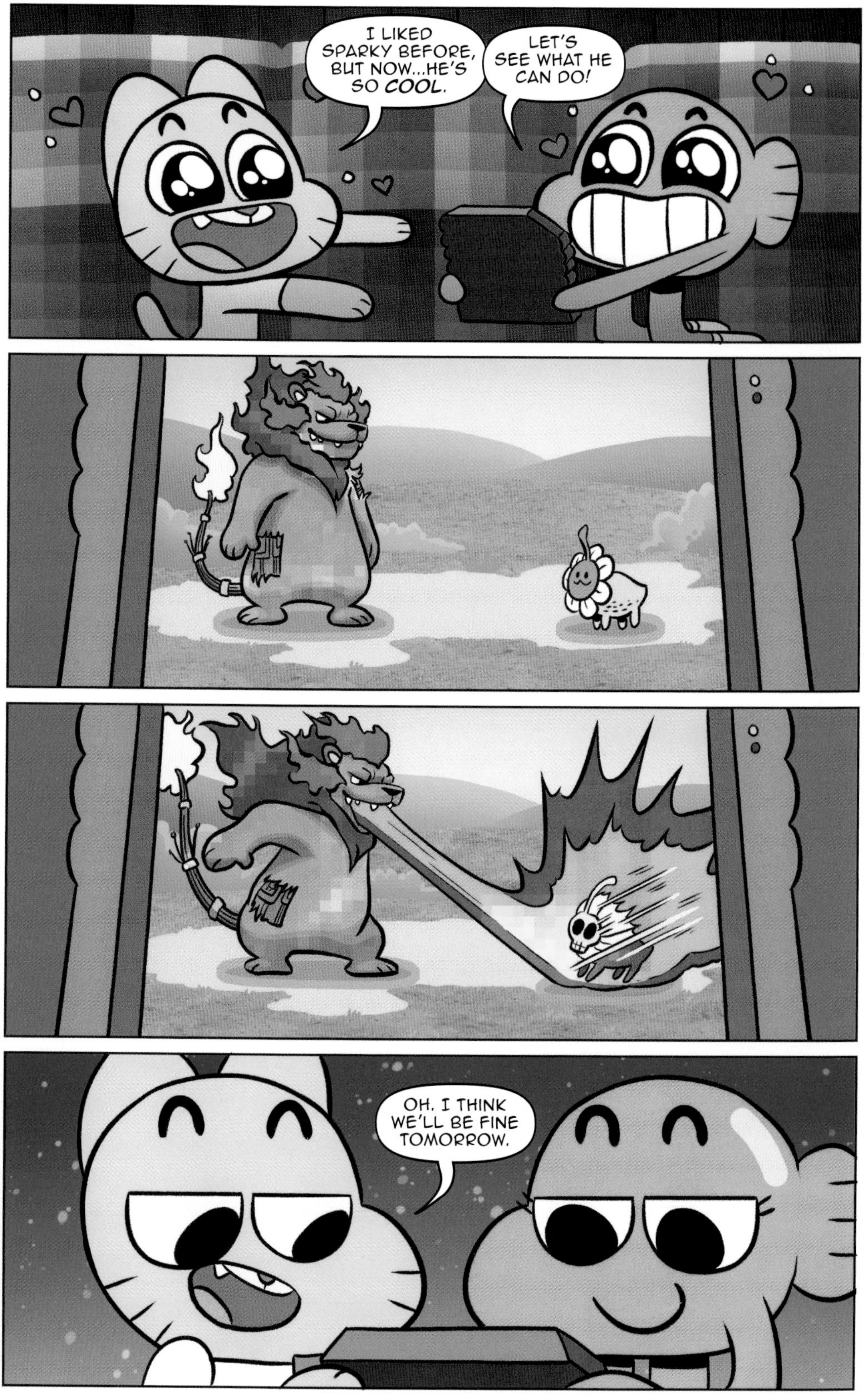

I LIKED SPARKY BEFORE, BUT NOW...HE'S SO *COOL*.
LET'S SEE WHAT HE CAN DO!
OH. I THINK WE'LL BE FINE TOMORROW.

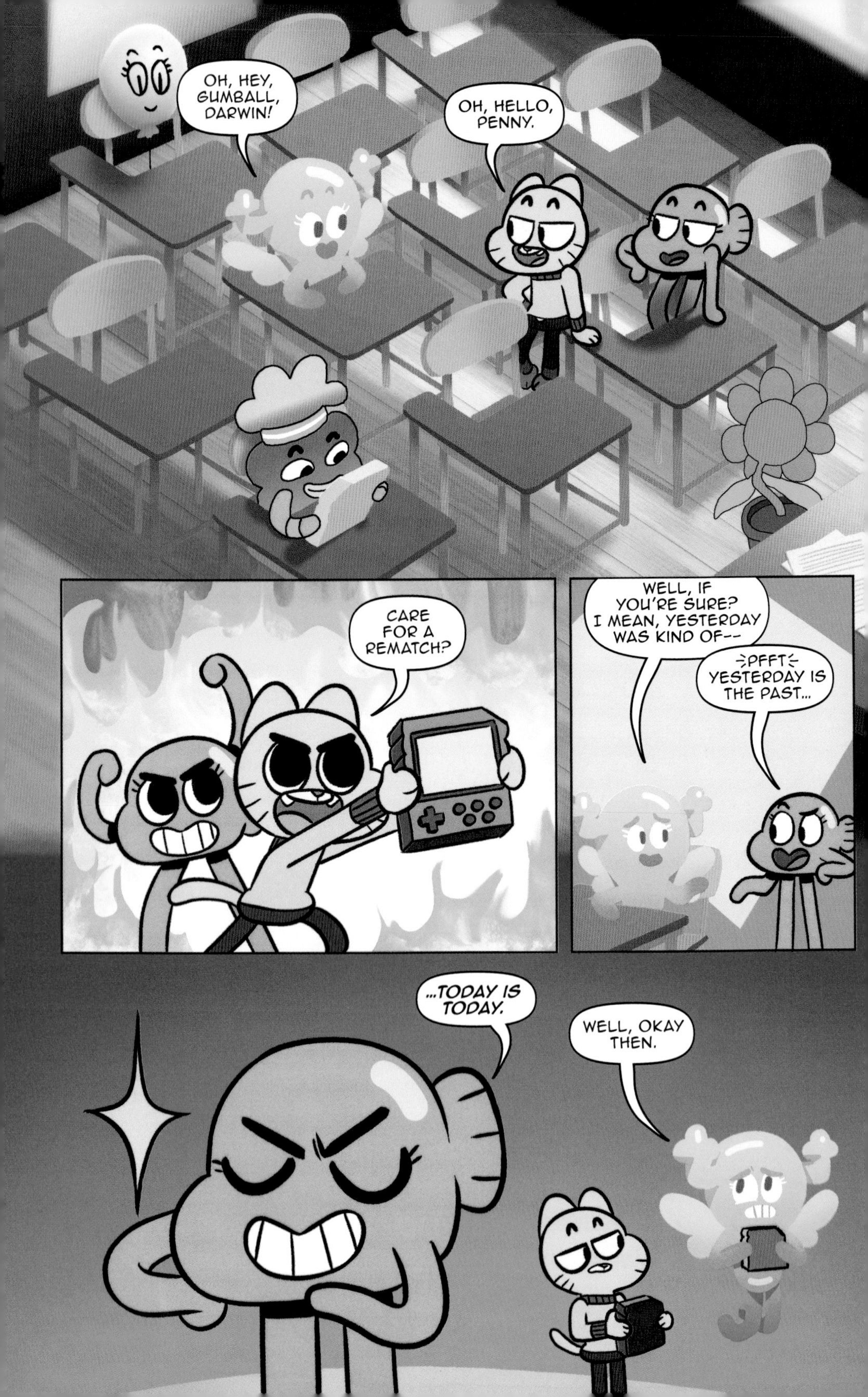
OH, HEY, GUMBALL, DARWIN!
OH, HELLO, PENNY.
CARE FOR A REMATCH?
WELL, IF YOU'RE SURE? I MEAN, YESTERDAY WAS KIND OF--
PFFT YESTERDAY IS THE PAST...
...TODAY IS TODAY.
WELL, OKAY THEN.

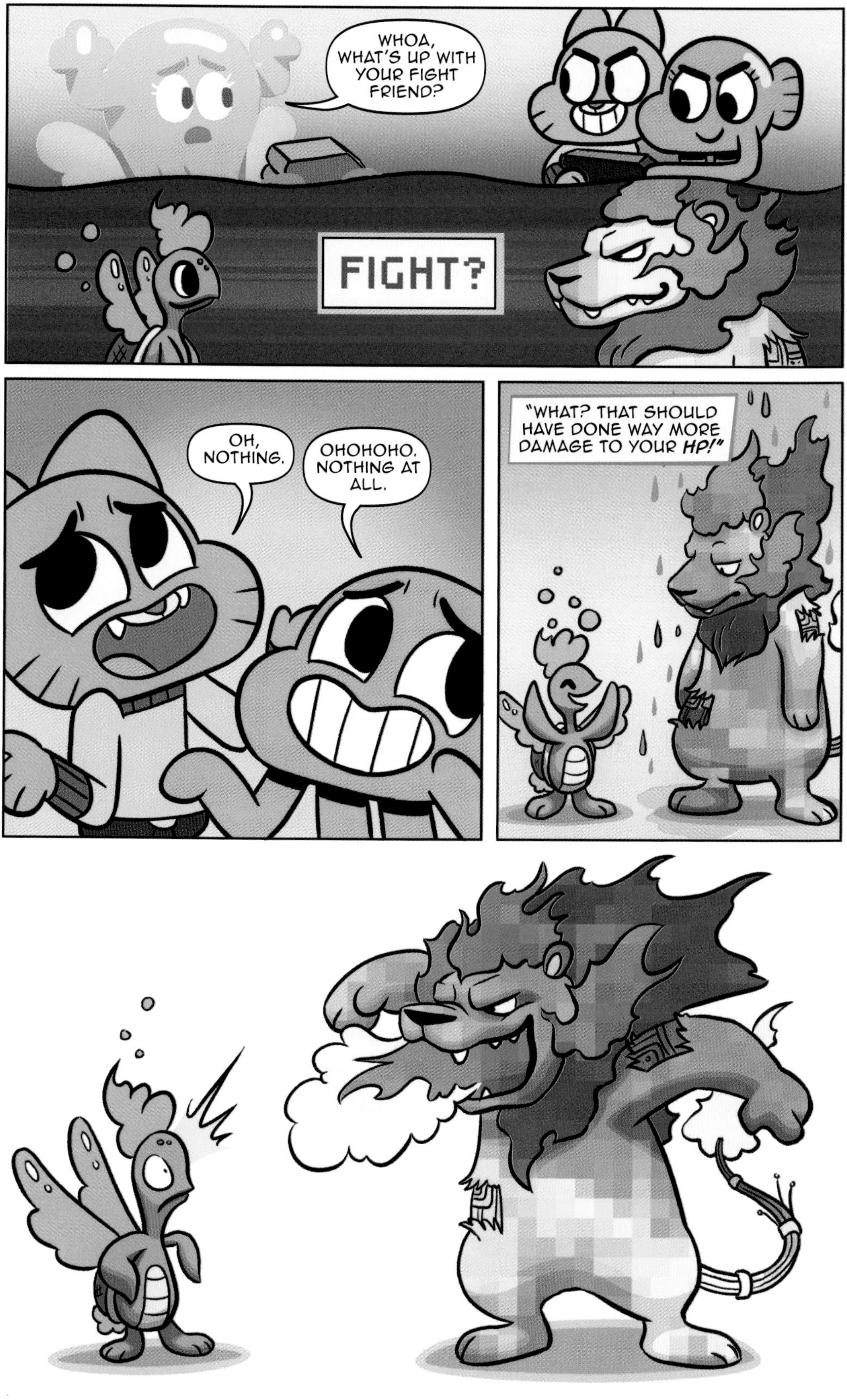

WHOA, WHAT'S UP WITH YOUR FIGHT FRIEND?
FIGHT?
OH, NOTHING.
OHOHOHO. NOTHING AT ALL.
"WHAT? THAT SHOULD HAVE DONE WAY MORE DAMAGE TO YOUR HP!"

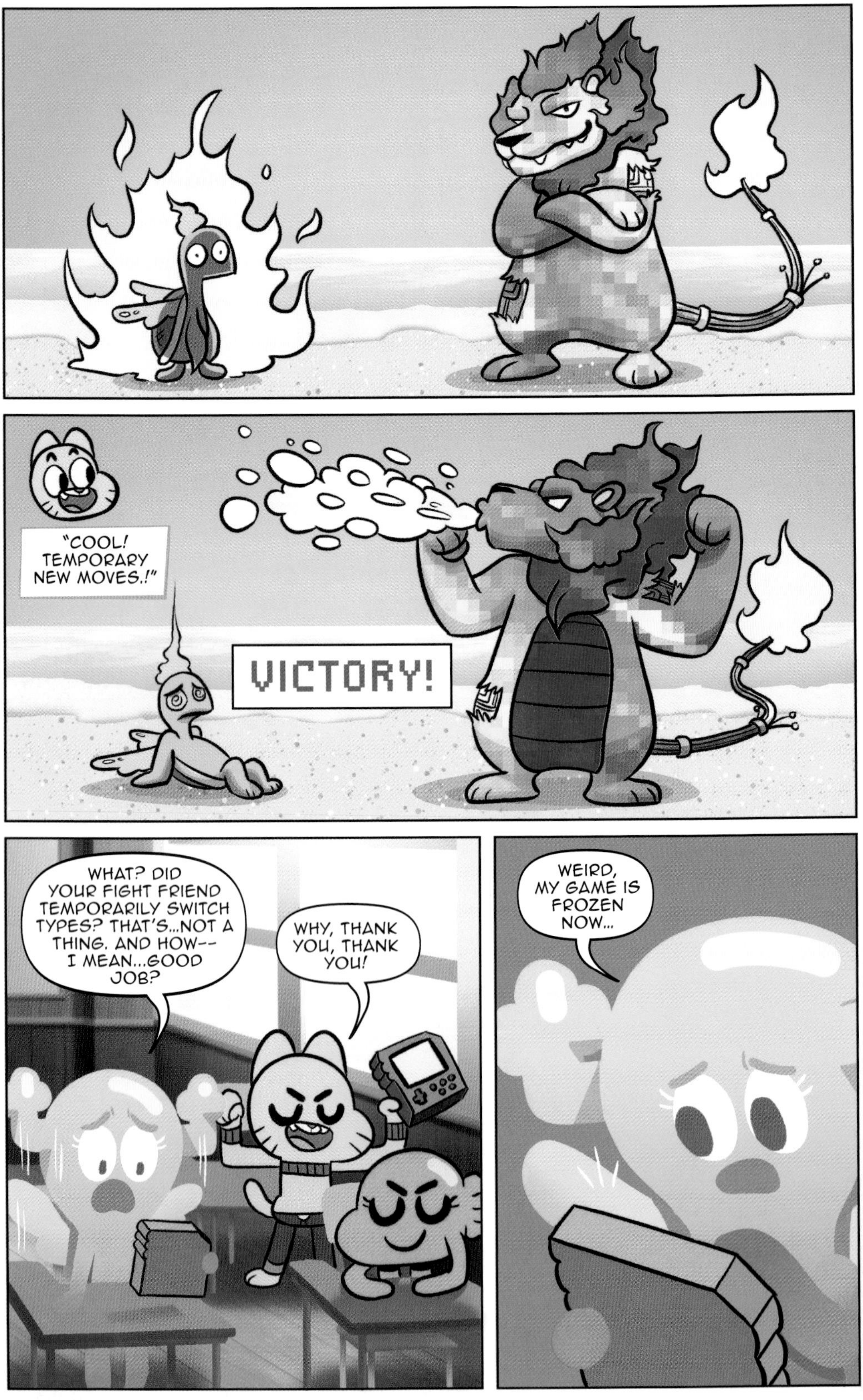
"COOL! TEMPORARY NEW MOVES.!"
VICTORY!
WHAT? DID YOUR FIGHT FRIEND TEMPORARILY SWITCH TYPES? THAT'S...NOT A THING. AND HOW-- I MEAN...GOOD JOB?
WHY, THANK YOU, THANK YOU!
WEIRD, MY GAME IS FROZEN NOW...

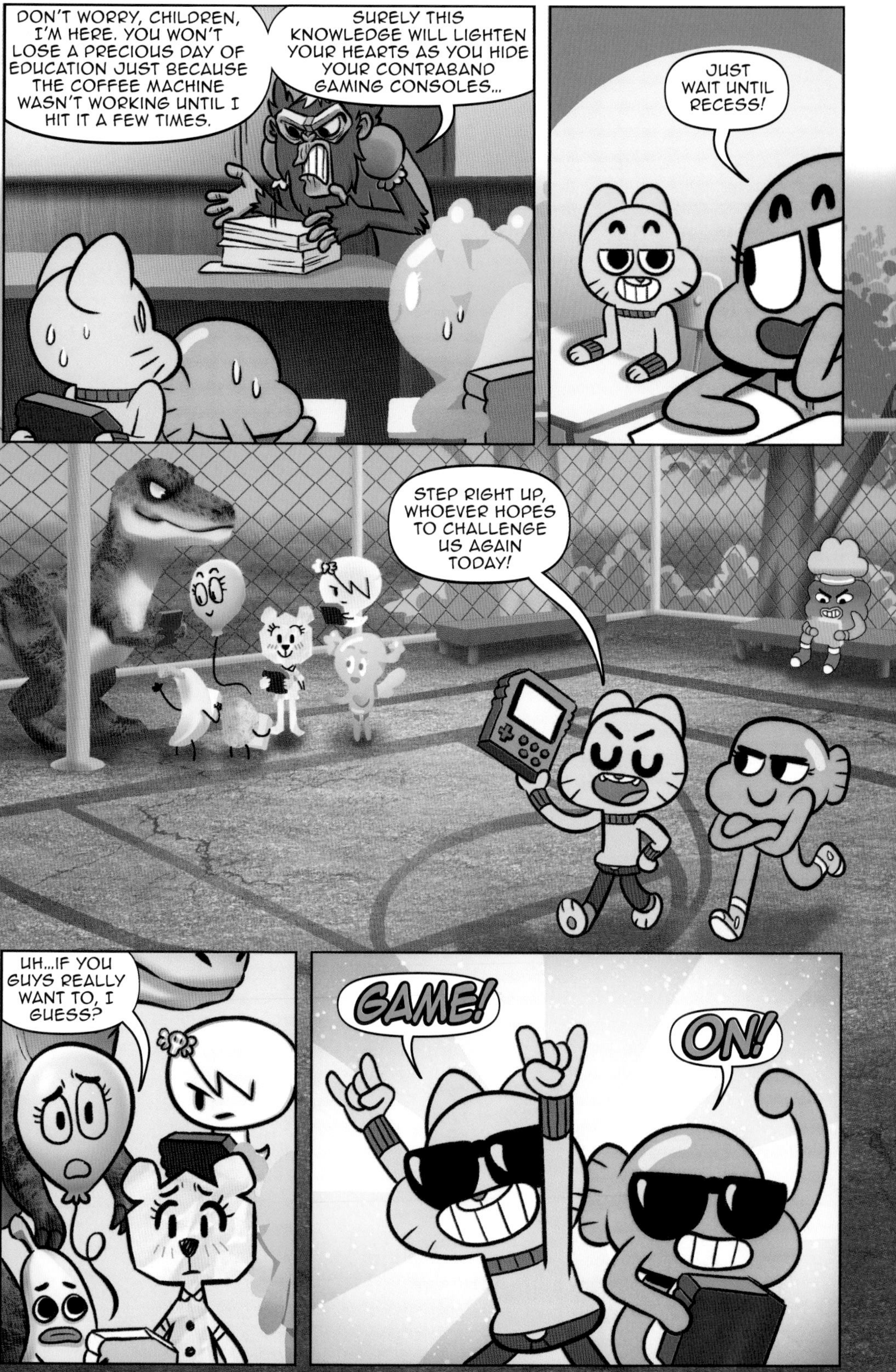
DON'T WORRY, CHILDREN, I'M HERE. YOU WON'T LOSE A PRECIOUS DAY OF EDUCATION JUST BECAUSE THE COFFEE MACHINE WASN'T WORKING UNTIL I HIT IT A FEW TIMES.
SURELY THIS KNOWLEDGE WILL LIGHTEN YOUR HEARTS AS YOU HIDE YOUR CONTRABAND GAMING CONSOLES...
JUST WAIT UNTIL RECESS!
STEP RIGHT UP, WHOEVER HOPES TO CHALLENGE US AGAIN TODAY!
UH...IF YOU GUYS REALLY WANT TO, I GUESS?
GAME!
ON!

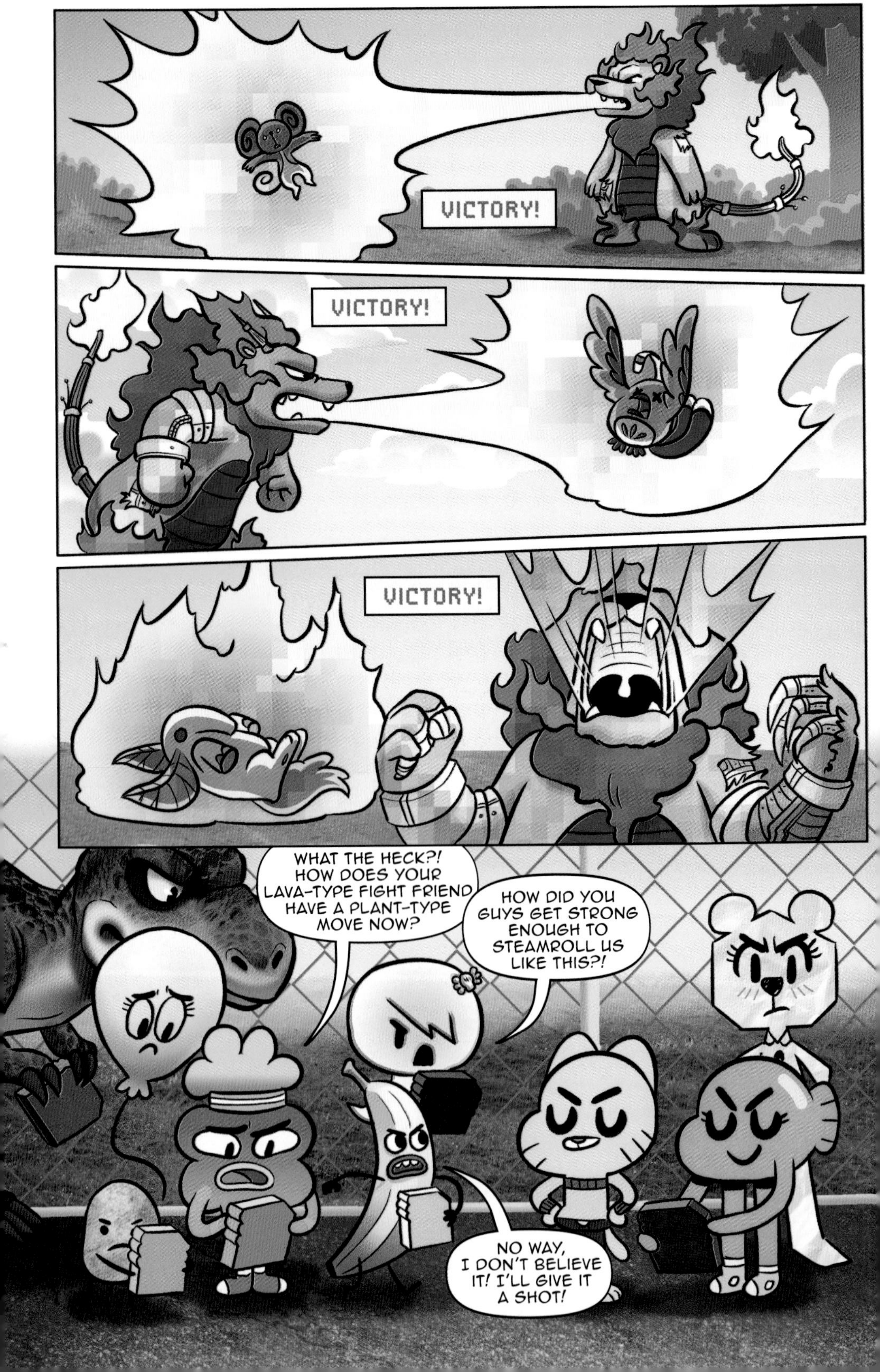
VICTORY!
VICTORY!
VICTORY!
WHAT THE HECK?! HOW DOES YOUR LAVA-TYPE FIGHT FRIEND HAVE A PLANT-TYPE MOVE NOW?
HOW DID YOU GUYS GET STRONG ENOUGH TO STEAMROLL US LIKE THIS?!
NO WAY, I DON'T BELIEVE IT! I'LL GIVE IT A SHOT!

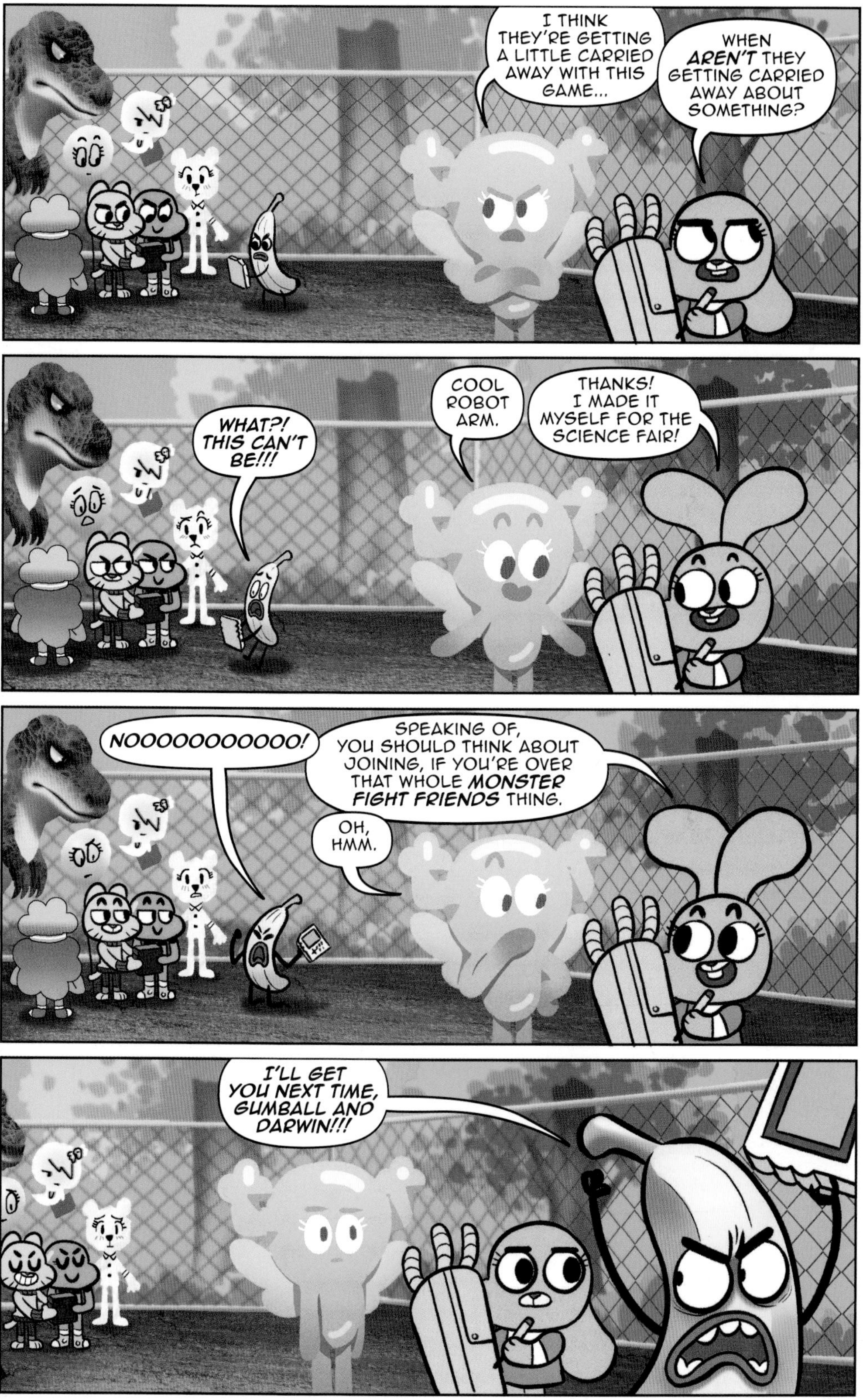
I THINK THEY'RE GETTING A LITTLE CARRIED AWAY WITH THIS GAME...
WHEN *AREN'T* THEY GETTING CARRIED AWAY ABOUT SOMETHING?
WHAT?! THIS CAN'T BE!!!
COOL ROBOT ARM.
THANKS! I MADE IT MYSELF FOR THE SCIENCE FAIR!
NOOOOOOOOOOO!
SPEAKING OF, YOU SHOULD THINK ABOUT JOINING, IF YOU'RE OVER THAT WHOLE *MONSTER FIGHT FRIENDS* THING.
OH, HMM.
I'LL GET YOU NEXT TIME, GUMBALL AND DARWIN!!!

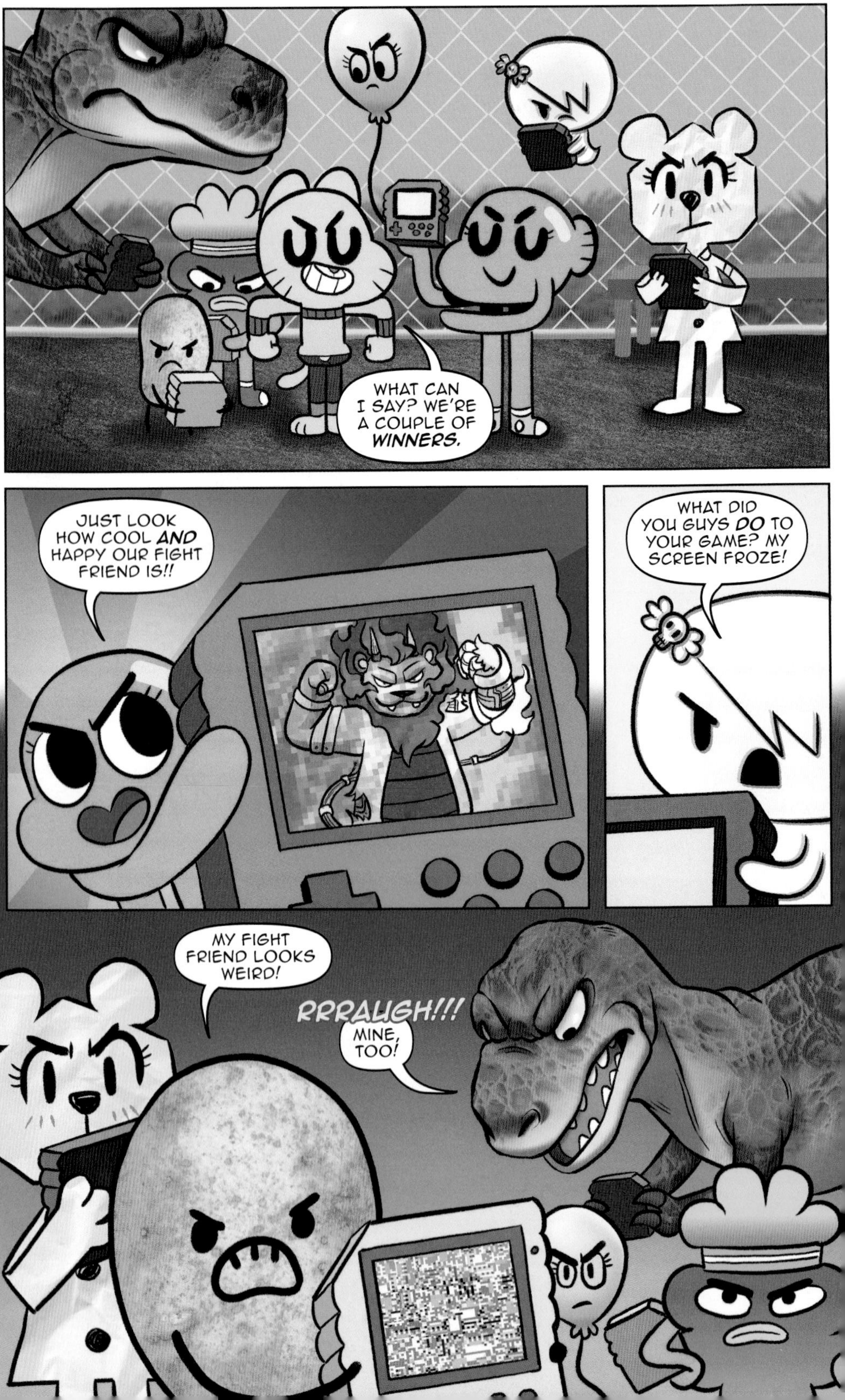
WHAT CAN I SAY? WE'RE A COUPLE OF *WINNERS.*
JUST LOOK HOW COOL **AND** HAPPY OUR FIGHT FRIEND IS!!
WHAT DID YOU GUYS **DO** TO YOUR GAME? MY SCREEN FROZE!
MY FIGHT FRIEND LOOKS WEIRD!
RRRAUGH!!!
MINE, TOO!

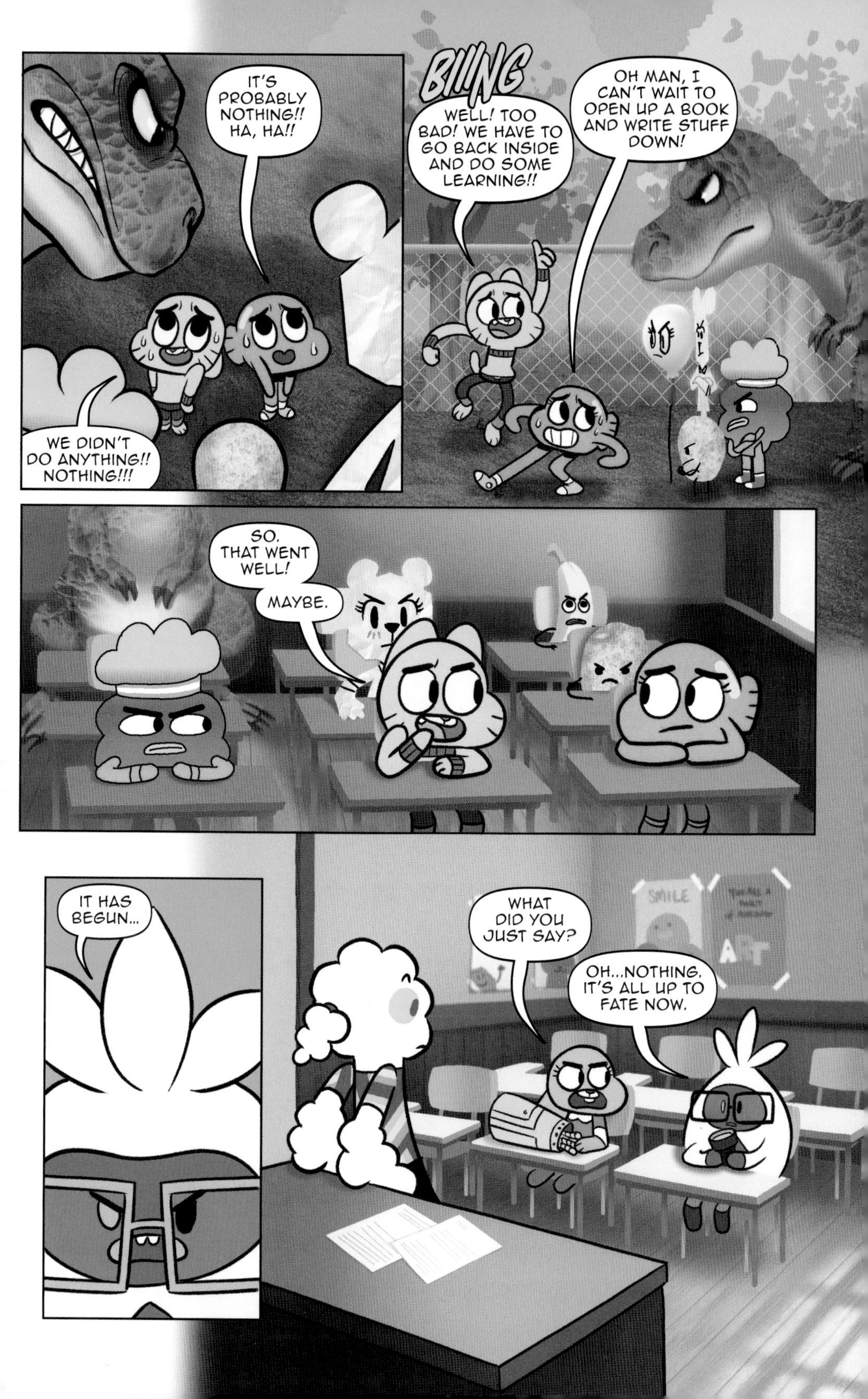
IT'S PROBABLY NOTHING!! HA, HA!!
WE DIDN'T DO ANYTHING!! NOTHING!!!
BIIING
WELL! TOO BAD! WE HAVE TO GO BACK INSIDE AND DO SOME LEARNING!!
OH MAN, I CAN'T WAIT TO OPEN UP A BOOK AND WRITE STUFF DOWN!
SO. THAT WENT WELL!
MAYBE.
IT HAS BEGUN...
WHAT DID YOU JUST SAY?
OH...NOTHING. IT'S ALL UP TO FATE NOW.
SMILE

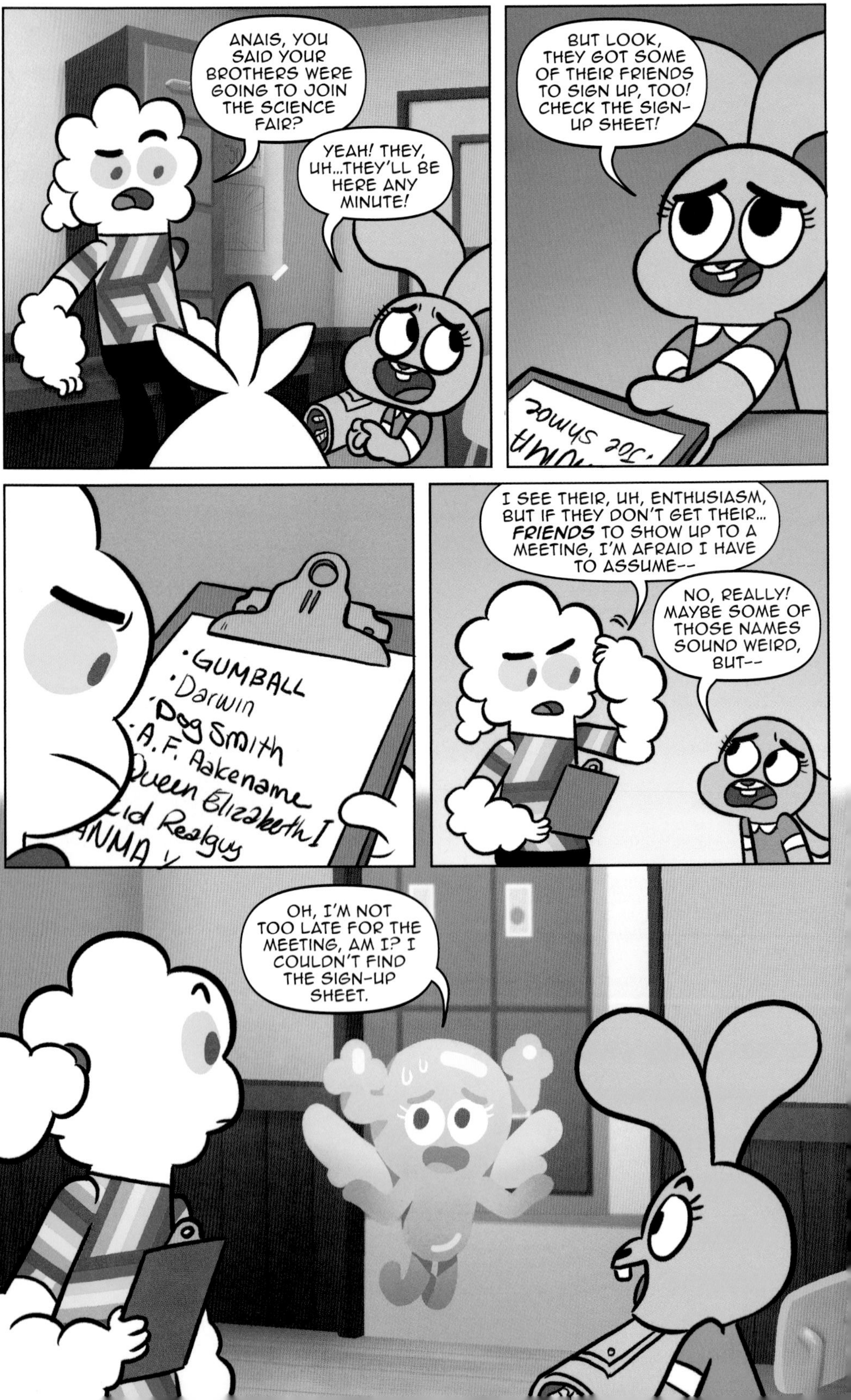
ANAIS, YOU SAID YOUR BROTHERS WERE GOING TO JOIN THE SCIENCE FAIR?
YEAH! THEY, UH...THEY'LL BE HERE ANY MINUTE!
BUT LOOK, THEY GOT SOME OF THEIR FRIENDS TO SIGN UP, TOO! CHECK THE SIGN-UP SHEET!
•GUMBALL
•Darwin
•Dog Smith
•A.F. Aakename
Queen Elizabeth I
I SEE THEIR, UH, ENTHUSIASM, BUT IF THEY DON'T GET THEIR... *FRIENDS* TO SHOW UP TO A MEETING, I'M AFRAID I HAVE TO ASSUME--
NO, REALLY! MAYBE SOME OF THOSE NAMES SOUND WEIRD, BUT--
OH, I'M NOT TOO LATE FOR THE MEETING, AM I? I COULDN'T FIND THE SIGN-UP SHEET.

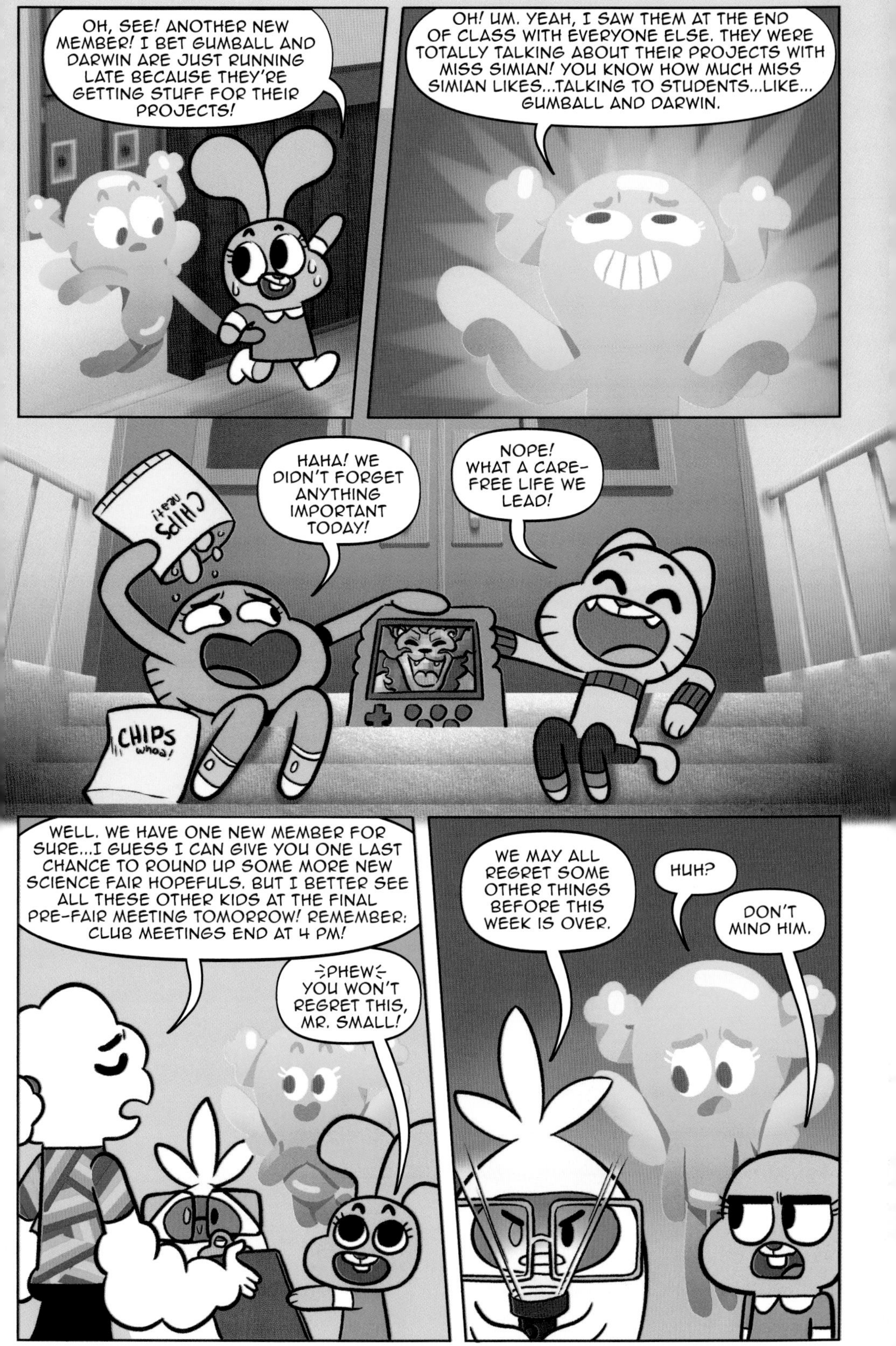
OH, SEE! ANOTHER NEW MEMBER! I BET GUMBALL AND DARWIN ARE JUST RUNNING LATE BECAUSE THEY'RE GETTING STUFF FOR THEIR PROJECTS!
OH! UM. YEAH, I SAW THEM AT THE END OF CLASS WITH EVERYONE ELSE. THEY WERE TOTALLY TALKING ABOUT THEIR PROJECTS WITH MISS SIMIAN! YOU KNOW HOW MUCH MISS SIMIAN LIKES...TALKING TO STUDENTS...LIKE... GUMBALL AND DARWIN.
CHIPS neat!
HAHA! WE DIDN'T FORGET ANYTHING IMPORTANT TODAY!
NOPE! WHAT A CARE-FREE LIFE WE LEAD!
CHIPS whoa!
WELL. WE HAVE ONE NEW MEMBER FOR SURE...I GUESS I CAN GIVE YOU ONE LAST CHANCE TO ROUND UP SOME MORE NEW SCIENCE FAIR HOPEFULS. BUT I BETTER SEE ALL THESE OTHER KIDS AT THE FINAL PRE-FAIR MEETING TOMORROW! REMEMBER: CLUB MEETINGS END AT 4 PM!
PHEW YOU WON'T REGRET THIS, MR. SMALL!
WE MAY ALL REGRET SOME OTHER THINGS BEFORE THIS WEEK IS OVER.
HUH?
DON'T MIND HIM.

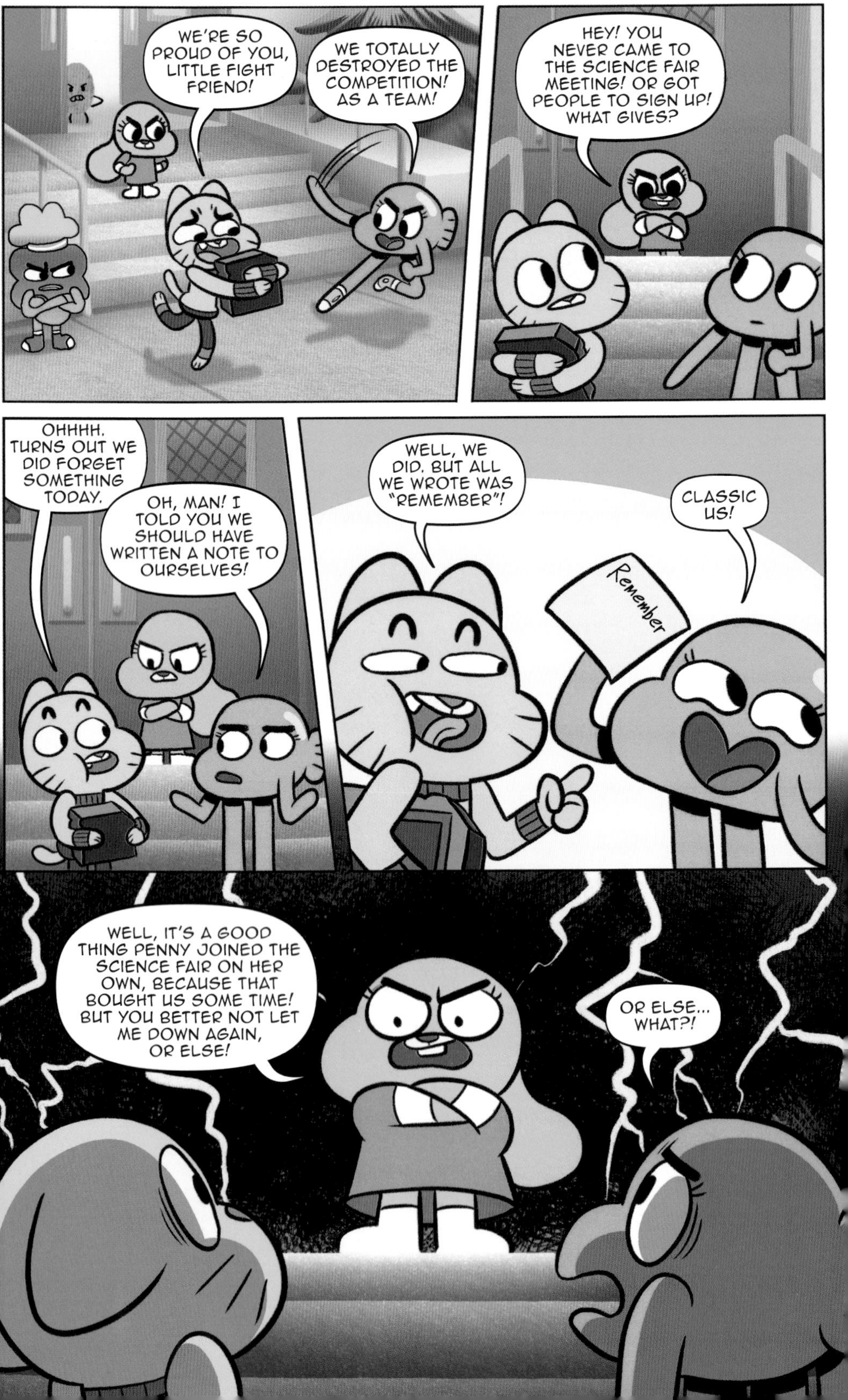
WE'RE SO PROUD OF YOU, LITTLE FIGHT FRIEND!
WE TOTALLY DESTROYED THE COMPETITION! AS A TEAM!
HEY! YOU NEVER CAME TO THE SCIENCE FAIR MEETING! OR GOT PEOPLE TO SIGN UP! WHAT GIVES?
OHHHH. TURNS OUT WE DID FORGET SOMETHING TODAY.
OH, MAN! I TOLD YOU WE SHOULD HAVE WRITTEN A NOTE TO OURSELVES!
WELL, WE DID. BUT ALL WE WROTE WAS "REMEMBER"!
CLASSIC US!
Remember
WELL, IT'S A GOOD THING PENNY JOINED THE SCIENCE FAIR ON HER OWN, BECAUSE THAT BOUGHT US SOME TIME! BUT YOU BETTER NOT LET ME DOWN AGAIN, OR ELSE!
OR ELSE... WHAT?!

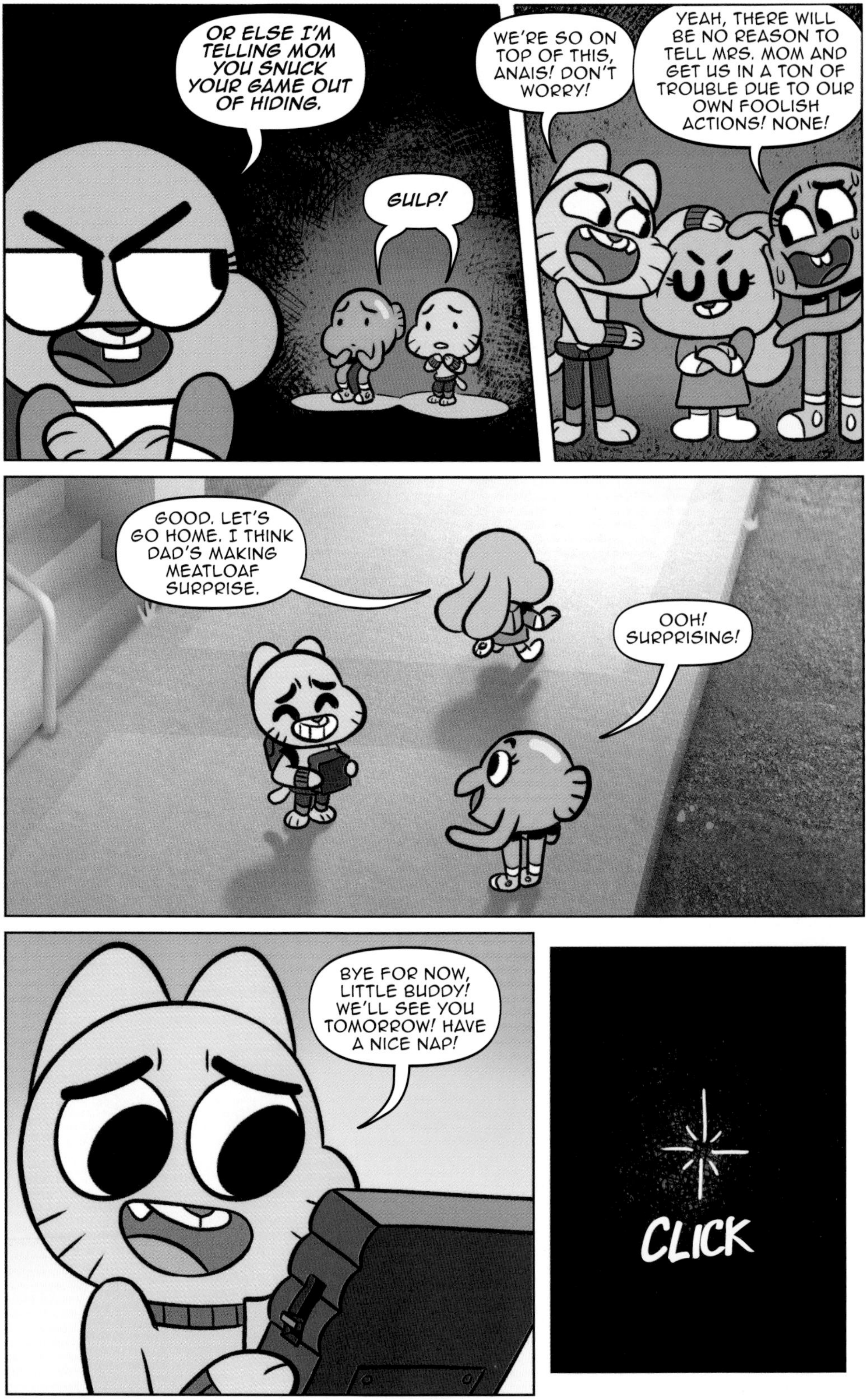
OR ELSE I'M TELLING MOM YOU SNUCK YOUR GAME OUT OF HIDING.
GULP!
WE'RE SO ON TOP OF THIS, ANAIS! DON'T WORRY!
YEAH, THERE WILL BE NO REASON TO TELL MRS. MOM AND GET US IN A TON OF TROUBLE DUE TO OUR OWN FOOLISH ACTIONS! NONE!
GOOD. LET'S GO HOME. I THINK DAD'S MAKING MEATLOAF SURPRISE.
OOH! SURPRISING!
BYE FOR NOW, LITTLE BUDDY! WE'LL SEE YOU TOMORROW! HAVE A NICE NAP!
CLICK

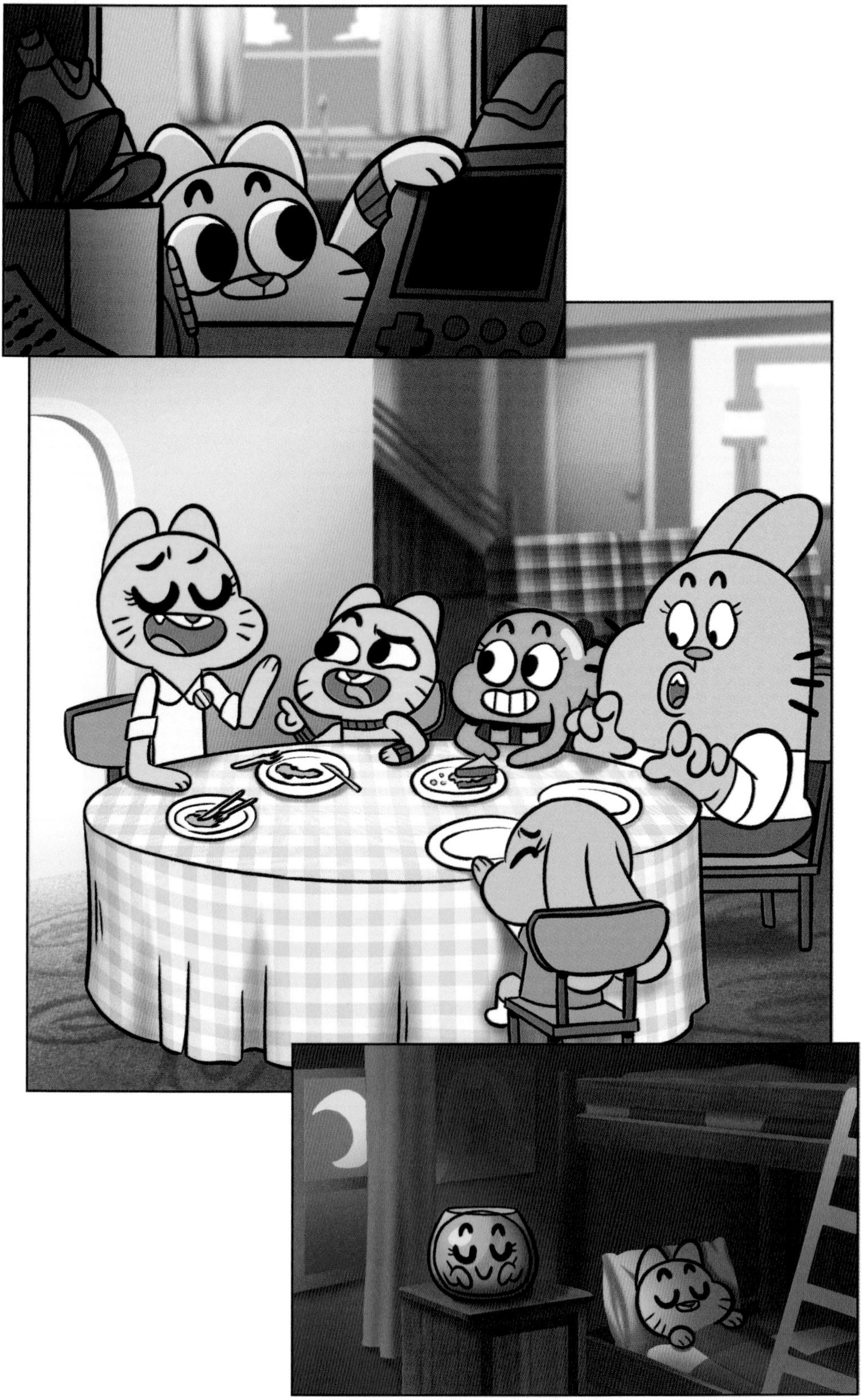

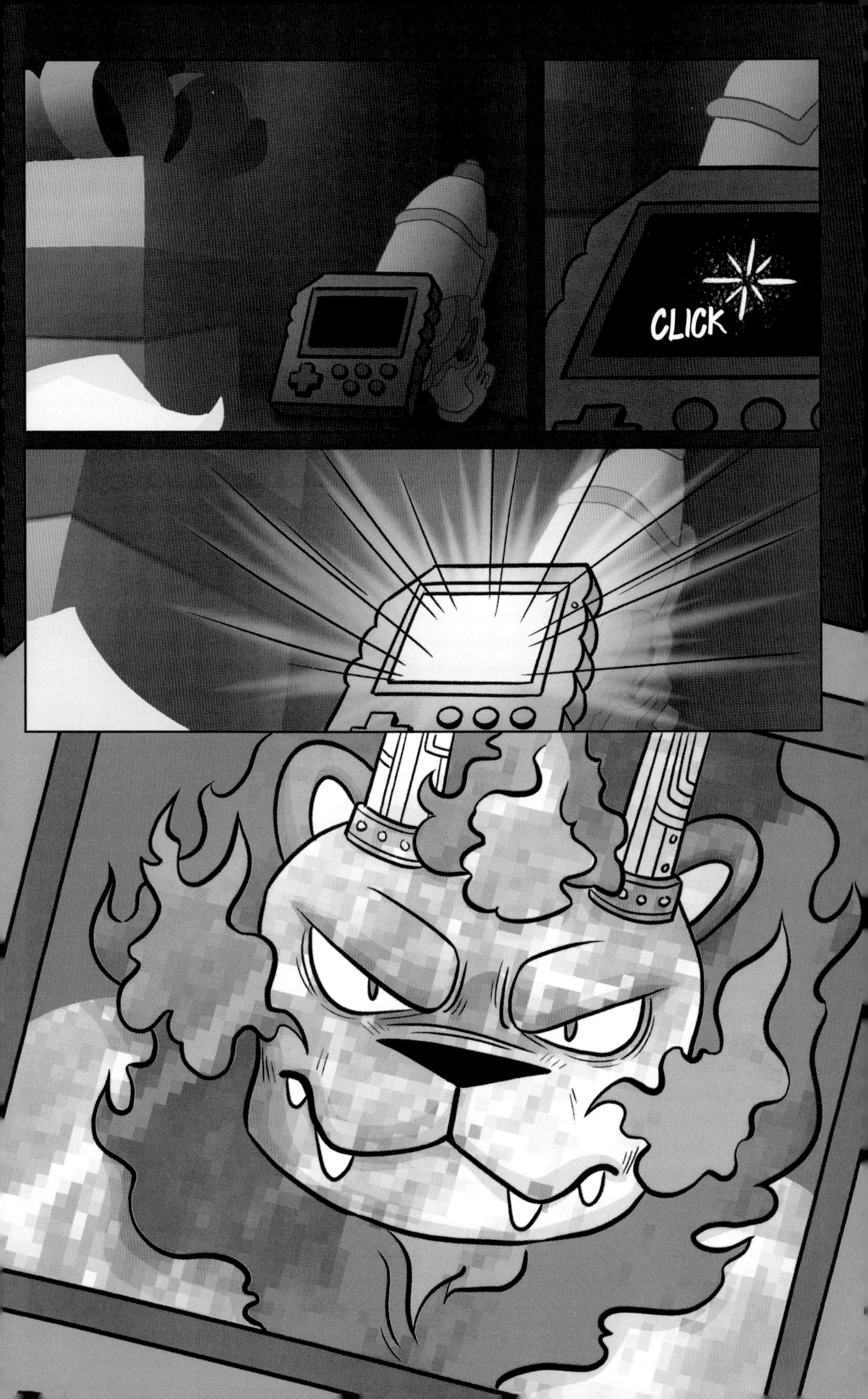
CLICK

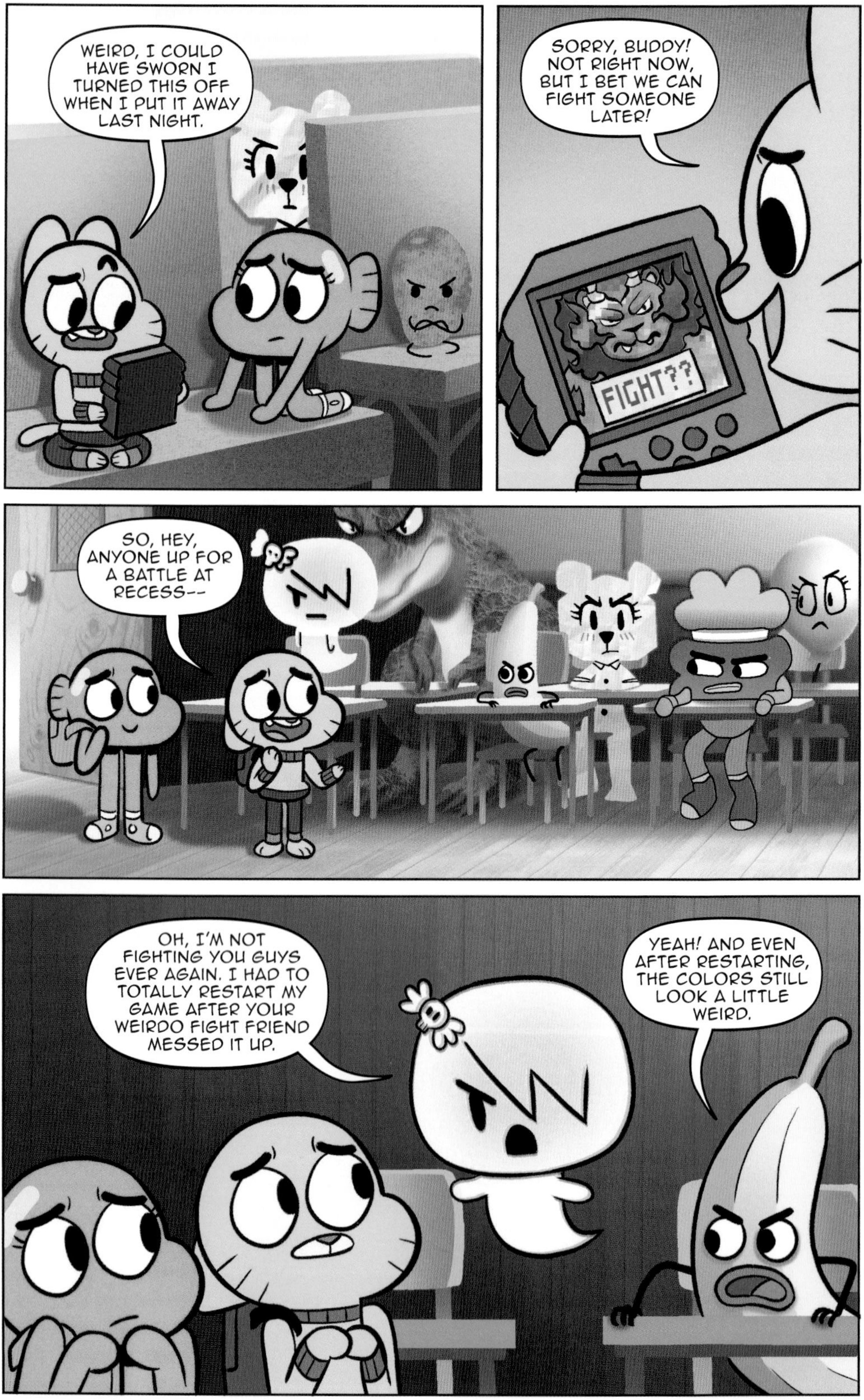
WEIRD, I COULD HAVE SWORN I TURNED THIS OFF WHEN I PUT IT AWAY LAST NIGHT.
SORRY, BUDDY! NOT RIGHT NOW, BUT I BET WE CAN FIGHT SOMEONE LATER!
FIGHT??
SO, HEY, ANYONE UP FOR A BATTLE AT RECESS--
OH, I'M NOT FIGHTING YOU GUYS EVER AGAIN. I HAD TO TOTALLY RESTART MY GAME AFTER YOUR WEIRDO FIGHT FRIEND MESSED IT UP.
YEAH! AND EVEN AFTER RESTARTING, THE COLORS STILL LOOK A LITTLE WEIRD.

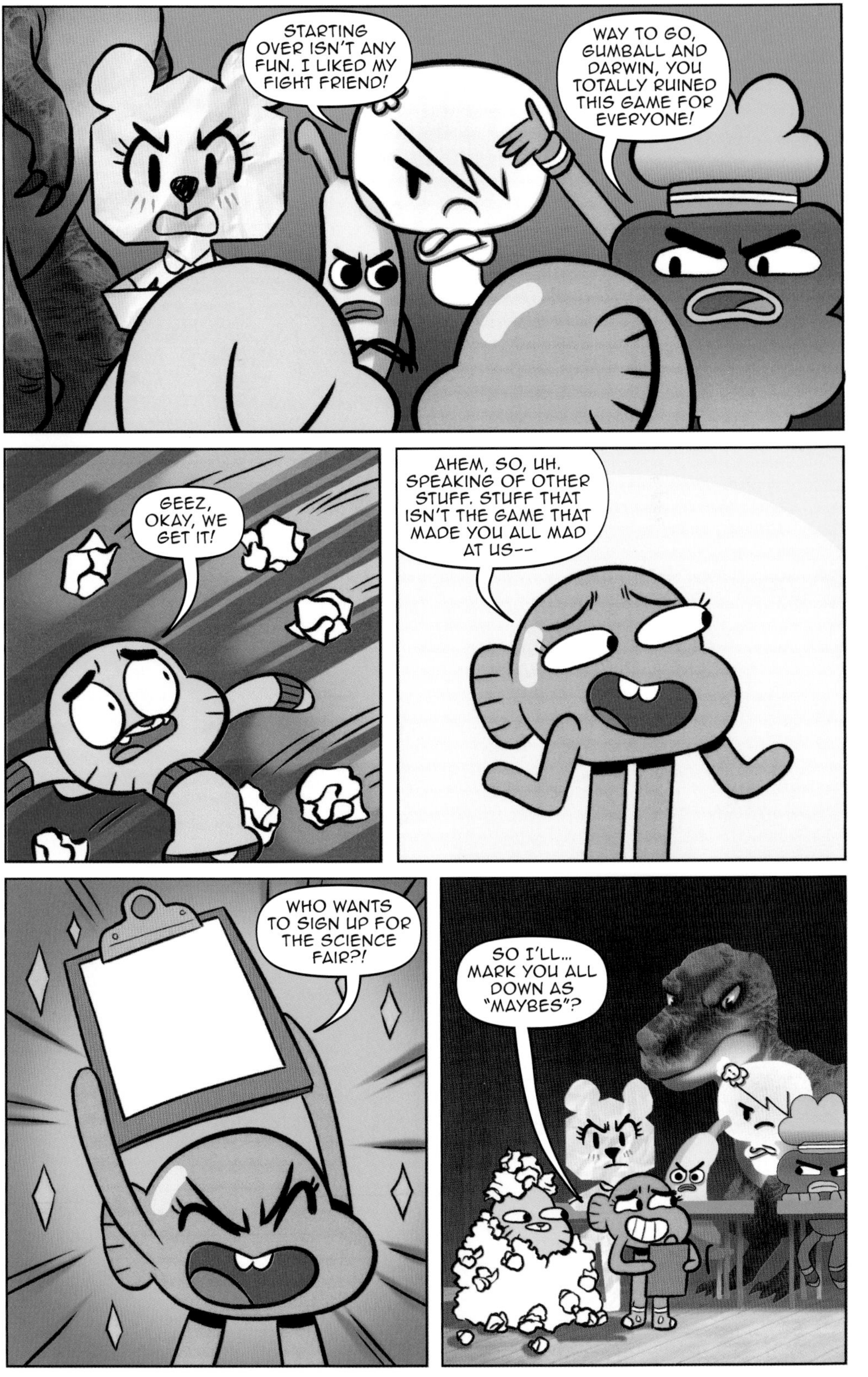
STARTING OVER ISN'T ANY FUN. I LIKED MY FIGHT FRIEND!
WAY TO GO, GUMBALL AND DARWIN, YOU TOTALLY RUINED THIS GAME FOR EVERYONE!
GEEZ, OKAY, WE GET IT!
AHEM, SO, UH. SPEAKING OF OTHER STUFF. STUFF THAT ISN'T THE GAME THAT MADE YOU ALL MAD AT US--
WHO WANTS TO SIGN UP FOR THE SCIENCE FAIR?!
SO I'LL... MARK YOU ALL DOWN AS "MAYBES"?

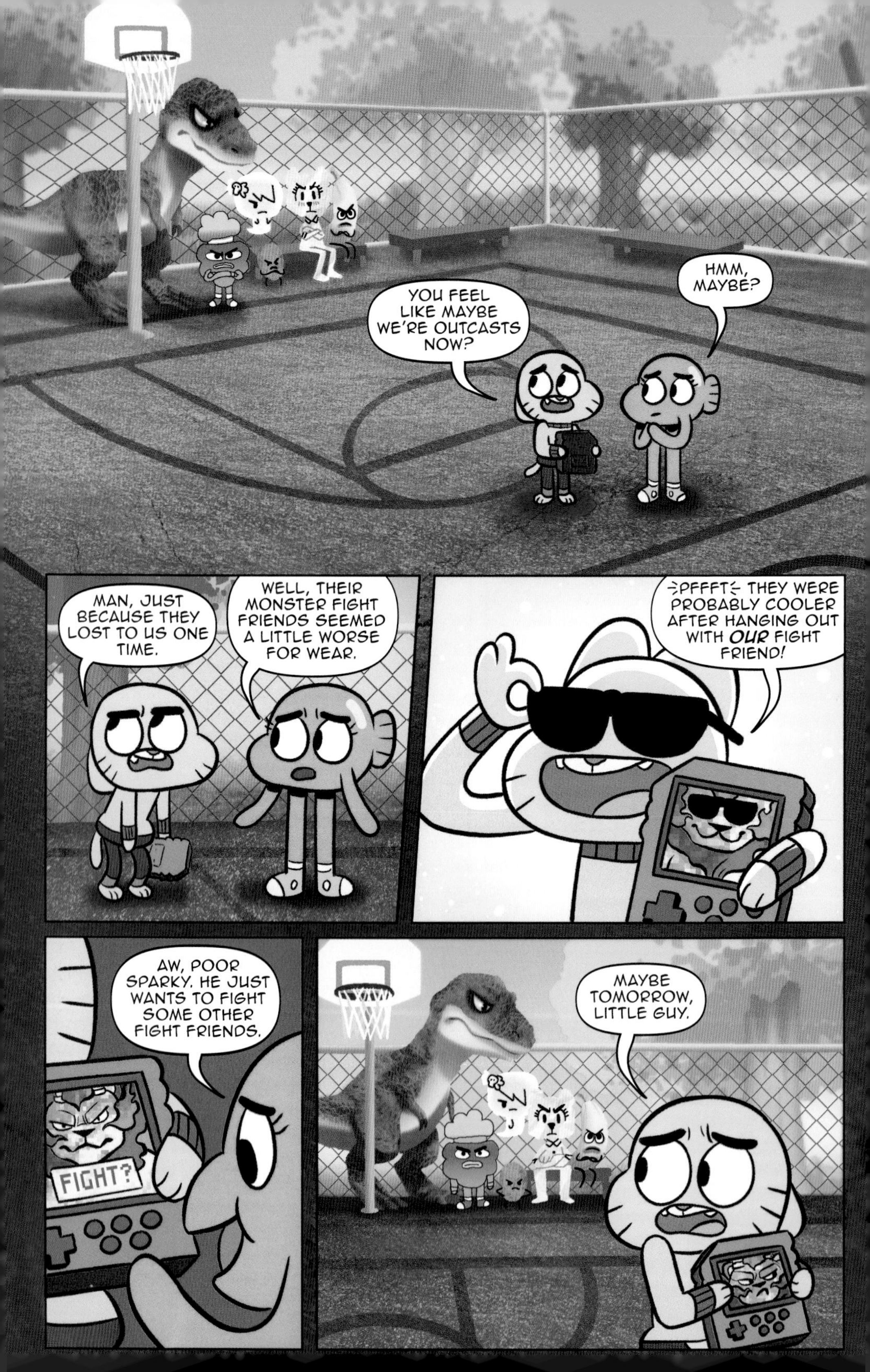
YOU FEEL LIKE MAYBE WE'RE OUTCASTS NOW?
HMM, MAYBE?
MAN, JUST BECAUSE THEY LOST TO US ONE TIME.
WELL, THEIR MONSTER FIGHT FRIENDS SEEMED A LITTLE WORSE FOR WEAR.
PFFFT THEY WERE PROBABLY COOLER AFTER HANGING OUT WITH OUR FIGHT FRIEND!
AW, POOR SPARKY. HE JUST WANTS TO FIGHT SOME OTHER FIGHT FRIENDS.
FIGHT?
MAYBE TOMORROW, LITTLE GUY.

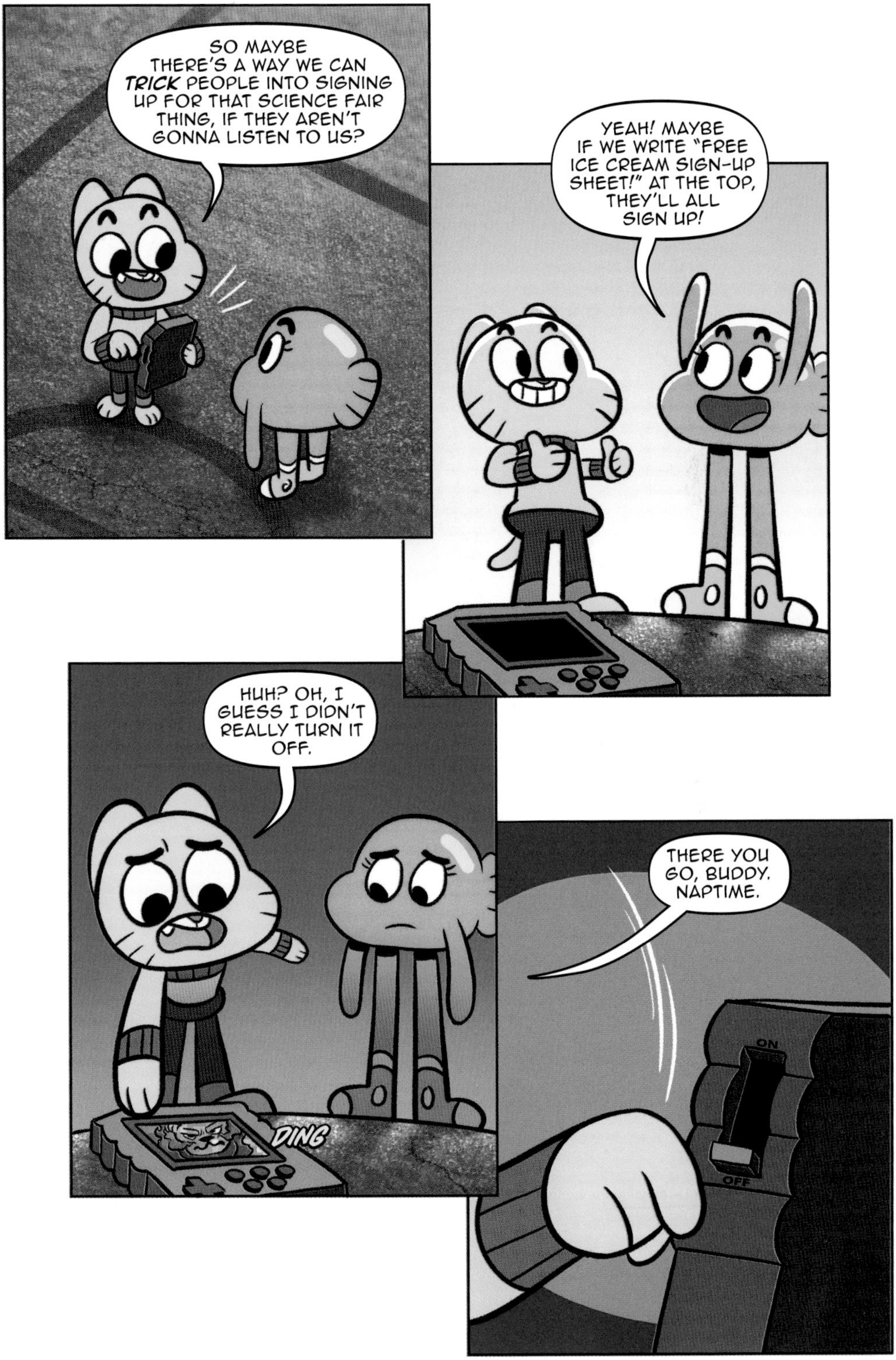

SO MAYBE THERE'S A WAY WE CAN *TRICK* PEOPLE INTO SIGNING UP FOR THAT SCIENCE FAIR THING, IF THEY AREN'T GONNA LISTEN TO US?
YEAH! MAYBE IF WE WRITE "FREE ICE CREAM SIGN-UP SHEET!" AT THE TOP, THEY'LL ALL SIGN UP!
HUH? OH, I GUESS I DIDN'T REALLY TURN IT OFF.
DING
THERE YOU GO, BUDDY. NAPTIME.
ON
OFF

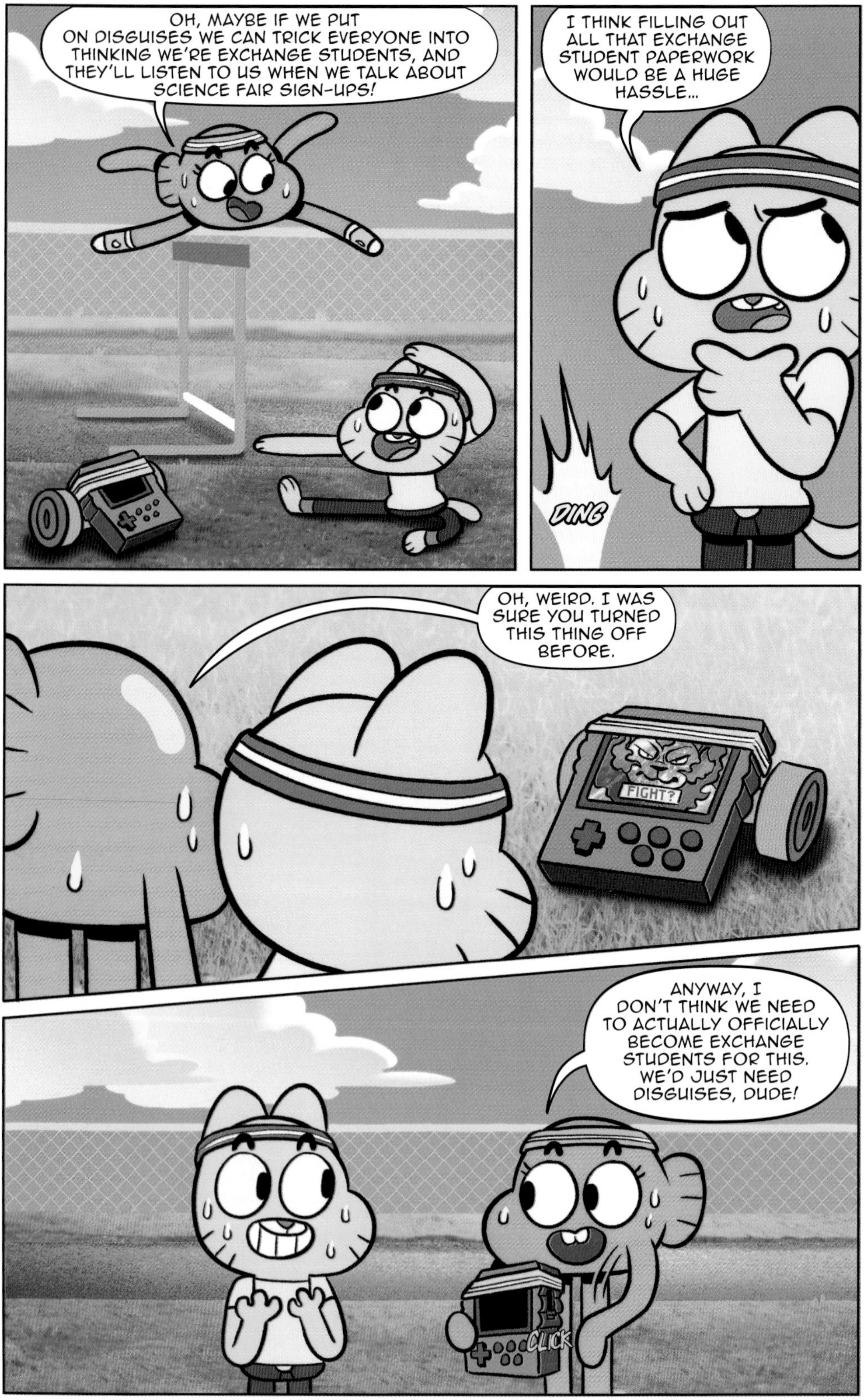
OH, MAYBE IF WE PUT ON DISGUISES WE CAN TRICK EVERYONE INTO THINKING WE'RE EXCHANGE STUDENTS, AND THEY'LL LISTEN TO US WHEN WE TALK ABOUT SCIENCE FAIR SIGN-UPS!
I THINK FILLING OUT ALL THAT EXCHANGE STUDENT PAPERWORK WOULD BE A HUGE HASSLE...
DING
OH, WEIRD. I WAS SURE YOU TURNED THIS THING OFF BEFORE.
FIGHT?
ANYWAY, I DON'T THINK WE NEED TO ACTUALLY OFFICIALLY BECOME EXCHANGE STUDENTS FOR THIS. WE'D JUST NEED DISGUISES, DUDE!
CLICK

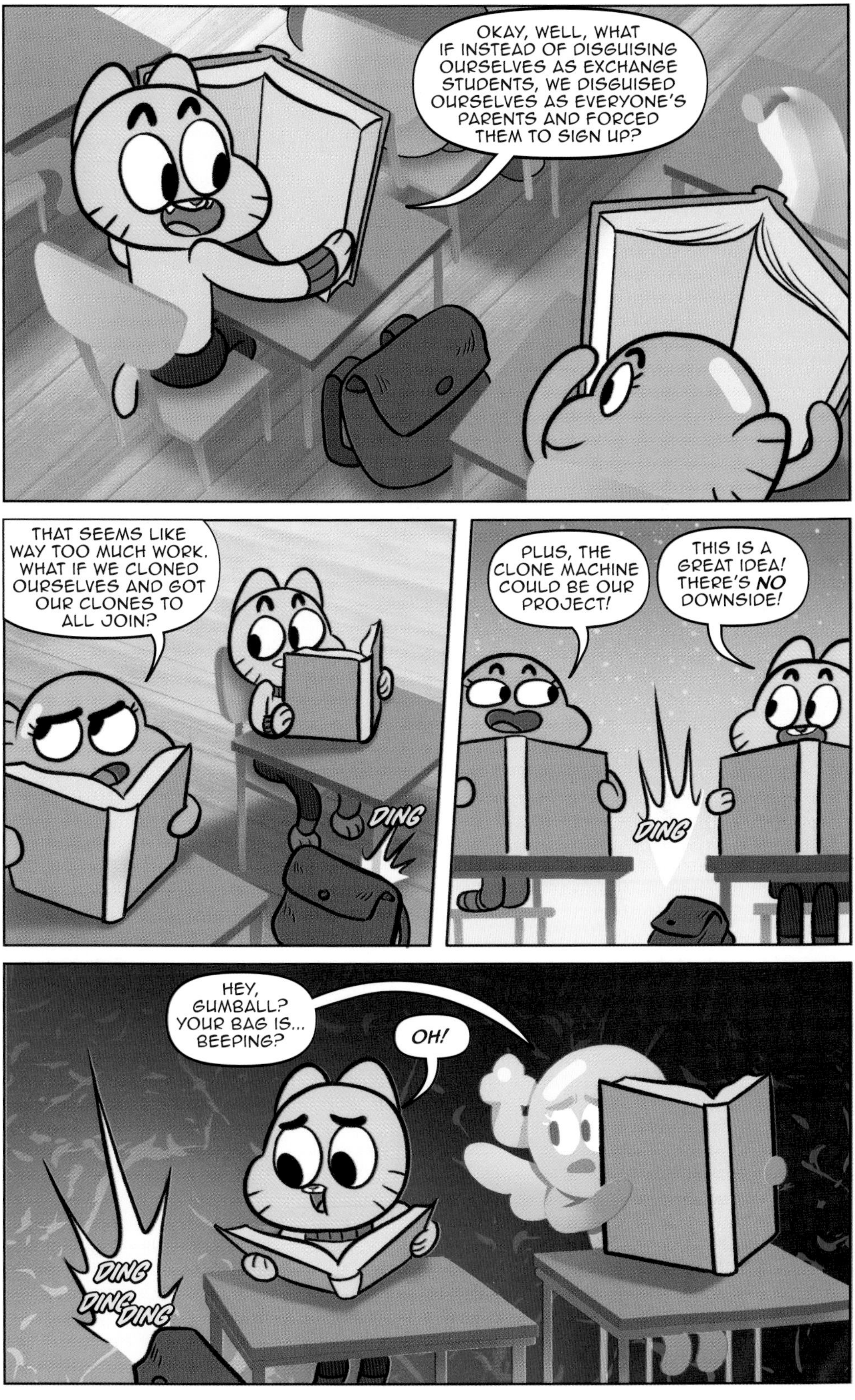

OKAY, WELL, WHAT IF INSTEAD OF DISGUISING OURSELVES AS EXCHANGE STUDENTS, WE DISGUISED OURSELVES AS EVERYONE'S PARENTS AND FORCED THEM TO SIGN UP?
THAT SEEMS LIKE WAY TOO MUCH WORK. WHAT IF WE CLONED OURSELVES AND GOT OUR CLONES TO ALL JOIN?
DING
PLUS, THE CLONE MACHINE COULD BE OUR PROJECT!
THIS IS A GREAT IDEA! THERE'S **NO** DOWNSIDE!
DING
HEY, GUMBALL? YOUR BAG IS... BEEPING?
OH!
DING
DING DING

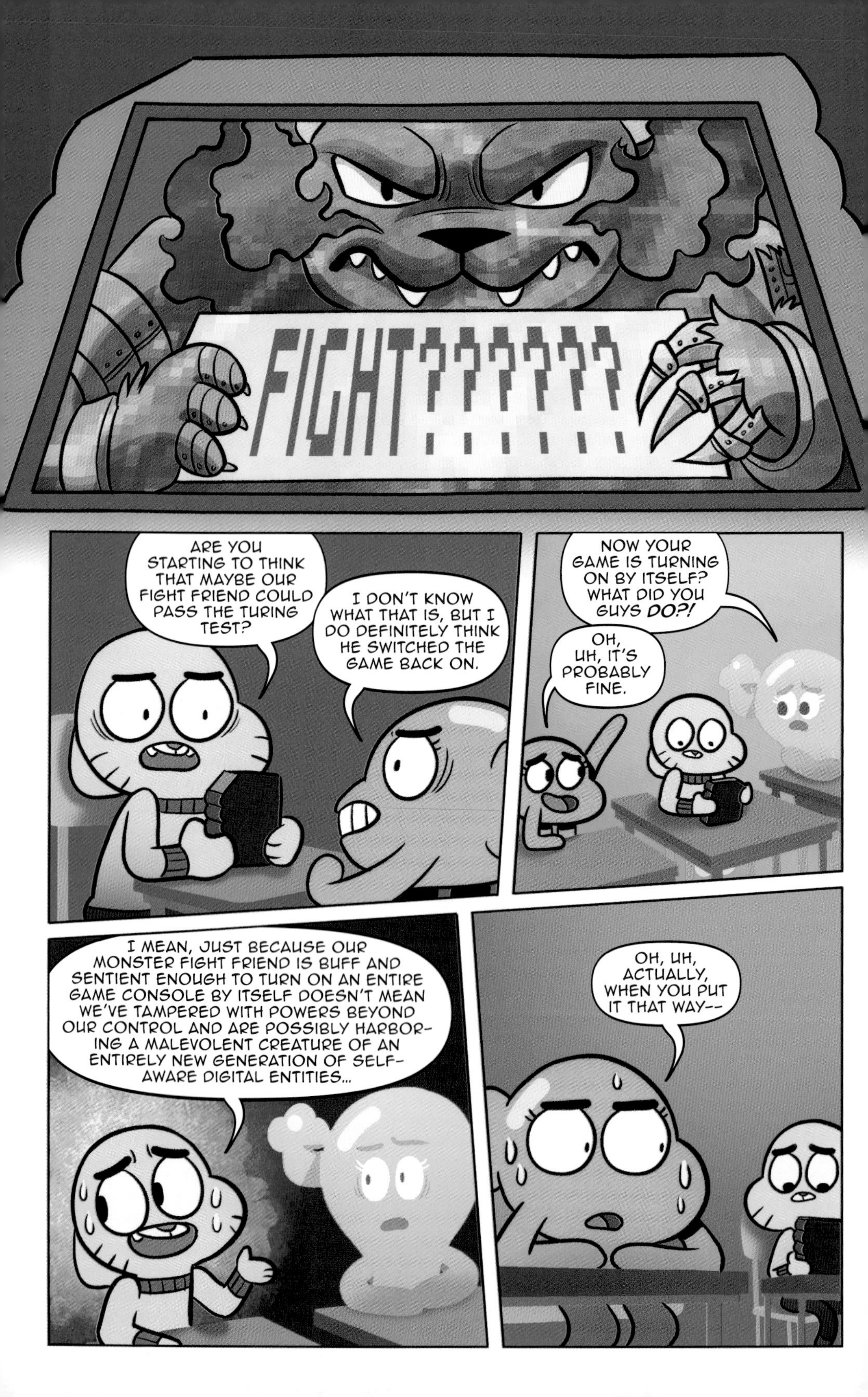
FIGHT??????
ARE YOU STARTING TO THINK THAT MAYBE OUR FIGHT FRIEND COULD PASS THE TURING TEST?
I DON'T KNOW WHAT THAT IS, BUT I DO DEFINITELY THINK HE SWITCHED THE GAME BACK ON.
NOW YOUR GAME IS TURNING ON BY ITSELF? WHAT DID YOU GUYS DO?!
OH, UH, IT'S PROBABLY FINE.
I MEAN, JUST BECAUSE OUR MONSTER FIGHT FRIEND IS BUFF AND SENTIENT ENOUGH TO TURN ON AN ENTIRE GAME CONSOLE BY ITSELF DOESN'T MEAN WE'VE TAMPERED WITH POWERS BEYOND OUR CONTROL AND ARE POSSIBLY HARBOR-ING A MALEVOLENT CREATURE OF AN ENTIRELY NEW GENERATION OF SELF-AWARE DIGITAL ENTITIES...
OH, UH, ACTUALLY, WHEN YOU PUT IT THAT WAY--

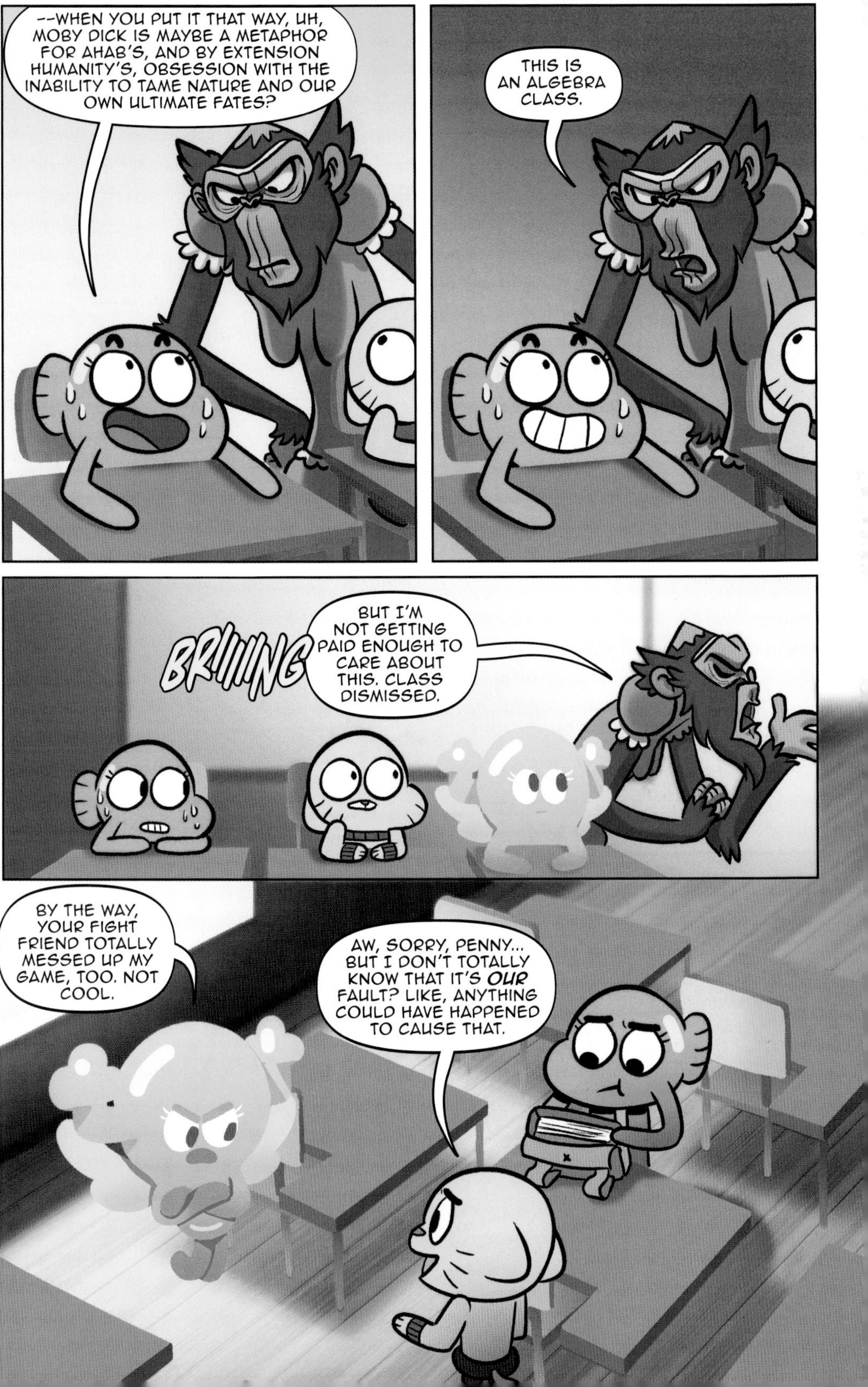
--WHEN YOU PUT IT THAT WAY, UH, MOBY DICK IS MAYBE A METAPHOR FOR AHAB'S, AND BY EXTENSION HUMANITY'S, OBSESSION WITH THE INABILITY TO TAME NATURE AND OUR OWN ULTIMATE FATES?
THIS IS AN ALGEBRA CLASS.
BRIIIING
BUT I'M NOT GETTING PAID ENOUGH TO CARE ABOUT THIS. CLASS DISMISSED.
BY THE WAY, YOUR FIGHT FRIEND TOTALLY MESSED UP MY GAME, TOO. NOT COOL.
AW, SORRY, PENNY... BUT I DON'T TOTALLY KNOW THAT IT'S *OUR* FAULT? LIKE, ANYTHING COULD HAVE HAPPENED TO CAUSE THAT.

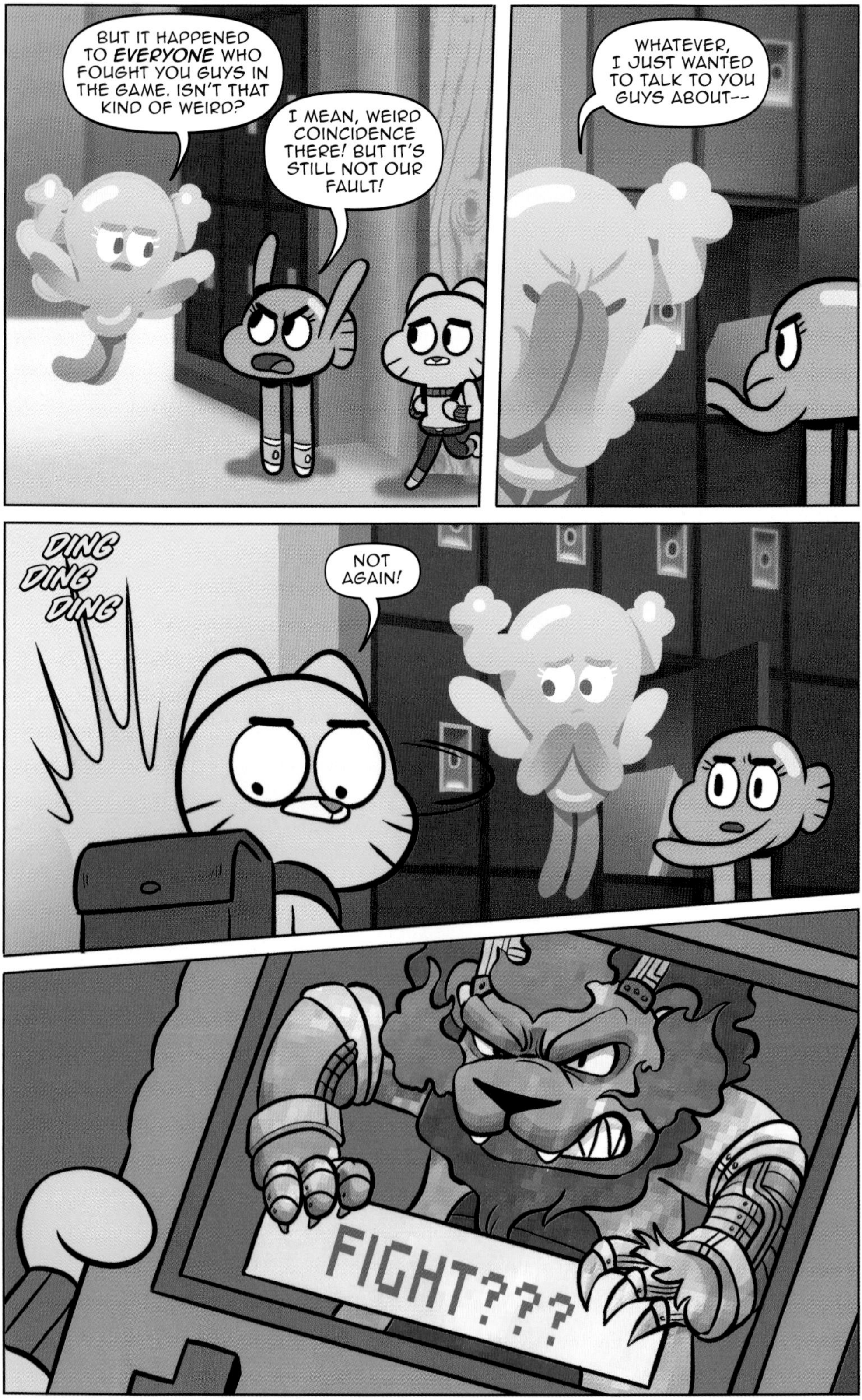
BUT IT HAPPENED TO ***EVERYONE*** WHO FOUGHT YOU GUYS IN THE GAME. ISN'T THAT KIND OF WEIRD?
I MEAN, WEIRD COINCIDENCE THERE! BUT IT'S STILL NOT OUR FAULT!
WHATEVER, I JUST WANTED TO TALK TO YOU GUYS ABOUT--
DING DING DING
NOT AGAIN!
FIGHT???

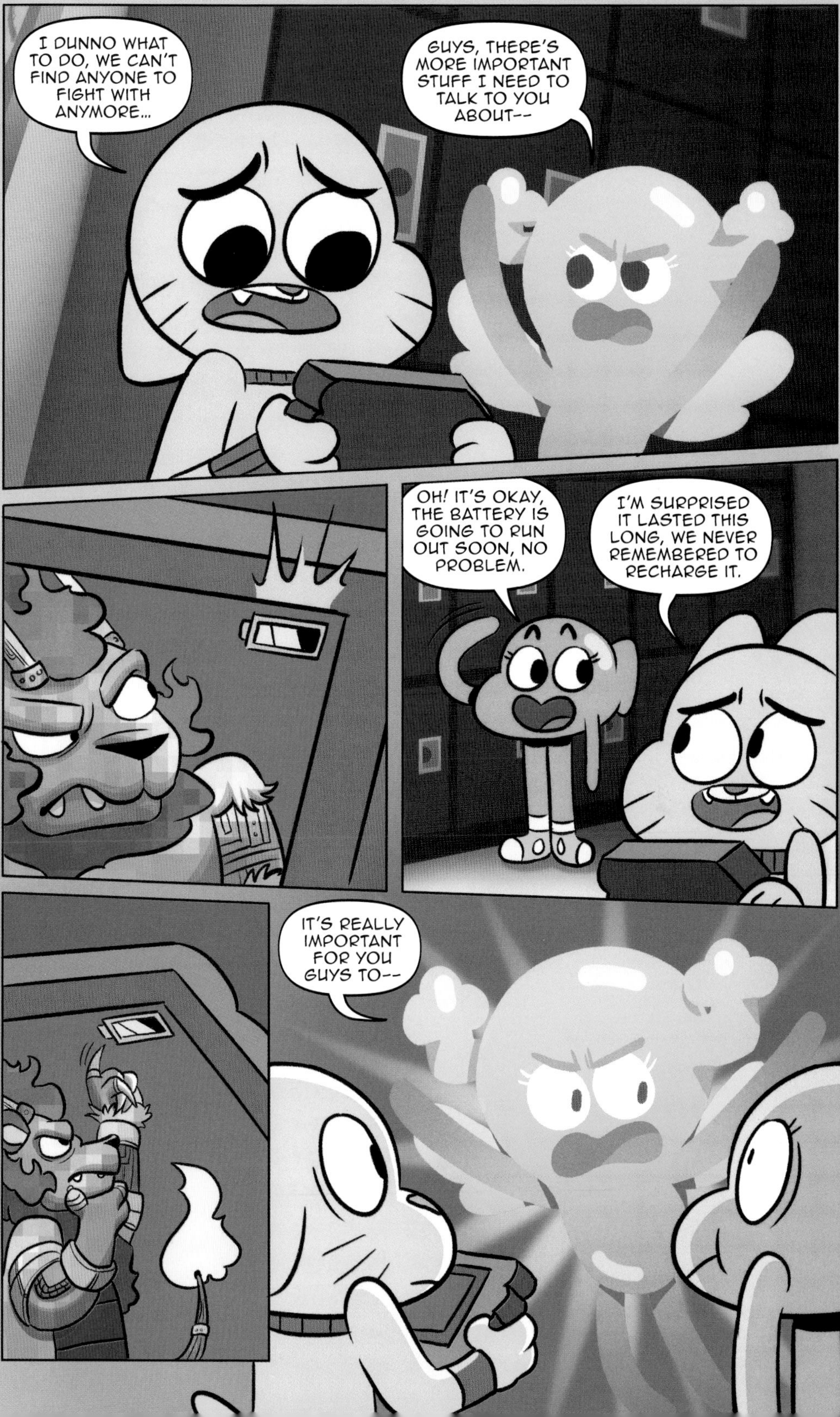
I DUNNO WHAT TO DO, WE CAN'T FIND ANYONE TO FIGHT WITH ANYMORE...
GUYS, THERE'S MORE IMPORTANT STUFF I NEED TO TALK TO YOU ABOUT--
OH! IT'S OKAY, THE BATTERY IS GOING TO RUN OUT SOON, NO PROBLEM.
I'M SURPRISED IT LASTED THIS LONG, WE NEVER REMEMBERED TO RECHARGE IT.
IT'S REALLY IMPORTANT FOR YOU GUYS TO--

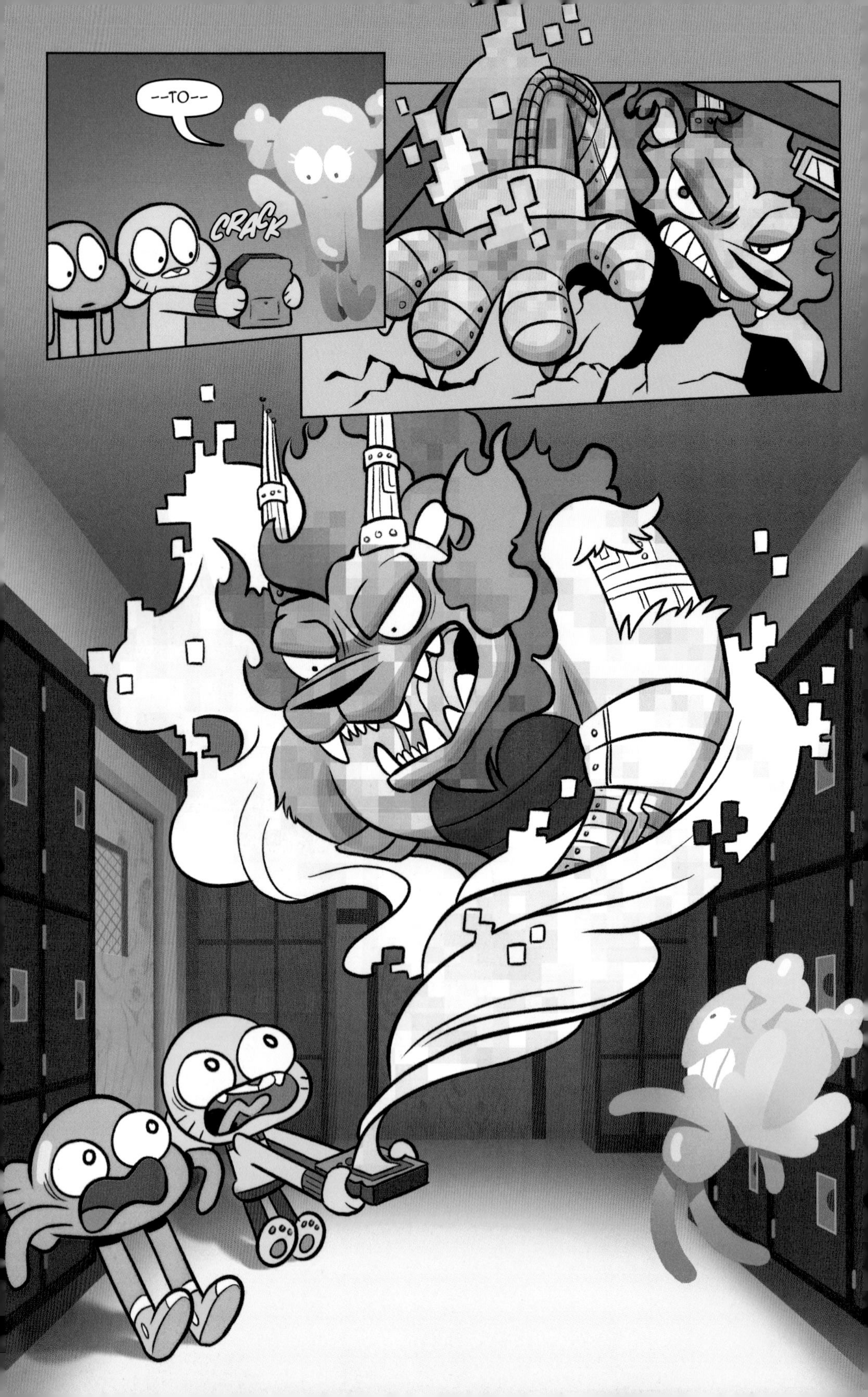
--TO--
CRACK

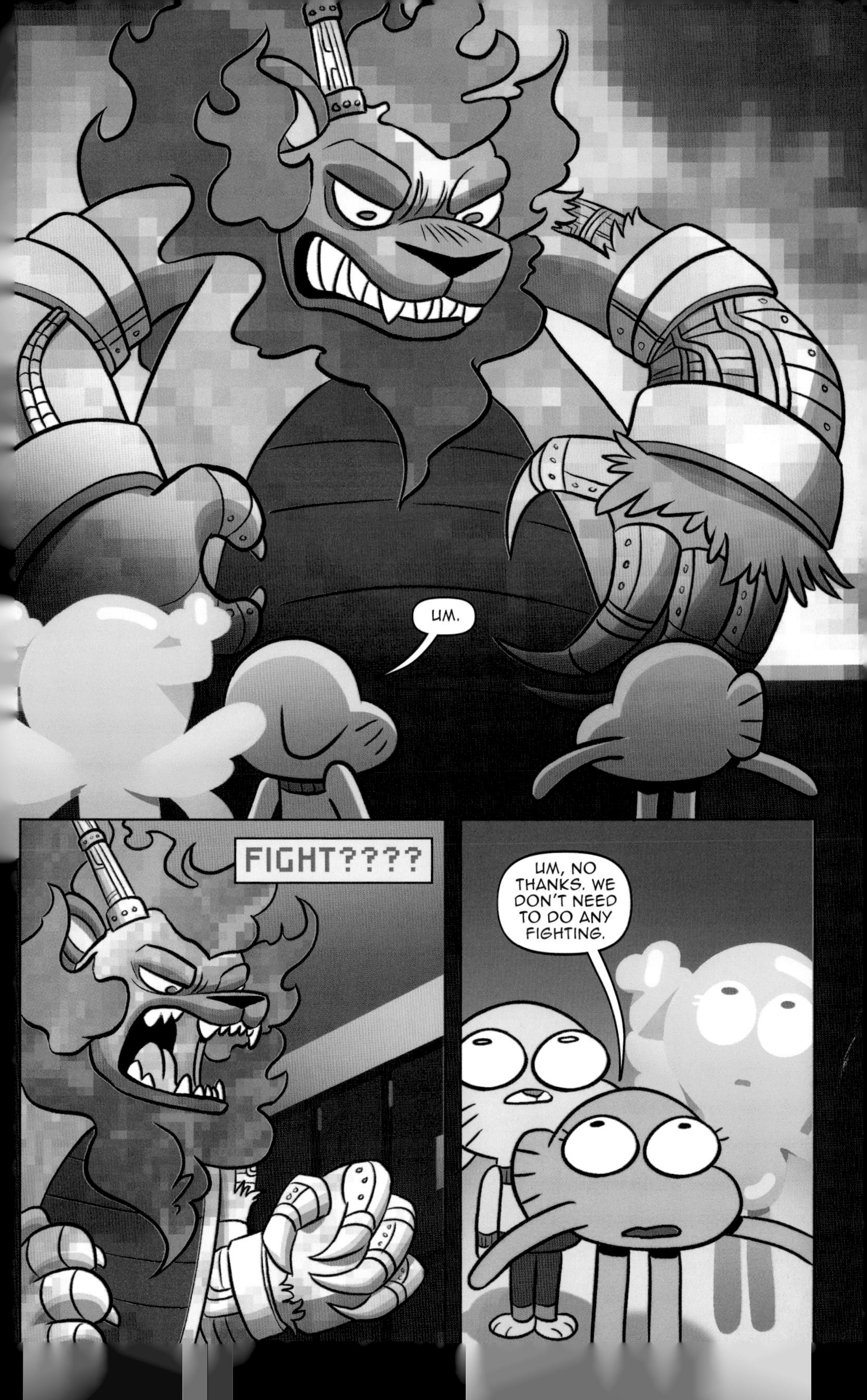
UM.
FIGHT????
UM, NO THANKS. WE DON'T NEED TO DO ANY FIGHTING.

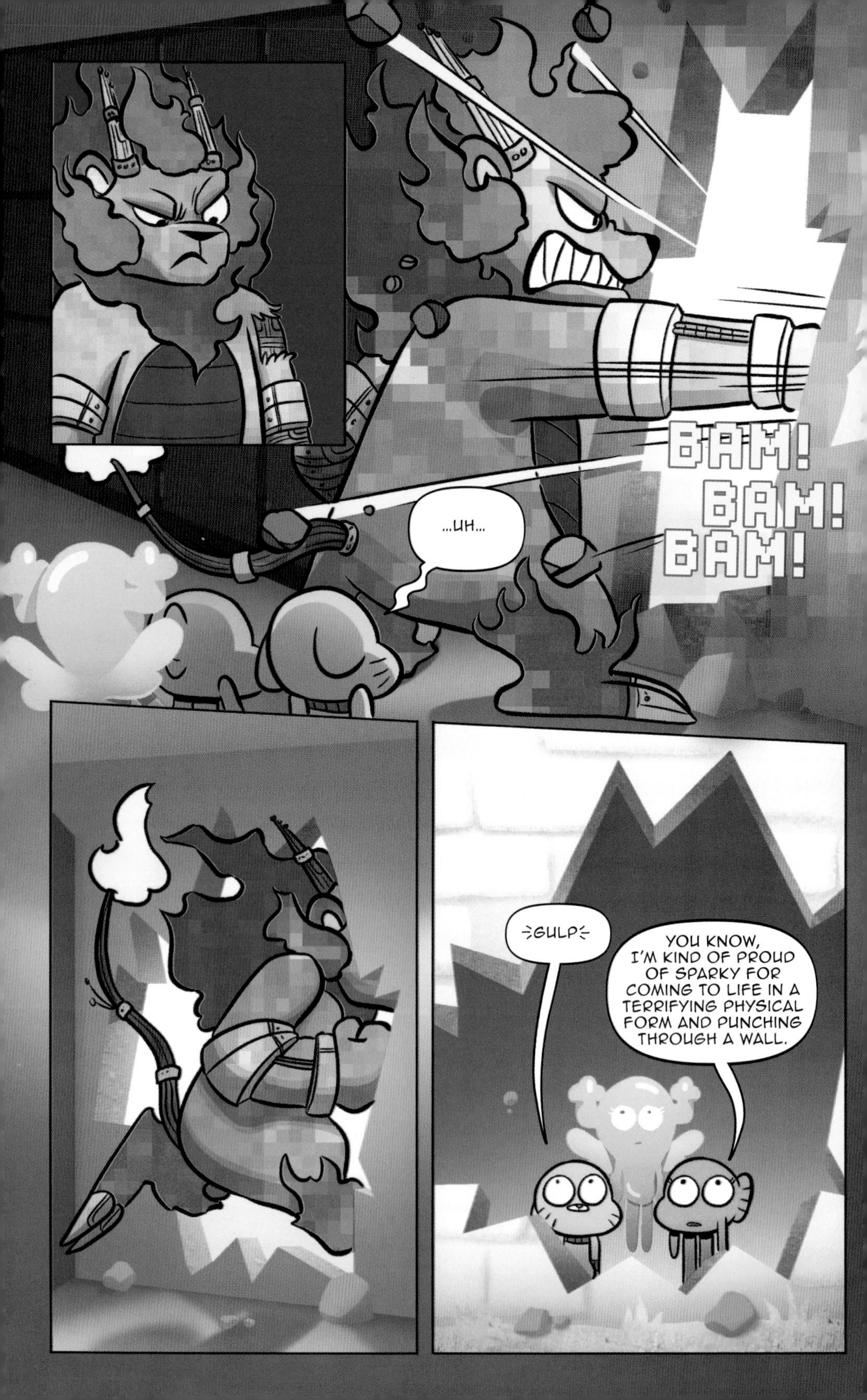
BAM!
BAM!
BAM!
...UH...
-GULP-
YOU KNOW, I'M KIND OF PROUD OF SPARKY FOR COMING TO LIFE IN A TERRIFYING PHYSICAL FORM AND PUNCHING THROUGH A WALL.

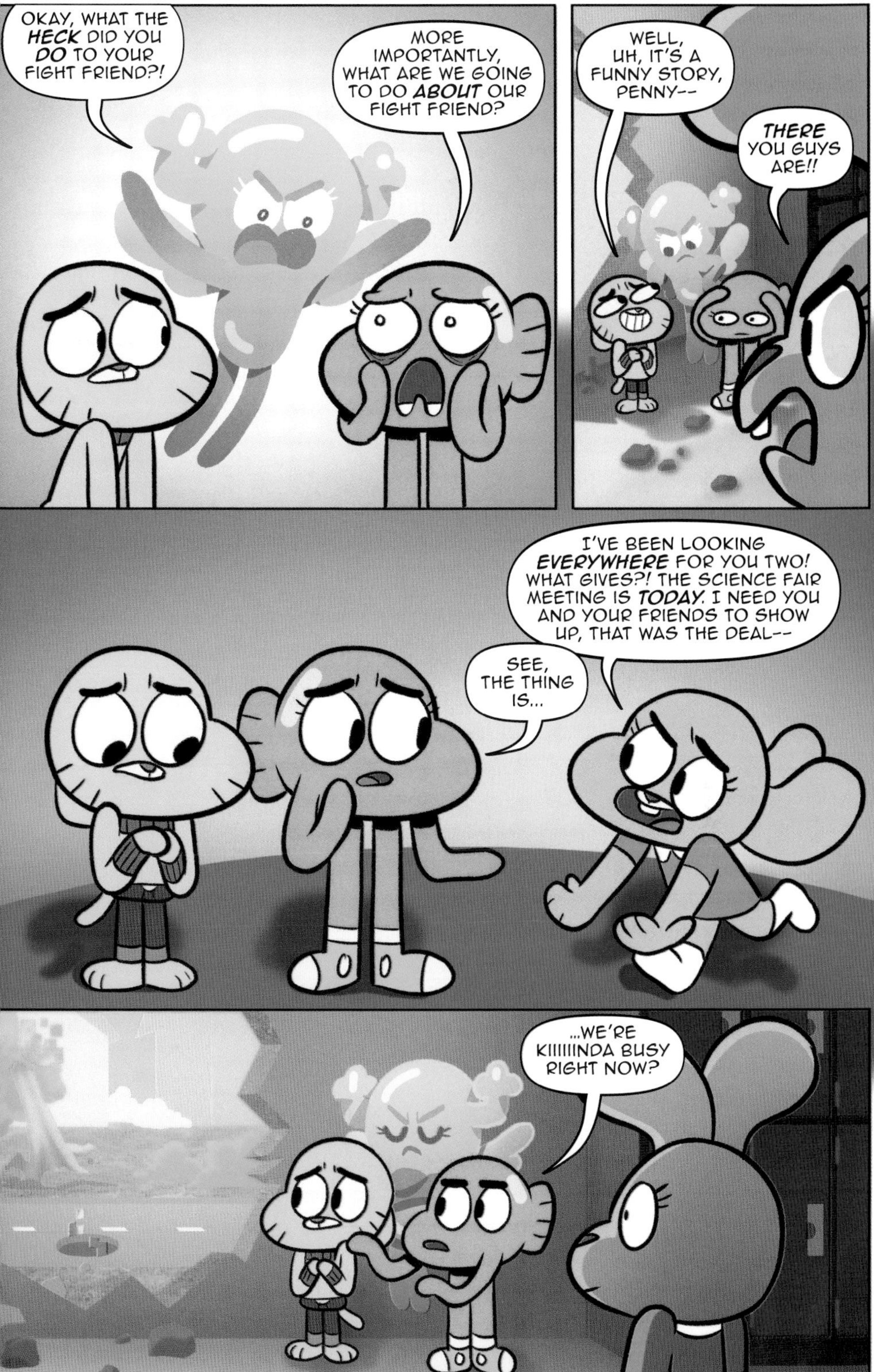
OKAY, WHAT THE HECK DID YOU DO TO YOUR FIGHT FRIEND?!
MORE IMPORTANTLY, WHAT ARE WE GOING TO DO ABOUT OUR FIGHT FRIEND?
WELL, UH, IT'S A FUNNY STORY, PENNY--
THERE YOU GUYS ARE!!
I'VE BEEN LOOKING EVERYWHERE FOR YOU TWO! WHAT GIVES?! THE SCIENCE FAIR MEETING IS TODAY. I NEED YOU AND YOUR FRIENDS TO SHOW UP, THAT WAS THE DEAL--
SEE, THE THING IS...
...WE'RE KIIIIIINDA BUSY RIGHT NOW?

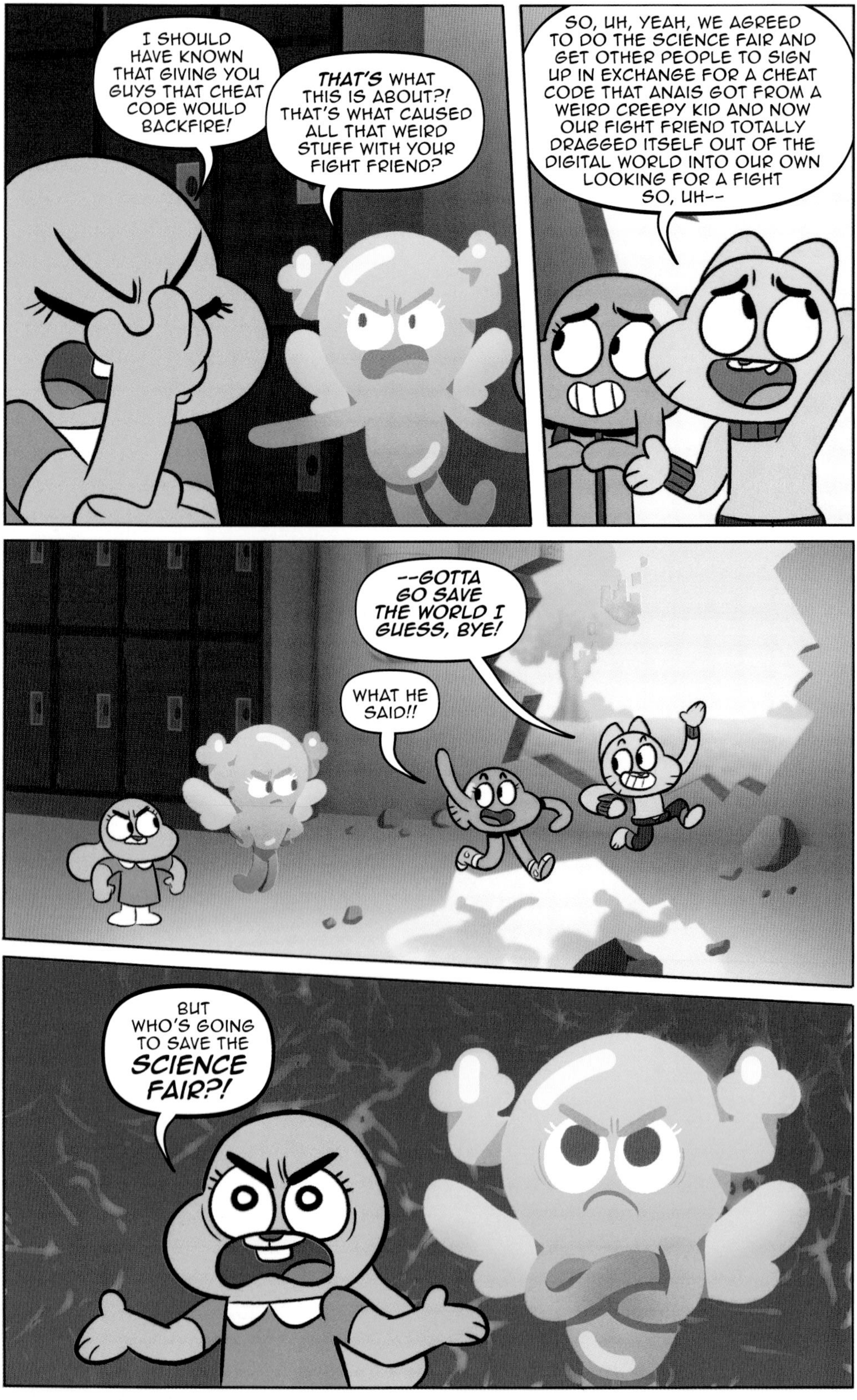
I SHOULD HAVE KNOWN THAT GIVING YOU GUYS THAT CHEAT CODE WOULD BACKFIRE!
THAT'S WHAT THIS IS ABOUT?! THAT'S WHAT CAUSED ALL THAT WEIRD STUFF WITH YOUR FIGHT FRIEND?
SO, UH, YEAH, WE AGREED TO DO THE SCIENCE FAIR AND GET OTHER PEOPLE TO SIGN UP IN EXCHANGE FOR A CHEAT CODE THAT ANAIS GOT FROM A WEIRD CREEPY KID AND NOW OUR FIGHT FRIEND TOTALLY DRAGGED ITSELF OUT OF THE DIGITAL WORLD INTO OUR OWN LOOKING FOR A FIGHT SO, UH--
--GOTTA GO SAVE THE WORLD I GUESS, BYE!
WHAT HE SAID!!
BUT WHO'S GOING TO SAVE THE SCIENCE FAIR?!

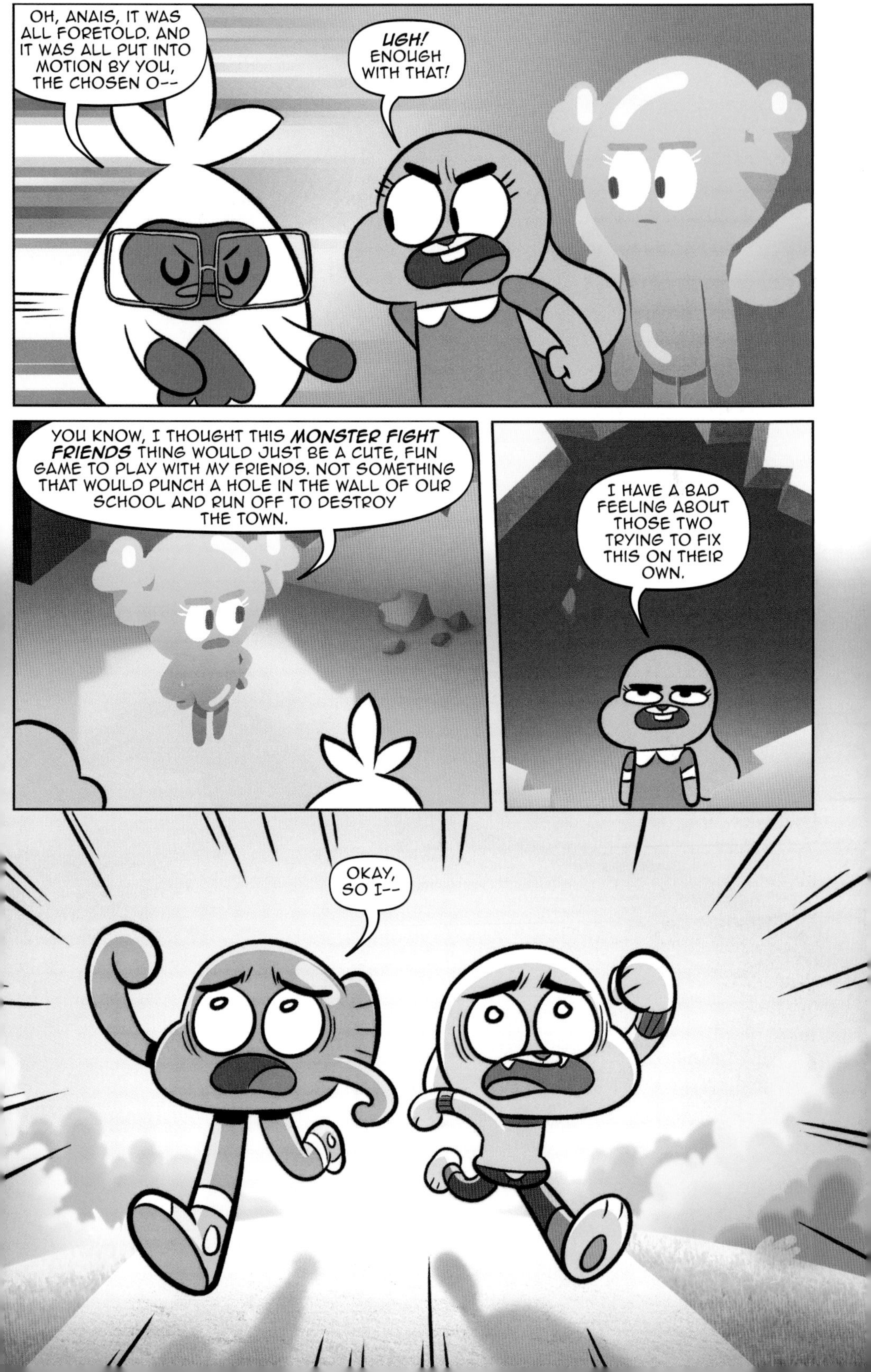
OH, ANAIS, IT WAS ALL FORETOLD. AND IT WAS ALL PUT INTO MOTION BY YOU, THE CHOSEN O--
UGH! ENOUGH WITH THAT!
YOU KNOW, I THOUGHT THIS MONSTER FIGHT FRIENDS THING WOULD JUST BE A CUTE, FUN GAME TO PLAY WITH MY FRIENDS. NOT SOMETHING THAT WOULD PUNCH A HOLE IN THE WALL OF OUR SCHOOL AND RUN OFF TO DESTROY THE TOWN.
I HAVE A BAD FEELING ABOUT THOSE TWO TRYING TO FIX THIS ON THEIR OWN.
OKAY, SO I--

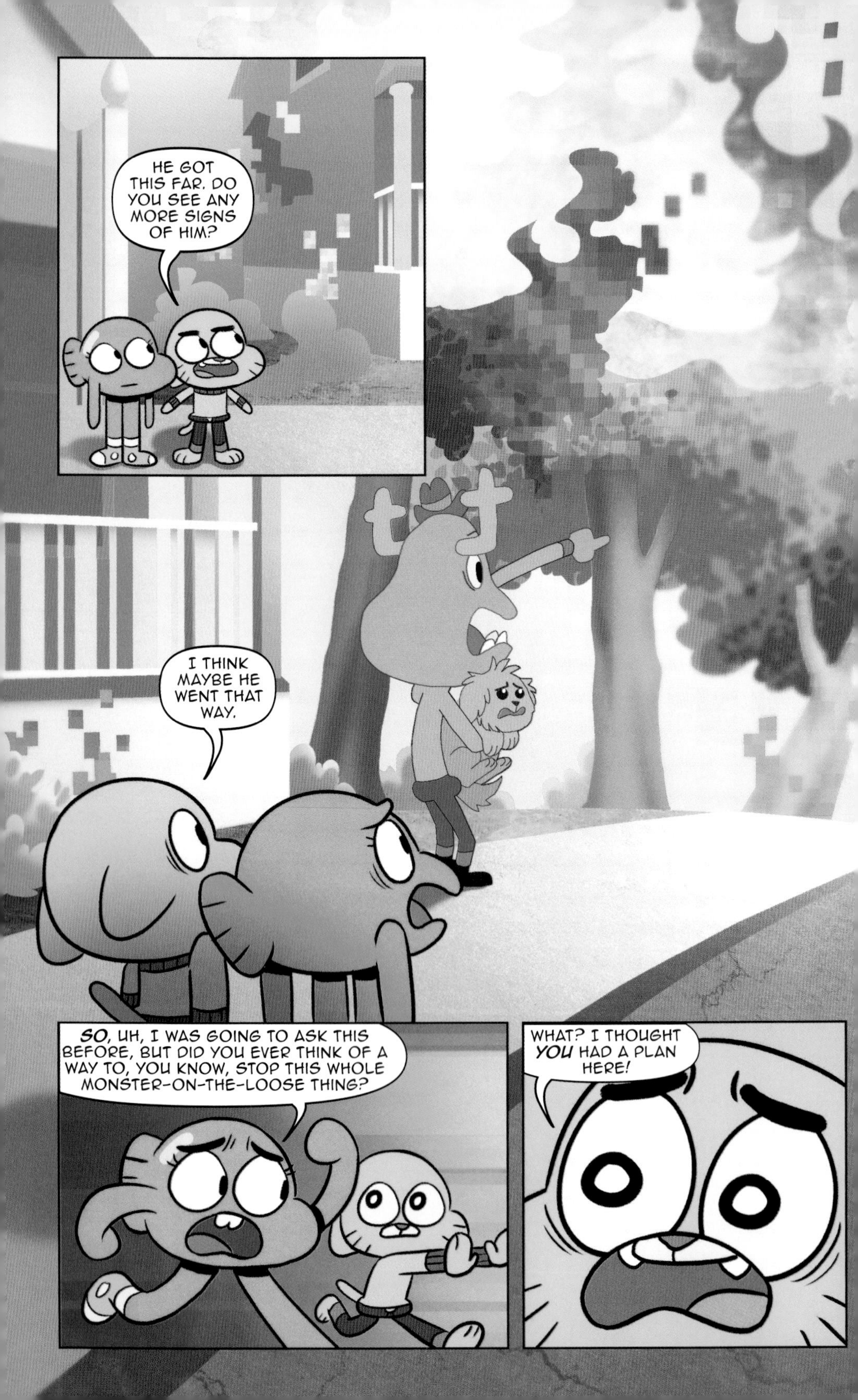
HE GOT THIS FAR. DO YOU SEE ANY MORE SIGNS OF HIM?
I THINK MAYBE HE WENT THAT WAY.
SO, UH, I WAS GOING TO ASK THIS BEFORE, BUT DID YOU EVER THINK OF A WAY TO, YOU KNOW, STOP THIS WHOLE MONSTER-ON-THE-LOOSE THING?
WHAT? I THOUGHT YOU HAD A PLAN HERE!

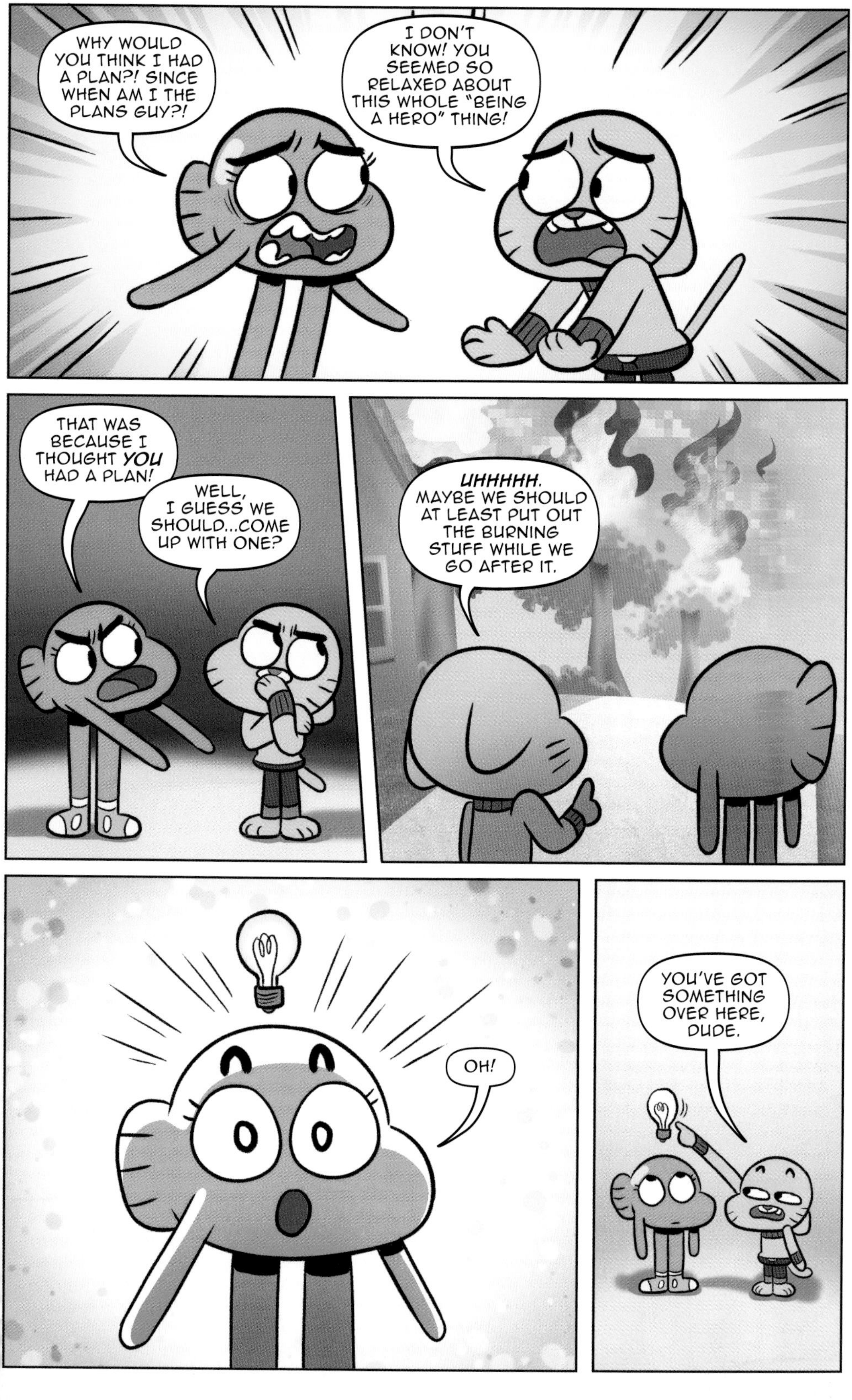
WHY WOULD YOU THINK I HAD A PLAN?! SINCE WHEN AM I THE PLANS GUY?!
I DON'T KNOW! YOU SEEMED SO RELAXED ABOUT THIS WHOLE "BEING A HERO" THING!
THAT WAS BECAUSE I THOUGHT *YOU* HAD A PLAN!
WELL, I GUESS WE SHOULD...COME UP WITH ONE?
UHHHHH. MAYBE WE SHOULD AT LEAST PUT OUT THE BURNING STUFF WHILE WE GO AFTER IT.
OH!
YOU'VE GOT SOMETHING OVER HERE, DUDE.

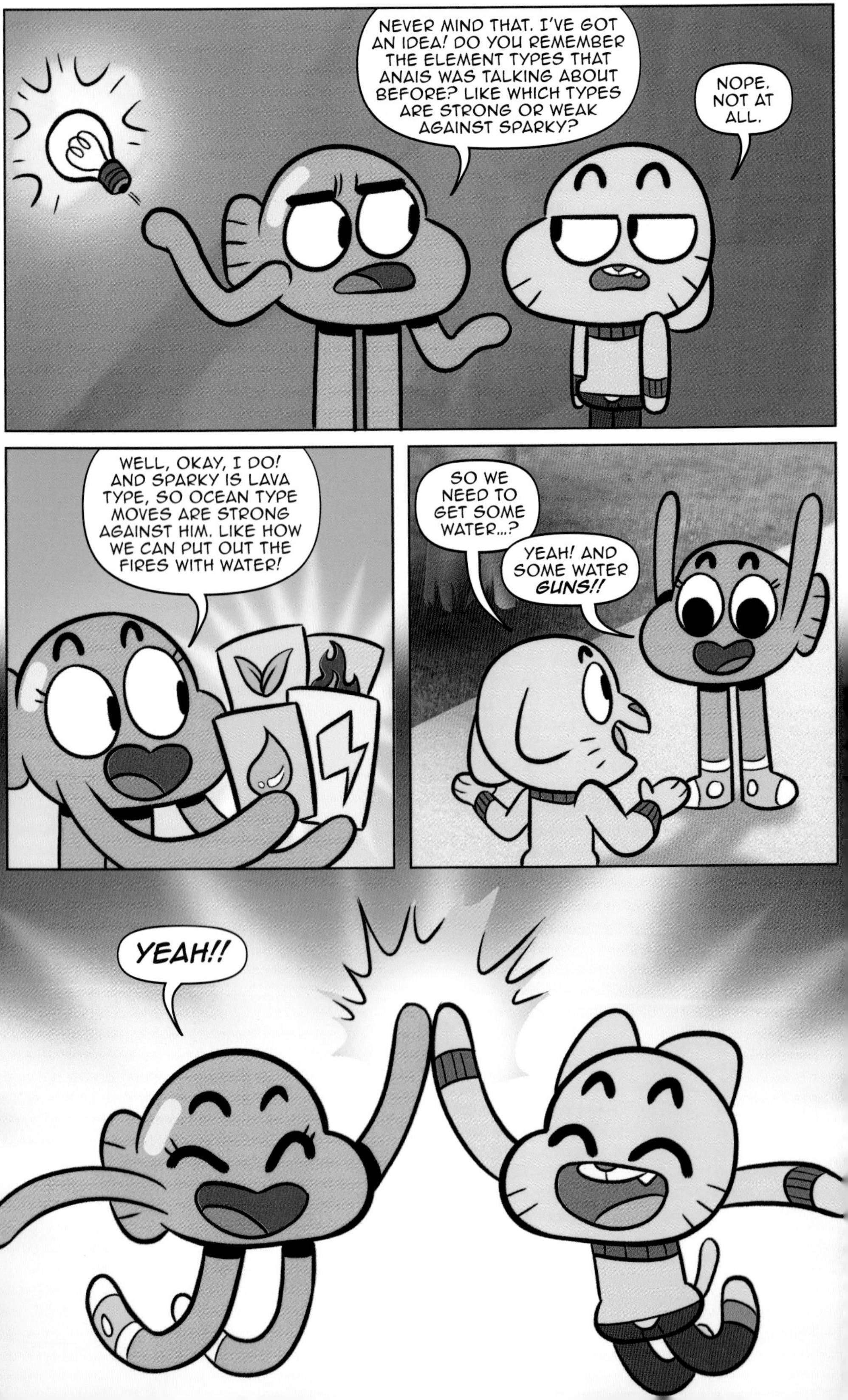
NEVER MIND THAT. I'VE GOT AN IDEA! DO YOU REMEMBER THE ELEMENT TYPES THAT ANAIS WAS TALKING ABOUT BEFORE? LIKE WHICH TYPES ARE STRONG OR WEAK AGAINST SPARKY?
NOPE. NOT AT ALL.
WELL, OKAY, I DO! AND SPARKY IS LAVA TYPE, SO OCEAN TYPE MOVES ARE STRONG AGAINST HIM. LIKE HOW WE CAN PUT OUT THE FIRES WITH WATER!
SO WE NEED TO GET SOME WATER...?
YEAH! AND SOME WATER GUNS!!
YEAH!!

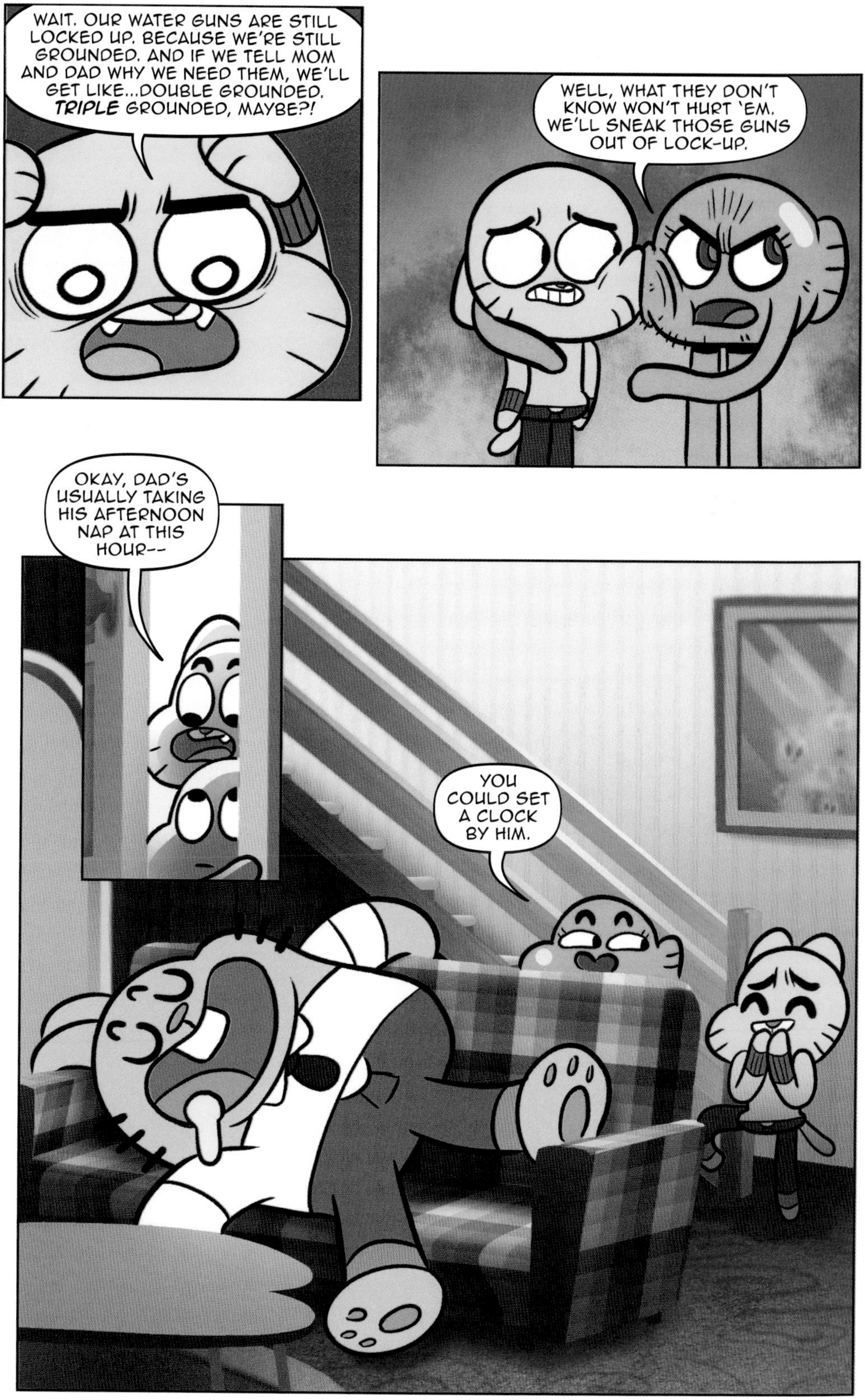
WAIT. OUR WATER GUNS ARE STILL LOCKED UP. BECAUSE WE'RE STILL GROUNDED. AND IF WE TELL MOM AND DAD WHY WE NEED THEM, WE'LL GET LIKE...DOUBLE GROUNDED. *TRIPLE* GROUNDED, MAYBE?!
WELL, WHAT THEY DON'T KNOW WON'T HURT 'EM. WE'LL SNEAK THOSE GUNS OUT OF LOCK-UP.
OKAY, DAD'S USUALLY TAKING HIS AFTERNOON NAP AT THIS HOUR--
YOU COULD SET A CLOCK BY HIM.

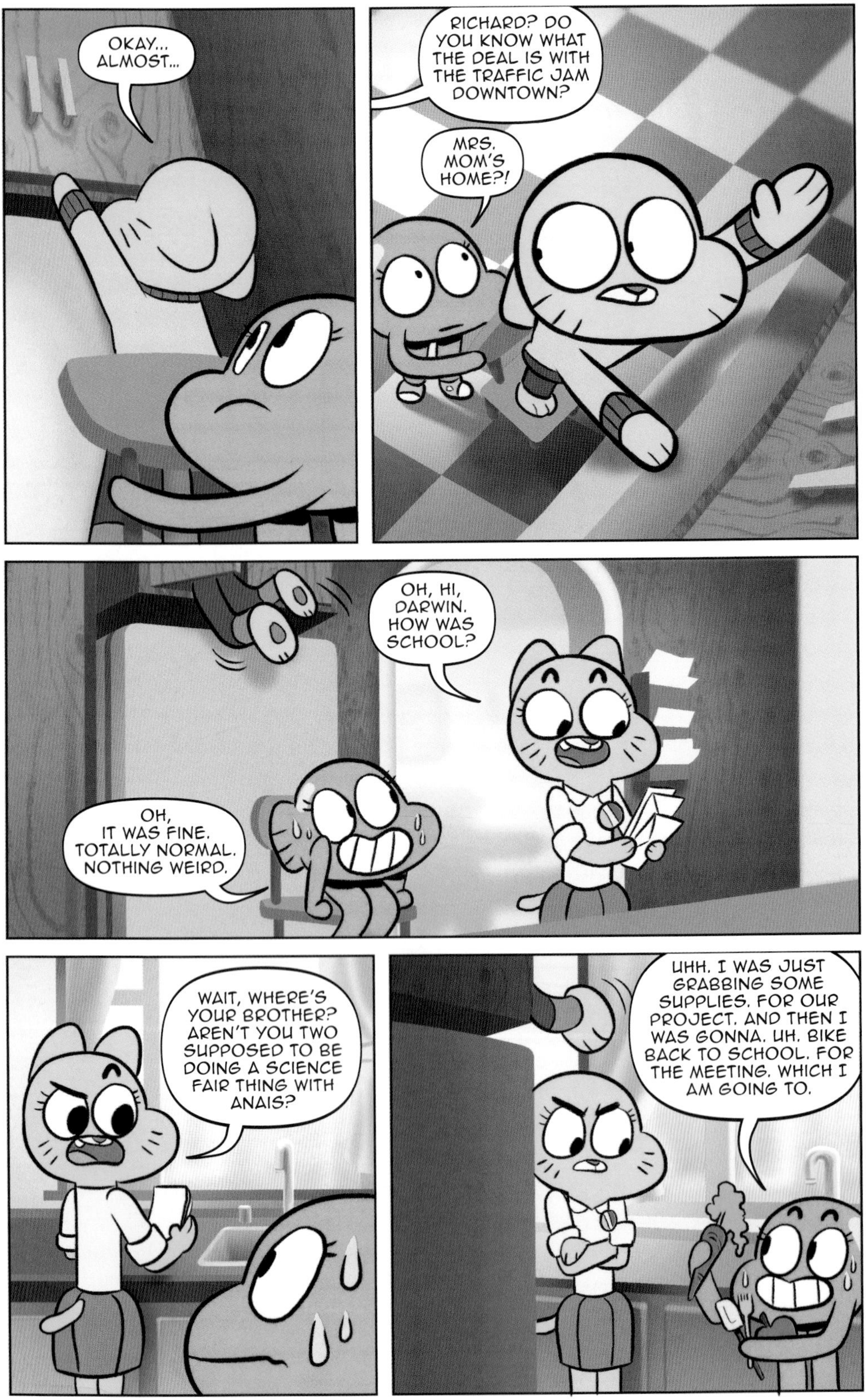
OKAY... ALMOST...
RICHARD? DO YOU KNOW WHAT THE DEAL IS WITH THE TRAFFIC JAM DOWNTOWN?
MRS. MOM'S HOME?!
OH, HI, DARWIN. HOW WAS SCHOOL?
OH, IT WAS FINE. TOTALLY NORMAL. NOTHING WEIRD.
WAIT, WHERE'S YOUR BROTHER? AREN'T YOU TWO SUPPOSED TO BE DOING A SCIENCE FAIR THING WITH ANAIS?
UHH. I WAS JUST GRABBING SOME SUPPLIES. FOR OUR PROJECT. AND THEN I WAS GONNA. UH. BIKE BACK TO SCHOOL. FOR THE MEETING. WHICH I AM GOING TO.

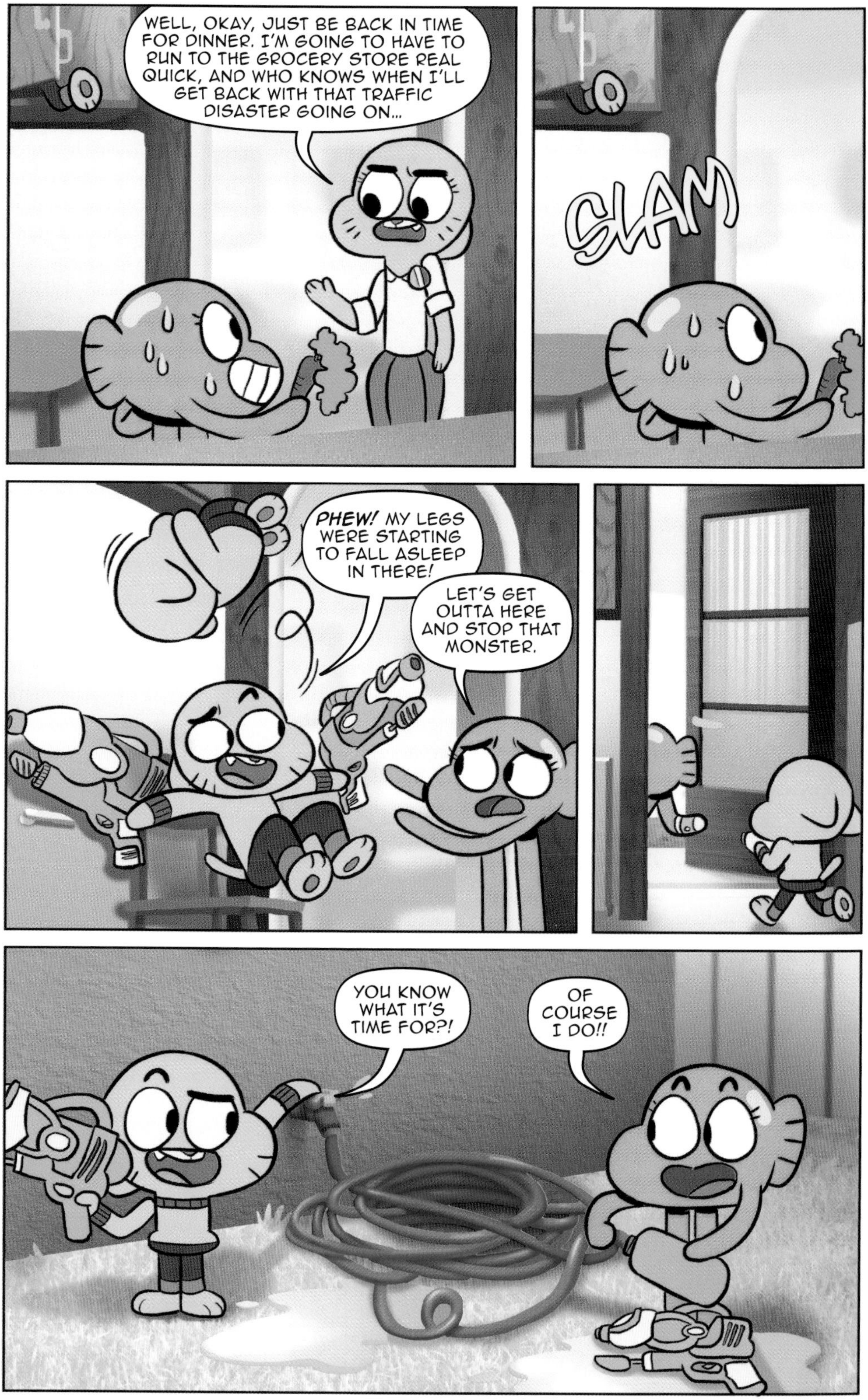
WELL, OKAY, JUST BE BACK IN TIME FOR DINNER. I'M GOING TO HAVE TO RUN TO THE GROCERY STORE REAL QUICK, AND WHO KNOWS WHEN I'LL GET BACK WITH THAT TRAFFIC DISASTER GOING ON...
SLAM
PHEW! MY LEGS WERE STARTING TO FALL ASLEEP IN THERE!
LET'S GET OUTTA HERE AND STOP THAT MONSTER.
YOU KNOW WHAT IT'S TIME FOR?!
OF COURSE I DO!!

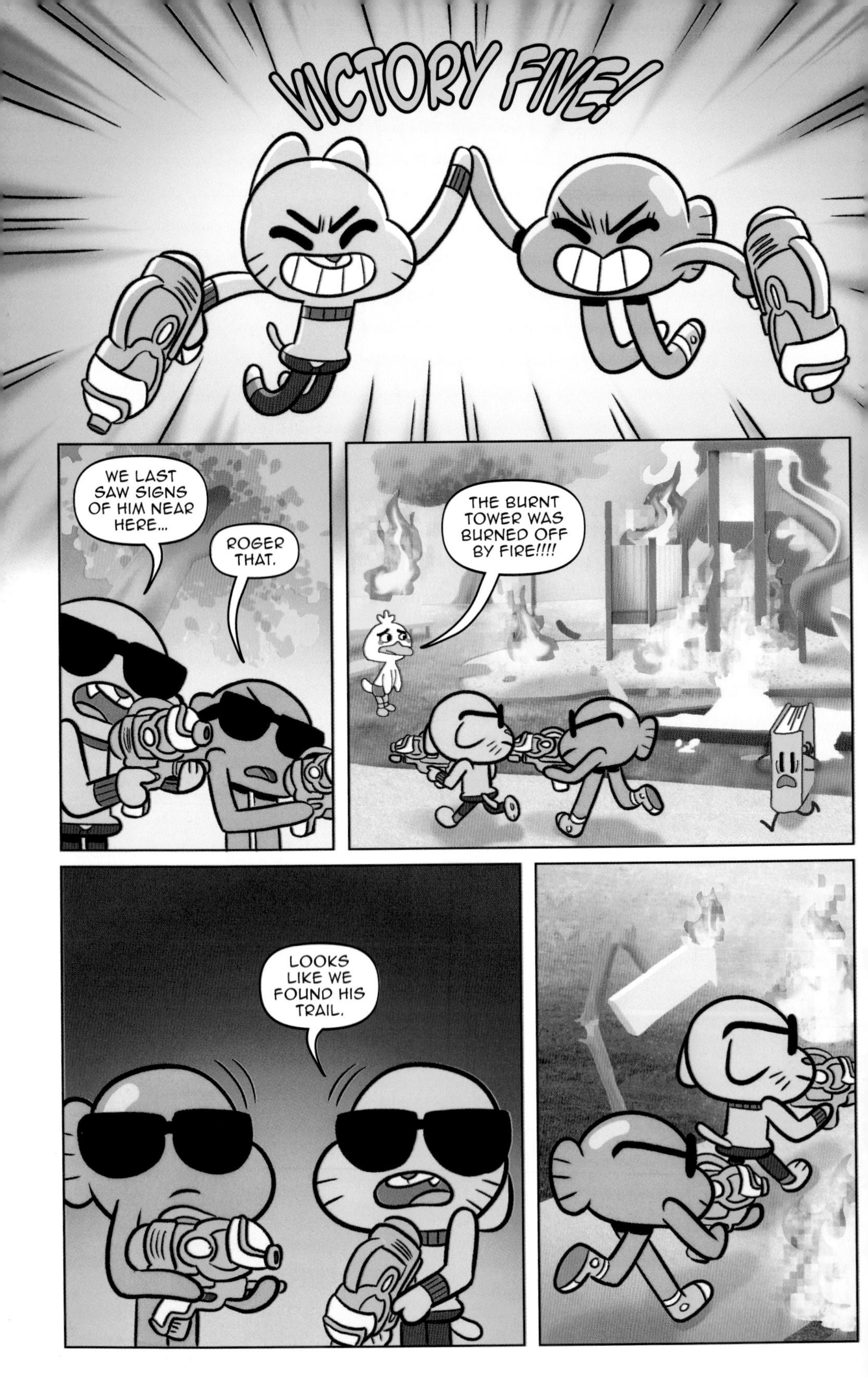
VICTORY FIVE!
WE LAST SAW SIGNS OF HIM NEAR HERE...
ROGER THAT.
THE BURNT TOWER WAS BURNED OFF BY FIRE!!!!
LOOKS LIKE WE FOUND HIS TRAIL.

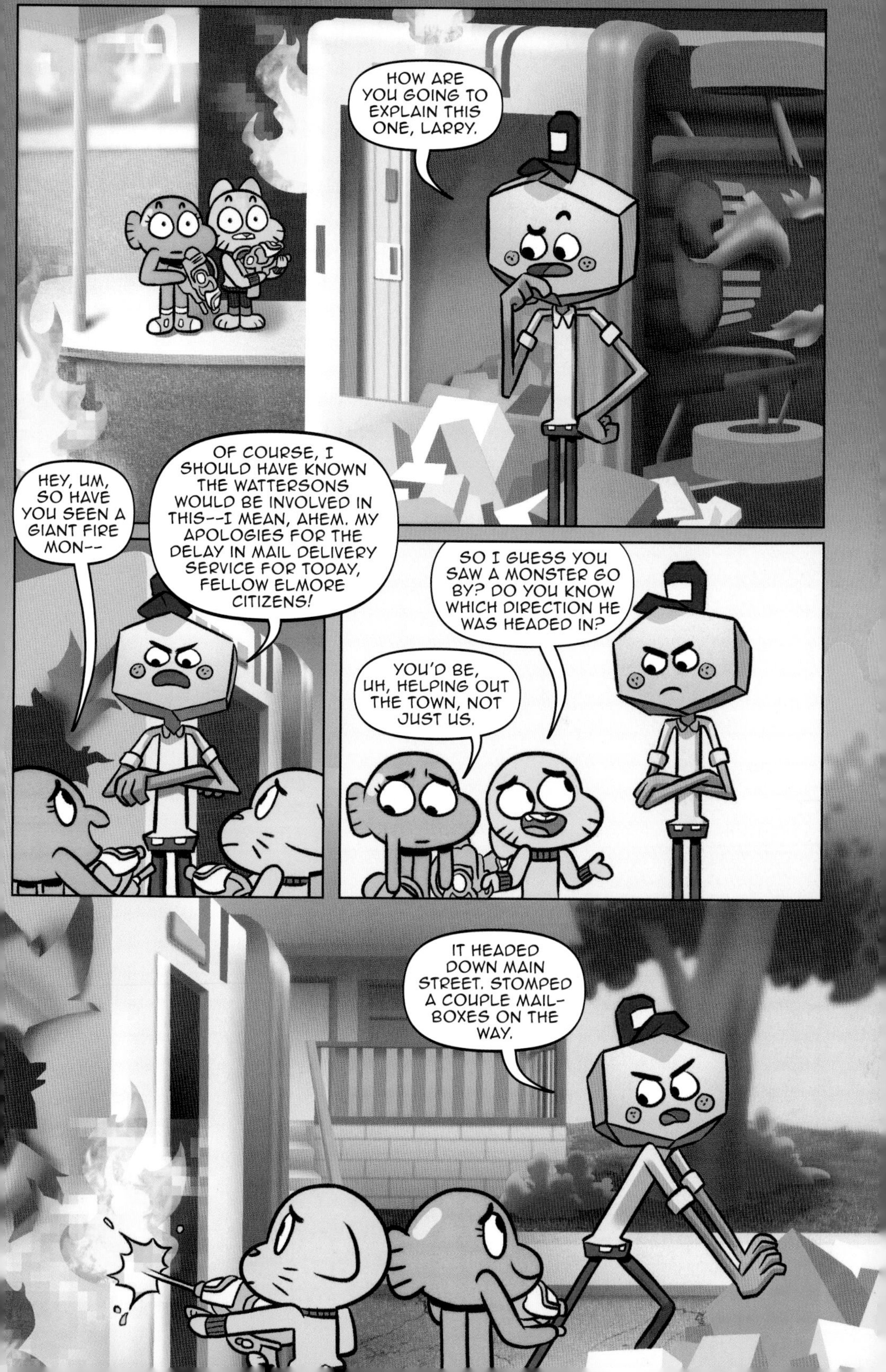
HOW ARE YOU GOING TO EXPLAIN THIS ONE, LARRY.
HEY, UM, SO HAVE YOU SEEN A GIANT FIRE MON--
OF COURSE, I SHOULD HAVE KNOWN THE WATTERSONS WOULD BE INVOLVED IN THIS--I MEAN, AHEM. MY APOLOGIES FOR THE DELAY IN MAIL DELIVERY SERVICE FOR TODAY, FELLOW ELMORE CITIZENS!
SO I GUESS YOU SAW A MONSTER GO BY? DO YOU KNOW WHICH DIRECTION HE WAS HEADED IN?
YOU'D BE, UH, HELPING OUT THE TOWN, NOT JUST US.
IT HEADED DOWN MAIN STREET. STOMPED A COUPLE MAIL-BOXES ON THE WAY.

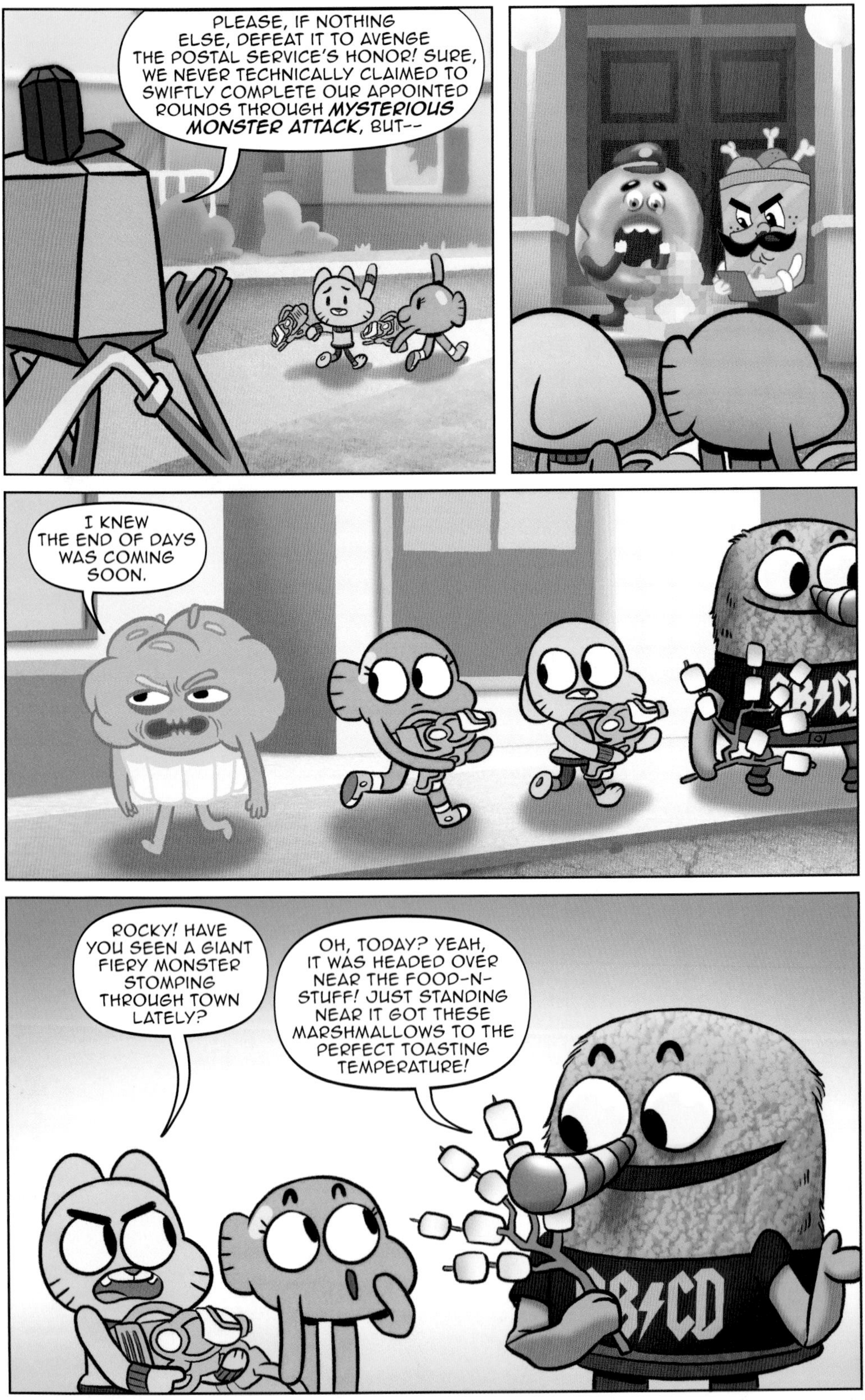
PLEASE, IF NOTHING ELSE, DEFEAT IT TO AVENGE THE POSTAL SERVICE'S HONOR! SURE, WE NEVER TECHNICALLY CLAIMED TO SWIFTLY COMPLETE OUR APPOINTED ROUNDS THROUGH *MYSTERIOUS MONSTER ATTACK*, BUT--
I KNEW THE END OF DAYS WAS COMING SOON.
ROCKY! HAVE YOU SEEN A GIANT FIERY MONSTER STOMPING THROUGH TOWN LATELY?
OH, TODAY? YEAH, IT WAS HEADED OVER NEAR THE FOOD-N-STUFF! JUST STANDING NEAR IT GOT THESE MARSHMALLOWS TO THE PERFECT TOASTING TEMPERATURE!

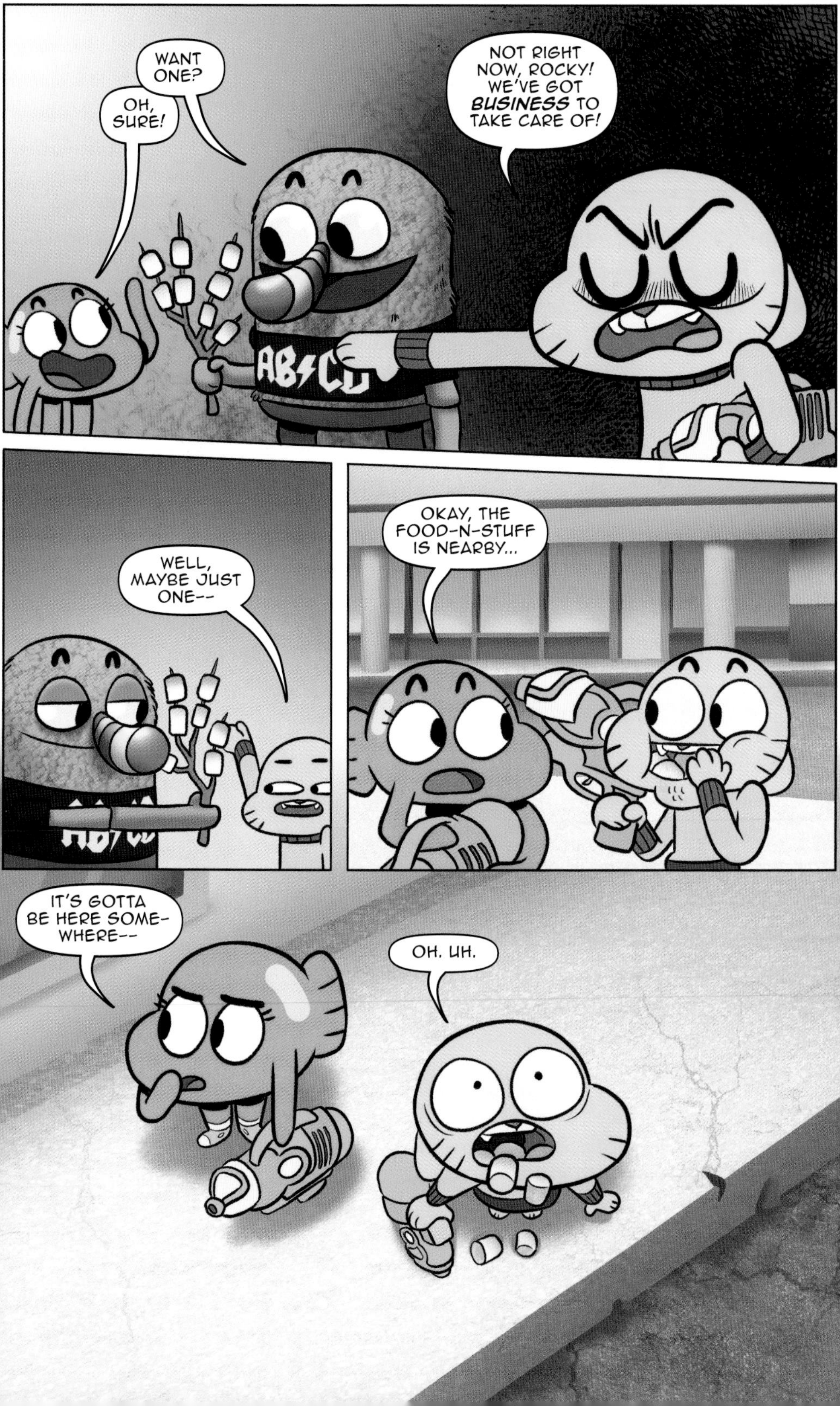
WANT ONE?
OH, SURE!
NOT RIGHT NOW, ROCKY! WE'VE GOT **BUSINESS** TO TAKE CARE OF!
AB/CD
WELL, MAYBE JUST ONE--
OKAY, THE FOOD-N-STUFF IS NEARBY...
IT'S GOTTA BE HERE SOME-WHERE--
OH. UH.

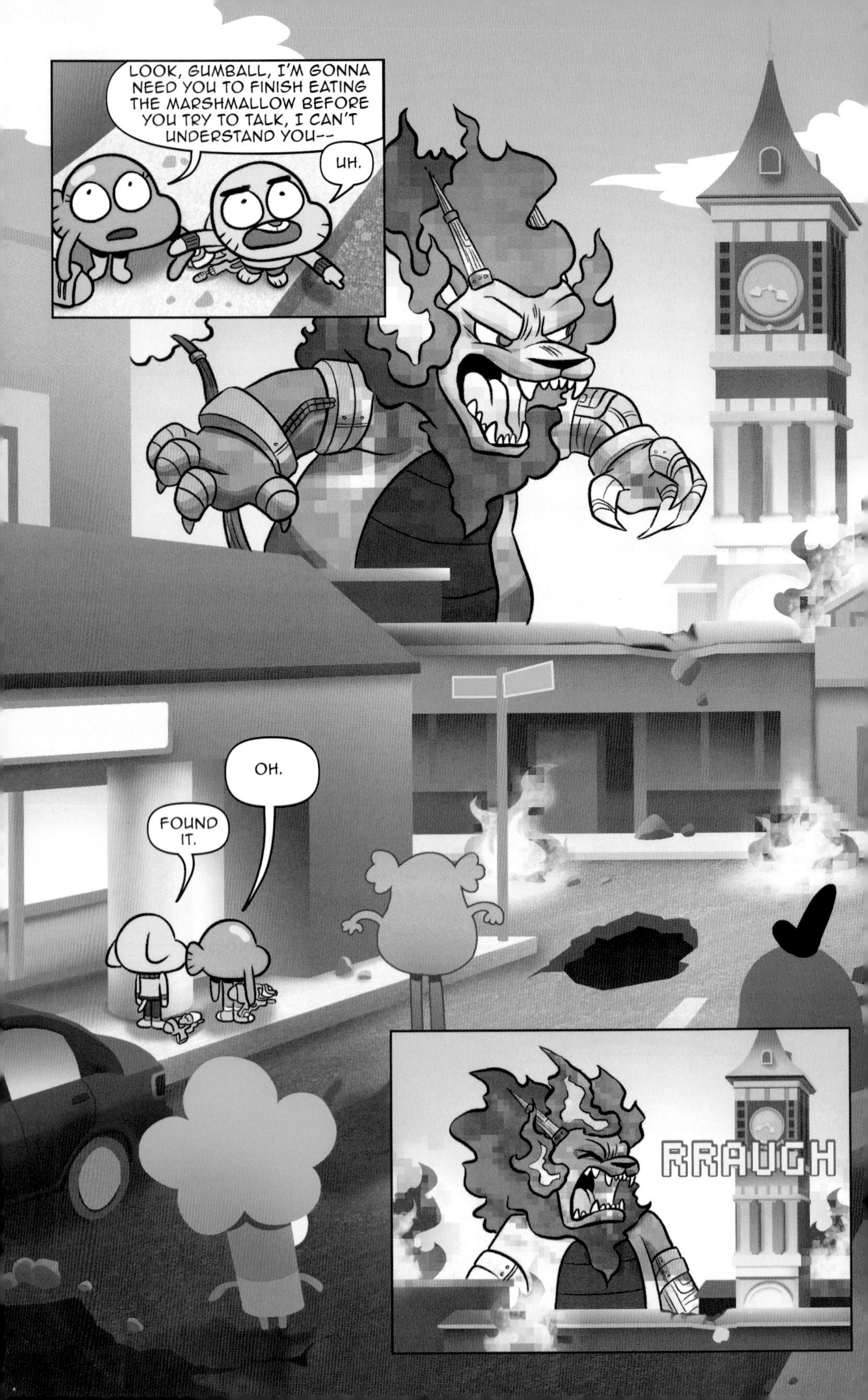
LOOK, GUMBALL, I'M GONNA NEED YOU TO FINISH EATING THE MARSHMALLOW BEFORE YOU TRY TO TALK, I CAN'T UNDERSTAND YOU--
UH.
OH.
FOUND IT.
RRAUGH

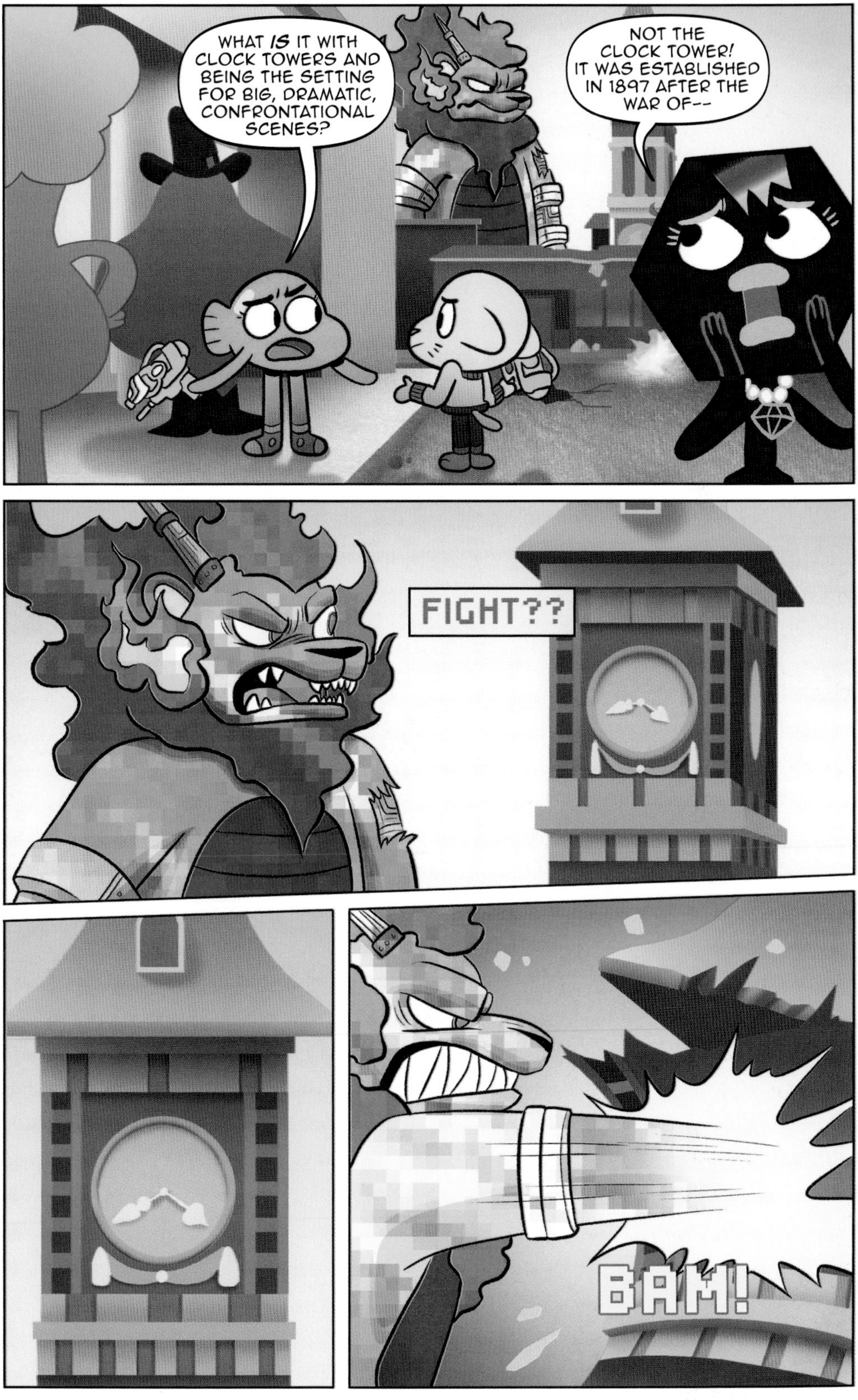
WHAT IS IT WITH CLOCK TOWERS AND BEING THE SETTING FOR BIG, DRAMATIC, CONFRONTATIONAL SCENES?
NOT THE CLOCK TOWER! IT WAS ESTABLISHED IN 1897 AFTER THE WAR OF--
FIGHT??
BAM!

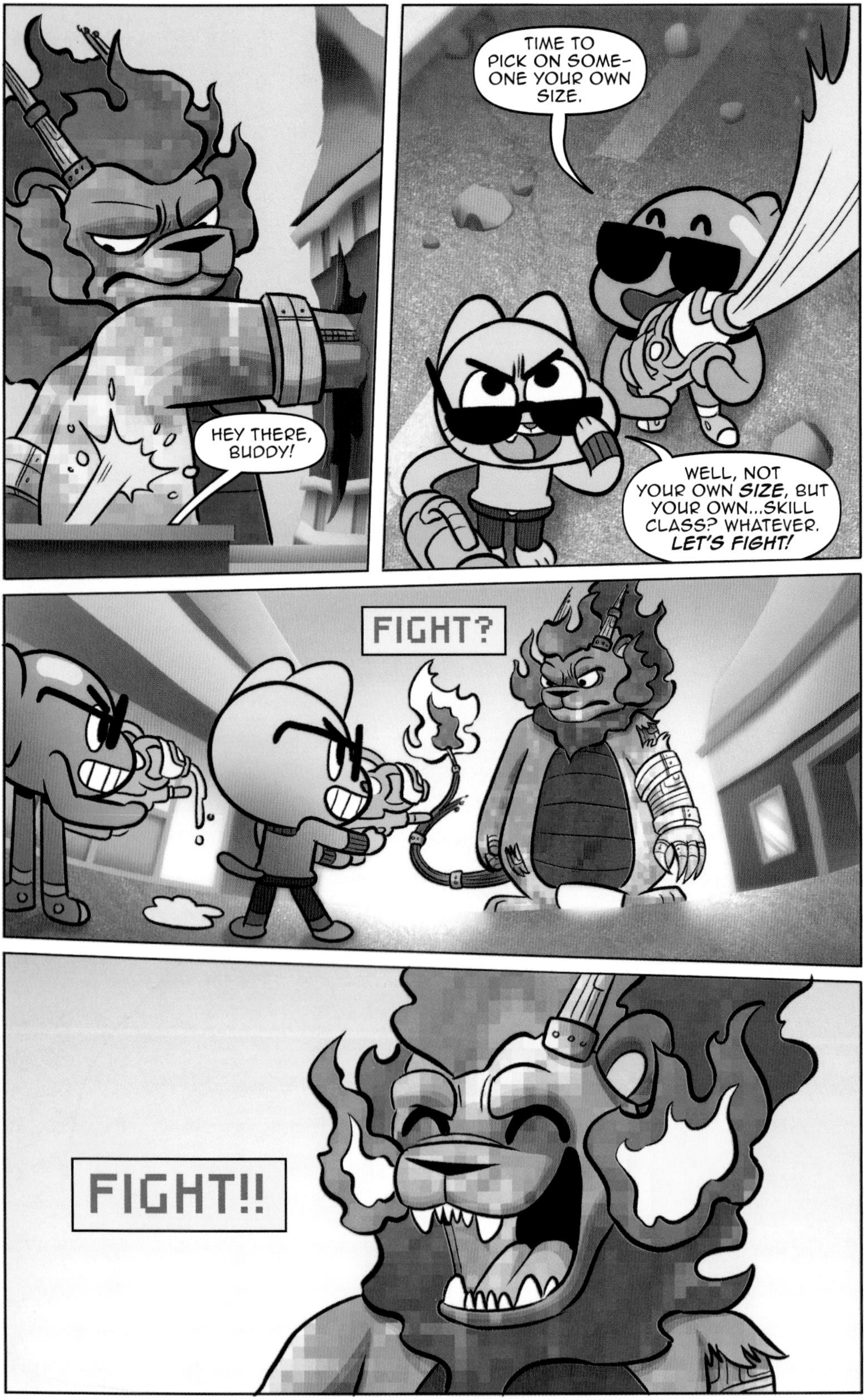
HEY THERE, BUDDY!
TIME TO PICK ON SOME-ONE YOUR OWN SIZE.
WELL, NOT YOUR OWN SIZE, BUT YOUR OWN...SKILL CLASS? WHATEVER. LET'S FIGHT!
FIGHT?
FIGHT!!

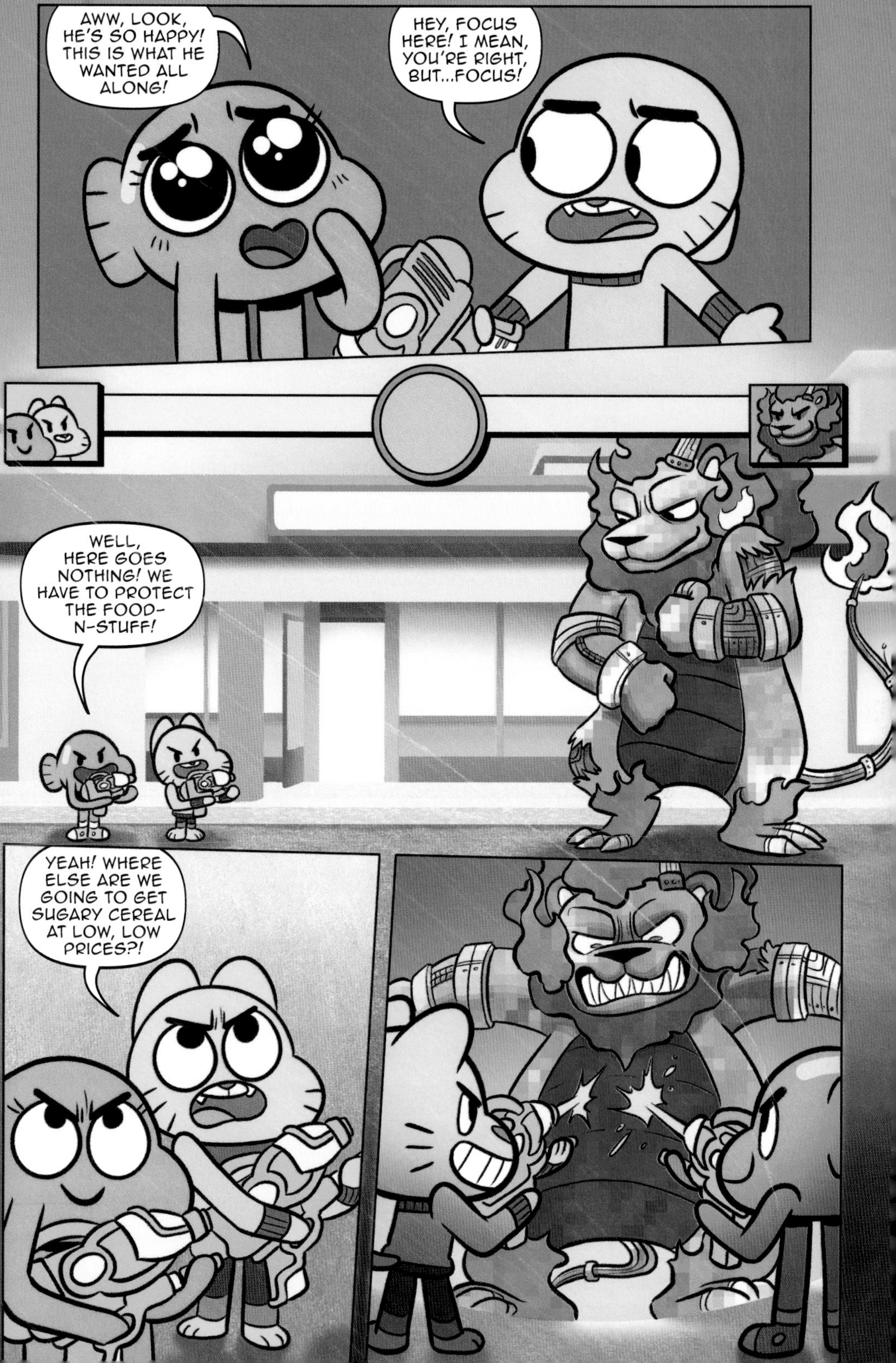
AWW, LOOK, HE'S SO HAPPY! THIS IS WHAT HE WANTED ALL ALONG!
HEY, FOCUS HERE! I MEAN, YOU'RE RIGHT, BUT...FOCUS!
WELL, HERE GOES NOTHING! WE HAVE TO PROTECT THE FOOD-N-STUFF!
YEAH! WHERE ELSE ARE WE GOING TO GET SUGARY CEREAL AT LOW, LOW PRICES?!

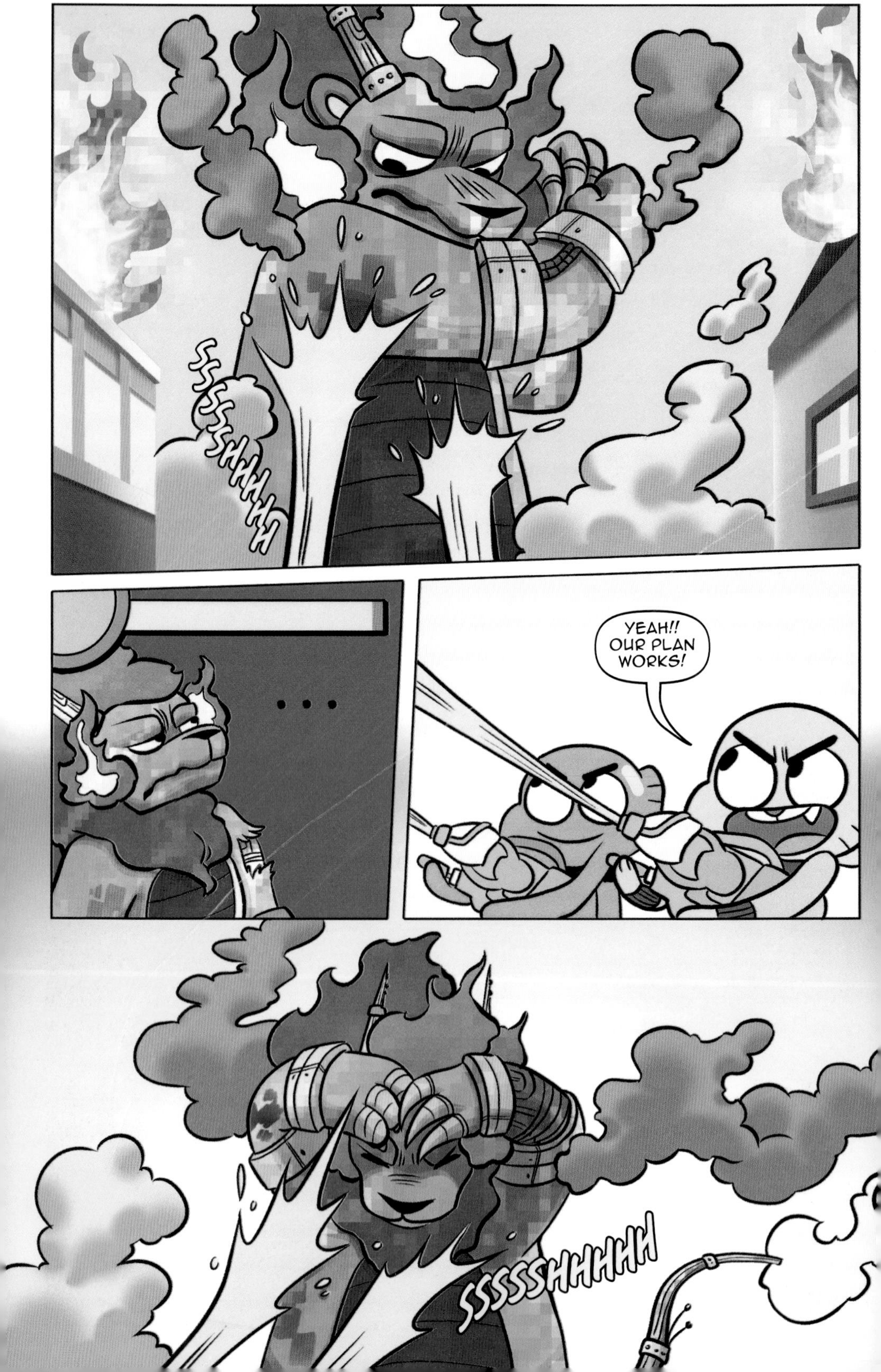
SSSSHHHHHH
...
YEAH!! OUR PLAN WORKS!
SSSSSHHHHHH

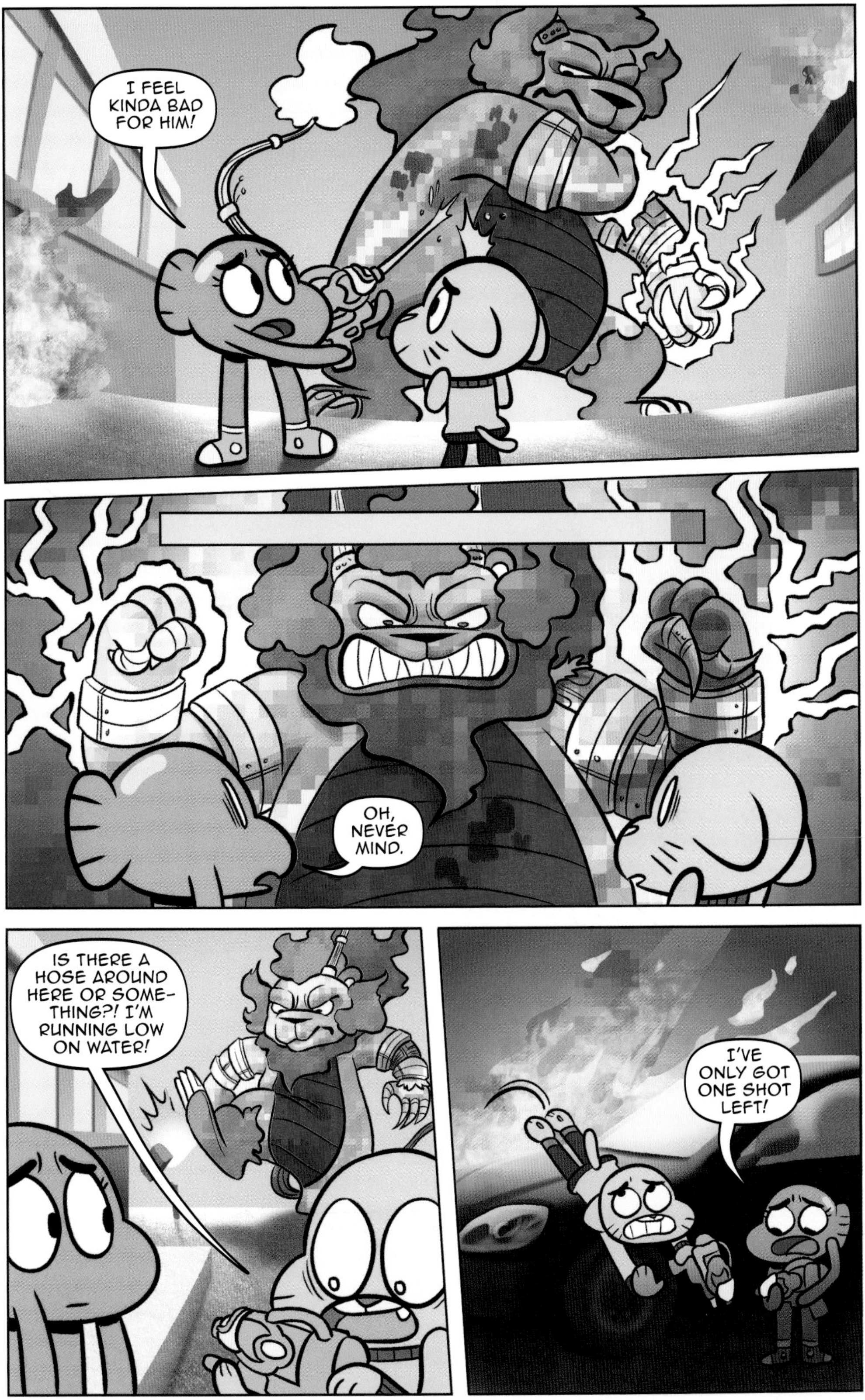
I FEEL KINDA BAD FOR HIM!
OH, NEVER MIND.
IS THERE A HOSE AROUND HERE OR SOME-THING?! I'M RUNNING LOW ON WATER!
I'VE ONLY GOT ONE SHOT LEFT!

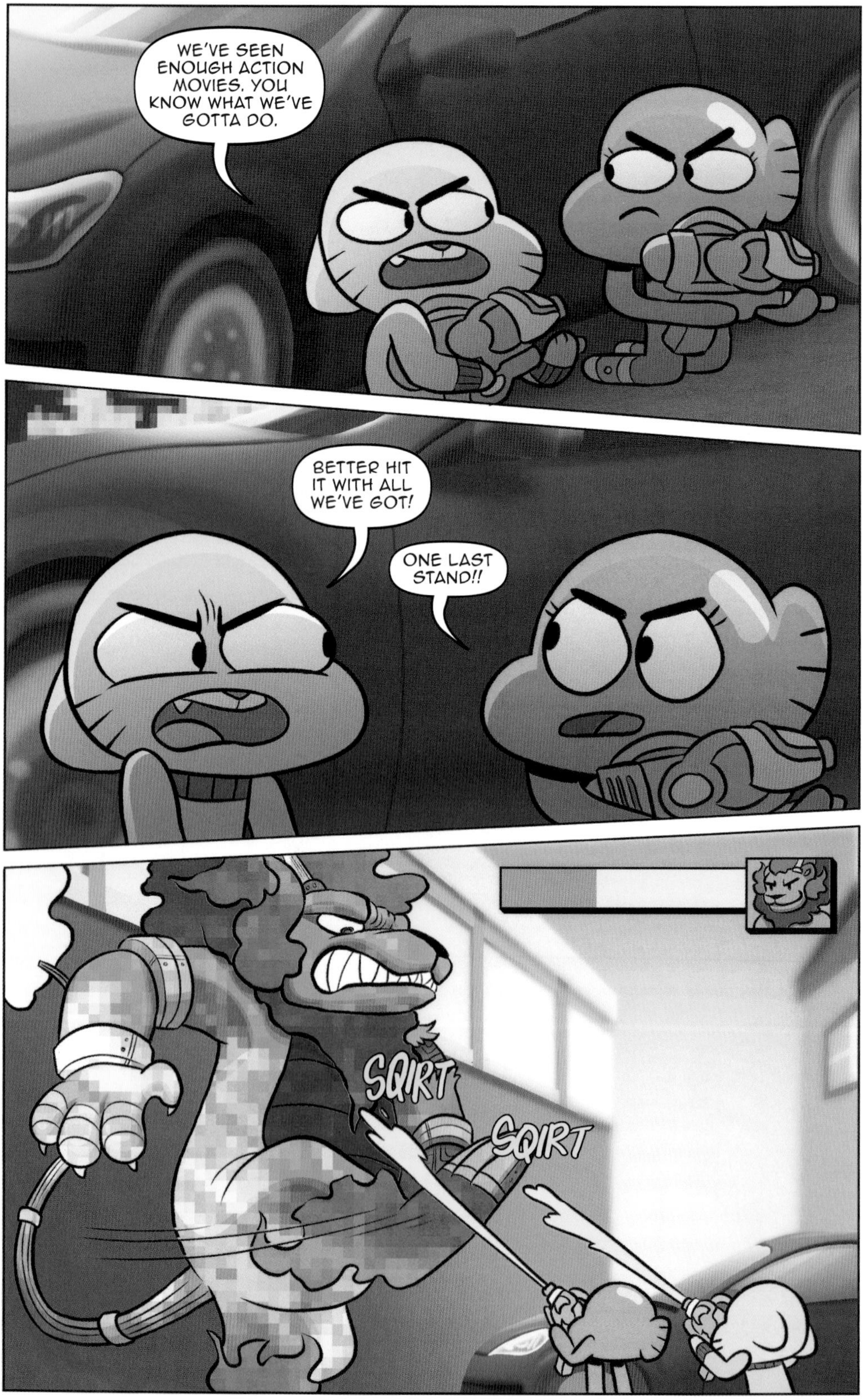
WE'VE SEEN ENOUGH ACTION MOVIES. YOU KNOW WHAT WE'VE GOTTA DO.
BETTER HIT IT WITH ALL WE'VE GOT!
ONE LAST STAND!!
SQIRT
SQIRT

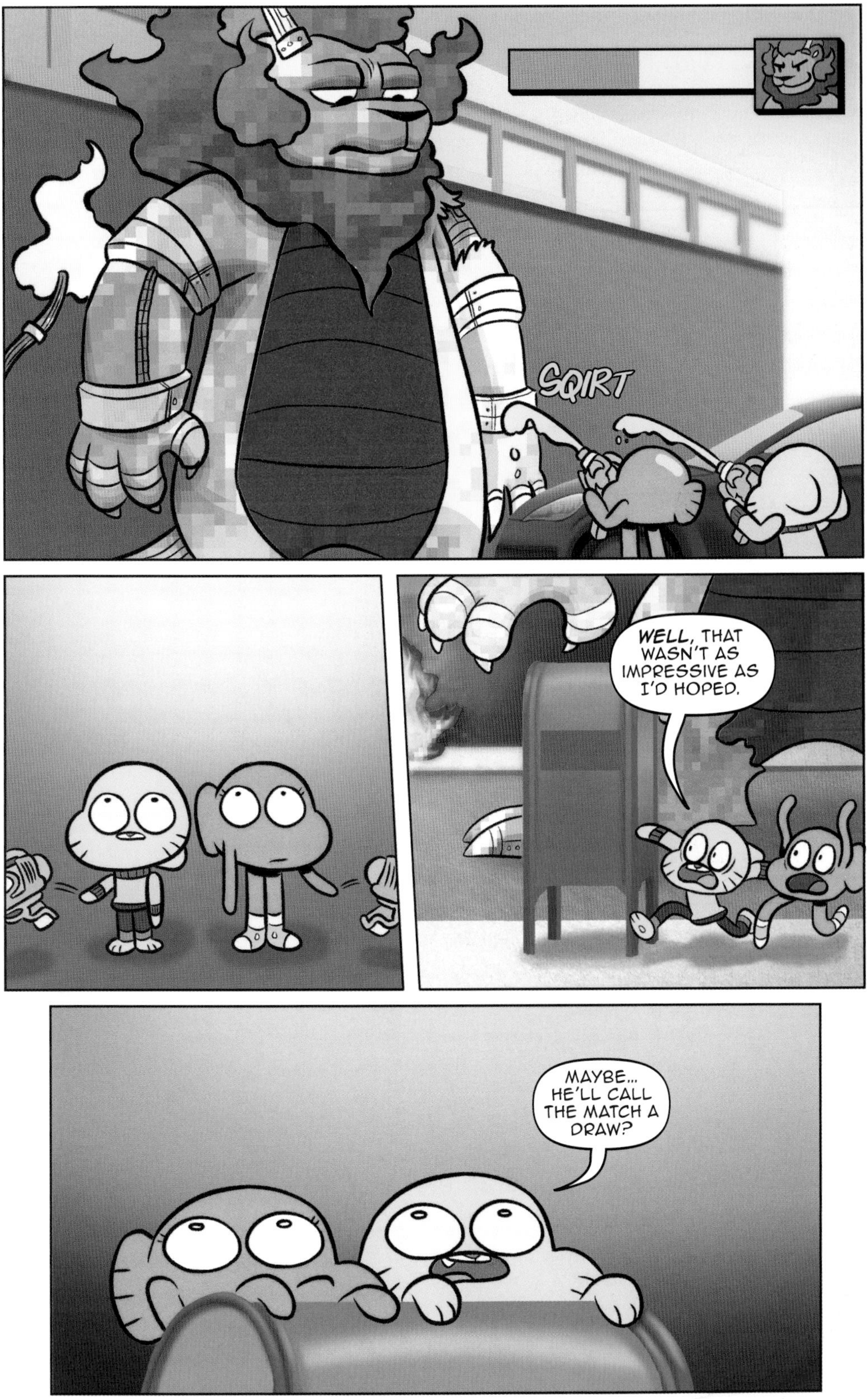
SQIRT
WELL, THAT WASN'T AS IMPRESSIVE AS I'D HOPED.
MAYBE... HE'LL CALL THE MATCH A DRAW?

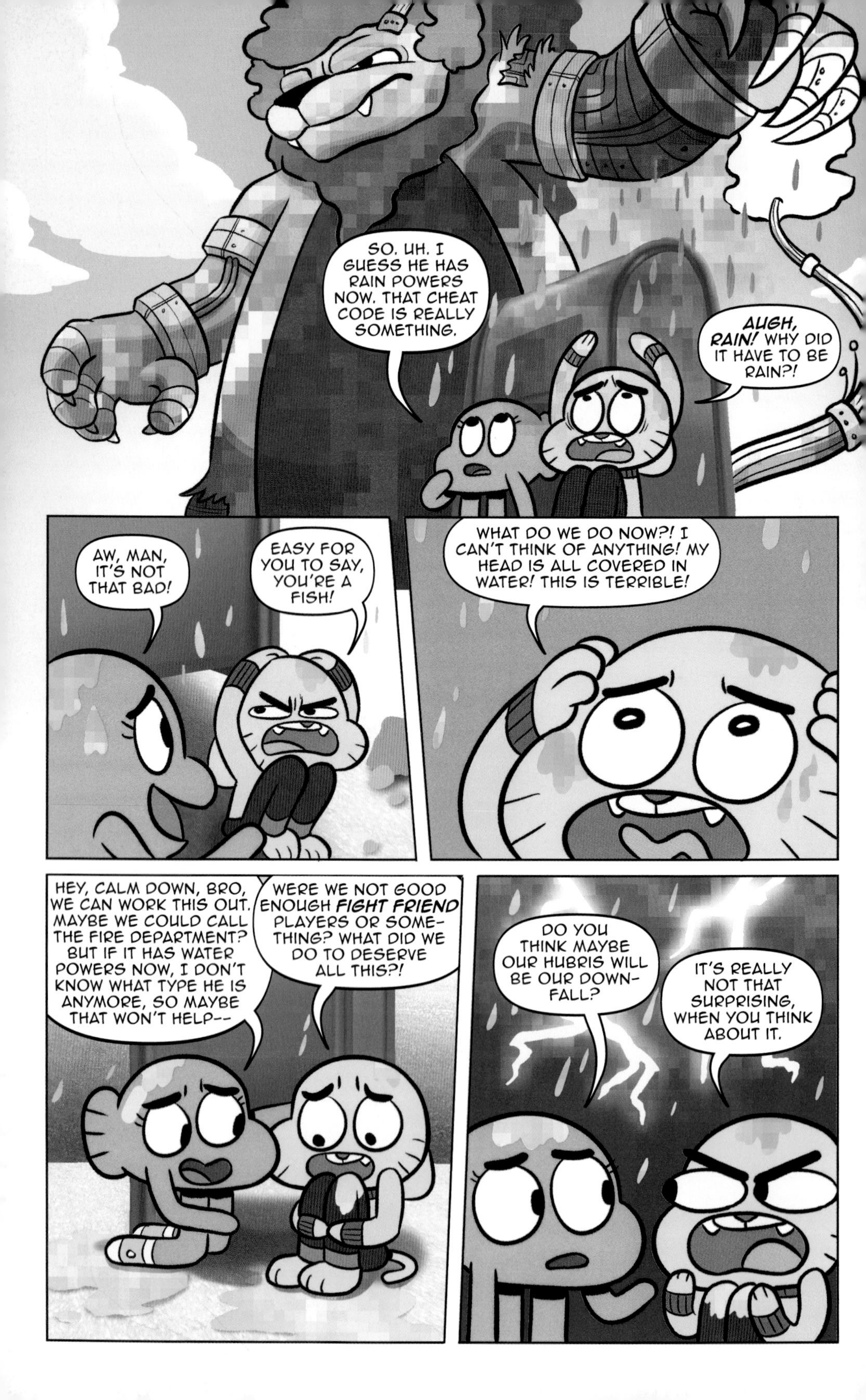
SO. UH. I GUESS HE HAS RAIN POWERS NOW. THAT CHEAT CODE IS REALLY SOMETHING.
AUGH, RAIN! WHY DID IT HAVE TO BE RAIN?!
AW, MAN, IT'S NOT THAT BAD!
EASY FOR YOU TO SAY, YOU'RE A FISH!
WHAT DO WE DO NOW?! I CAN'T THINK OF ANYTHING! MY HEAD IS ALL COVERED IN WATER! THIS IS TERRIBLE!
HEY, CALM DOWN, BRO, WE CAN WORK THIS OUT. MAYBE WE COULD CALL THE FIRE DEPARTMENT? BUT IF IT HAS WATER POWERS NOW, I DON'T KNOW WHAT TYPE HE IS ANYMORE, SO MAYBE THAT WON'T HELP--
WERE WE NOT GOOD ENOUGH FIGHT FRIEND PLAYERS OR SOME-THING? WHAT DID WE DO TO DESERVE ALL THIS?!
DO YOU THINK MAYBE OUR HUBRIS WILL BE OUR DOWN-FALL?
IT'S REALLY NOT THAT SURPRISING, WHEN YOU THINK ABOUT IT.

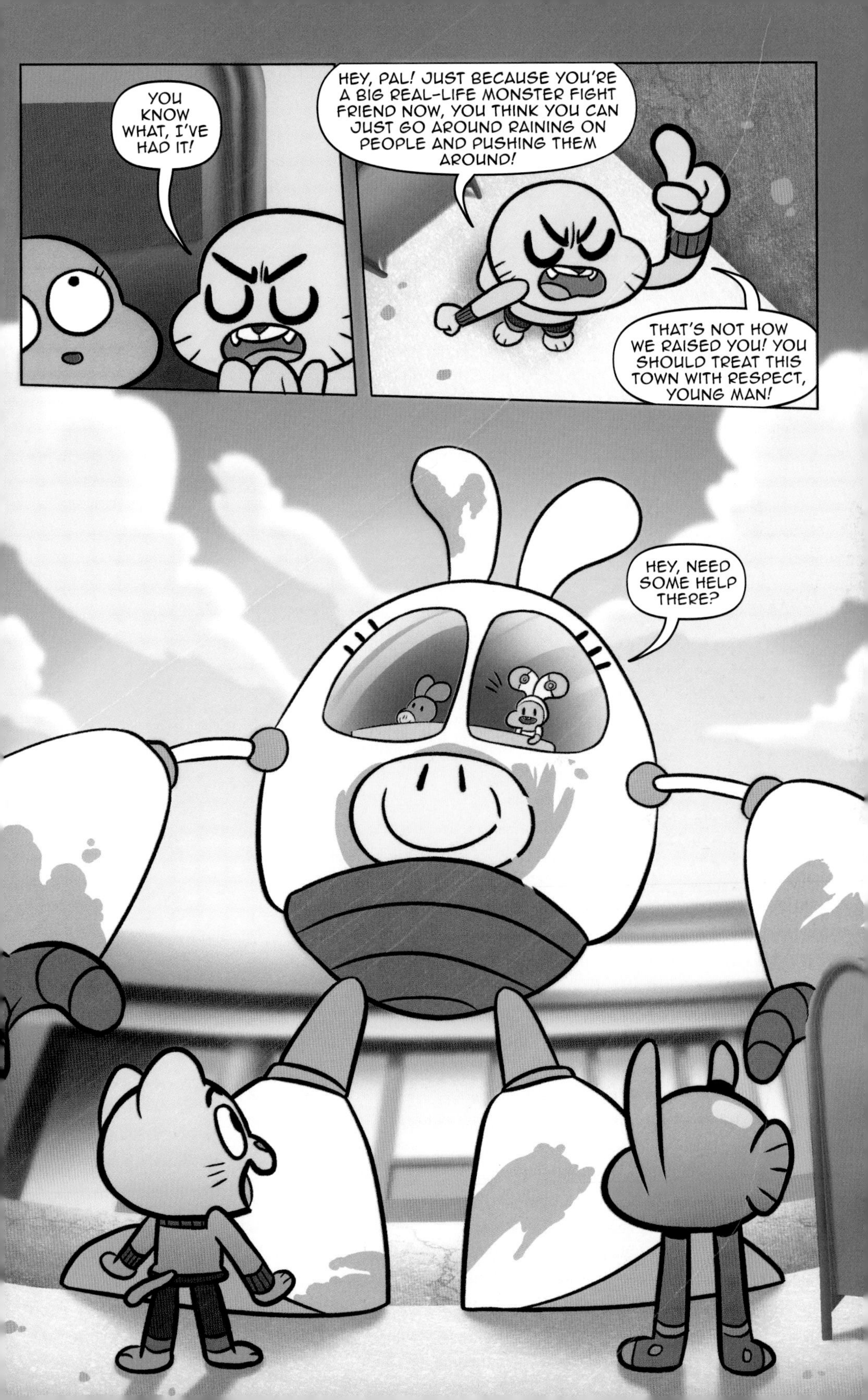
YOU KNOW WHAT, I'VE HAD IT!
HEY, PAL! JUST BECAUSE YOU'RE A BIG REAL-LIFE MONSTER FIGHT FRIEND NOW, YOU THINK YOU CAN JUST GO AROUND RAINING ON PEOPLE AND PUSHING THEM AROUND!
THAT'S NOT HOW WE RAISED YOU! YOU SHOULD TREAT THIS TOWN WITH RESPECT, YOUNG MAN!
HEY, NEED SOME HELP THERE?

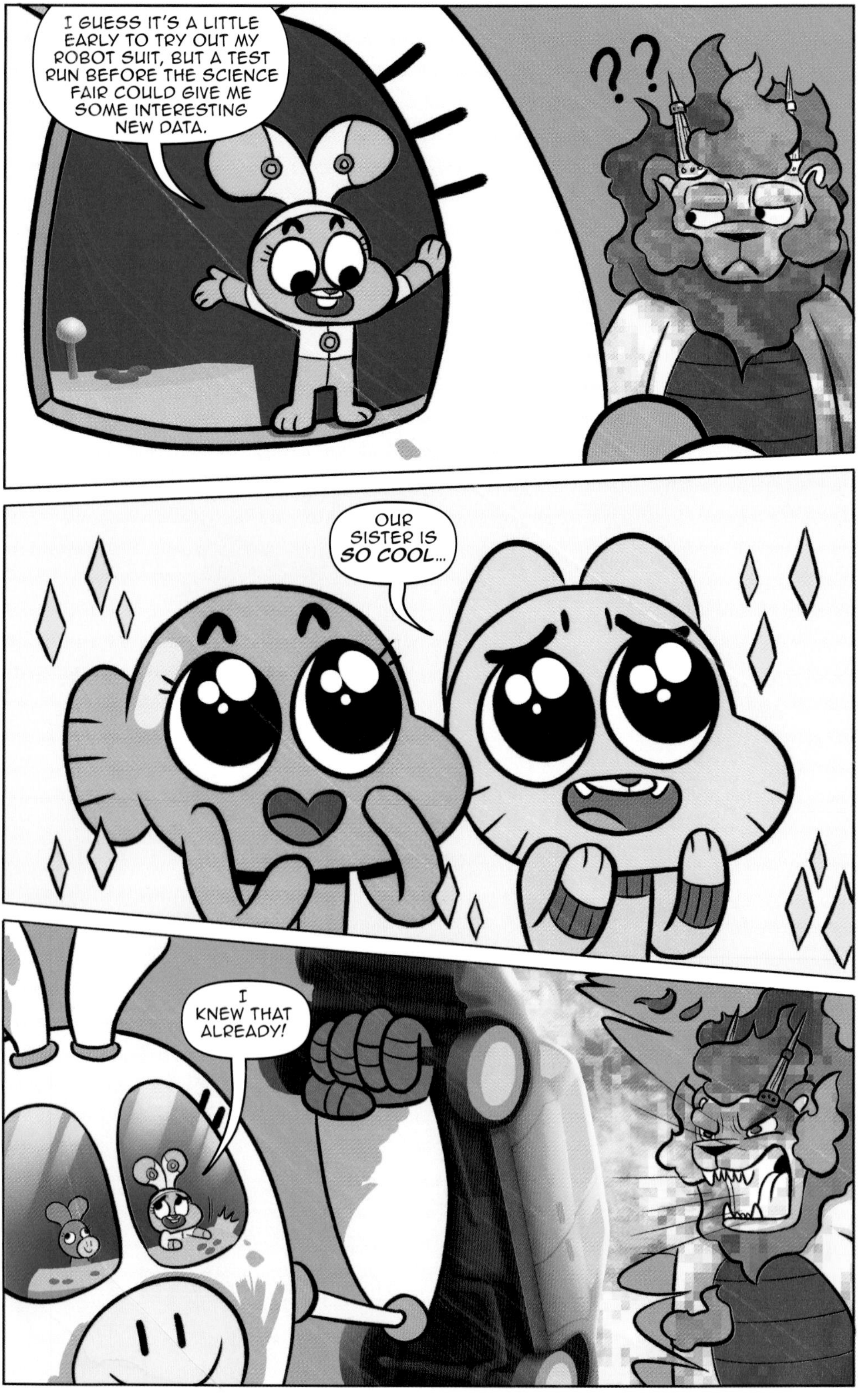
I GUESS IT'S A LITTLE EARLY TO TRY OUT MY ROBOT SUIT, BUT A TEST RUN BEFORE THE SCIENCE FAIR COULD GIVE ME SOME INTERESTING NEW DATA.
??
OUR SISTER IS *SO COOL*...
I KNEW THAT ALREADY!

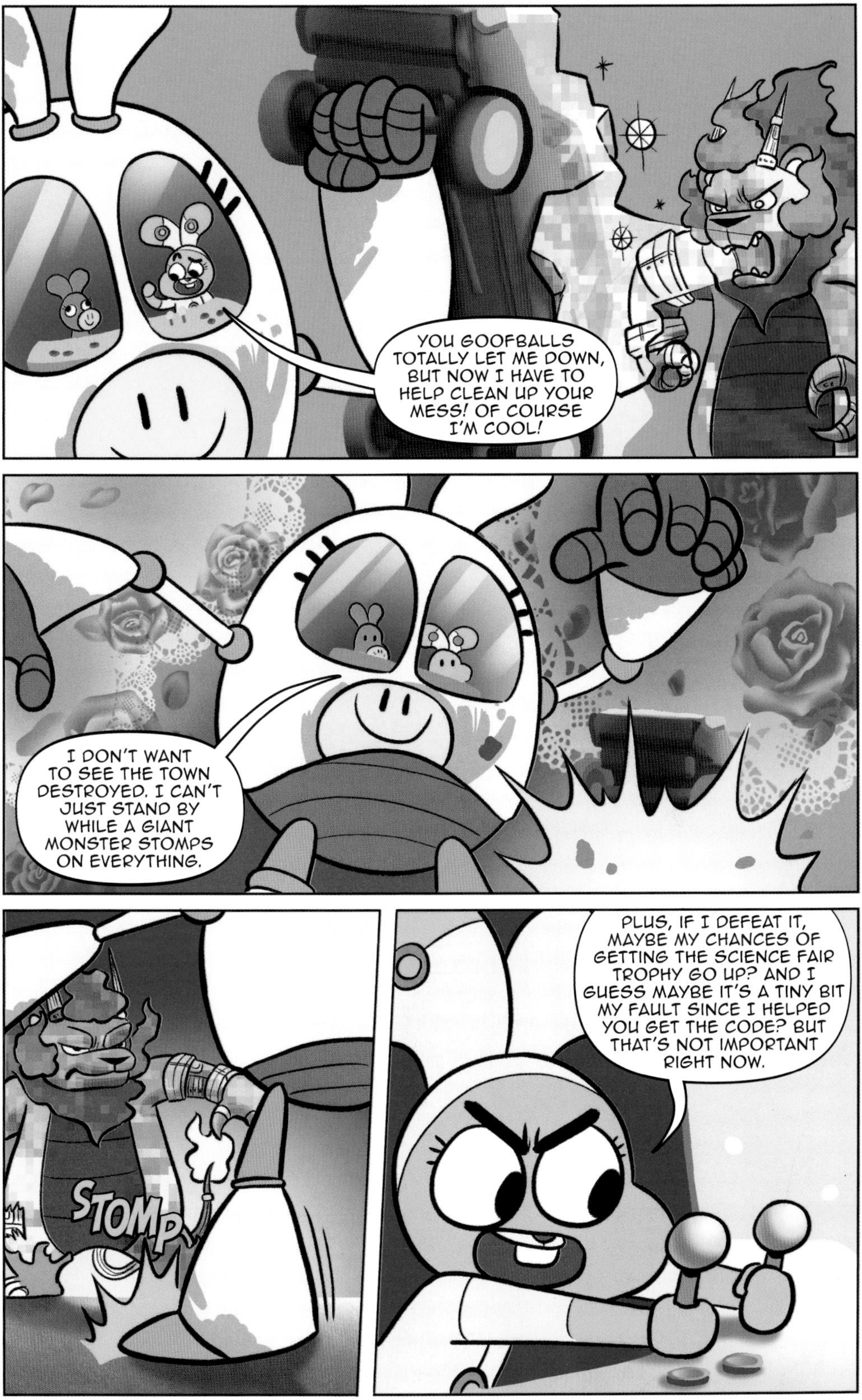
YOU GOOFBALLS TOTALLY LET ME DOWN, BUT NOW I HAVE TO HELP CLEAN UP YOUR MESS! OF COURSE I'M COOL!
I DON'T WANT TO SEE THE TOWN DESTROYED. I CAN'T JUST STAND BY WHILE A GIANT MONSTER STOMPS ON EVERYTHING.
STOMP
PLUS, IF I DEFEAT IT, MAYBE MY CHANCES OF GETTING THE SCIENCE FAIR TROPHY GO UP? AND I GUESS MAYBE IT'S A TINY BIT MY FAULT SINCE I HELPED YOU GET THE CODE? BUT THAT'S NOT IMPORTANT RIGHT NOW.

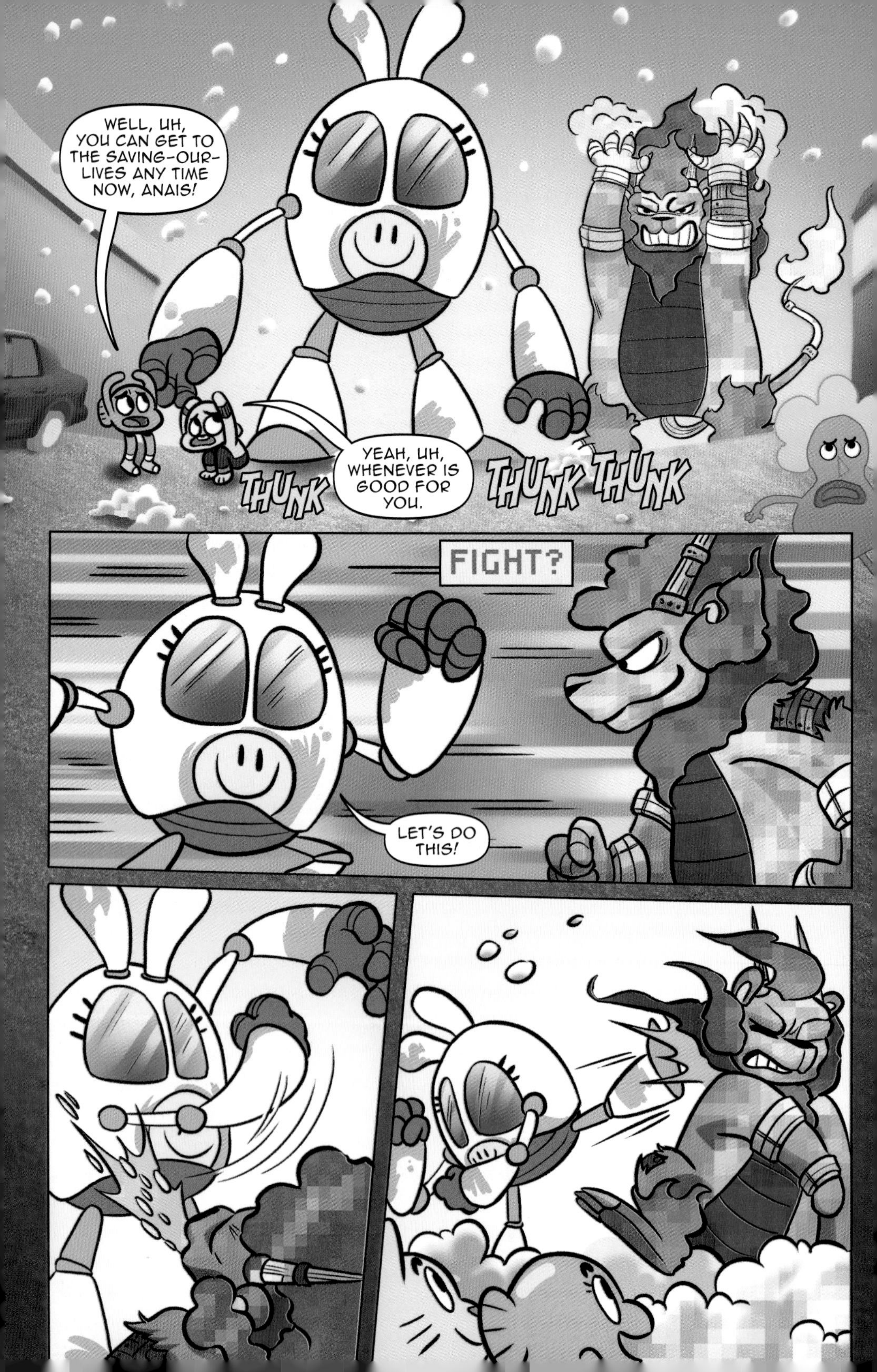
WELL, UH, YOU CAN GET TO THE SAVING-OUR-LIVES ANY TIME NOW, ANAIS!
THUNK
YEAH, UH, WHENEVER IS GOOD FOR YOU.
THUNK THUNK
FIGHT?
LET'S DO THIS!

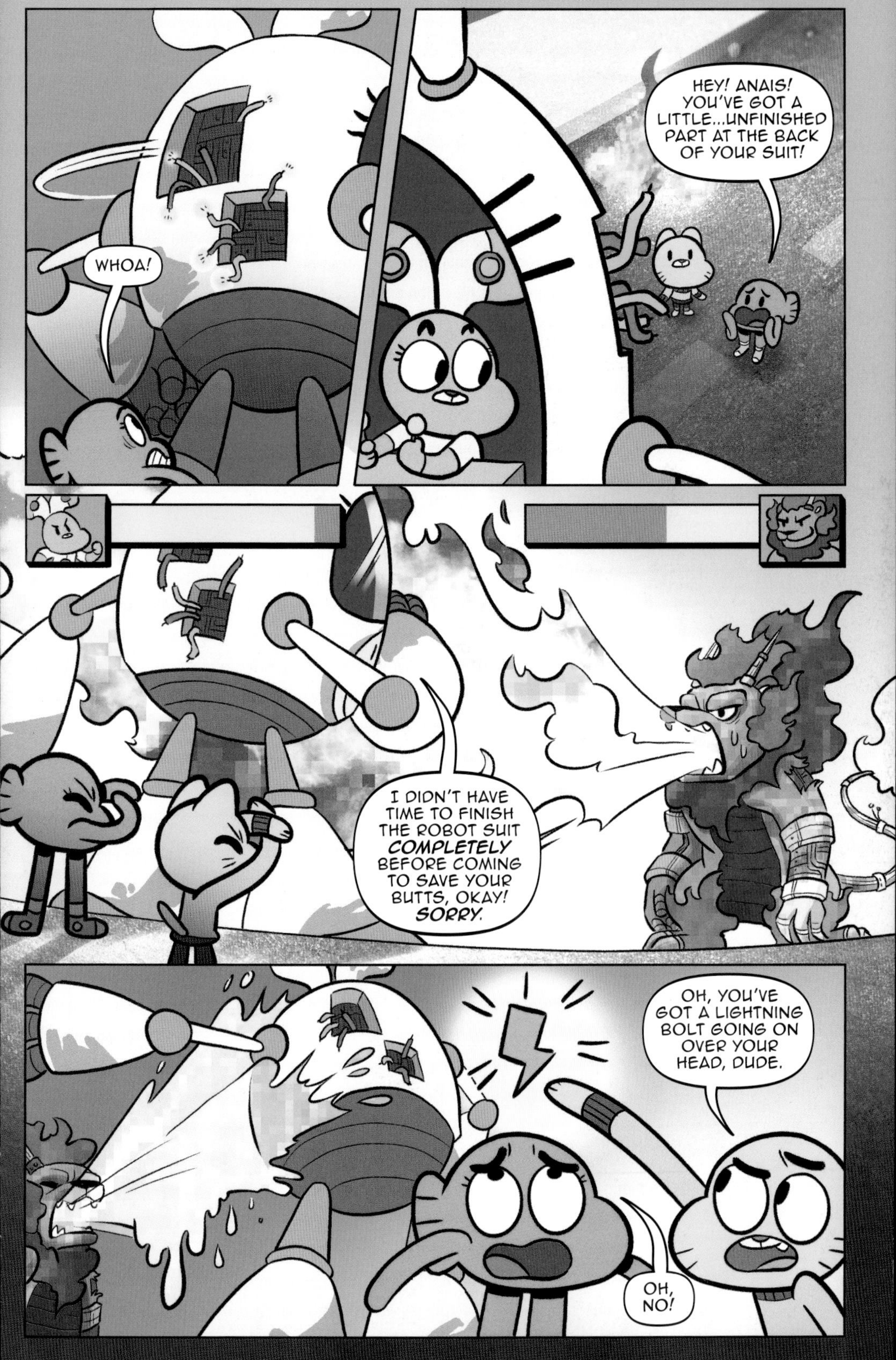
WHOA!
HEY! ANAIS! YOU'VE GOT A LITTLE...UNFINISHED PART AT THE BACK OF YOUR SUIT!
I DIDN'T HAVE TIME TO FINISH THE ROBOT SUIT ***COMPLETELY*** BEFORE COMING TO SAVE YOUR BUTTS, OKAY! ***SORRY.***
OH, YOU'VE GOT A LIGHTNING BOLT GOING ON OVER YOUR HEAD, DUDE.
OH, NO!

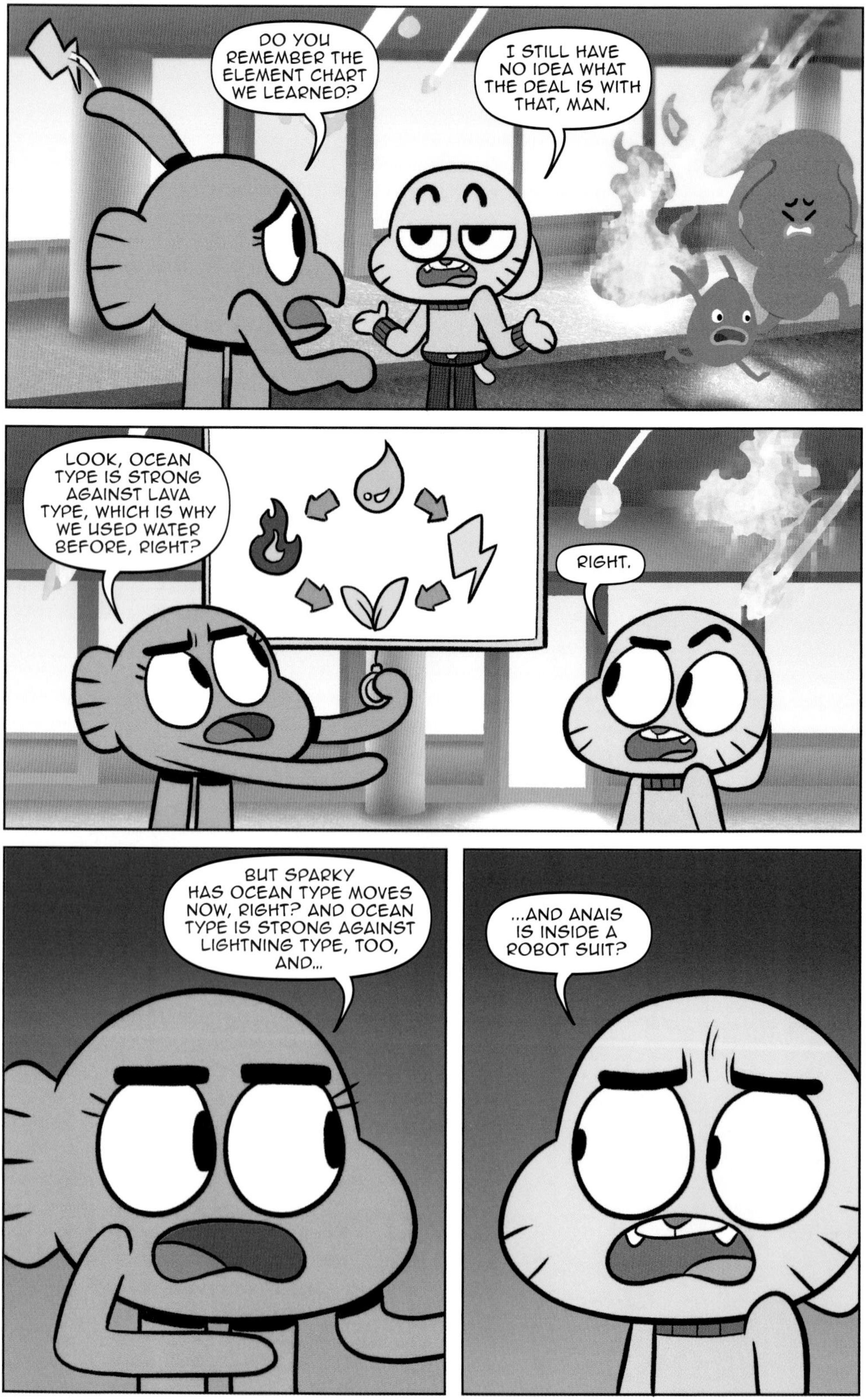
DO YOU REMEMBER THE ELEMENT CHART WE LEARNED?
I STILL HAVE NO IDEA WHAT THE DEAL IS WITH THAT, MAN.
LOOK, OCEAN TYPE IS STRONG AGAINST LAVA TYPE, WHICH IS WHY WE USED WATER BEFORE, RIGHT?
RIGHT.
BUT SPARKY HAS OCEAN TYPE MOVES NOW, RIGHT? AND OCEAN TYPE IS STRONG AGAINST LIGHTNING TYPE, TOO, AND...
...AND ANAIS IS INSIDE A ROBOT SUIT?

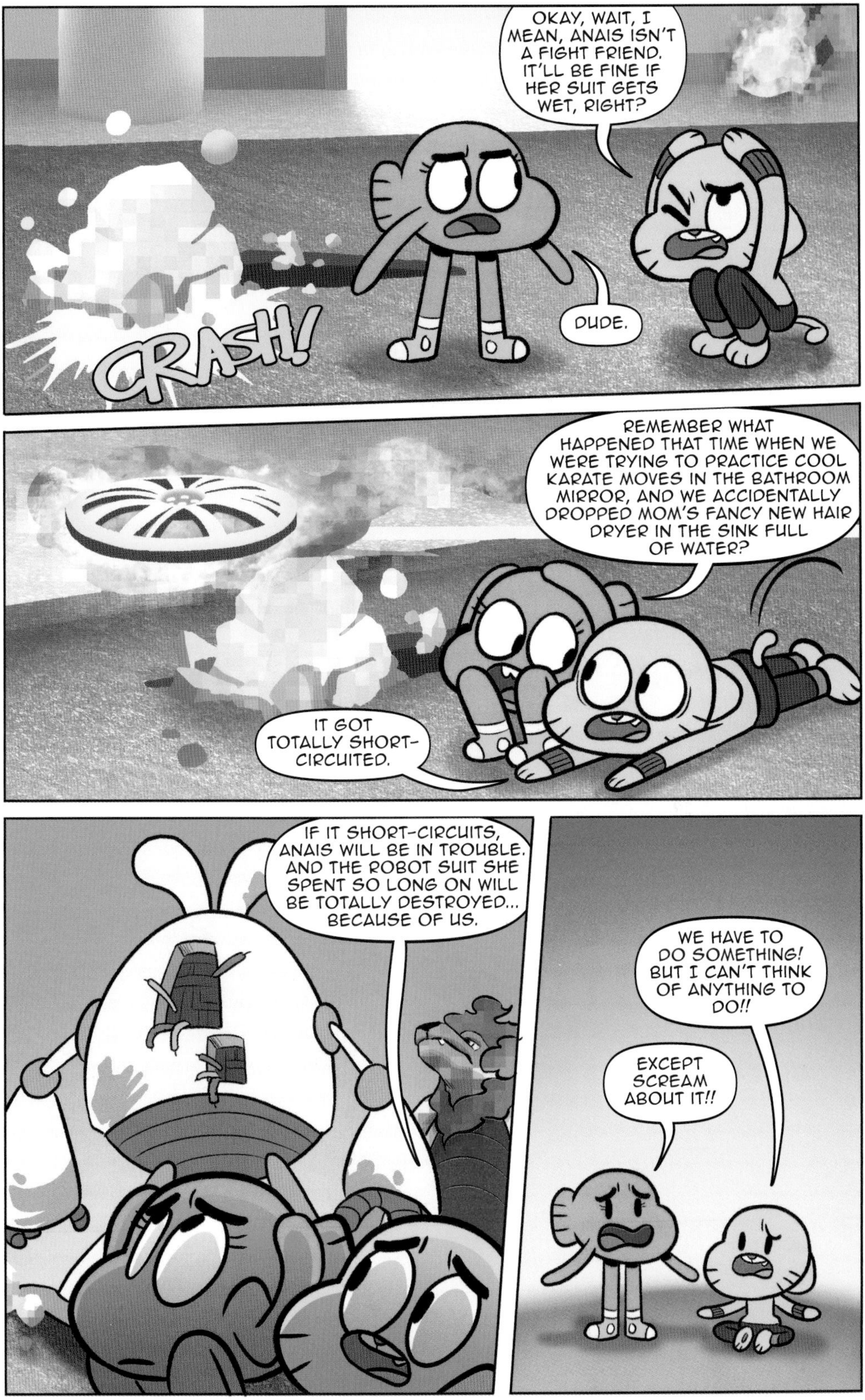
OKAY, WAIT, I MEAN, ANAIS ISN'T A FIGHT FRIEND. IT'LL BE FINE IF HER SUIT GETS WET, RIGHT?
CRASH!
DUDE.
REMEMBER WHAT HAPPENED THAT TIME WHEN WE WERE TRYING TO PRACTICE COOL KARATE MOVES IN THE BATHROOM MIRROR, AND WE ACCIDENTALLY DROPPED MOM'S FANCY NEW HAIR DRYER IN THE SINK FULL OF WATER?
IT GOT TOTALLY SHORT-CIRCUITED.
IF IT SHORT-CIRCUITS, ANAIS WILL BE IN TROUBLE. AND THE ROBOT SUIT SHE SPENT SO LONG ON WILL BE TOTALLY DESTROYED... BECAUSE OF US.
WE HAVE TO DO SOMETHING! BUT I CAN'T THINK OF ANYTHING TO DO!!
EXCEPT SCREAM ABOUT IT!!

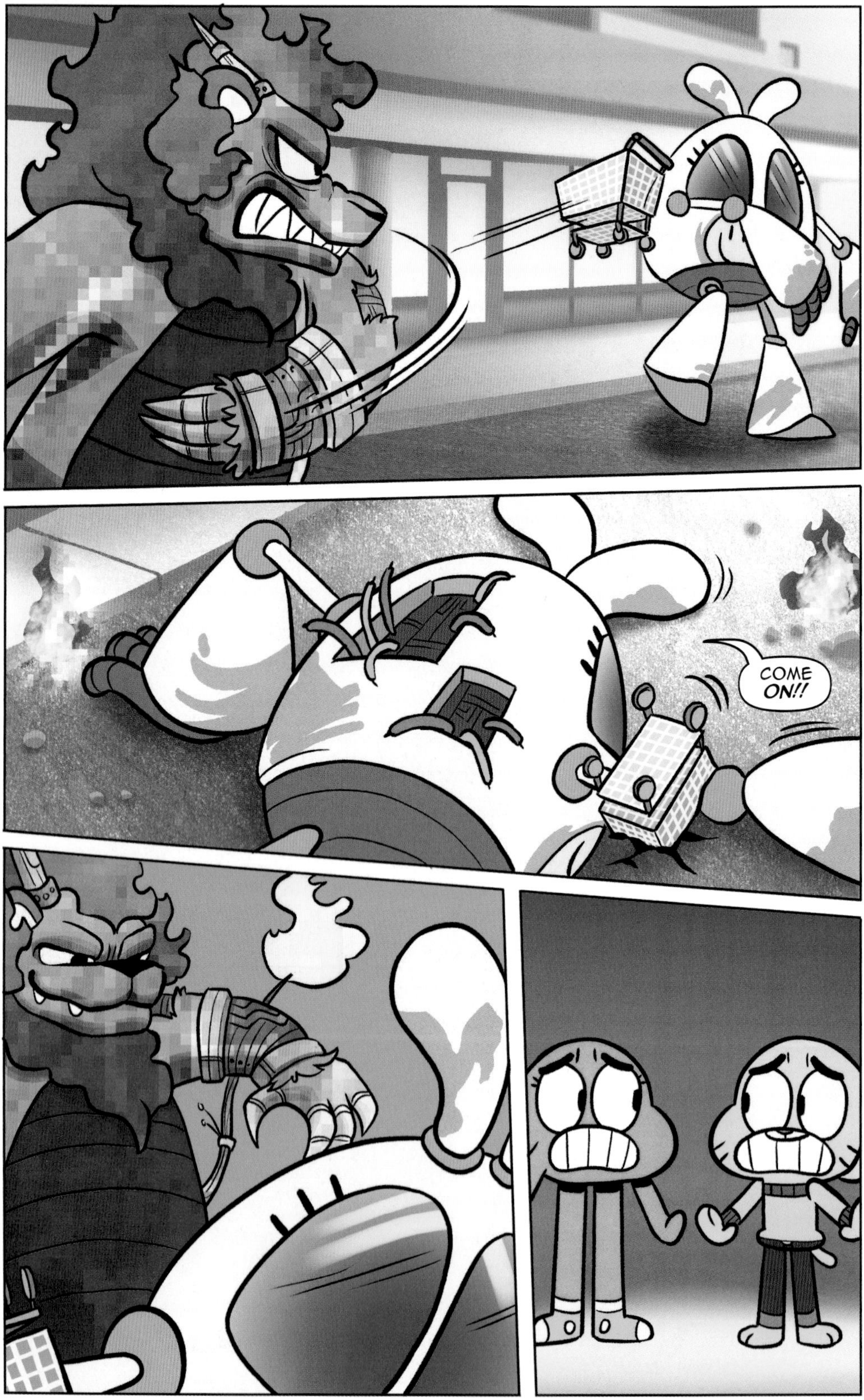
COME ON!!

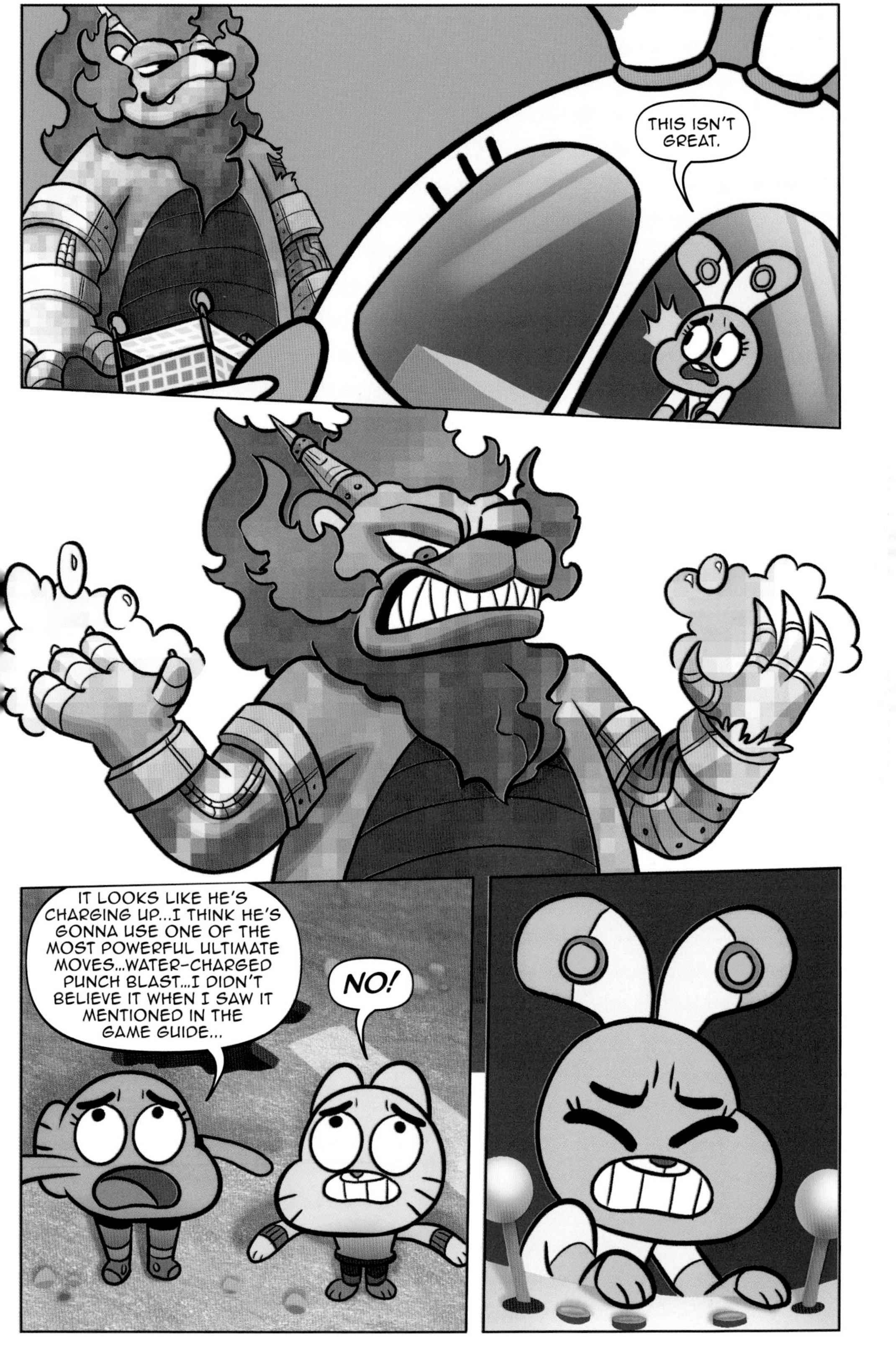
THIS ISN'T GREAT.
IT LOOKS LIKE HE'S CHARGING UP...I THINK HE'S GONNA USE ONE OF THE MOST POWERFUL ULTIMATE MOVES...WATER-CHARGED PUNCH BLAST...I DIDN'T BELIEVE IT WHEN I SAW IT MENTIONED IN THE GAME GUIDE...
NO!

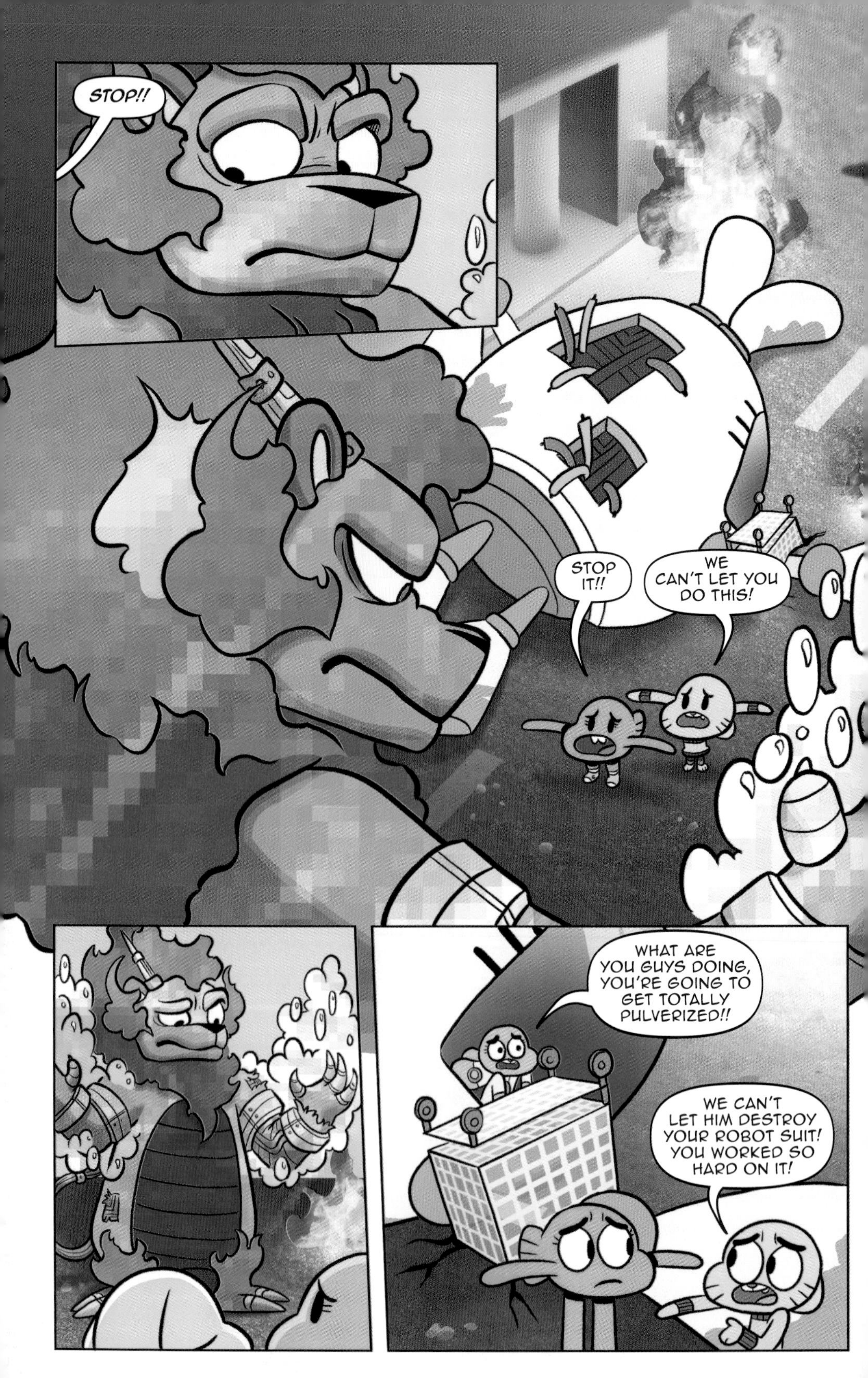
STOP!!
STOP IT!!
WE CAN'T LET YOU DO THIS!
WHAT ARE YOU GUYS DOING, YOU'RE GOING TO GET TOTALLY PULVERIZED!!
WE CAN'T LET HIM DESTROY YOUR ROBOT SUIT! YOU WORKED SO HARD ON IT!

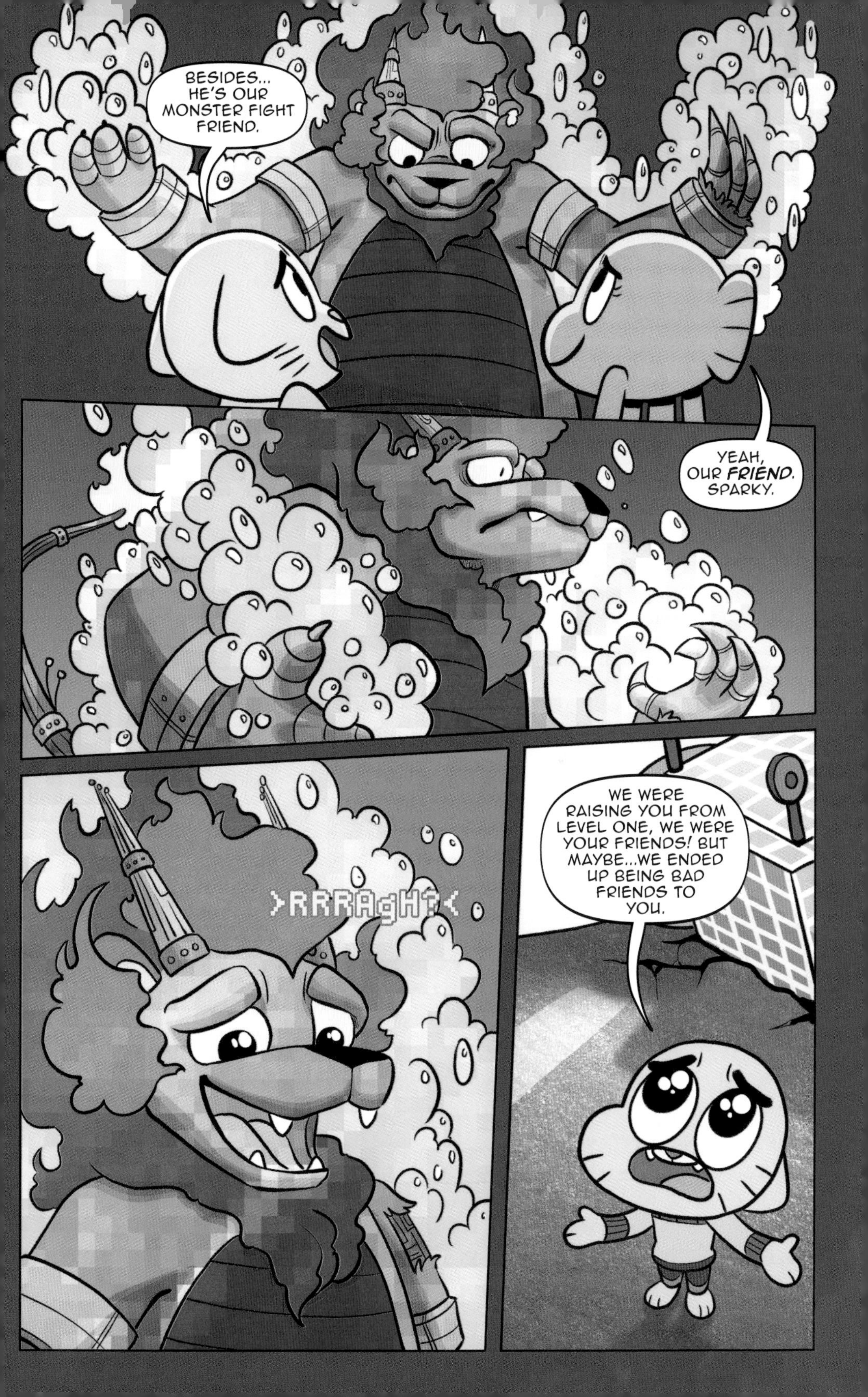
BESIDES... HE'S OUR MONSTER FIGHT FRIEND.
YEAH, OUR FRIEND. SPARKY.
>RRRAgH?<
WE WERE RAISING YOU FROM LEVEL ONE, WE WERE YOUR FRIENDS! BUT MAYBE...WE ENDED UP BEING BAD FRIENDS TO YOU.

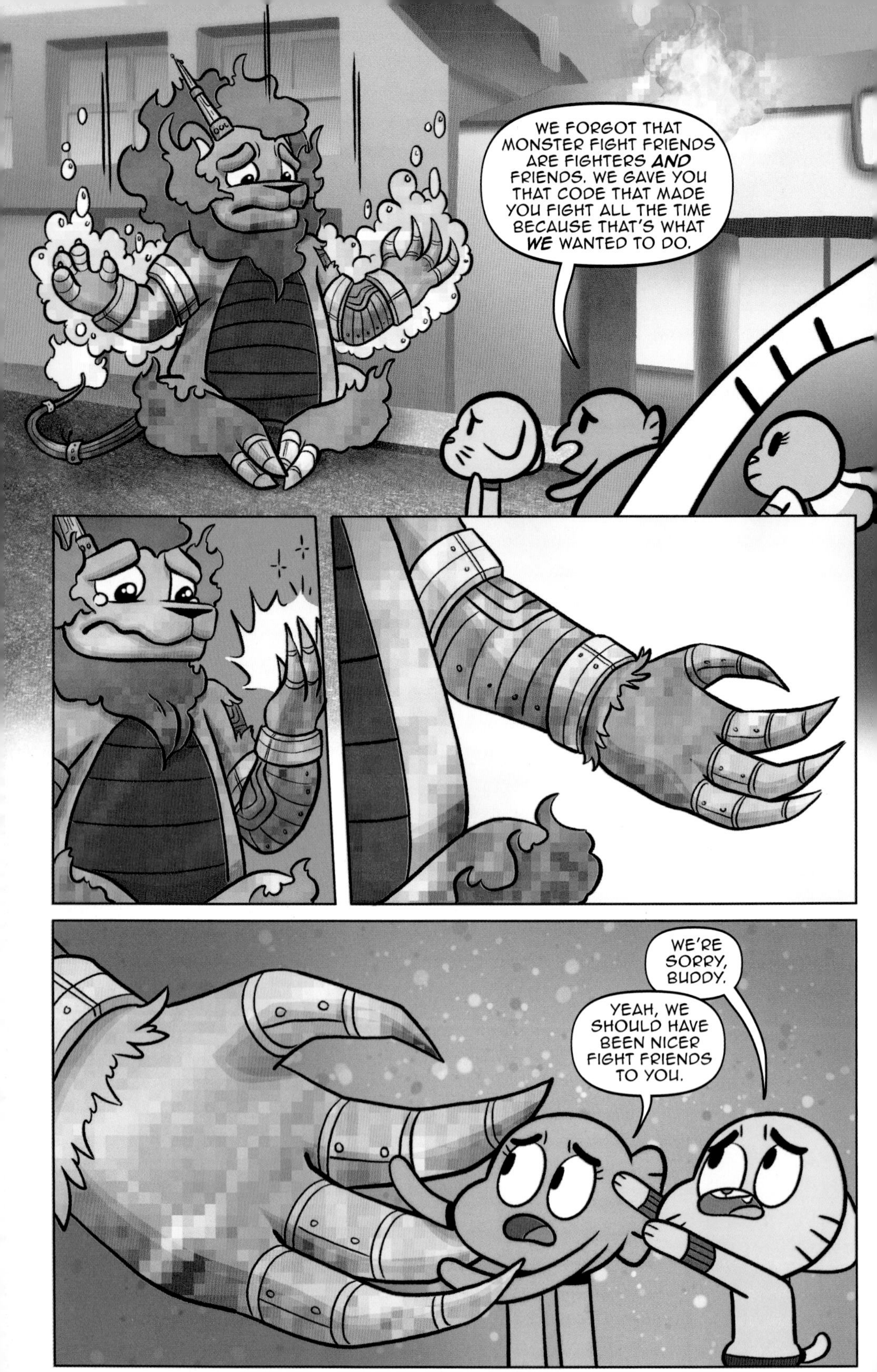
WE FORGOT THAT MONSTER FIGHT FRIENDS ARE FIGHTERS AND FRIENDS. WE GAVE YOU THAT CODE THAT MADE YOU FIGHT ALL THE TIME BECAUSE THAT'S WHAT WE WANTED TO DO.
WE'RE SORRY, BUDDY.
YEAH, WE SHOULD HAVE BEEN NICER FIGHT FRIENDS TO YOU.

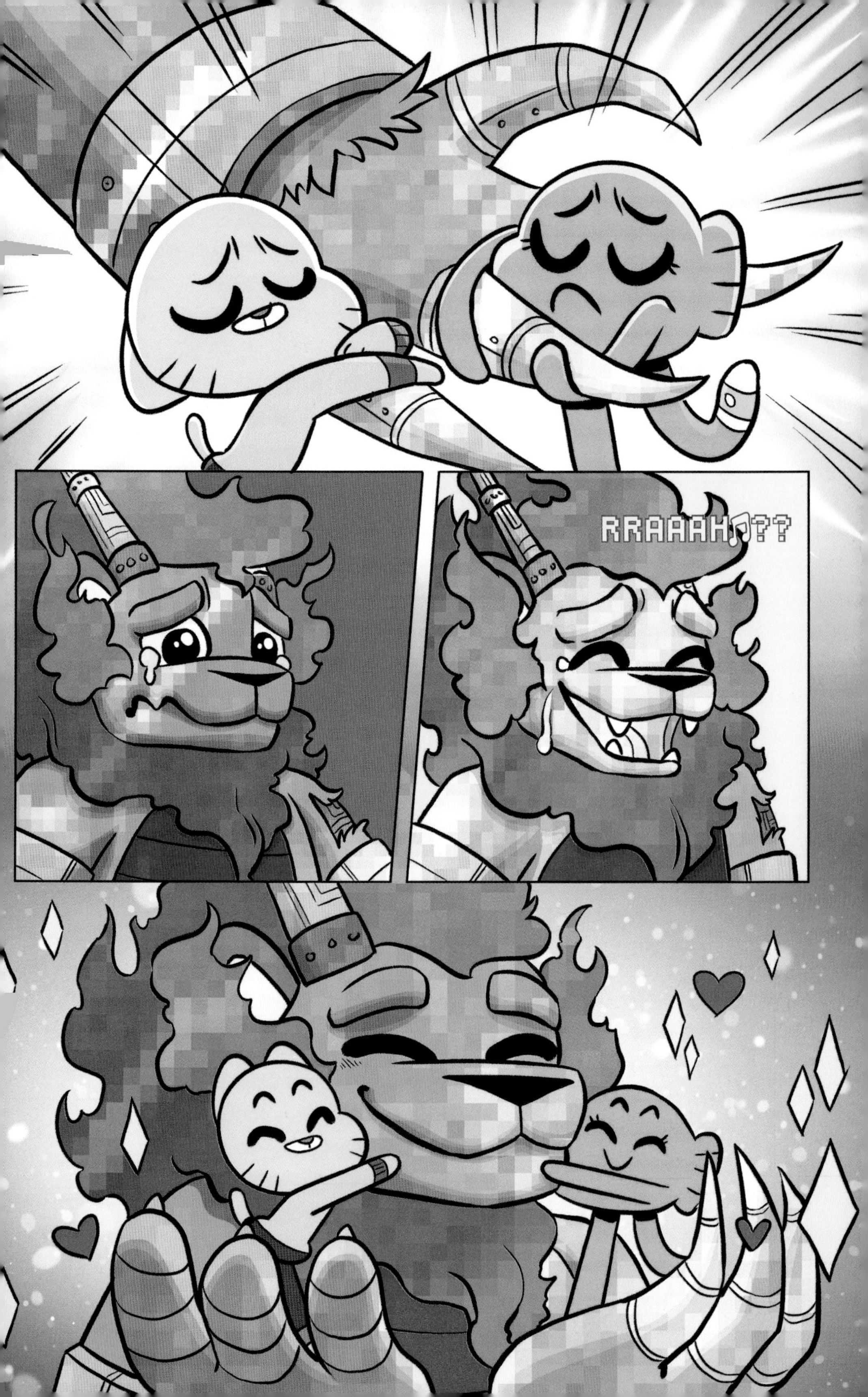
RRAAAAH♫??

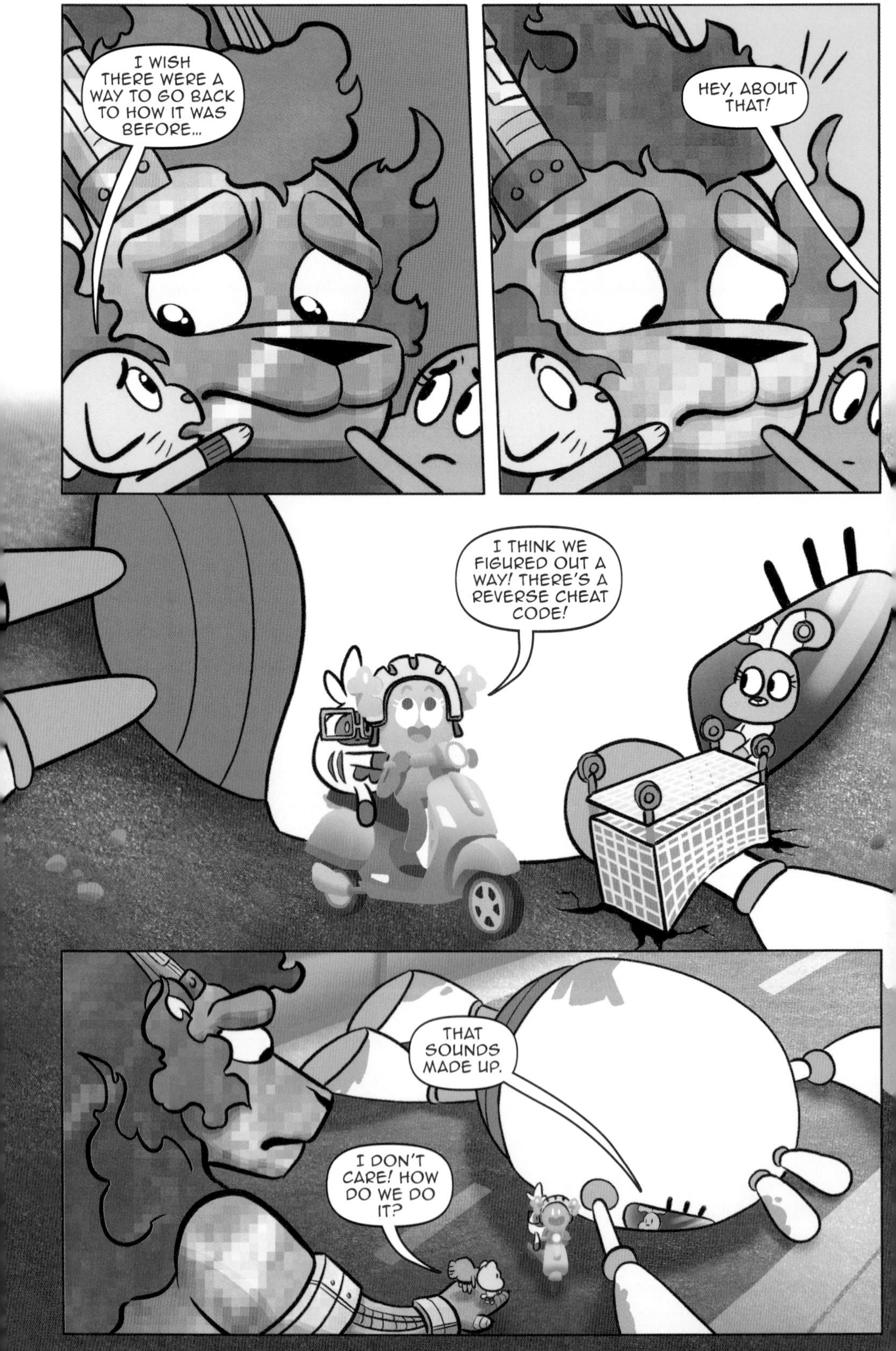
I WISH THERE WERE A WAY TO GO BACK TO HOW IT WAS BEFORE...
HEY, ABOUT THAT!
I THINK WE FIGURED OUT A WAY! THERE'S A REVERSE CHEAT CODE!
THAT SOUNDS MADE UP.
I DON'T CARE! HOW DO WE DO IT?

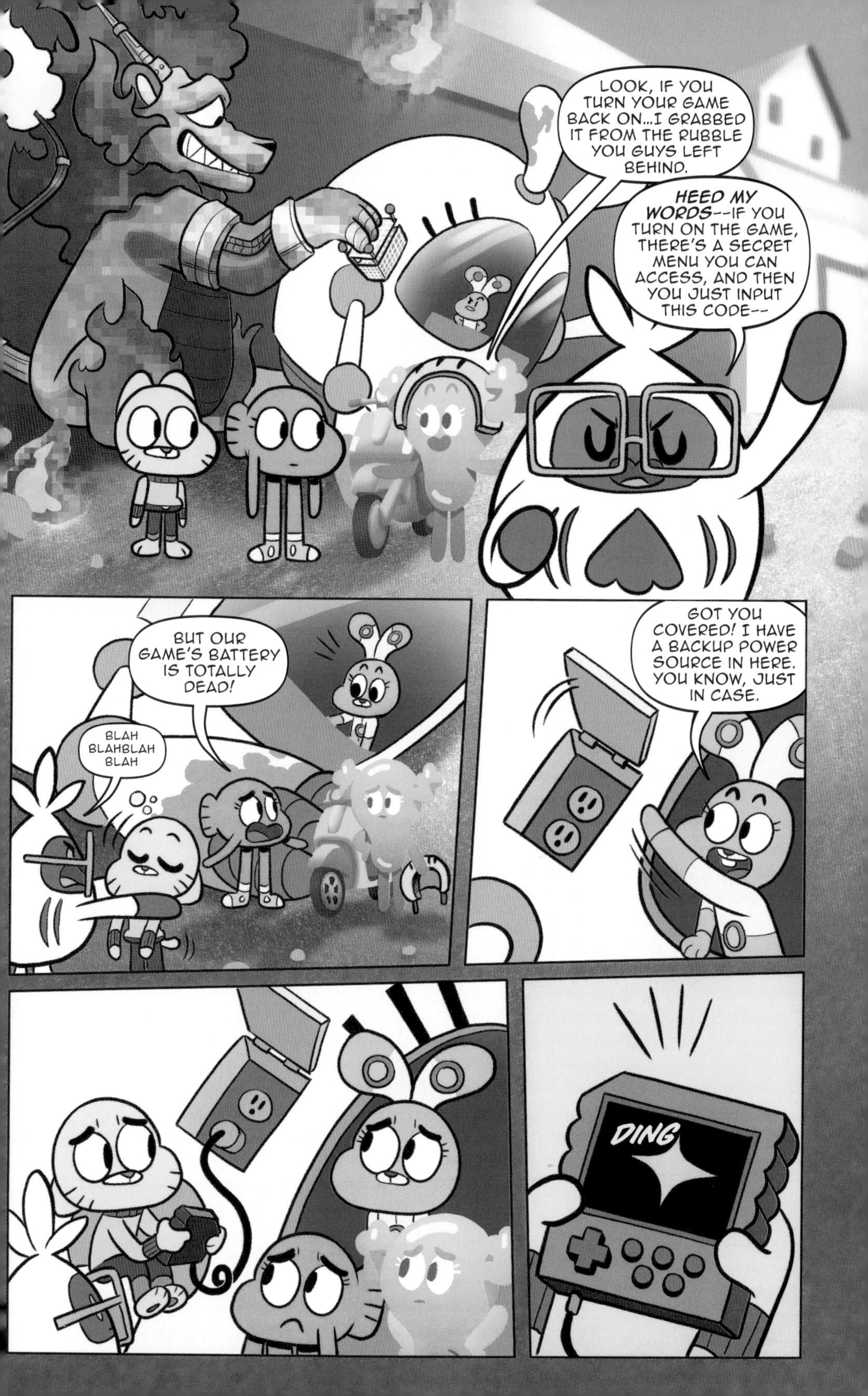
LOOK, IF YOU TURN YOUR GAME BACK ON...I GRABBED IT FROM THE RUBBLE YOU GUYS LEFT BEHIND.
HEED MY WORDS--IF YOU TURN ON THE GAME, THERE'S A SECRET MENU YOU CAN ACCESS, AND THEN YOU JUST INPUT THIS CODE--
BLAH BLAHBLAH BLAH
BUT OUR GAME'S BATTERY IS TOTALLY DEAD!
GOT YOU COVERED! I HAVE A BACKUP POWER SOURCE IN HERE. YOU KNOW, JUST IN CASE.
DING

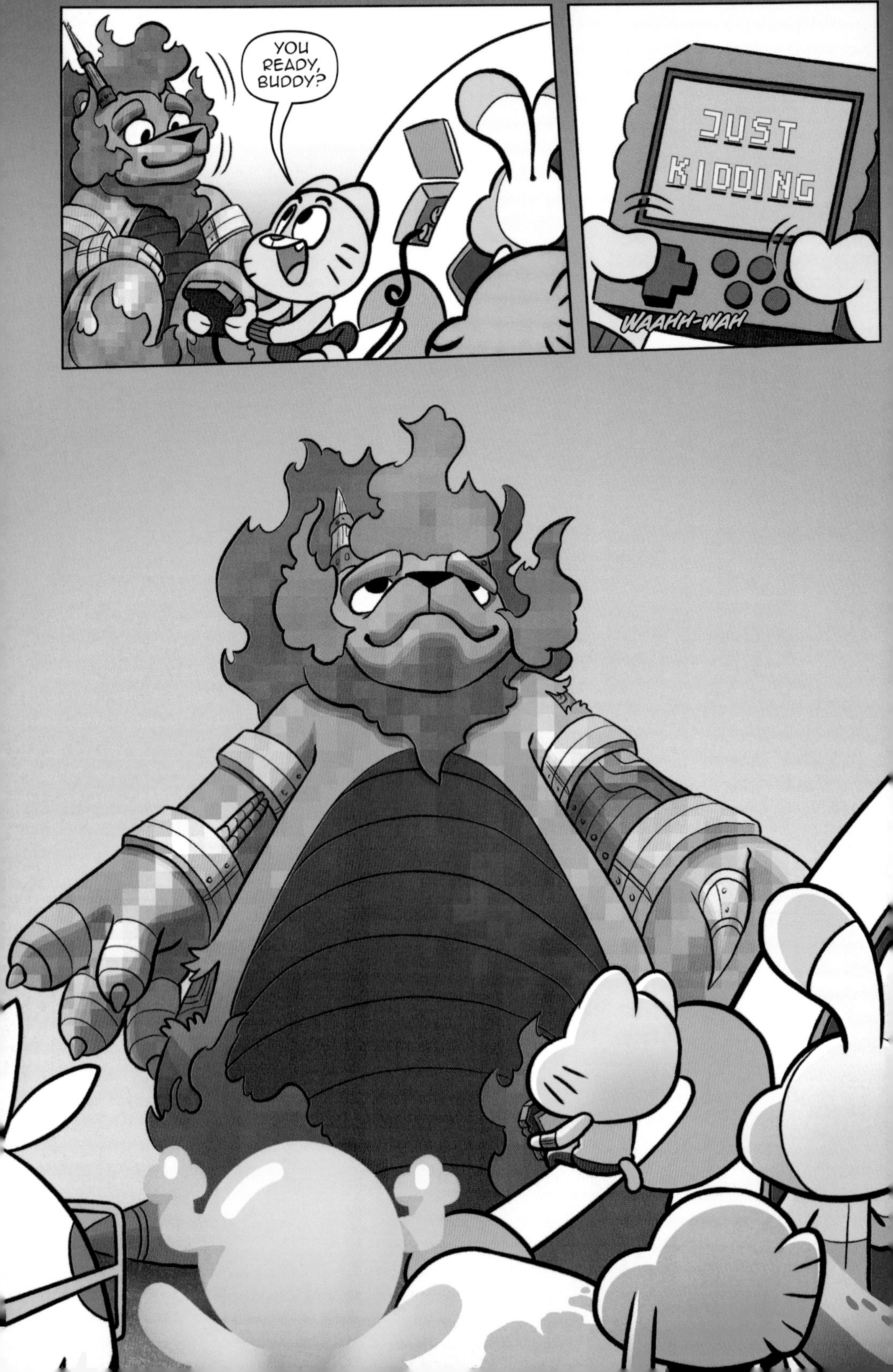
YOU READY, BUDDY?
JUST KIDDING
WAAHH-WAH

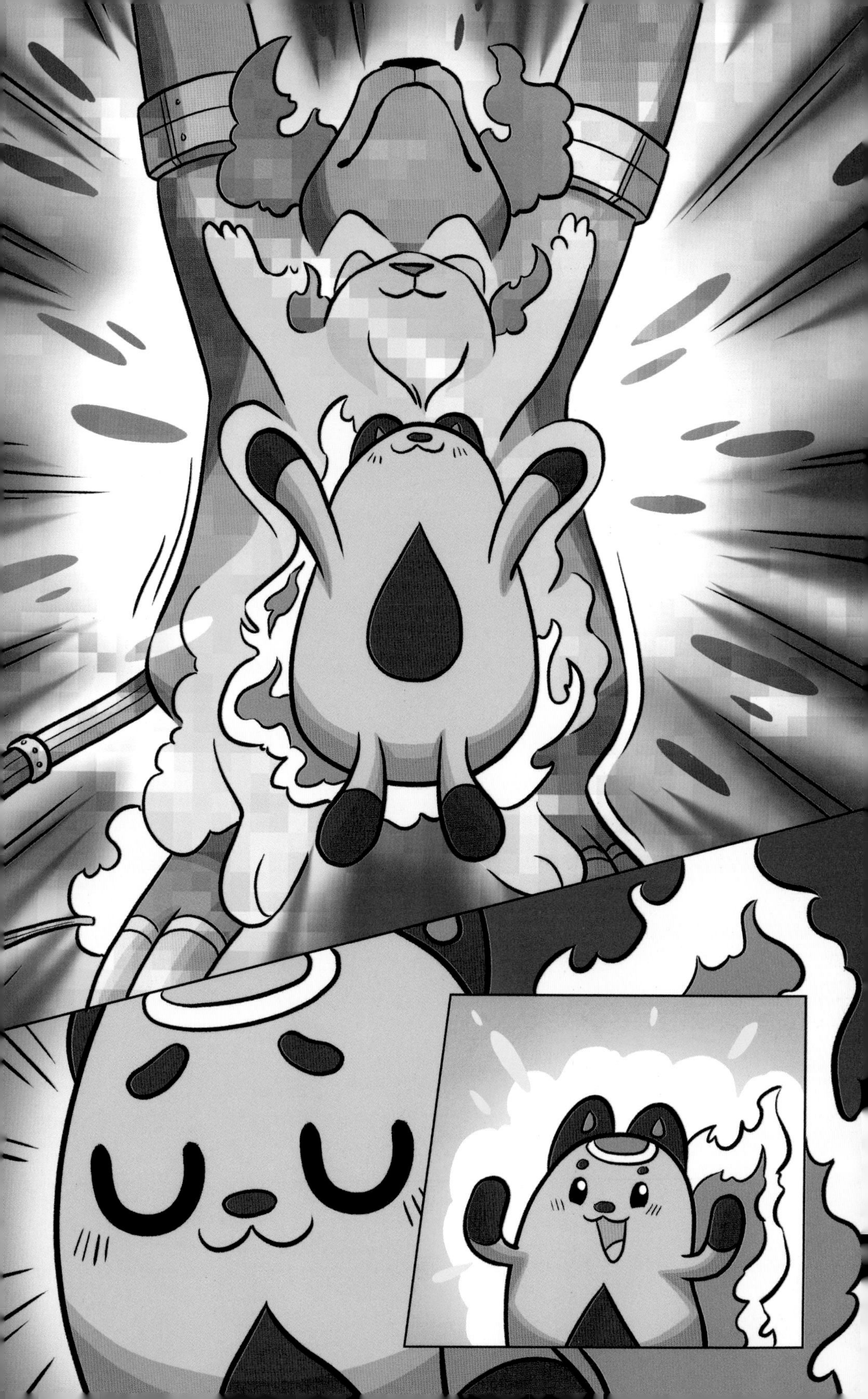

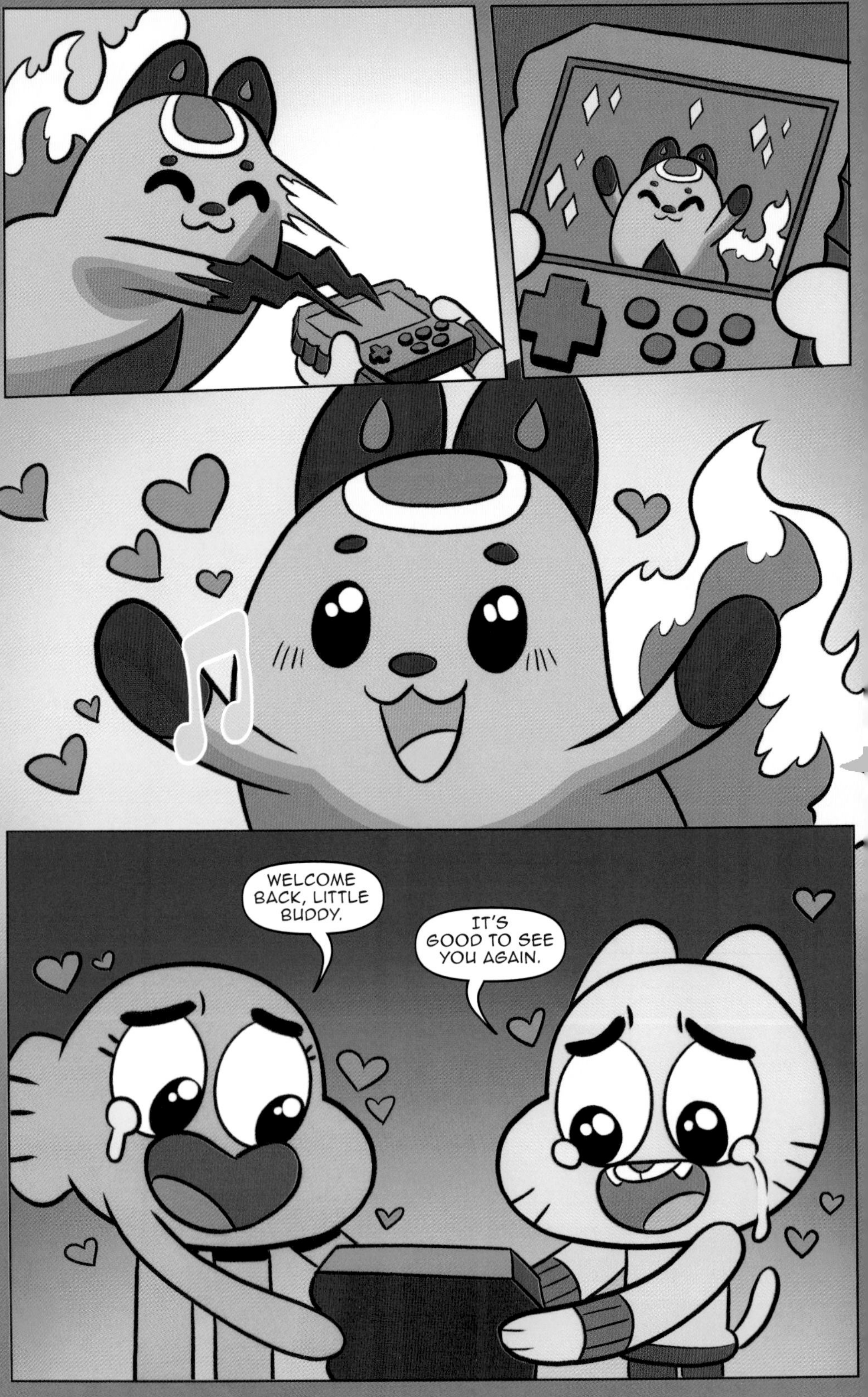
WELCOME BACK, LITTLE BUDDY.
IT'S GOOD TO SEE YOU AGAIN.

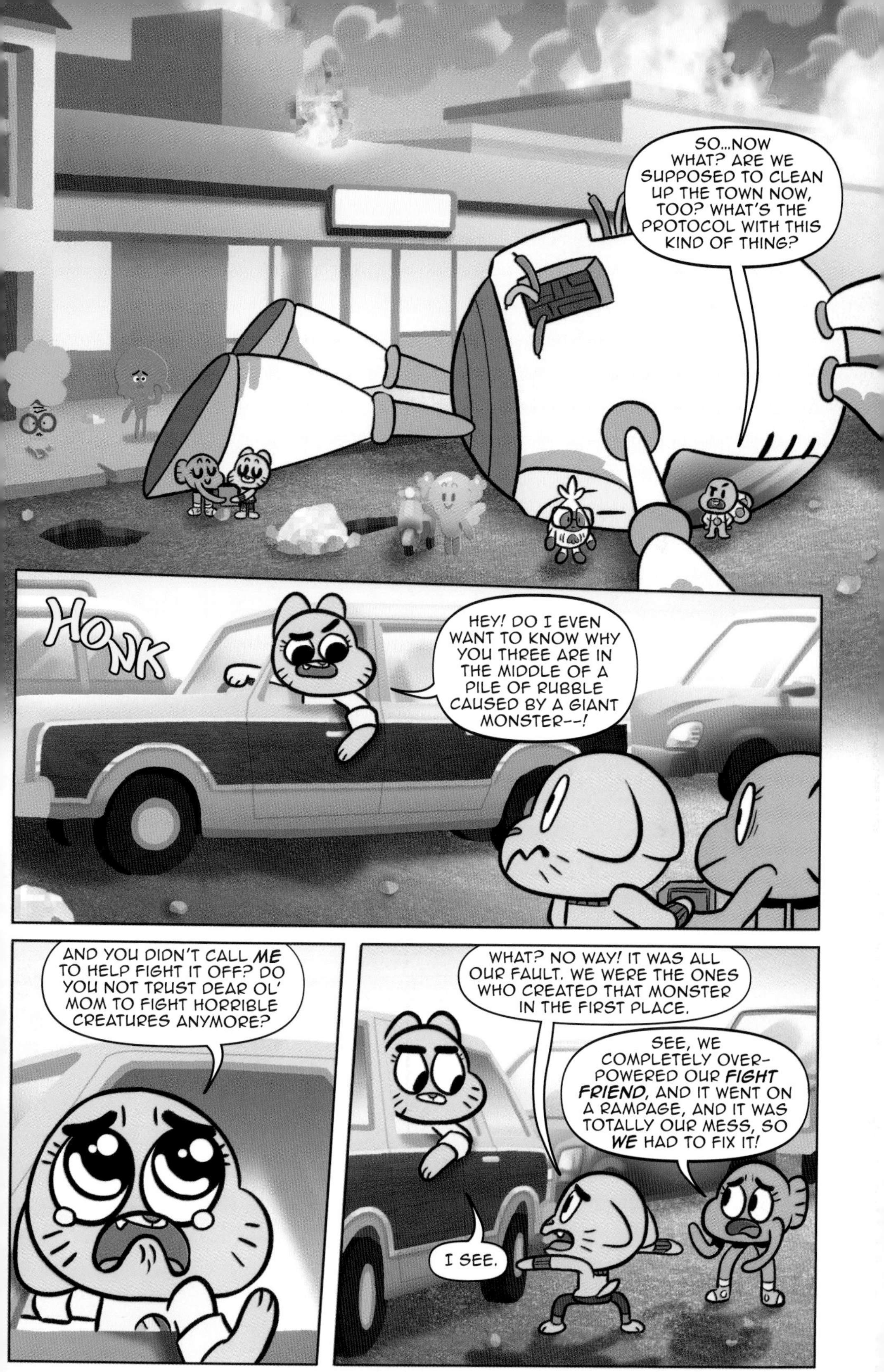
SO...NOW WHAT? ARE WE SUPPOSED TO CLEAN UP THE TOWN NOW, TOO? WHAT'S THE PROTOCOL WITH THIS KIND OF THING?
HONK
HEY! DO I EVEN WANT TO KNOW WHY YOU THREE ARE IN THE MIDDLE OF A PILE OF RUBBLE CAUSED BY A GIANT MONSTER--!
AND YOU DIDN'T CALL *ME* TO HELP FIGHT IT OFF? DO YOU NOT TRUST DEAR OL' MOM TO FIGHT HORRIBLE CREATURES ANYMORE?
WHAT? NO WAY! IT WAS ALL OUR FAULT. WE WERE THE ONES WHO CREATED THAT MONSTER IN THE FIRST PLACE.
SEE, WE COMPLETELY OVER-POWERED OUR ***FIGHT FRIEND***, AND IT WENT ON A RAMPAGE, AND IT WAS TOTALLY OUR MESS, SO ***WE*** HAD TO FIX IT!
I SEE.

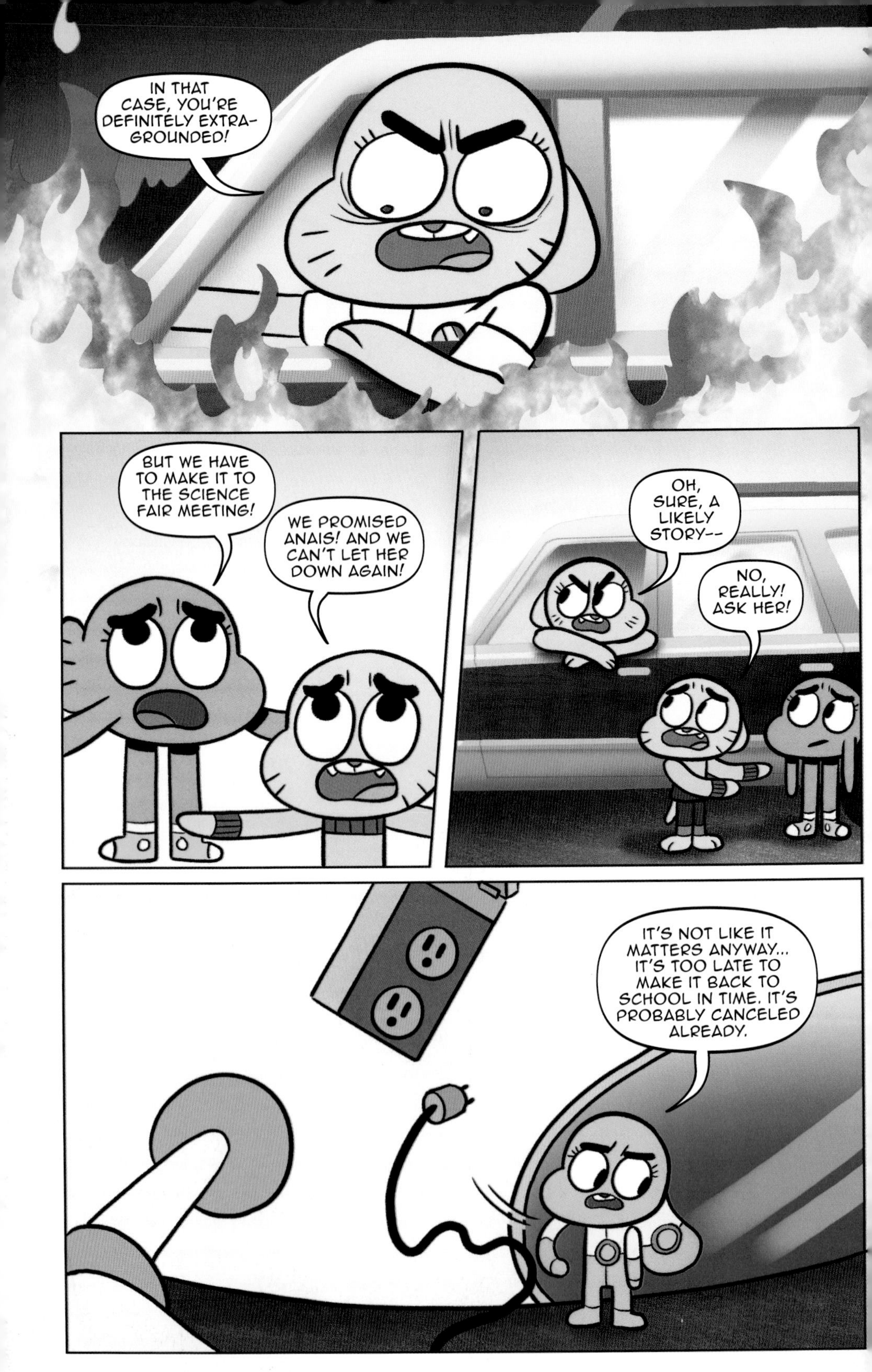
IN THAT CASE, YOU'RE DEFINITELY EXTRA-GROUNDED!
BUT WE HAVE TO MAKE IT TO THE SCIENCE FAIR MEETING!
WE PROMISED ANAIS! AND WE CAN'T LET HER DOWN AGAIN!
OH, SURE, A LIKELY STORY--
NO, REALLY! ASK HER!
IT'S NOT LIKE IT MATTERS ANYWAY... IT'S TOO LATE TO MAKE IT BACK TO SCHOOL IN TIME. IT'S PROBABLY CANCELED ALREADY.

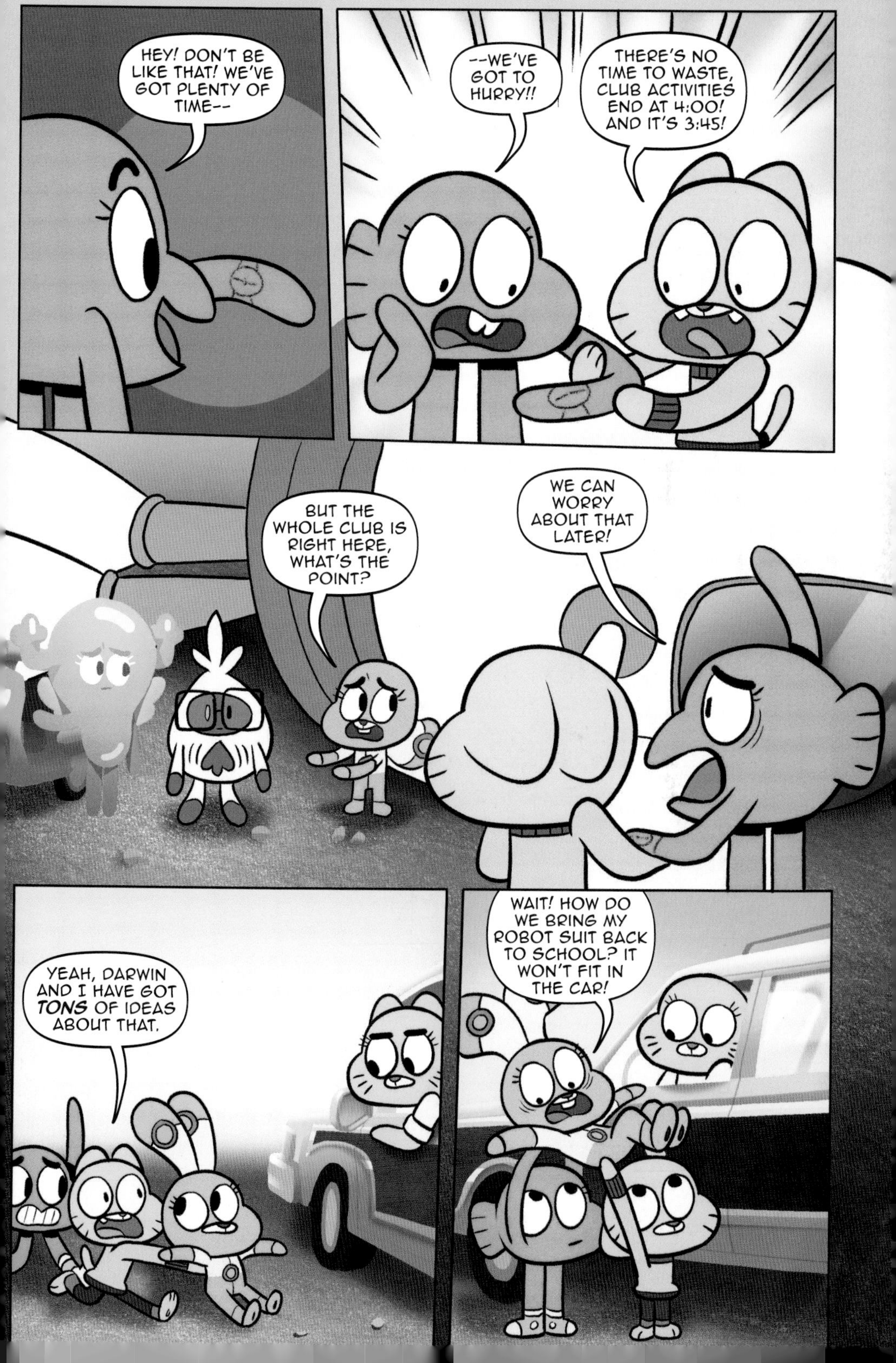
HEY! DON'T BE LIKE THAT! WE'VE GOT PLENTY OF TIME--
--WE'VE GOT TO HURRY!!
THERE'S NO TIME TO WASTE, CLUB ACTIVITIES END AT 4:00! AND IT'S 3:45!
BUT THE WHOLE CLUB IS RIGHT HERE, WHAT'S THE POINT?
WE CAN WORRY ABOUT THAT LATER!
YEAH, DARWIN AND I HAVE GOT *TONS* OF IDEAS ABOUT THAT.
WAIT! HOW DO WE BRING MY ROBOT SUIT BACK TO SCHOOL? IT WON'T FIT IN THE CAR!

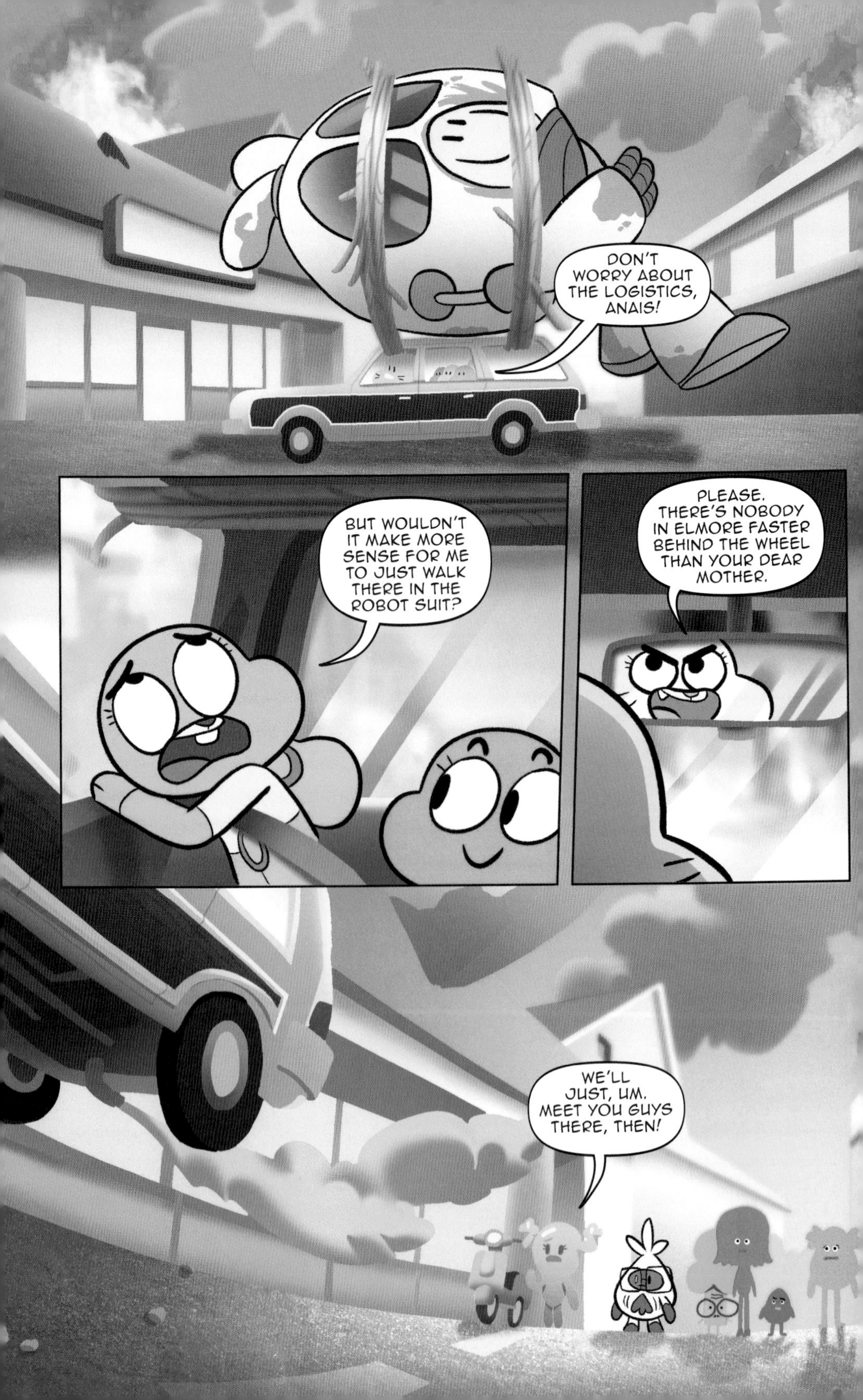
DON'T WORRY ABOUT THE LOGISTICS, ANAIS!
BUT WOULDN'T IT MAKE MORE SENSE FOR ME TO JUST WALK THERE IN THE ROBOT SUIT?
PLEASE. THERE'S NOBODY IN ELMORE FASTER BEHIND THE WHEEL THAN YOUR DEAR MOTHER.
WE'LL JUST, UM. MEET YOU GUYS THERE, THEN!

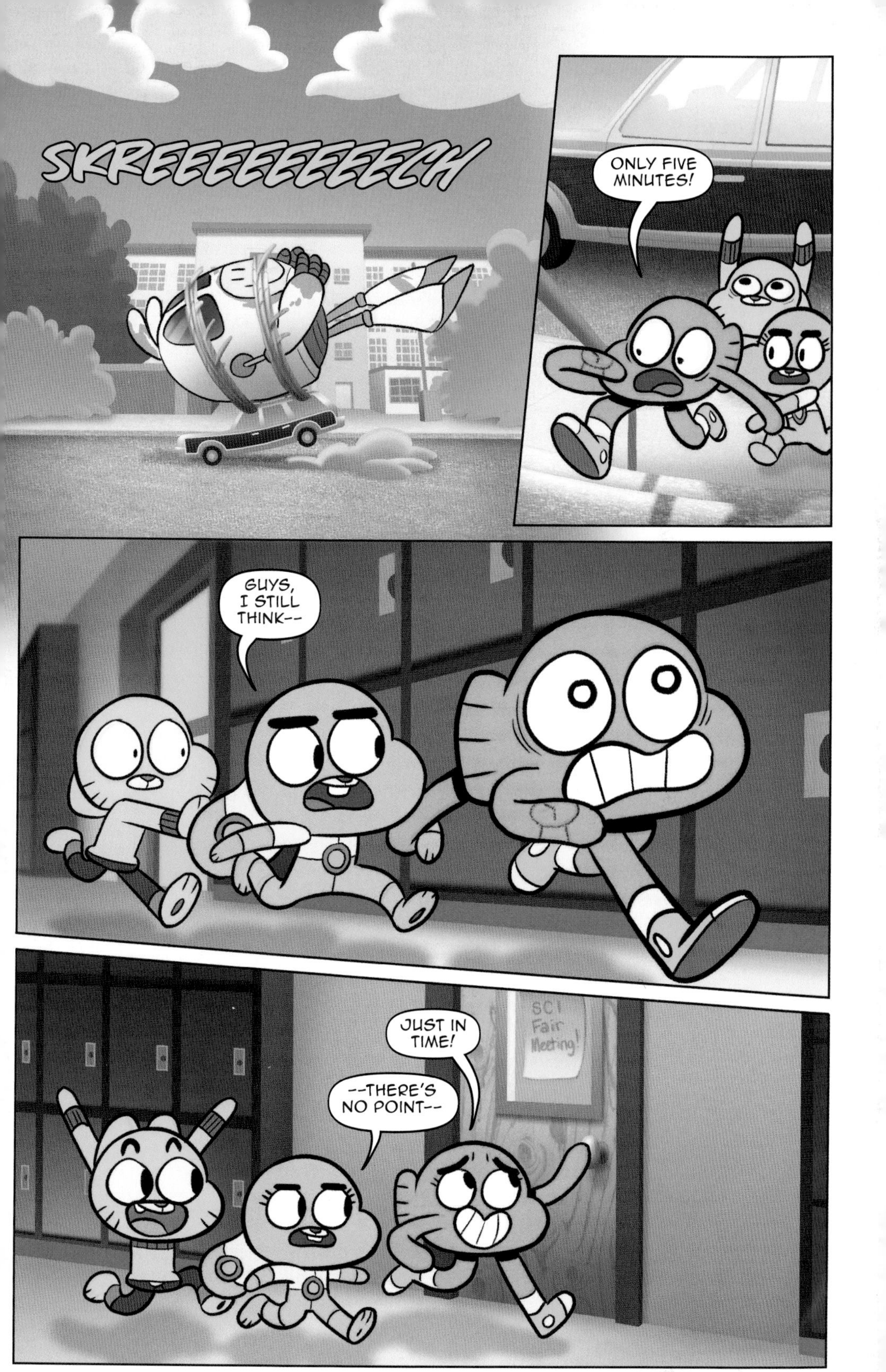
SKREEEEEEEEEECH
ONLY FIVE MINUTES!
GUYS, I STILL THINK--
JUST IN TIME!
--THERE'S NO POINT--
SCI Fair Meeting!

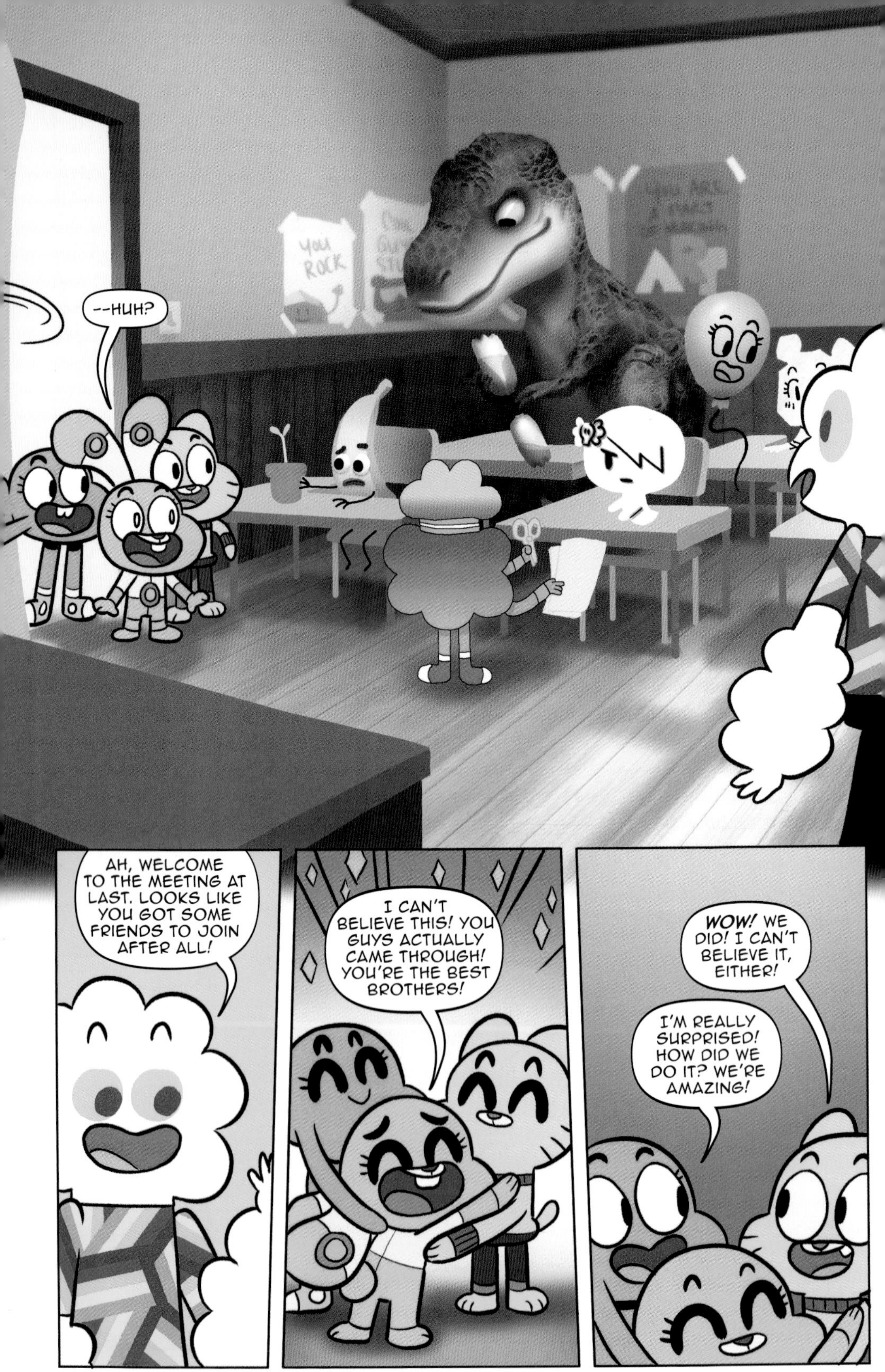
--HUH?
AH, WELCOME TO THE MEETING AT LAST. LOOKS LIKE YOU GOT SOME FRIENDS TO JOIN AFTER ALL!
I CAN'T BELIEVE THIS! YOU GUYS ACTUALLY CAME THROUGH! YOU'RE THE BEST BROTHERS!
WOW! WE DID! I CAN'T BELIEVE IT, EITHER!
I'M REALLY SURPRISED! HOW DID WE DO IT? WE'RE AMAZING!

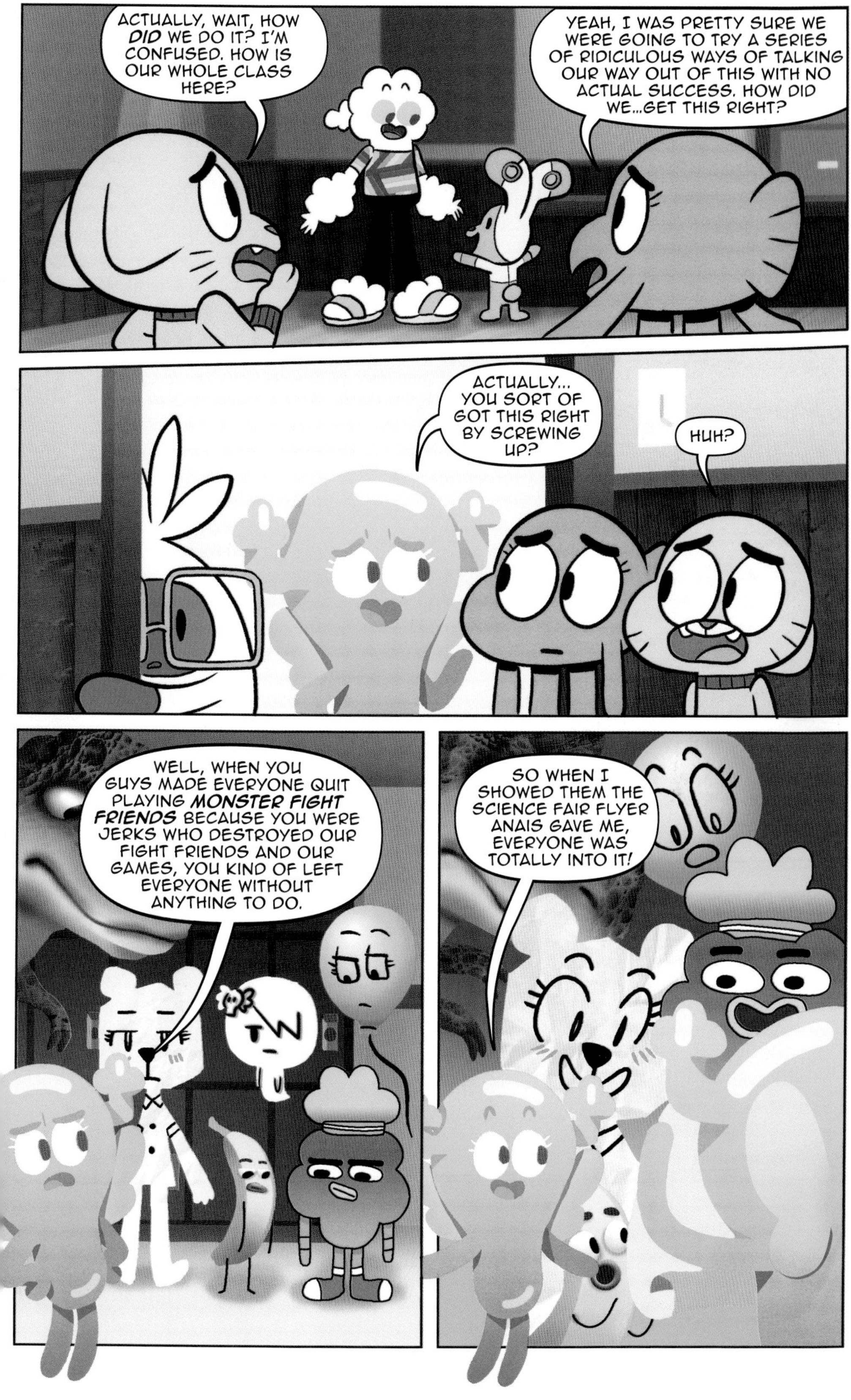
ACTUALLY, WAIT, HOW *DID* WE DO IT? I'M CONFUSED. HOW IS OUR WHOLE CLASS HERE?
YEAH, I WAS PRETTY SURE WE WERE GOING TO TRY A SERIES OF RIDICULOUS WAYS OF TALKING OUR WAY OUT OF THIS WITH NO ACTUAL SUCCESS. HOW DID WE...GET THIS RIGHT?
ACTUALLY... YOU SORT OF GOT THIS RIGHT BY SCREWING UP?
HUH?
WELL, WHEN YOU GUYS MADE EVERYONE QUIT PLAYING ***MONSTER FIGHT FRIENDS*** BECAUSE YOU WERE JERKS WHO DESTROYED OUR FIGHT FRIENDS AND OUR GAMES, YOU KIND OF LEFT EVERYONE WITHOUT ANYTHING TO DO.
SO WHEN I SHOWED THEM THE SCIENCE FAIR FLYER ANAIS GAVE ME, EVERYONE WAS TOTALLY INTO IT!

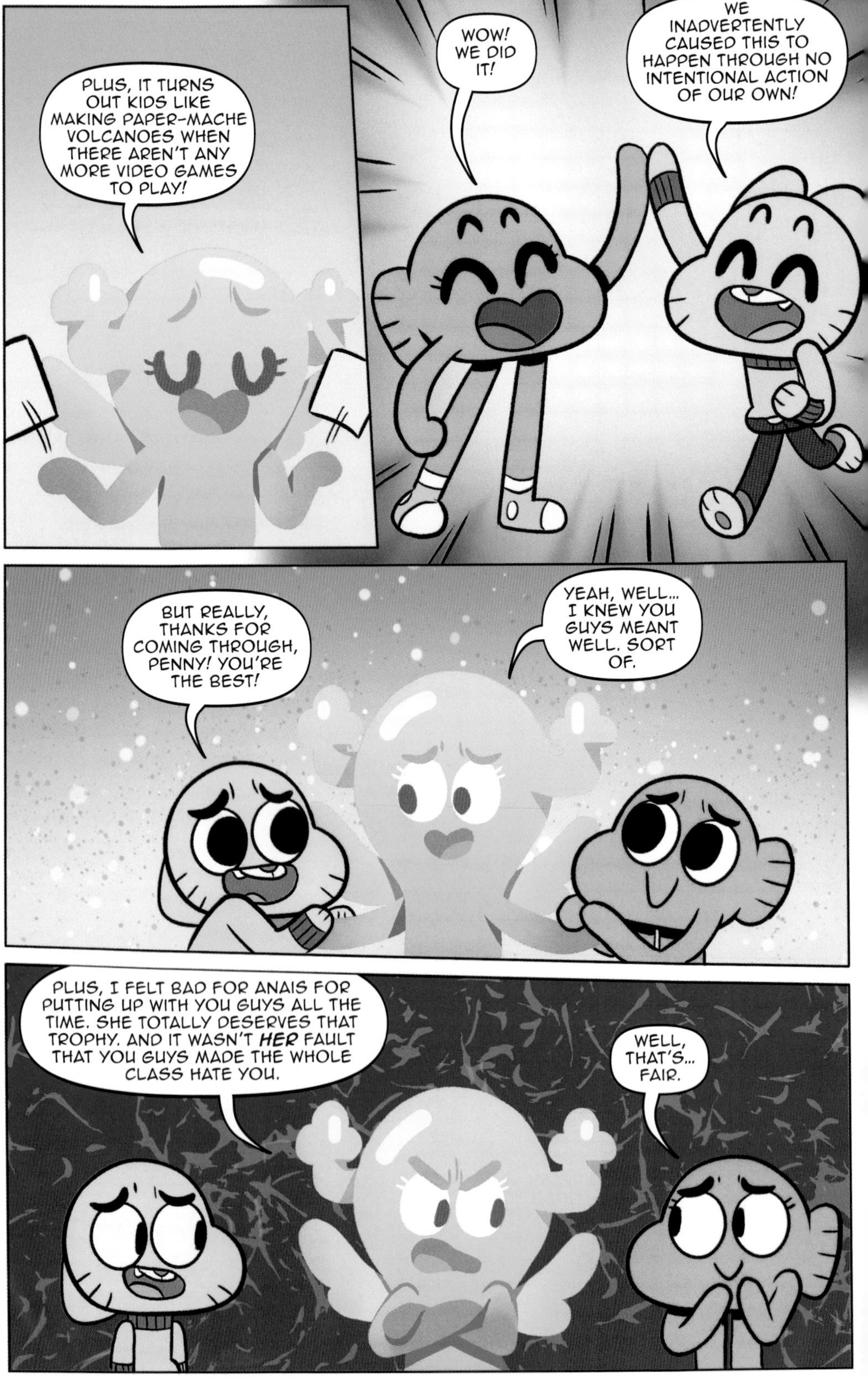
PLUS, IT TURNS OUT KIDS LIKE MAKING PAPER-MACHE VOLCANOES WHEN THERE AREN'T ANY MORE VIDEO GAMES TO PLAY!
WOW! WE DID IT!
WE INADVERTENTLY CAUSED THIS TO HAPPEN THROUGH NO INTENTIONAL ACTION OF OUR OWN!
BUT REALLY, THANKS FOR COMING THROUGH, PENNY! YOU'RE THE BEST!
YEAH, WELL... I KNEW YOU GUYS MEANT WELL. SORT OF.
PLUS, I FELT BAD FOR ANAIS FOR PUTTING UP WITH YOU GUYS ALL THE TIME. SHE TOTALLY DESERVES THAT TROPHY. AND IT WASN'T HER FAULT THAT YOU GUYS MADE THE WHOLE CLASS HATE YOU.
WELL, THAT'S... FAIR.

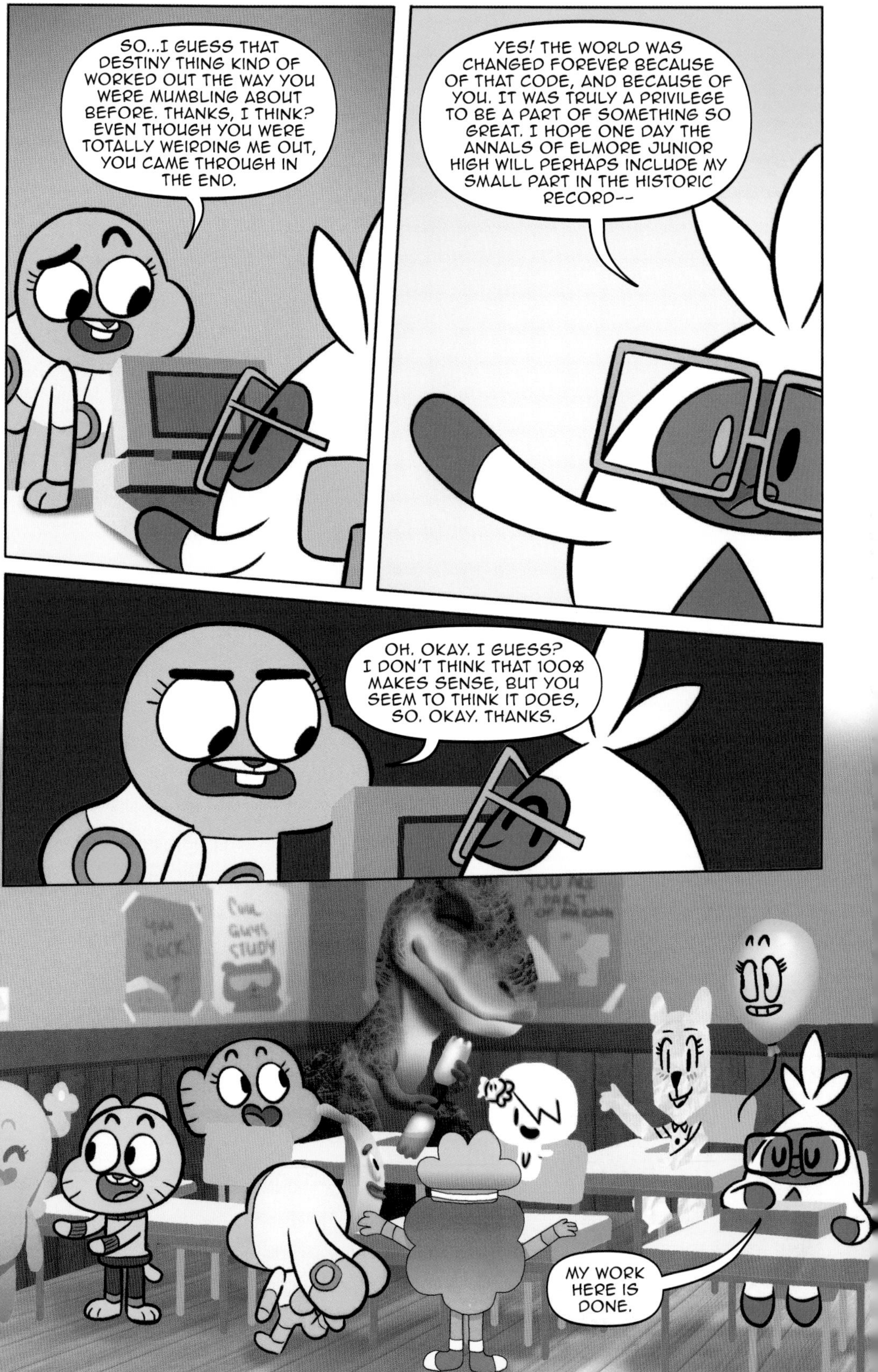
SO...I GUESS THAT DESTINY THING KIND OF WORKED OUT THE WAY YOU WERE MUMBLING ABOUT BEFORE. THANKS, I THINK? EVEN THOUGH YOU WERE TOTALLY WEIRDING ME OUT, YOU CAME THROUGH IN THE END.
YES! THE WORLD WAS CHANGED FOREVER BECAUSE OF THAT CODE, AND BECAUSE OF YOU. IT WAS TRULY A PRIVILEGE TO BE A PART OF SOMETHING SO GREAT. I HOPE ONE DAY THE ANNALS OF ELMORE JUNIOR HIGH WILL PERHAPS INCLUDE MY SMALL PART IN THE HISTORIC RECORD--
OH. OKAY. I GUESS? I DON'T THINK THAT 100% MAKES SENSE, BUT YOU SEEM TO THINK IT DOES, SO. OKAY. THANKS.
MY WORK HERE IS DONE.

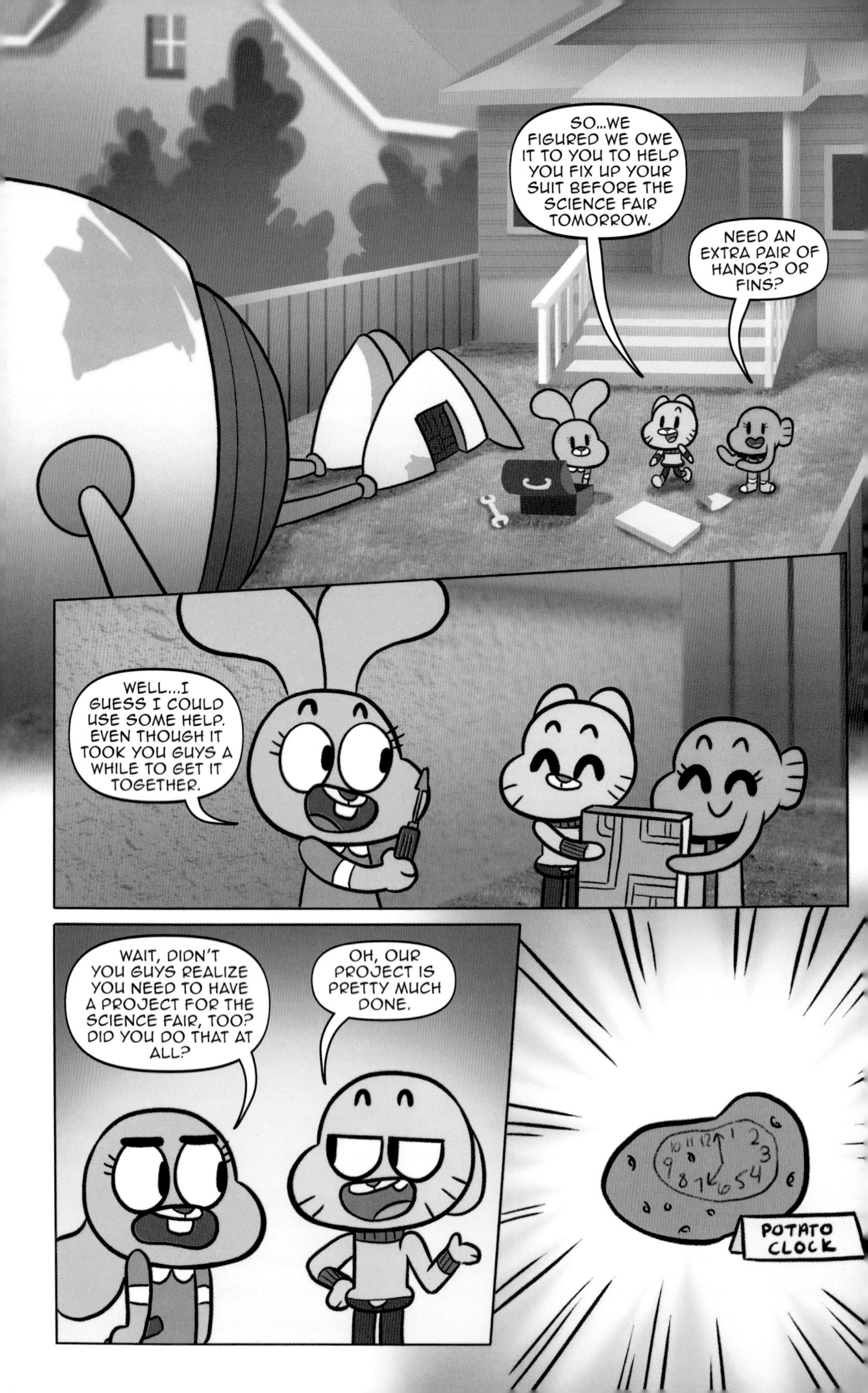
SO...WE FIGURED WE OWE IT TO YOU TO HELP YOU FIX UP YOUR SUIT BEFORE THE SCIENCE FAIR TOMORROW.
NEED AN EXTRA PAIR OF HANDS? OR FINS?
WELL...I GUESS I COULD USE SOME HELP. EVEN THOUGH IT TOOK YOU GUYS A WHILE TO GET IT TOGETHER.
WAIT, DIDN'T YOU GUYS REALIZE YOU NEED TO HAVE A PROJECT FOR THE SCIENCE FAIR, TOO? DID YOU DO THAT AT ALL?
OH, OUR PROJECT IS PRETTY MUCH DONE.
POTATO CLOCK

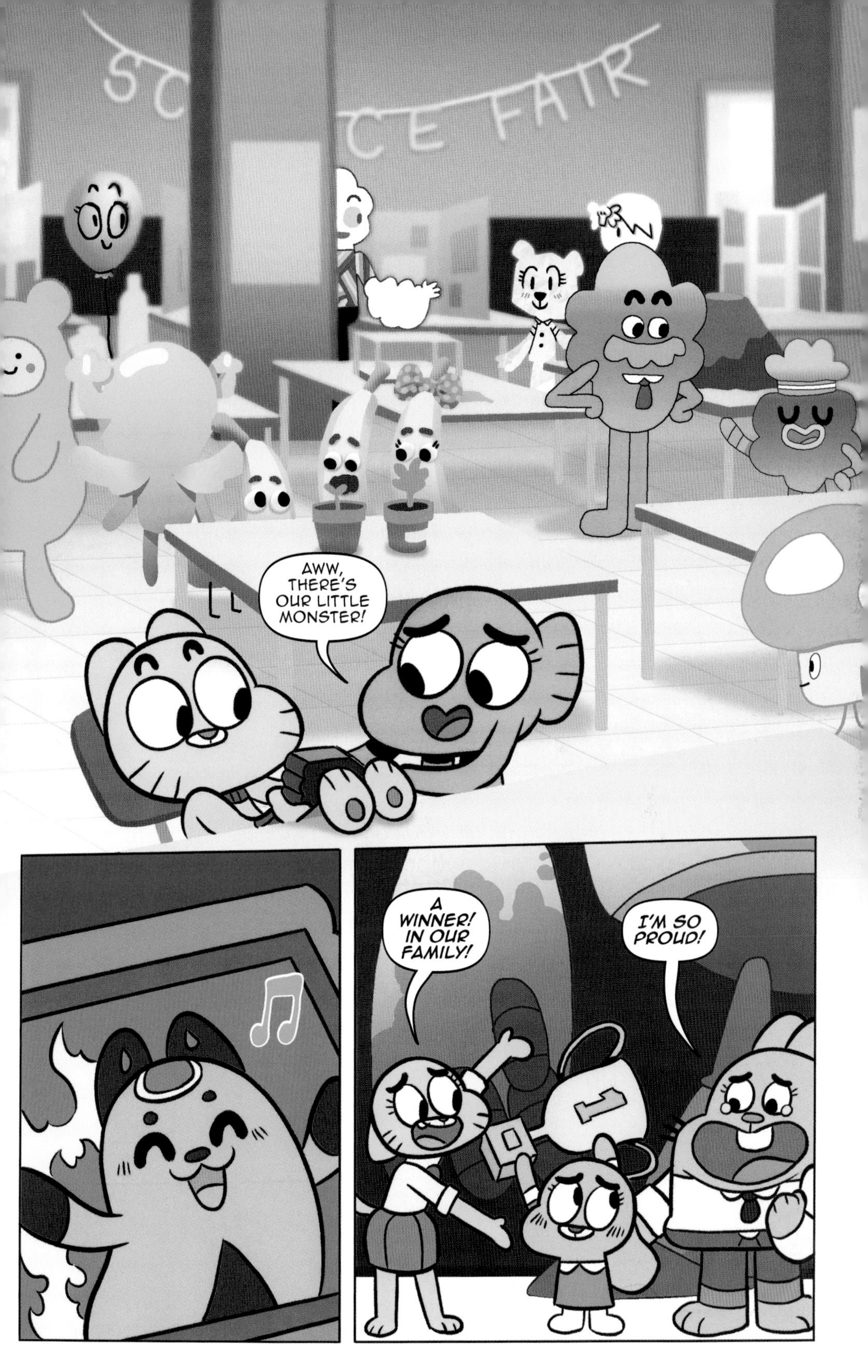
SC CE FAIR
AWW, THERE'S OUR LITTLE MONSTER!
A WINNER! IN OUR FAMILY!
I'M SO PROUD!

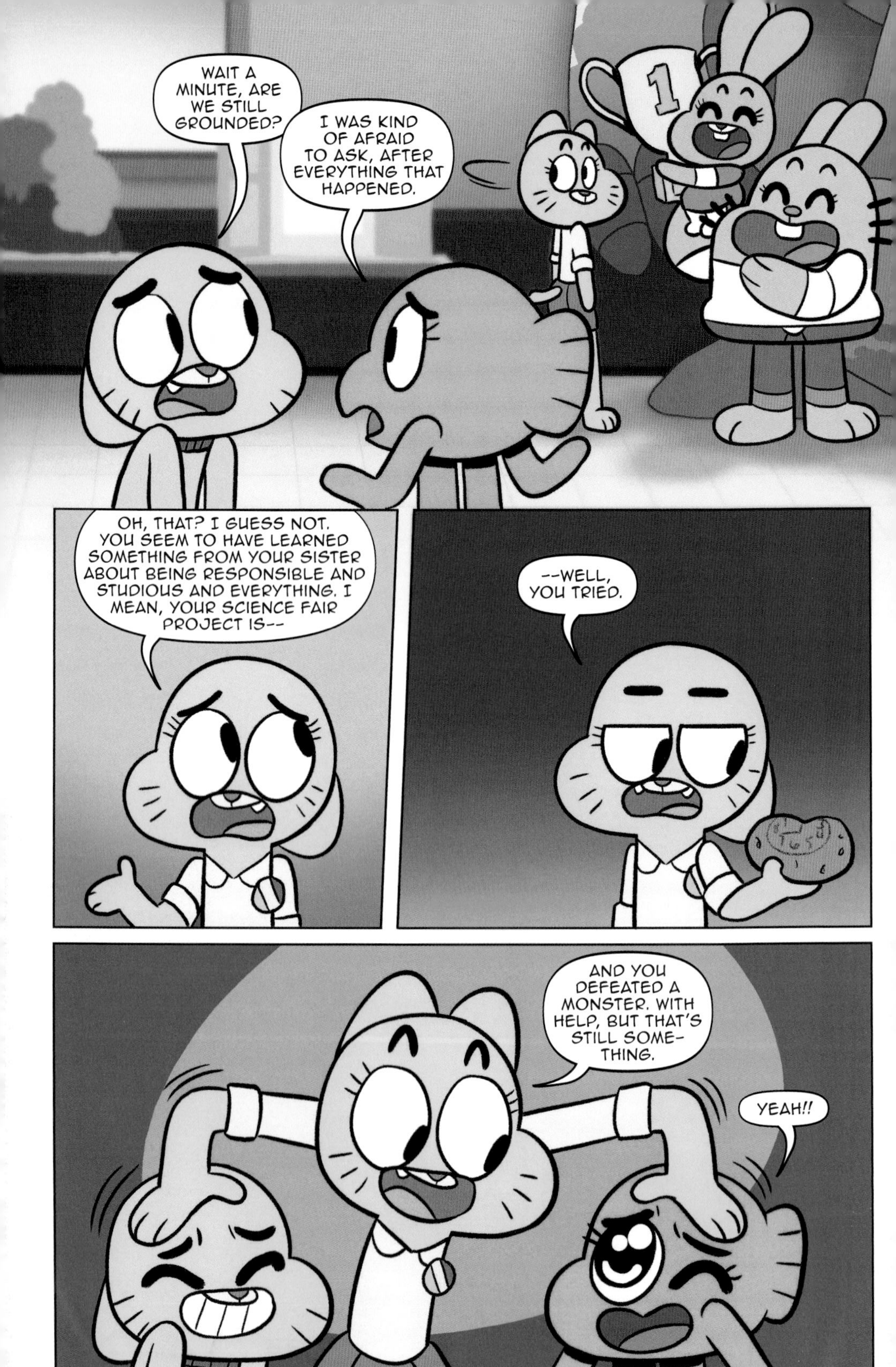
WAIT A MINUTE, ARE WE STILL GROUNDED?
I WAS KIND OF AFRAID TO ASK, AFTER EVERYTHING THAT HAPPENED.
OH, THAT? I GUESS NOT. YOU SEEM TO HAVE LEARNED SOMETHING FROM YOUR SISTER ABOUT BEING RESPONSIBLE AND STUDIOUS AND EVERYTHING. I MEAN, YOUR SCIENCE FAIR PROJECT IS--
--WELL, YOU TRIED.
AND YOU DEFEATED A MONSTER. WITH HELP, BUT THAT'S STILL SOME-THING.
YEAH!!

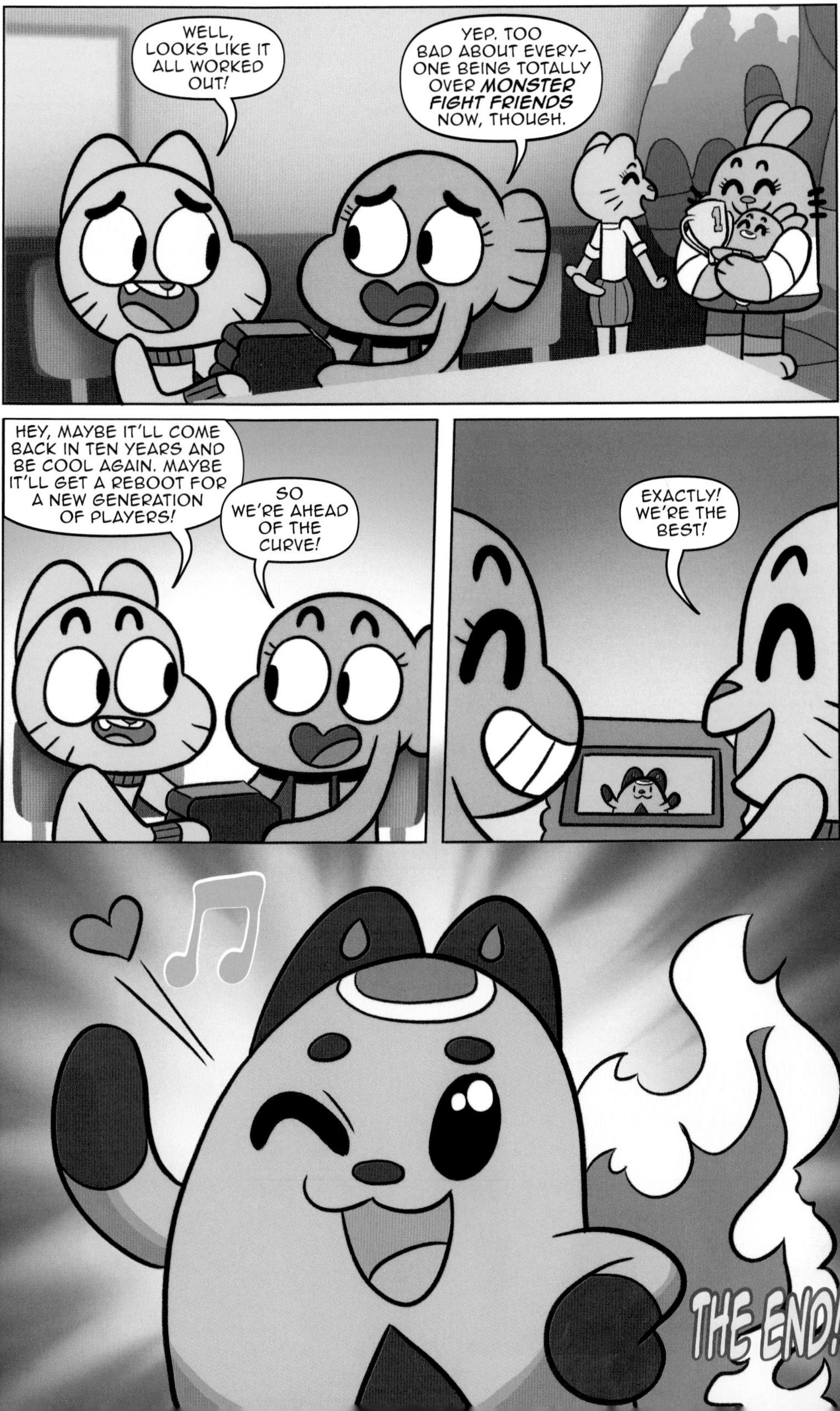
WELL, LOOKS LIKE IT ALL WORKED OUT!
YEP. TOO BAD ABOUT EVERY-ONE BEING TOTALLY OVER MONSTER FIGHT FRIENDS NOW, THOUGH.
HEY, MAYBE IT'LL COME BACK IN TEN YEARS AND BE COOL AGAIN. MAYBE IT'LL GET A REBOOT FOR A NEW GENERATION OF PLAYERS!
SO WE'RE AHEAD OF THE CURVE!
EXACTLY! WE'RE THE BEST!
THE END!

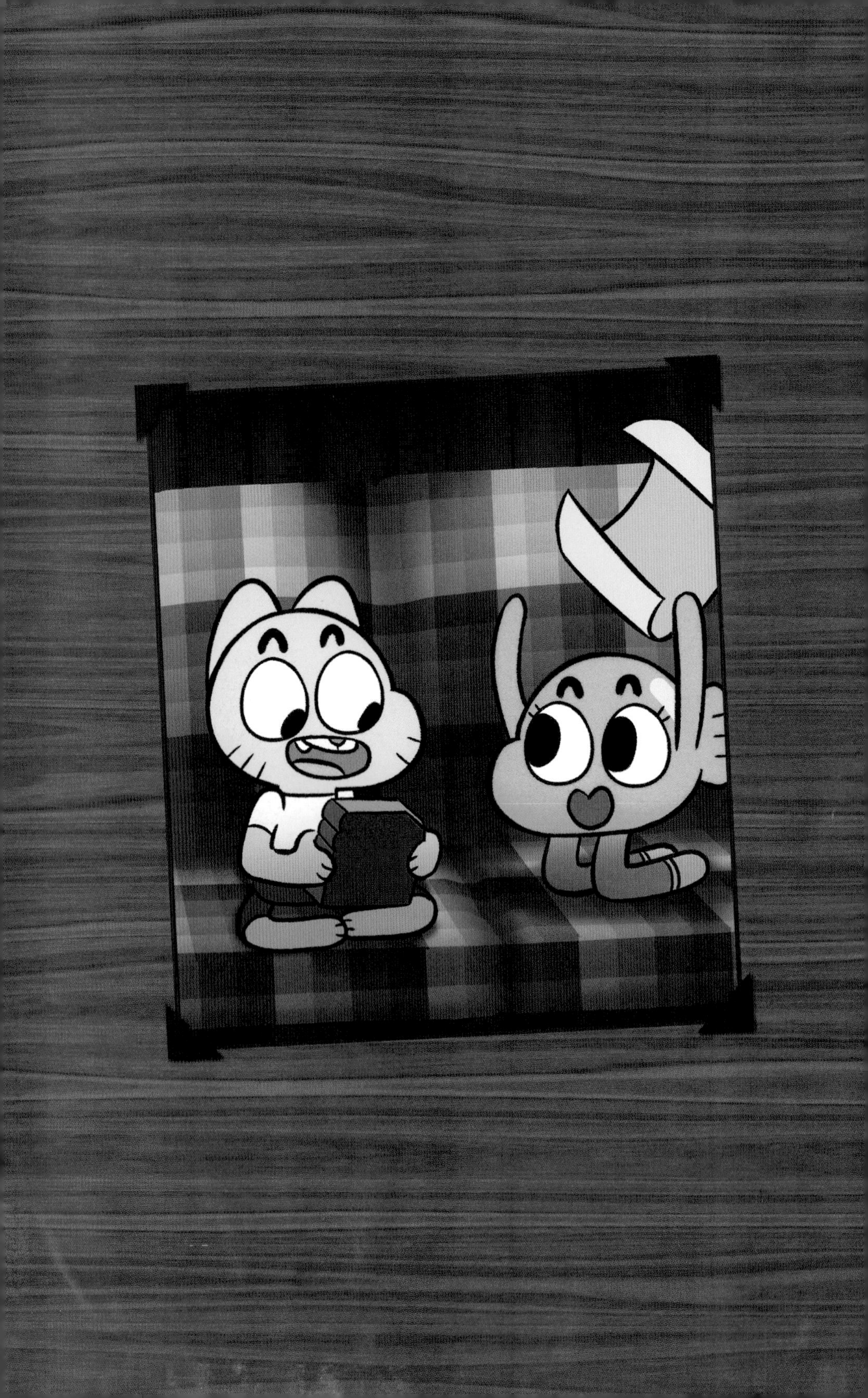

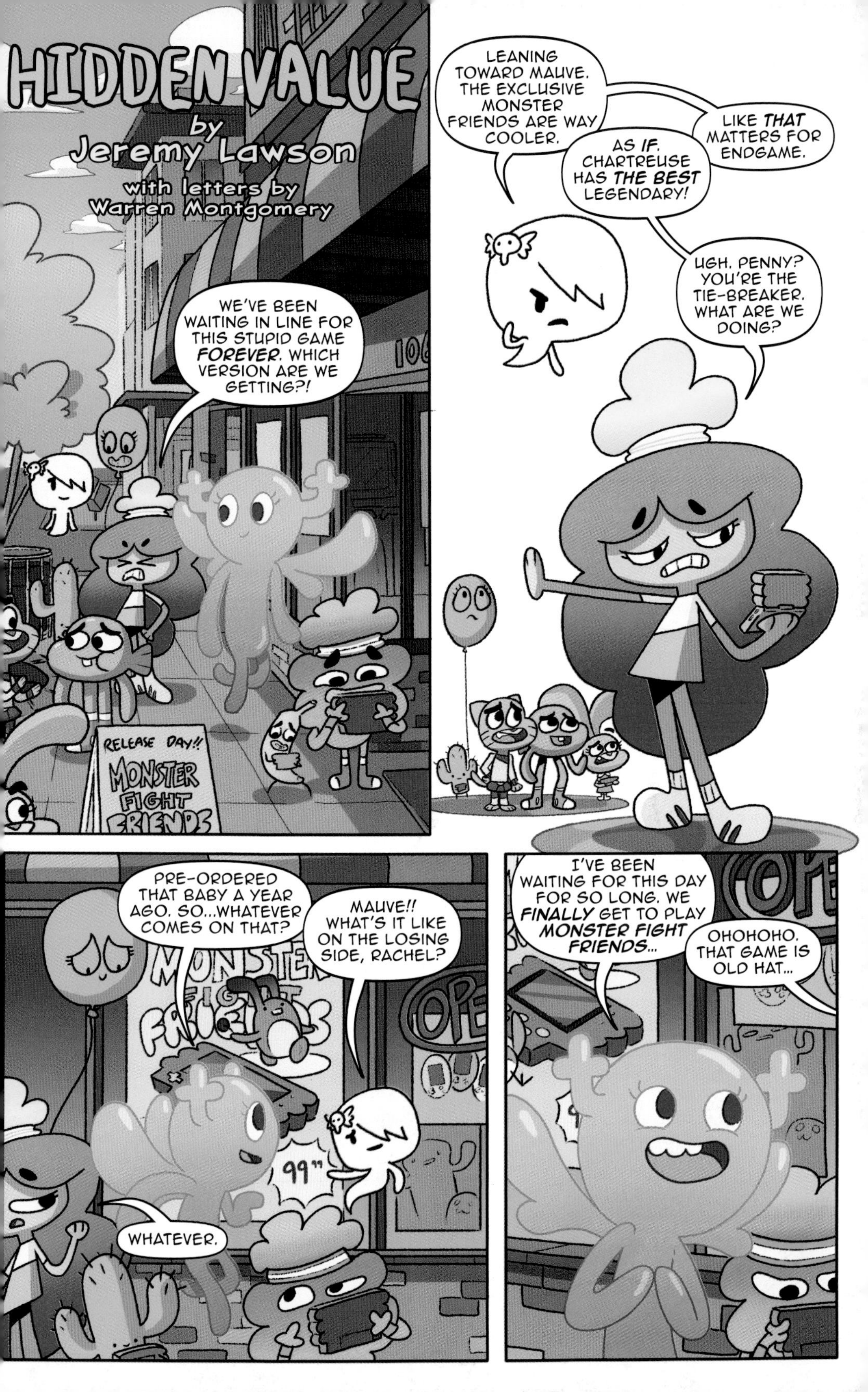
HIDDEN VALUE
by Jeremy Lawson
with letters by Warren Montgomery
WE'VE BEEN WAITING IN LINE FOR THIS STUPID GAME *FOREVER*. WHICH VERSION ARE WE GETTING?!
RELEASE DAY!!
MONSTER FIGHT FRIENDS
LEANING TOWARD MAUVE. THE EXCLUSIVE MONSTER FRIENDS ARE WAY COOLER.
LIKE *THAT* MATTERS FOR ENDGAME.
AS *IF*. CHARTREUSE HAS ***THE BEST*** LEGENDARY!
UGH. PENNY? YOU'RE THE TIE-BREAKER. WHAT ARE WE DOING?
PRE-ORDERED THAT BABY A YEAR AGO. SO...WHATEVER COMES ON THAT?
MAUVE!! WHAT'S IT LIKE ON THE LOSING SIDE, RACHEL?
WHATEVER.
I'VE BEEN WAITING FOR THIS DAY FOR SO LONG. WE ***FINALLY*** GET TO PLAY ***MONSTER FIGHT FRIENDS***...
OHOHOHO. THAT GAME IS OLD HAT...

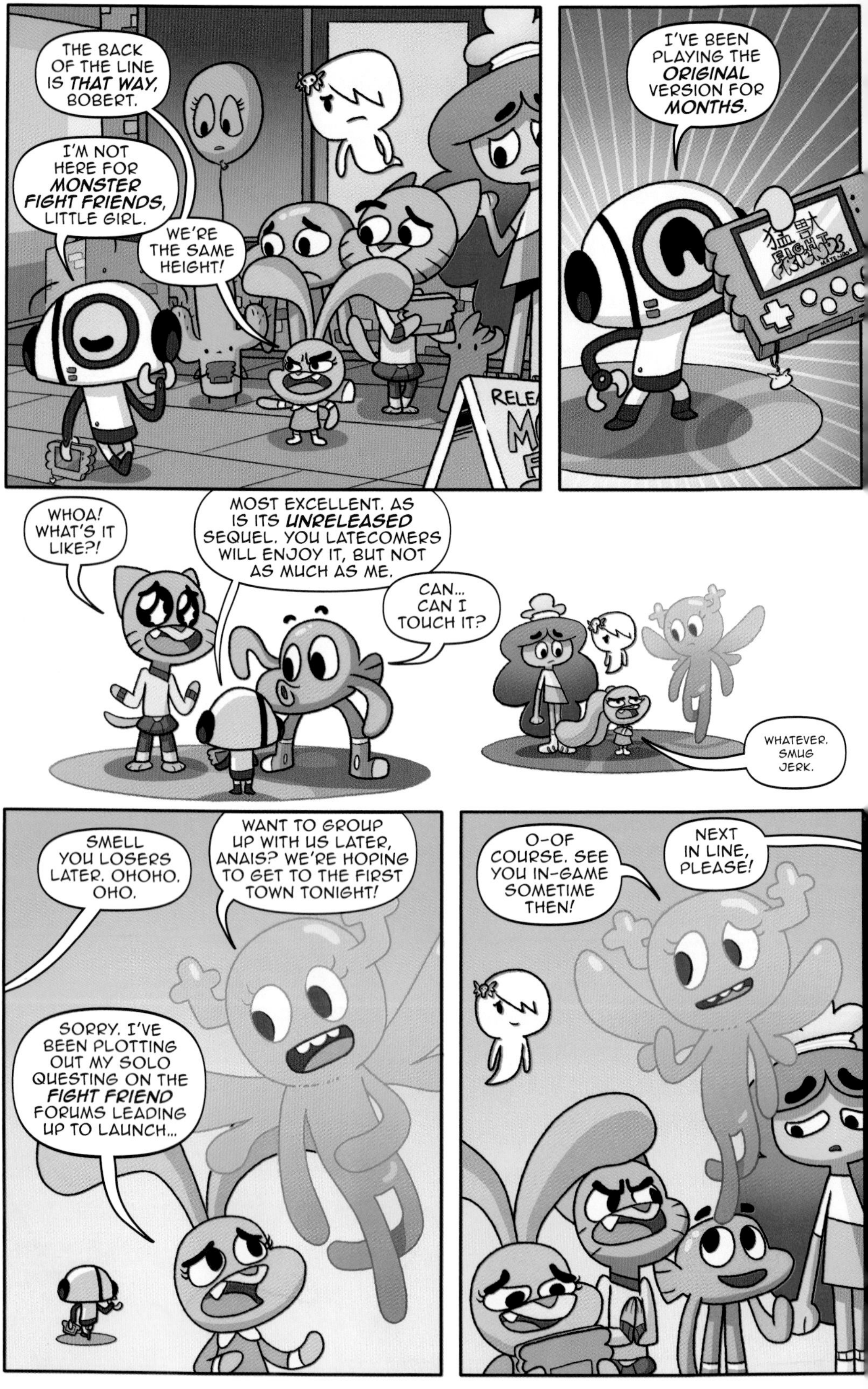
THE BACK OF THE LINE IS THAT WAY, BOBERT.
I'M NOT HERE FOR MONSTER FIGHT FRIENDS, LITTLE GIRL.
WE'RE THE SAME HEIGHT!
RELEA
I'VE BEEN PLAYING THE ORIGINAL VERSION FOR MONTHS.
WHOA! WHAT'S IT LIKE?!
MOST EXCELLENT. AS IS ITS UNRELEASED SEQUEL. YOU LATECOMERS WILL ENJOY IT, BUT NOT AS MUCH AS ME.
CAN... CAN I TOUCH IT?
WHATEVER. SMUG JERK.
SMELL YOU LOSERS LATER. OHOHO. OHO.
WANT TO GROUP UP WITH US LATER, ANAIS? WE'RE HOPING TO GET TO THE FIRST TOWN TONIGHT!
SORRY. I'VE BEEN PLOTTING OUT MY SOLO QUESTING ON THE FIGHT FRIEND FORUMS LEADING UP TO LAUNCH...
O-OF COURSE. SEE YOU IN-GAME SOMETIME THEN!
NEXT IN LINE, PLEASE!

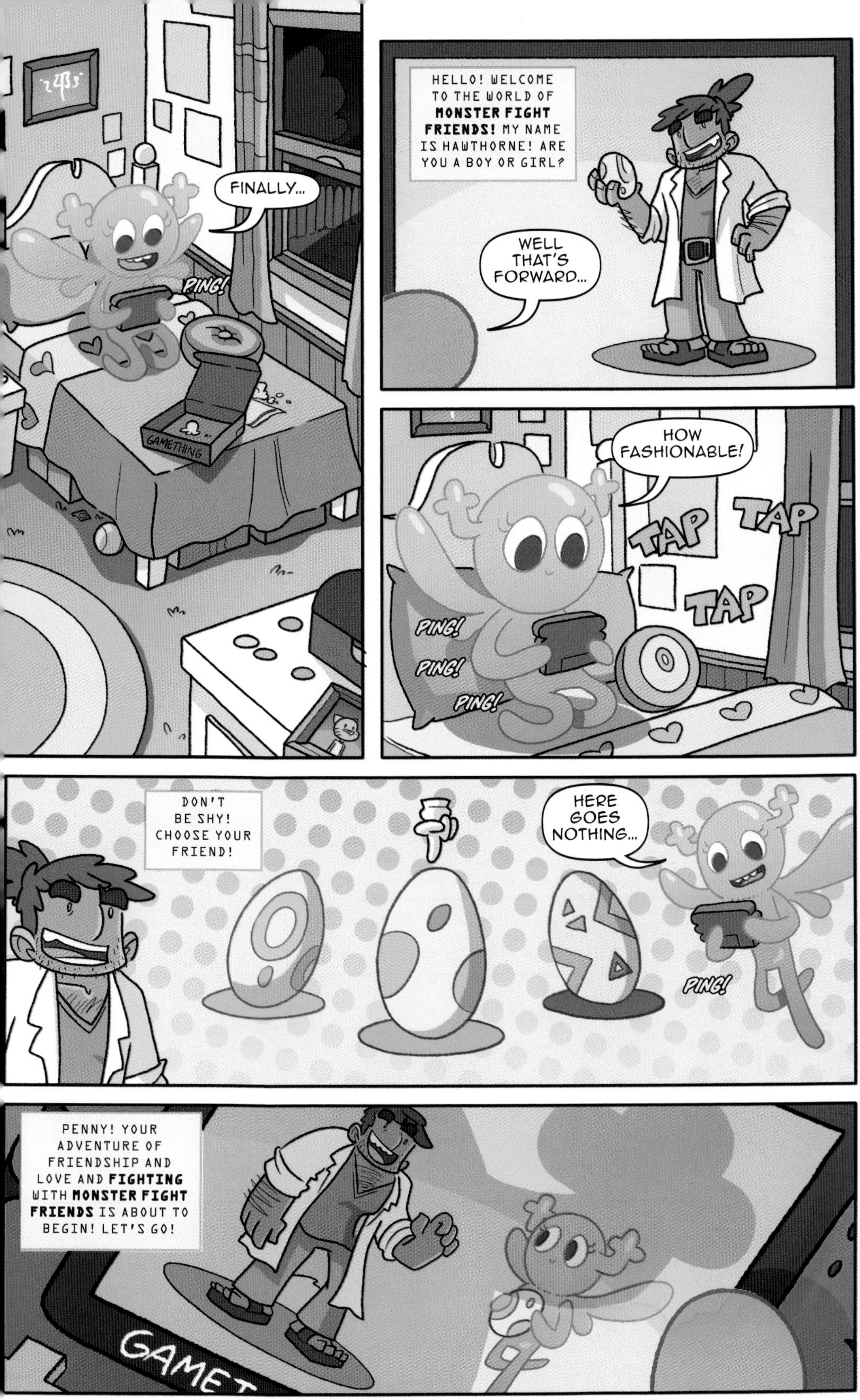
FINALLY...
PING!
GAMETHING
HELLO! WELCOME TO THE WORLD OF **MONSTER FIGHT FRIENDS!** MY NAME IS HAWTHORNE! ARE YOU A BOY OR GIRL?
WELL THAT'S FORWARD...
HOW FASHIONABLE!
TAP
TAP
TAP
PING!
PING!
PING!
DON'T BE SHY! CHOOSE YOUR FRIEND!
HERE GOES NOTHING...
PING!
PENNY! YOUR ADVENTURE OF FRIENDSHIP AND LOVE AND **FIGHTING** WITH **MONSTER FIGHT FRIENDS** IS ABOUT TO BEGIN! LET'S GO!
GAMET

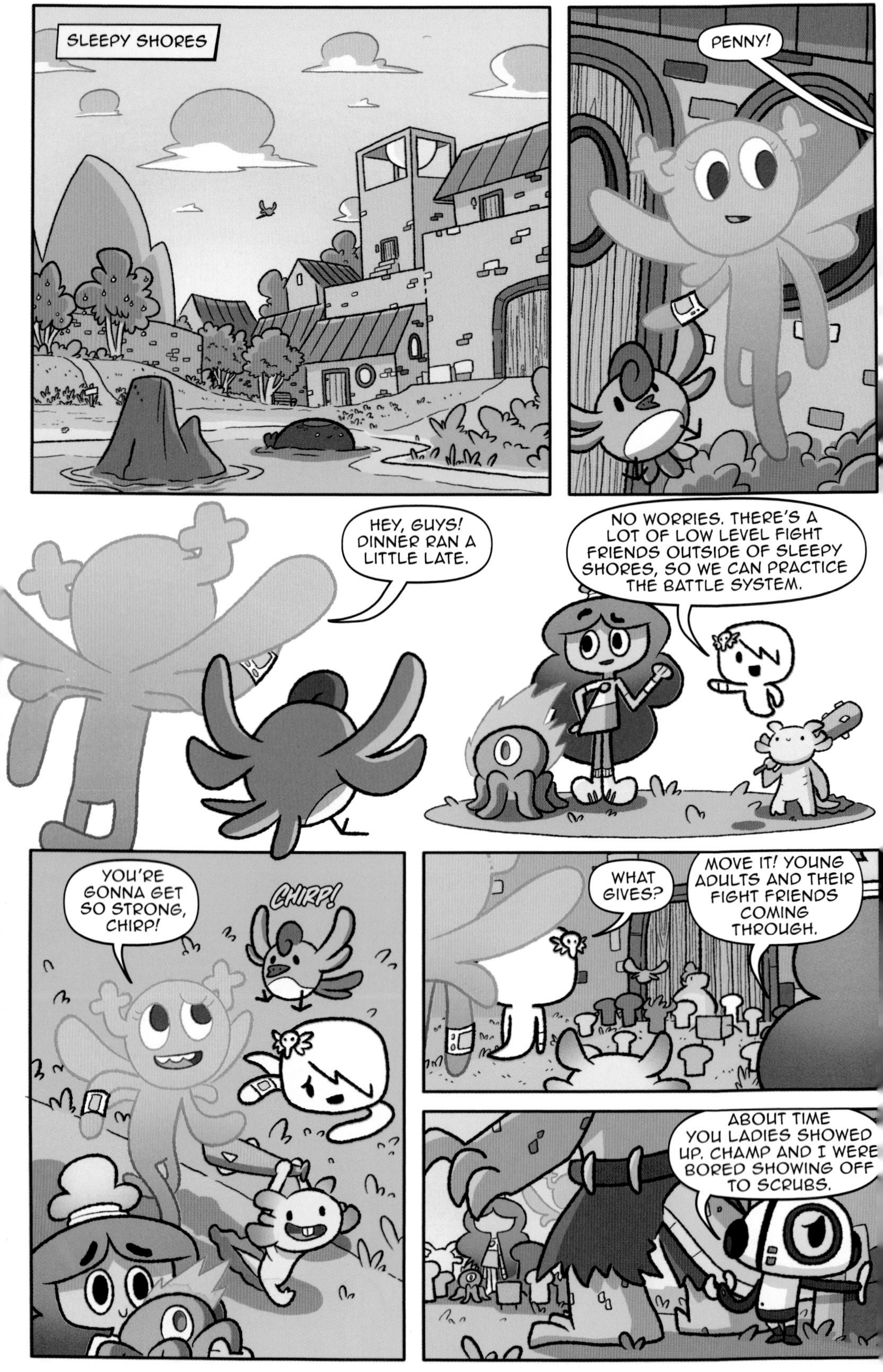
SLEEPY SHORES
PENNY!
HEY, GUYS! DINNER RAN A LITTLE LATE.
NO WORRIES. THERE'S A LOT OF LOW LEVEL FIGHT FRIENDS OUTSIDE OF SLEEPY SHORES, SO WE CAN PRACTICE THE BATTLE SYSTEM.
YOU'RE GONNA GET SO STRONG, CHIRP!
CHIRP!
WHAT GIVES?
MOVE IT! YOUNG ADULTS AND THEIR FIGHT FRIENDS COMING THROUGH.
ABOUT TIME YOU LADIES SHOWED UP. CHAMP AND I WERE BORED SHOWING OFF TO SCRUBS.

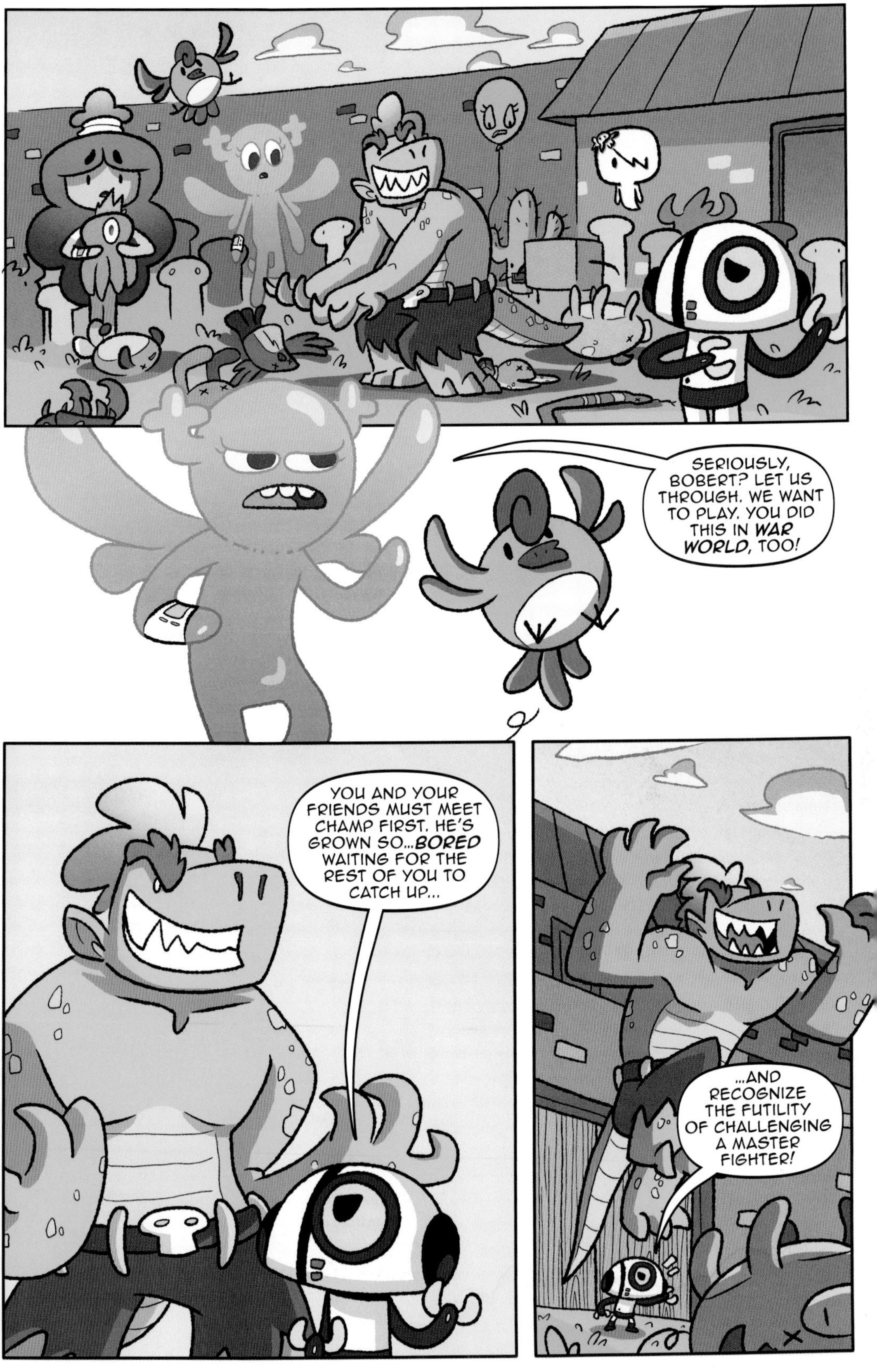
SERIOUSLY, BOBERT? LET US THROUGH. WE WANT TO PLAY. YOU DID THIS IN WAR WORLD, TOO!
YOU AND YOUR FRIENDS MUST MEET CHAMP FIRST. HE'S GROWN SO...BORED WAITING FOR THE REST OF YOU TO CATCH UP...
...AND RECOGNIZE THE FUTILITY OF CHALLENGING A MASTER FIGHTER!

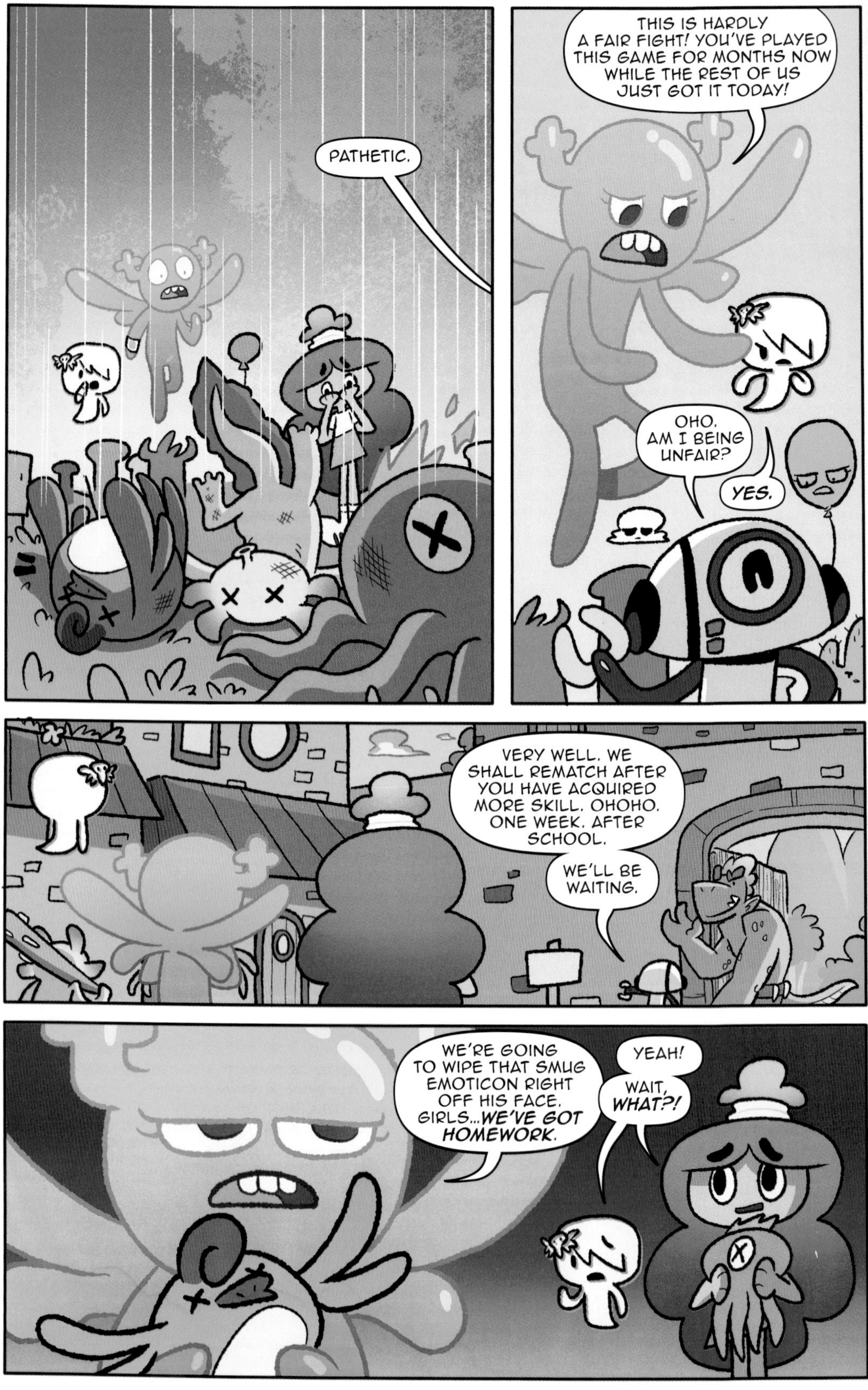
PATHETIC.
THIS IS HARDLY A FAIR FIGHT! YOU'VE PLAYED THIS GAME FOR MONTHS NOW WHILE THE REST OF US JUST GOT IT TODAY!
OHO. AM I BEING UNFAIR?
YES.
VERY WELL. WE SHALL REMATCH AFTER YOU HAVE ACQUIRED MORE SKILL. OHOHO. ONE WEEK. AFTER SCHOOL.
WE'LL BE WAITING.
WE'RE GOING TO WIPE THAT SMUG EMOTICON RIGHT OFF HIS FACE. GIRLS...WE'VE GOT HOMEWORK.
YEAH!
WAIT, WHAT?!

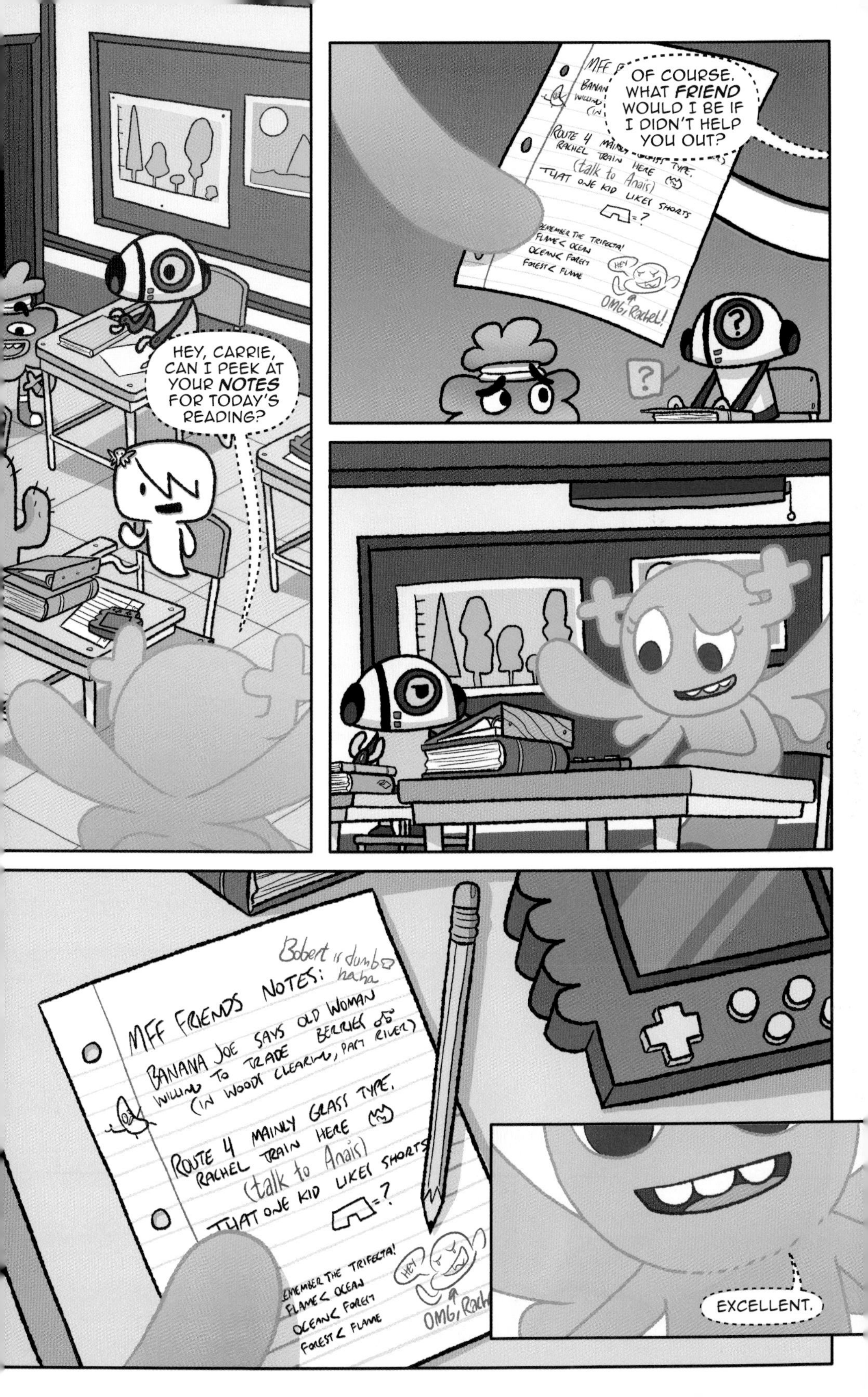

HEY, CARRIE, CAN I PEEK AT YOUR NOTES FOR TODAY'S READING?
OF COURSE. WHAT FRIEND WOULD I BE IF I DIDN'T HELP YOU OUT?
?
Bobert is dumb haha
MFF FRIENDS NOTES:
BANANA JOE SAYS OLD WOMAN WILLING TO TRADE BERRIES (IN WOODS CLEARING, PAST RIVER)
ROUTE 4 MAINLY GRASS TYPE. RACHEL TRAIN HERE
(talk to Anais)
THAT ONE KID LIKES SHORTS
=?
REMEMBER THE TRIFECTA!
FLAME < OCEAN
OCEAN < FOREST
FOREST < FLAME
HEY
OMG, Rachel!
EXCELLENT.

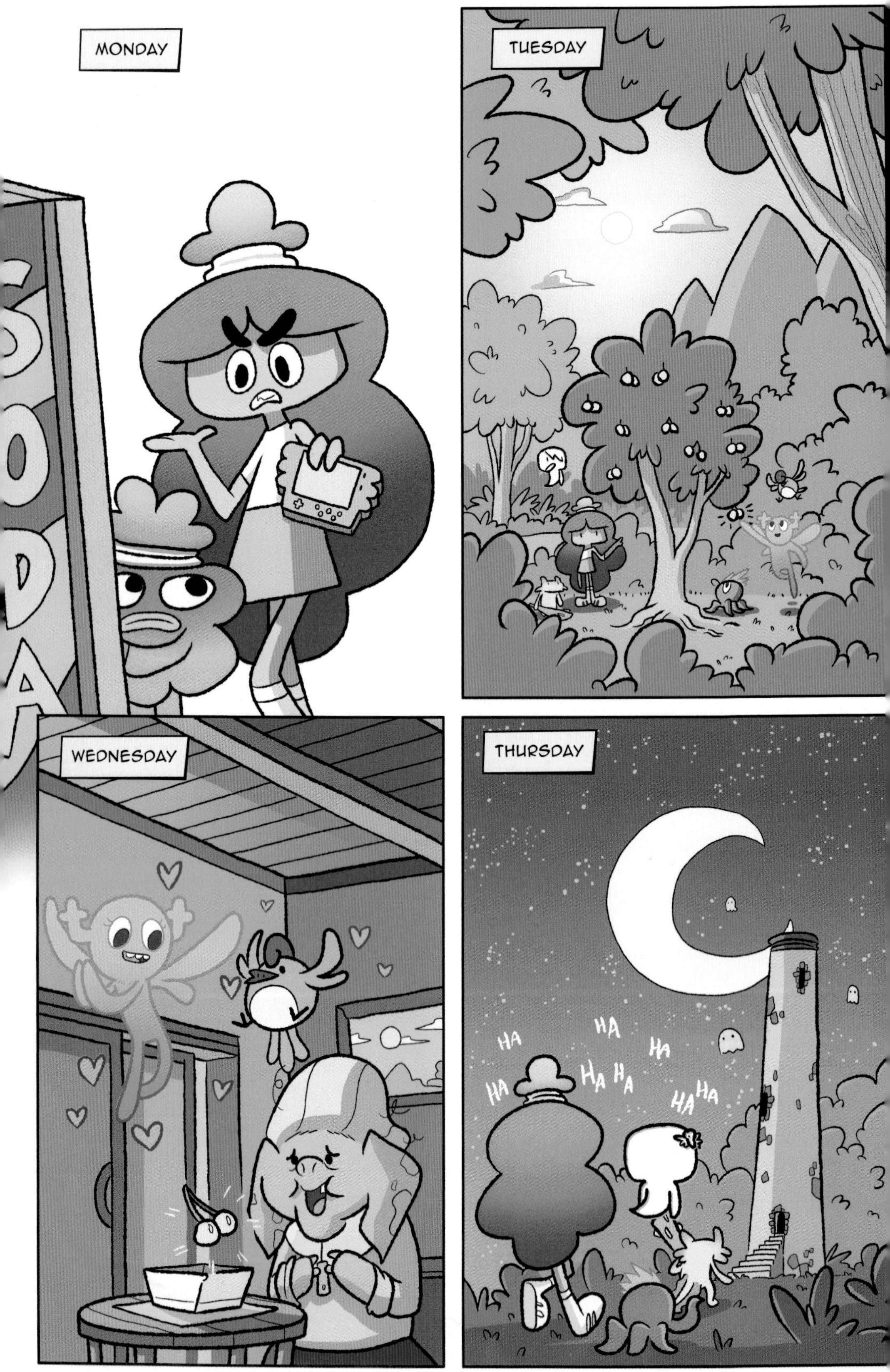
MONDAY
TUESDAY
WEDNESDAY
THURSDAY
HA
HA
HA
HA
HA HA
HA
HA HA

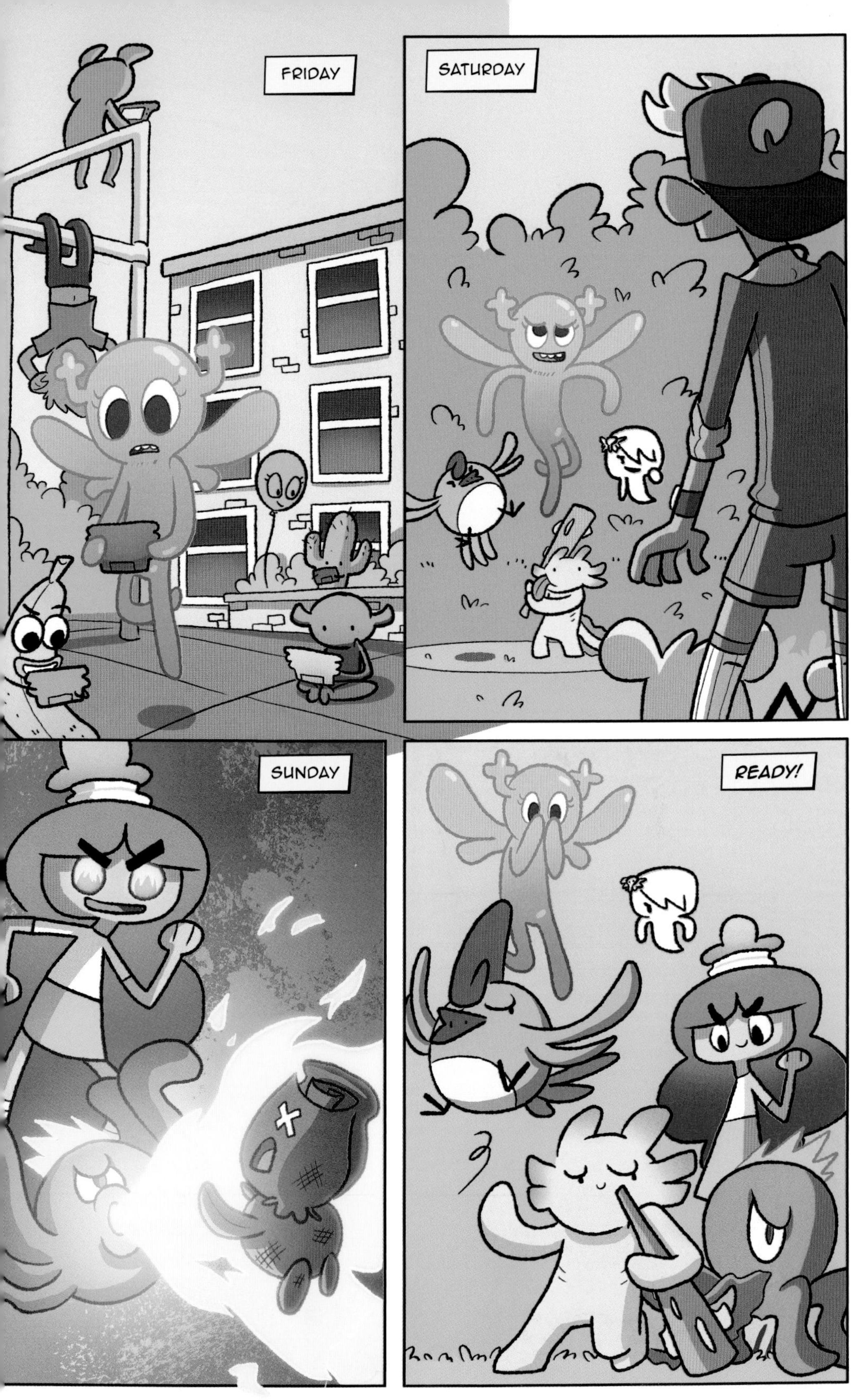
FRIDAY
SATURDAY
SUNDAY
READY!

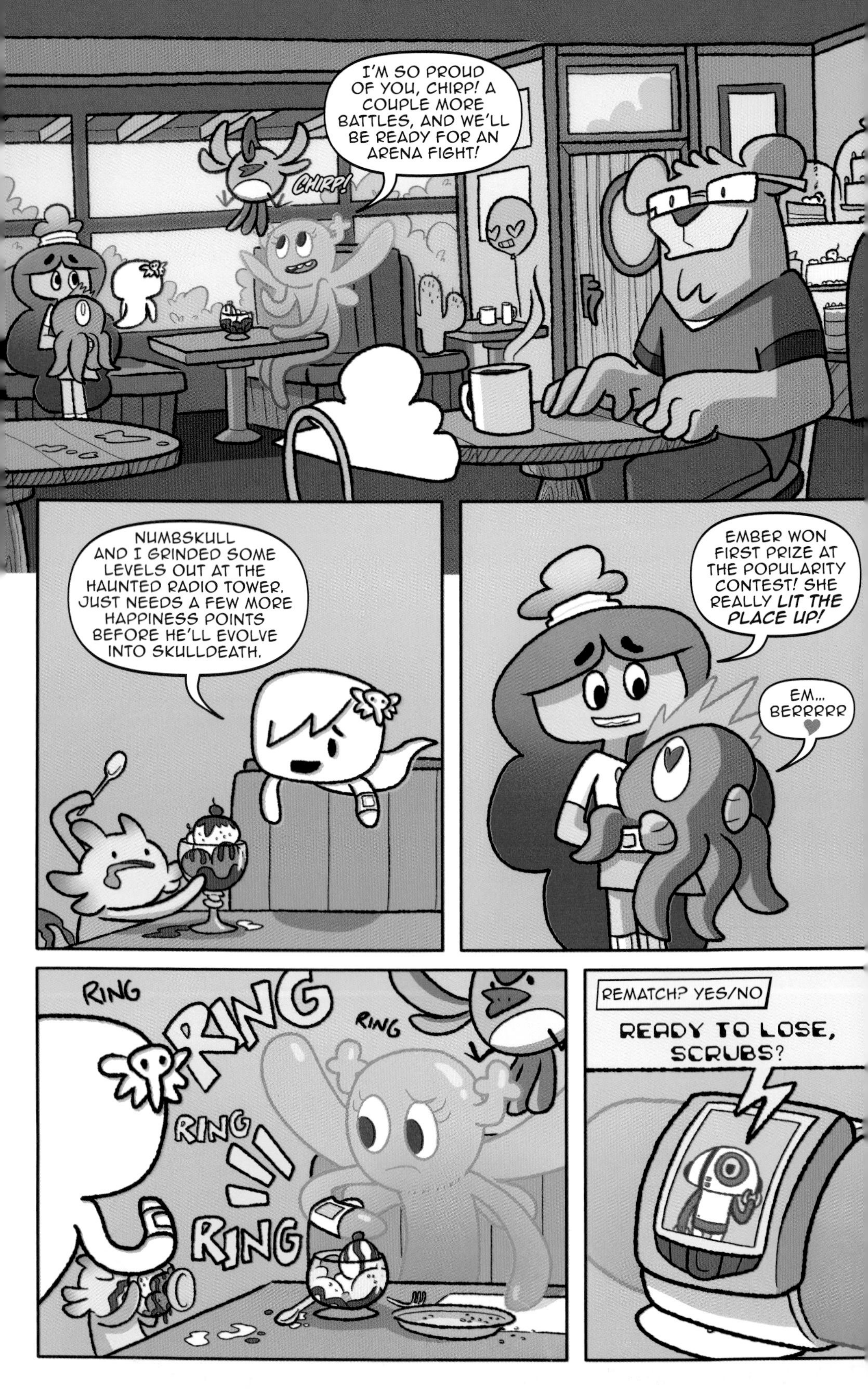
I'M SO PROUD OF YOU, CHIRP! A COUPLE MORE BATTLES, AND WE'LL BE READY FOR AN ARENA FIGHT!
CHIRP!
NUMBSKULL AND I GRINDED SOME LEVELS OUT AT THE HAUNTED RADIO TOWER. JUST NEEDS A FEW MORE HAPPINESS POINTS BEFORE HE'LL EVOLVE INTO SKULLDEATH.
EMBER WON FIRST PRIZE AT THE POPULARITY CONTEST! SHE REALLY *LIT THE PLACE UP!*
EM... BERRRRR
RING
RING
RING
RING
RING
REMATCH? YES/NO
READY TO LOSE, SCRUBS?

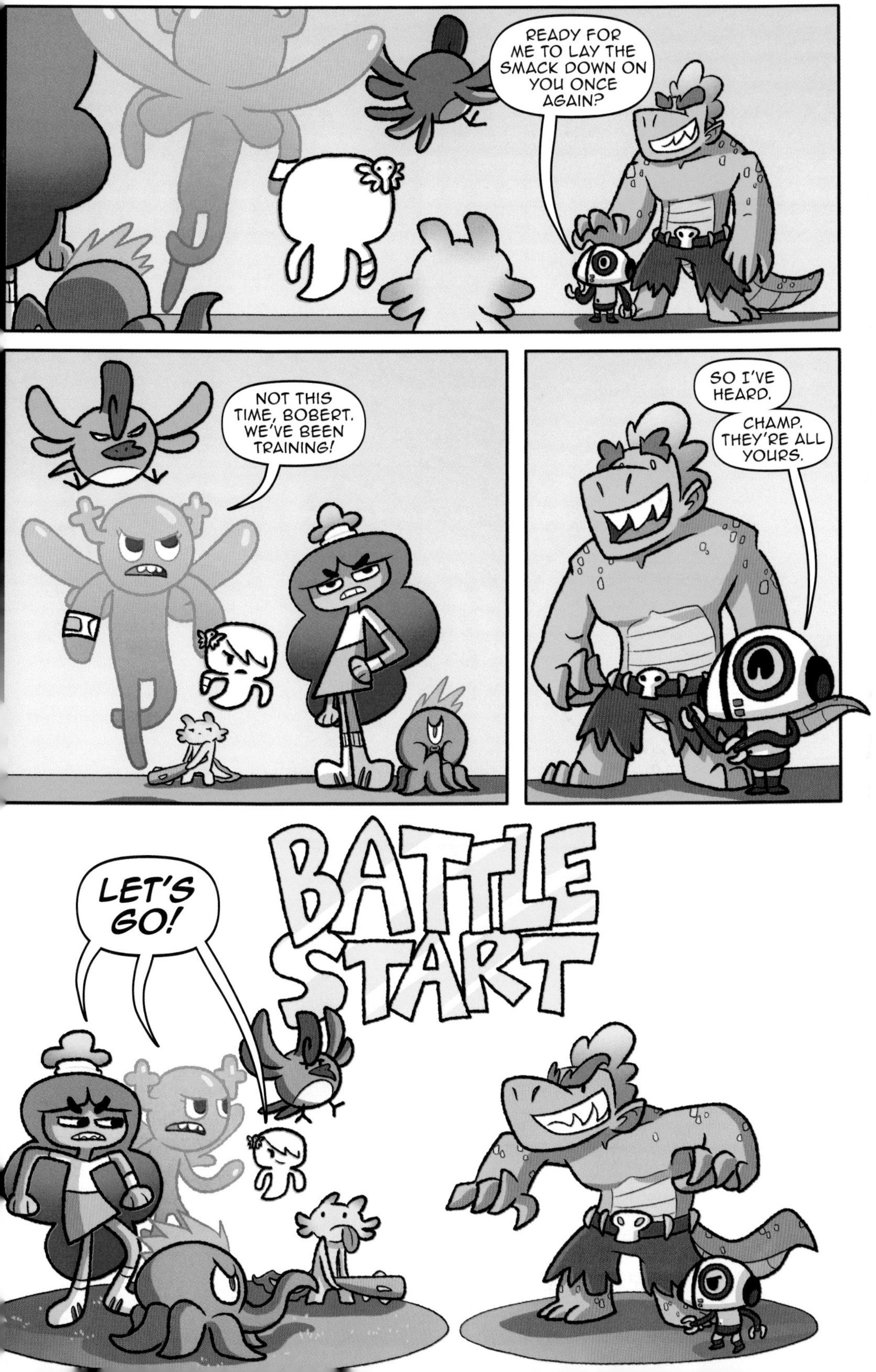
READY FOR ME TO LAY THE SMACK DOWN ON YOU ONCE AGAIN?
NOT THIS TIME, BOBERT. WE'VE BEEN TRAINING!
SO I'VE HEARD.
CHAMP. THEY'RE ALL YOURS.
LET'S GO!
BATTLE START

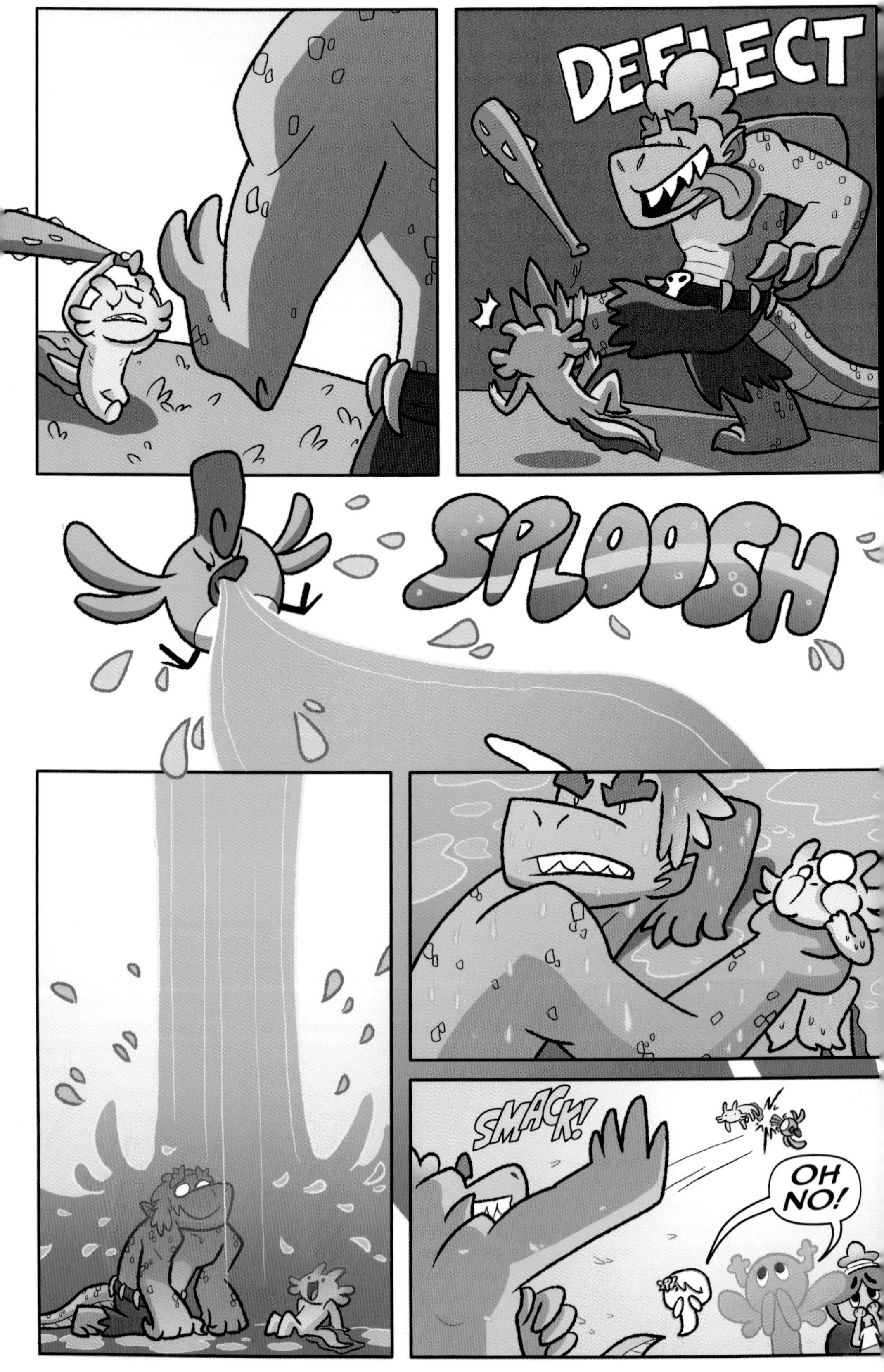
DEFLECT
SPLOOSH
SMACK!
OH NO!

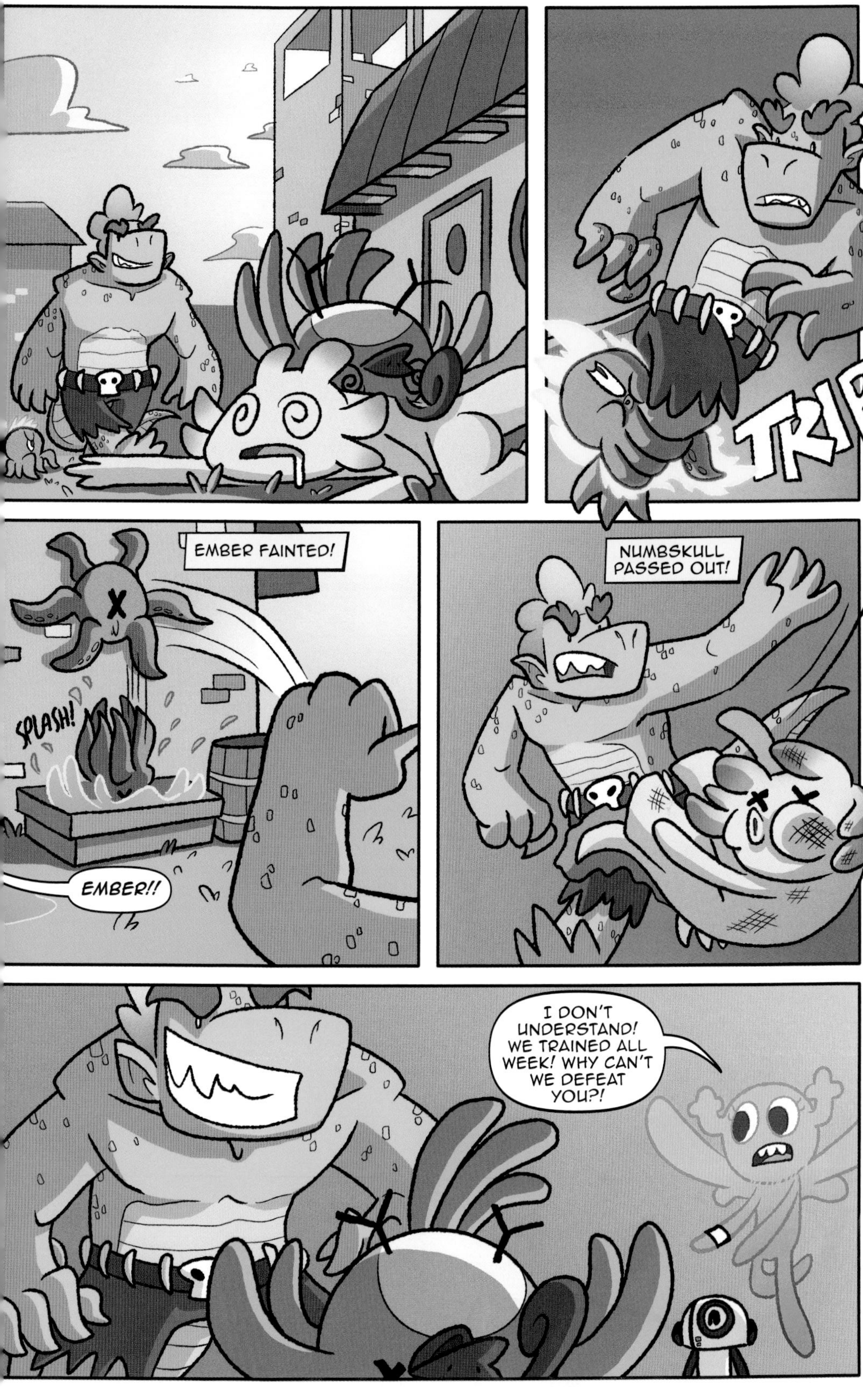
TRIP
EMBER FAINTED!
SPLASH!
EMBER!!
NUMBSKULL PASSED OUT!
I DON'T UNDERSTAND! WE TRAINED ALL WEEK! WHY CAN'T WE DEFEAT YOU?!

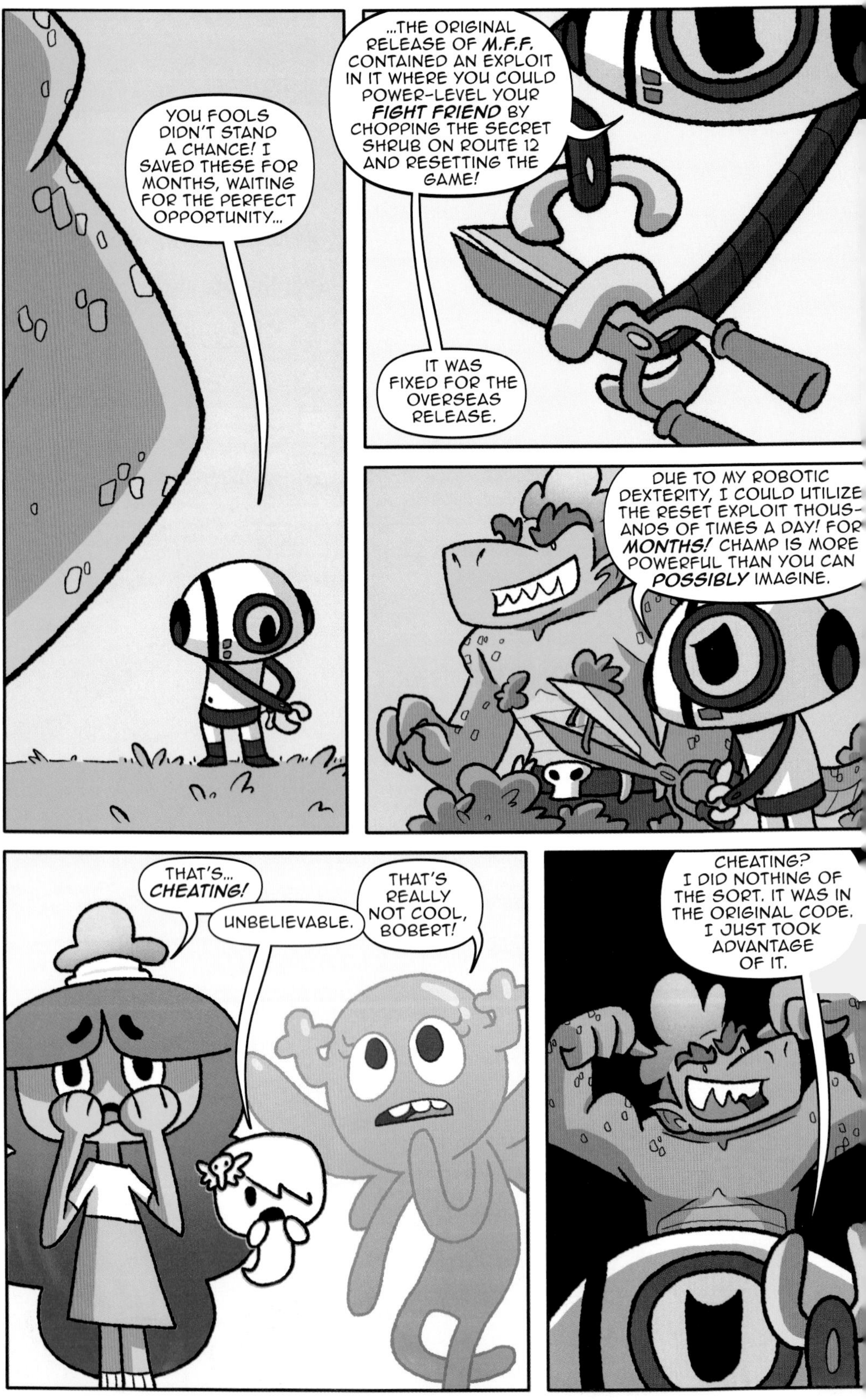
YOU FOOLS DIDN'T STAND A CHANCE! I SAVED THESE FOR MONTHS, WAITING FOR THE PERFECT OPPORTUNITY...
...THE ORIGINAL RELEASE OF *M.F.F.* CONTAINED AN EXPLOIT IN IT WHERE YOU COULD POWER-LEVEL YOUR ***FIGHT FRIEND*** BY CHOPPING THE SECRET SHRUB ON ROUTE 12 AND RESETTING THE GAME!
IT WAS FIXED FOR THE OVERSEAS RELEASE.
DUE TO MY ROBOTIC DEXTERITY, I COULD UTILIZE THE RESET EXPLOIT THOUSANDS OF TIMES A DAY! FOR ***MONTHS!*** CHAMP IS MORE POWERFUL THAN YOU CAN ***POSSIBLY*** IMAGINE.
THAT'S... ***CHEATING!***
UNBELIEVABLE.
THAT'S REALLY NOT COOL, BOBERT!
CHEATING? I DID NOTHING OF THE SORT. IT WAS IN THE ORIGINAL CODE. I JUST TOOK ADVANTAGE OF IT.

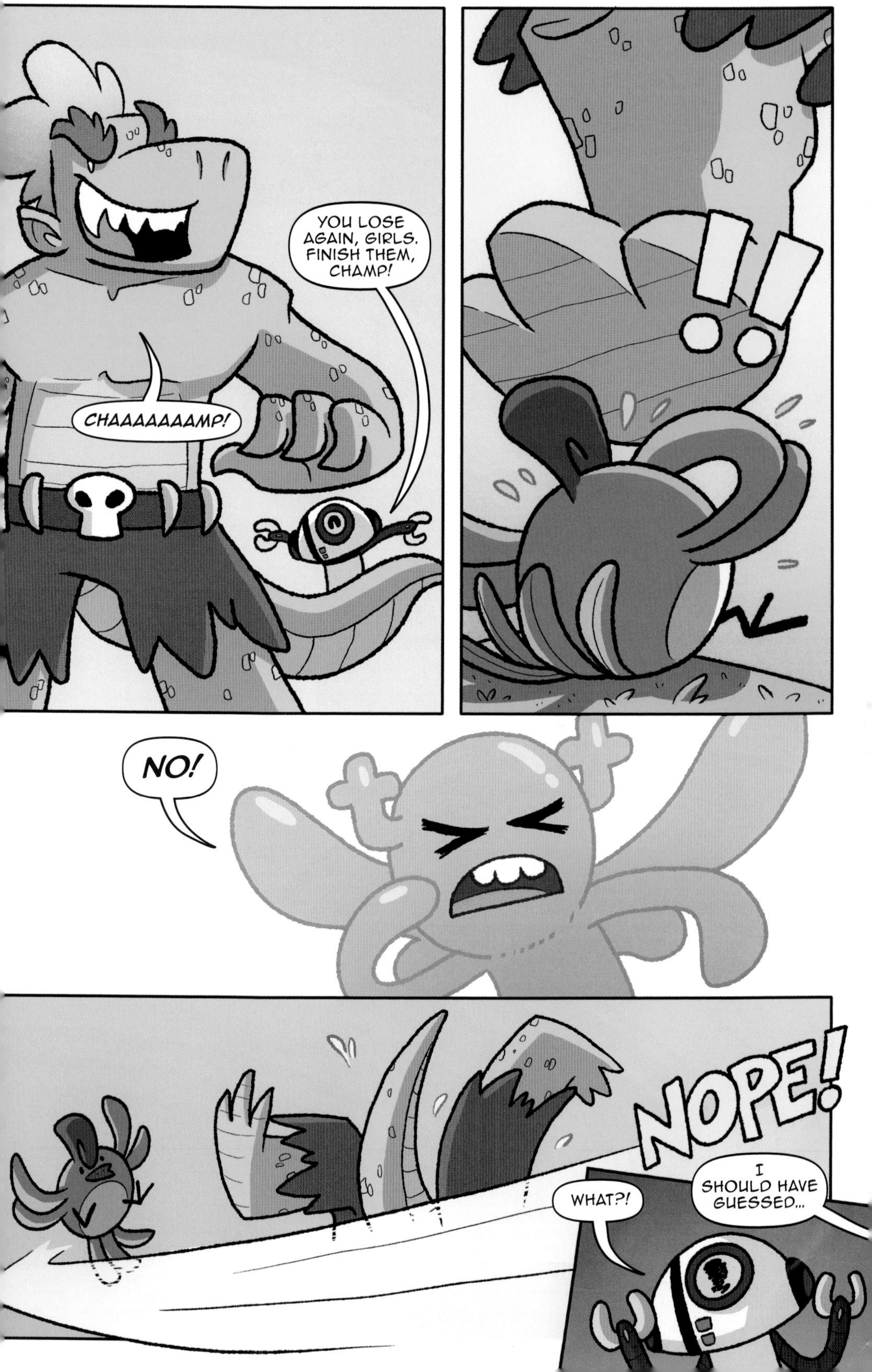
YOU LOSE AGAIN, GIRLS. FINISH THEM, CHAMP!
CHAAAAAAAAMP!
!!
NO!
NOPE!
WHAT?!
I SHOULD HAVE GUESSED...

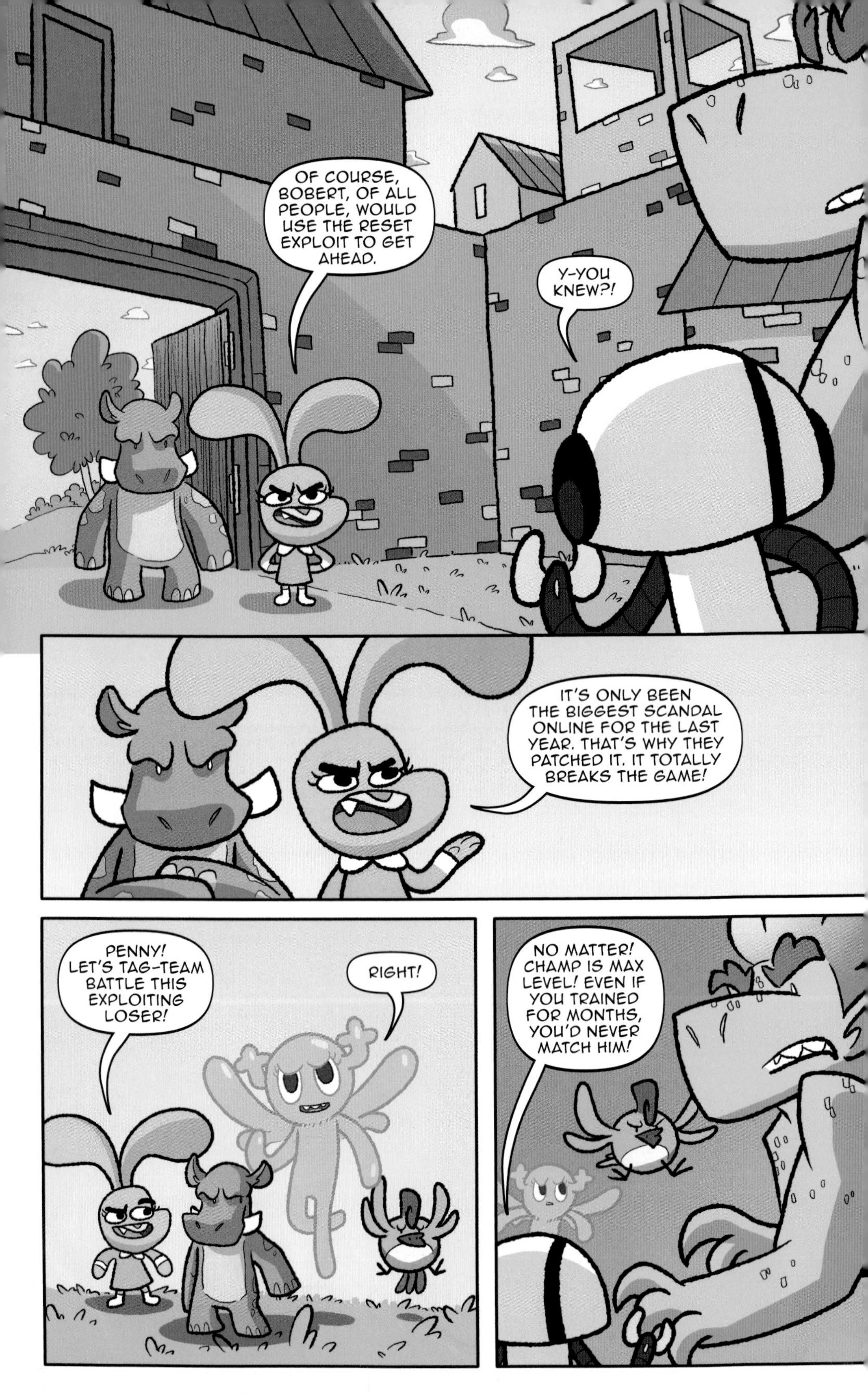
OF COURSE, BOBERT, OF ALL PEOPLE, WOULD USE THE RESET EXPLOIT TO GET AHEAD.
Y-YOU KNEW?!
IT'S ONLY BEEN THE BIGGEST SCANDAL ONLINE FOR THE LAST YEAR. THAT'S WHY THEY PATCHED IT. IT TOTALLY BREAKS THE GAME!
PENNY! LET'S TAG-TEAM BATTLE THIS EXPLOITING LOSER!
RIGHT!
NO MATTER! CHAMP IS MAX LEVEL! EVEN IF YOU TRAINED FOR MONTHS, YOU'D NEVER MATCH HIM!

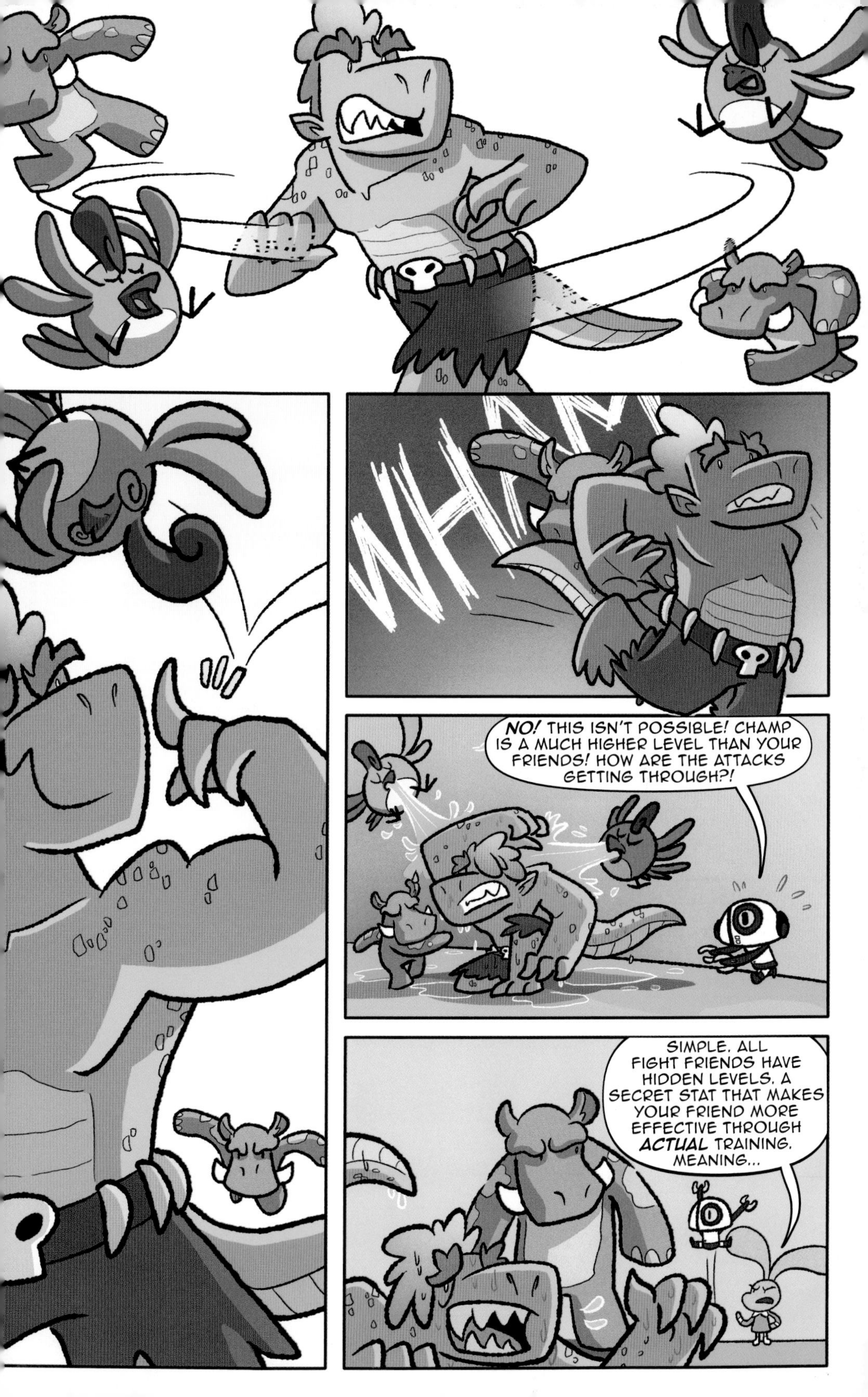
WHAM
NO! THIS ISN'T POSSIBLE! CHAMP IS A MUCH HIGHER LEVEL THAN YOUR FRIENDS! HOW ARE THE ATTACKS GETTING THROUGH?!
SIMPLE. ALL FIGHT FRIENDS HAVE HIDDEN LEVELS. A SECRET STAT THAT MAKES YOUR FRIEND MORE EFFECTIVE THROUGH ACTUAL TRAINING. MEANING...

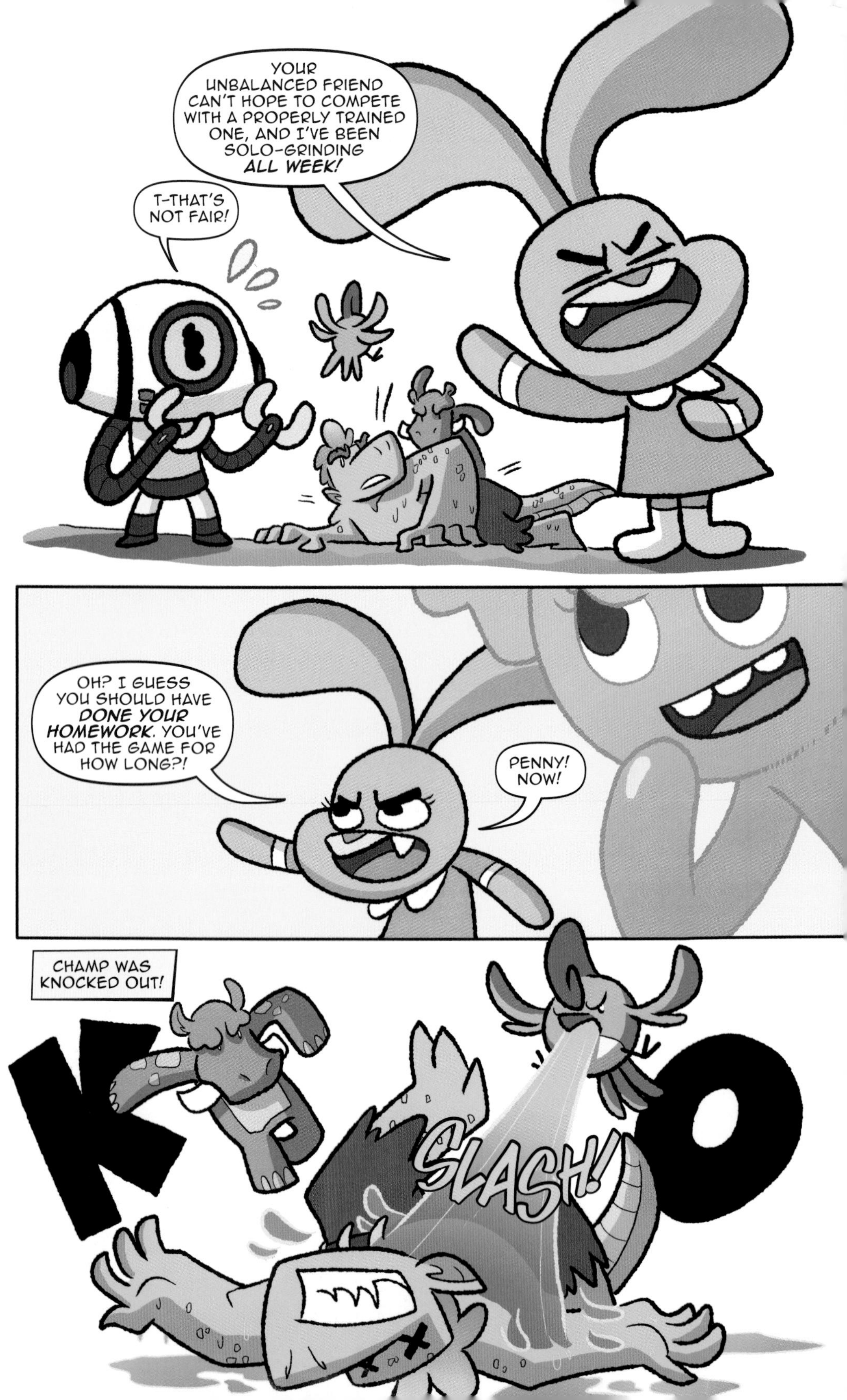
YOUR UNBALANCED FRIEND CAN'T HOPE TO COMPETE WITH A PROPERLY TRAINED ONE, AND I'VE BEEN SOLO-GRINDING *ALL WEEK!*
T-THAT'S NOT FAIR!
OH? I GUESS YOU SHOULD HAVE *DONE YOUR HOMEWORK*. YOU'VE HAD THE GAME FOR HOW LONG?!
PENNY! NOW!
CHAMP WAS KNOCKED OUT!
KO
SLASH!

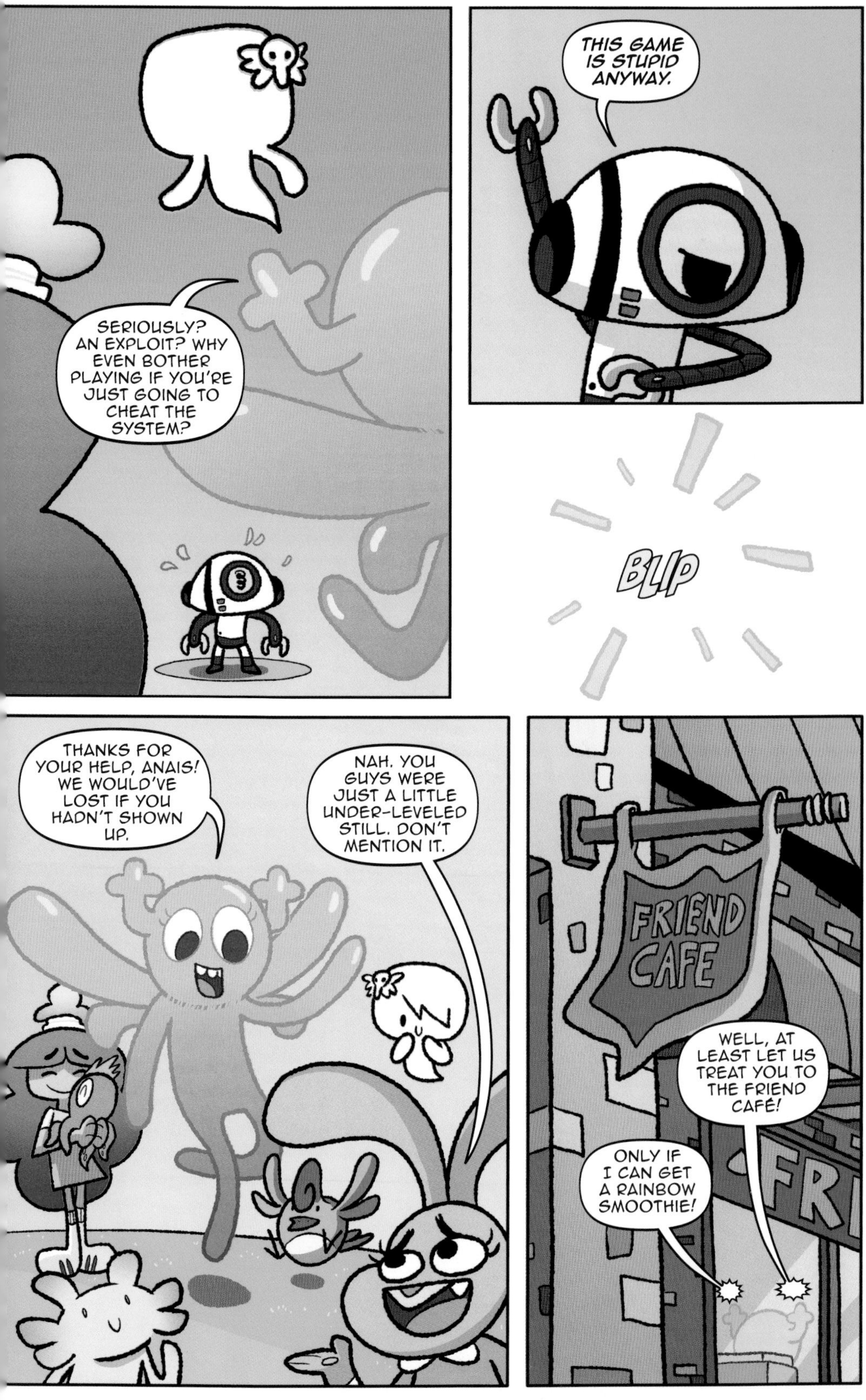

SERIOUSLY? AN EXPLOIT? WHY EVEN BOTHER PLAYING IF YOU'RE JUST GOING TO CHEAT THE SYSTEM?
THIS GAME IS STUPID ANYWAY.
BLIP
THANKS FOR YOUR HELP, ANAIS! WE WOULD'VE LOST IF YOU HADN'T SHOWN UP.
NAH. YOU GUYS WERE JUST A LITTLE UNDER-LEVELED STILL. DON'T MENTION IT.
FRIEND CAFE
WELL, AT LEAST LET US TREAT YOU TO THE FRIEND CAFÉ!
ONLY IF I CAN GET A RAINBOW SMOOTHIE!

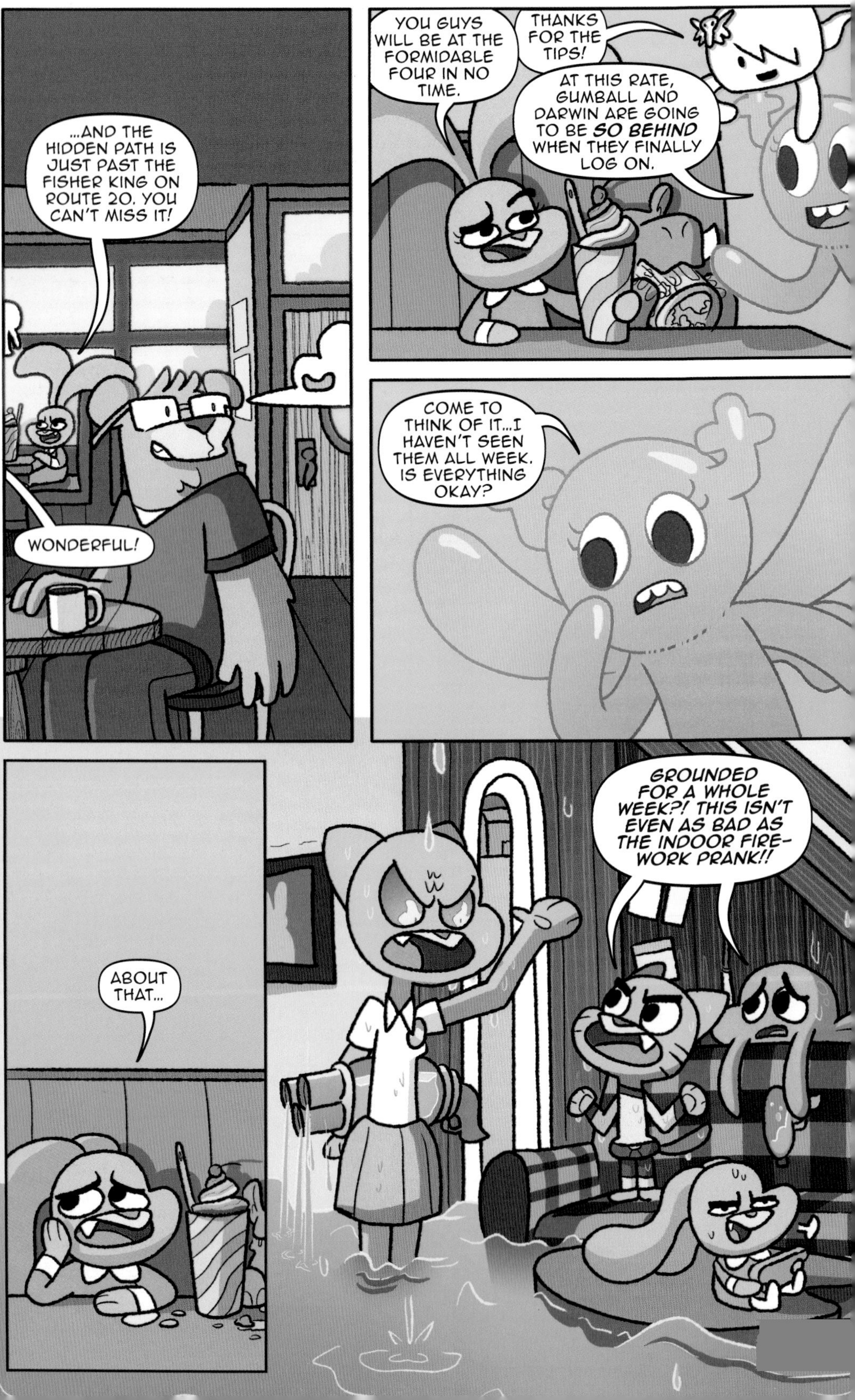
...AND THE HIDDEN PATH IS JUST PAST THE FISHER KING ON ROUTE 20. YOU CAN'T MISS IT!
WONDERFUL!
YOU GUYS WILL BE AT THE FORMIDABLE FOUR IN NO TIME.
THANKS FOR THE TIPS!
AT THIS RATE, GUMBALL AND DARWIN ARE GOING TO BE SO BEHIND WHEN THEY FINALLY LOG ON.
COME TO THINK OF IT...I HAVEN'T SEEN THEM ALL WEEK. IS EVERYTHING OKAY?
ABOUT THAT...
GROUNDED FOR A WHOLE WEEK?! THIS ISN'T EVEN AS BAD AS THE INDOOR FIRE-WORK PRANK!!

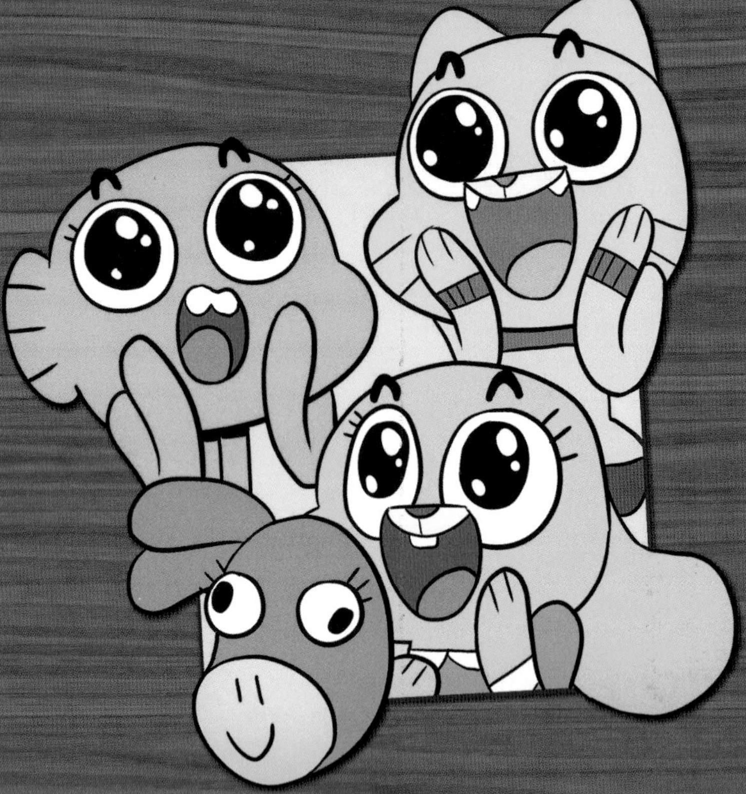

The AMAZING WORLD OF GUMBALL™

CONTINUES SUMMER 2017